HIPPO **ANiMAL**

Santa Paws

Nicholas Edwards

Hippo

Scholastic Children's Books,
Commonwealth House,
1-19 New Oxford Street,
London WC1A 1NU, UK
A division of Scholastic Ltd
London ~ New York ~ Toronto ~ Sydney ~ Auckland

First published in the USA by Scholastic Inc., 1995
First published in the UK by Scholastic Ltd, 1996
This edition, 1997

Text copyright © Ellen Emerson White, 1995

ISBN 0 590 11118 3

Typeset by TW Typesetting, Midsomer Norton, Avon
Printed by Cox and Wyman Ltd, Reading, Berkshire

10 9 8 7 6 5 4 3 2 1

Chapter 1

When the dog woke up, it was very cold. On winter nights, his mother always brought him, along with his brother and sisters, to some safe place out of the wind. She would scratch up some dry leaves to make them a little nest, and they would all cuddle up together. Then, in the morning, his mother would go off and try to find food for them. Sometimes she would let them come along, although they were too small to be much help. Mostly, she would forage for food while he and his siblings would scuffle and play somewhere nearby.

Once, his mother had lived in a big, nice house with a lot of college students. But then, when it got warm, they all left. She wasn't sure why they hadn't wanted her to come with them. Some of the students had even left without patting her, or saying goodbye. Her favourite, Jason, had filled up her water dish, given her some biscuits and told her what a good dog she was. But then, he got in his car and drove away, too.

She had waited in front of the house for a long time, but none of them came back. Ever since then, she had lived on the streets. Sometimes, nice people would give her food, but more often, she was on her own. There were even times when people would be mean and throw things at her, or chase her away.

Then, when he and his siblings were born, she had to spend most of her time taking care of them. She had a special route of rubbish bins and other places she would check for discarded food. If she found anything, like stale bread or old doughnuts, she would drag the food back and they would all gobble it down. On special days, she might even find some meat in funny plastic packages. They would tear them open and gulp down the old hamburger or bacon or chicken. He and his siblings would always fight playfully over the last little bits, but when his mother growled at them, they would stop right away and be good. The days when she brought home meat were the best days of all. Too often though, when they went to sleep, they were all still very hungry.

He was the smallest of the four puppies, but he had the biggest appetite and slept the most, too. Lots of mornings, he would wake up and be the only one left under the abandoned porch, or in a deep gully, or wherever they had spent the night. Lately, they had been sleeping in an old forgotten shed, behind a house where no people lived. It was safer that way. Lots of times, even if they wagged their tails, people would yell at them or act afraid. But when he saw big scary cars speed by, with happy dogs looking out the windows, he wished he knew *those* people. He also liked the people who would saunter down the street, with dogs on leashes walking proudly next to them. He really wanted to *be* one of those lucky dogs.

But, he wasn't, and he was happy, anyway. His mother always took care of them, and he loved his brother and sisters. They were a family, and as long as they were together, they were safe.

On this particular morning, he yawned a few times, and then rolled to his feet. None of the others were around, but he was sure they would be back soon with some breakfast. Maybe today they would even find some meat! Once he had stood up, he stretched a few times and yawned again. It was *really* cold, and he shivered a little. In fact, it would be nice to curl up again and get some more sleep. But he decided that he was more thirsty than he was sleepy and that it was time to go outside.

There was a hole in the back part of the old shed that they used for a door. He squirmed through it and immediately felt ice-cold snow under his paws. He shivered again, and shook the snow off each paw. It was *much* windier outside than it had been in the shed and he stepped tentatively through the fresh drifts of snow.

In the woods nearby, there was a small stream, where they would always drink. On some mornings lately, the water would be frozen, but his mother had shown him how to stamp his paw on the ice to break it. Today, there was so much snow that he couldn't even *find* the water at first. Then, when he did, he couldn't break the ice. He jumped with all four feet, slipping and sliding, but nothing happened. The ice was just too thick. Finally, he gave up and sat down in the snow, whimpering a little. Now he was going to be hungry *and* thirsty.

He swallowed a few mouthfuls of snow, but he still felt thirsty. The snow also made his insides feel cold. Where was his mother? Where were his brother and sisters? They had never left him for such a long time before. He ran back and forth in front of the frozen stream, whining anxiously. What if they were lost? What if they were hurt? What if they *never* came back? What would happen to him?

Maybe they were back at the shed, waiting for him. Maybe they had brought back food, and he and his brother could roll and play and pretend to fight over it. He should have waited for them, instead of wandering away.

He ran through the woods to the shed. Some of the snowdrifts were so tall that they were almost over his head and it took a lot of energy to bound through them. No, they would never go away and forget him. Never, ever.

But the shed was still deserted. He barked a few times, then waited for answering barks. Lately, his bark had been getting bigger and deeper, so he filled his chest with air and tried again. His bark echoed loudly through the silent backyard and woods. When there was still no answer, he whimpered and lay down to wait for them.

He rested his head on his numb front paws. They would probably come back through the big field behind the shed, and he watched the empty acres miserably. If he moved, he might miss them, so he would just stay here and wait. No matter how long it took, he would stay.

The sun was out and shining on him, which made him feel better. He waited patiently, staring at the field with his ears pricked forward alertly. He could hear birds, and squirrels, and faraway cars – but no dogs. He lifted his nose to try and catch their scent in the air, but he couldn't smell them, either.

So, he just waited. And waited, and waited, and waited. The sun went away after a while, and dark grey clouds rolled in to cover the sky. But still, he waited.

A light snow started falling, but he didn't abandon his post. He wanted to be able to *see* his family the second they came back. Every so often he would stand up to shake off the fresh flakes of snow that had landed on his fur. Then he would shiver, stamp out a new bed for himself, and lie back down. He had never felt so cold, and lonely, and miserable in his life.

Once it began to get dark, he couldn't help whimpering some more and yelping a few times. Something very bad must have happened to his family. Maybe, instead of waiting so long, he should have tried to follow their trail. Maybe they were hurt somewhere, or trapped. But if he went to look for them, they might come back while he was gone and think *he* was lost for good. Then they might go away and he would *never* find them.

There was a street running in front of the boarded-up house and a car was cruising slowly by. A bright beam of light flashed across the house and yard. The dog cringed and tried to duck out of the way. His mother had taught them that when people came around, it was usually safer to hide, just in case.

The car braked to a stop and two big men in uniforms got out. They were both local police officers, out on their nightly patrol.

"Come on, Steve," the man who had been driving said, as he stood by the squad car. "I didn't see anything."

Steve, who was about thirty years old with thick dark hair, aimed his torch around the yard. "We've had three break-ins in the last week," he answered. "If we have drifters in town, this is the kind of place where they might hide out."

"I know," the other cop, who was named Bill, said, sounding defensive. He was heavier than Steve was, with thinning blond hair and a neatly trimmed moustache. "I went to the academy, too, remember?"

Steve grinned at him. "Well, yeah, Bill," he agreed. "But *I* studied."

Bill laughed and snapped on his own torch. "OK, fair enough," he said, and directed the beam at the boarded-up windows of the house. "But, come on. Oceanport isn't exactly a high crime area."

"Law and order," Steve said cheerfully. "That's our job, pal."

The men sounded friendly, but the dog uneasily hung back in the shadows. One of the lights passed over him, paused, and came whipping back.

"There!" Steve said, and pointed towards the shed. "I told you I saw something!"

"Whoa, a *dog*," Bill said, his voice a little sarcastic. "We'd better call for back-up."

Steve ignored him and walked further into the yard. "It must be one of those strays," he said. "I thought Charlie finally managed to round all of them up this morning." Charlie was the animal control officer in Oceanport.

Bill shrugged. "So, he missed one. We'll

put a report in, and he can come back out here tomorrow."

"It's *cold*," Steve said. "You really want to leave the poor thing out here all night? He looks like he's only a puppy."

Bill made a face. "I don't feel like chasing around after him in the snow, either. Let Charlie do it. He needs the exercise."

Steve crouched down, holding his gloved hand out. "Come here, boy! Come on, pup!"

The dog hung back. What did they want? Should he go over there, or run away and hide? His mother would know. He whined quietly and kept his distance.

"He's wild, Steve," Bill said. "This'll take all night."

Steve shook his head, still holding his hand out. "Charlie said they were just scared. He figured once the vet checked them over and they got a few decent meals, they'd be fine." He snapped his fingers. "Come here, boy. Come on."

The dog shifted his weight and stayed where he was. He had to be careful. It might be some kind of trap.

10

"He's pretty mangy-looking," Bill said critically.

Steve frowned at him. "Are you kidding? That dog's at least half German shepherd. Clean him up a little, and he'd be something to see. And he's young, too. He'd be easy to train."

Bill looked dubious. "Maybe. Give me a good retriever, any day."

Steve stood up abruptly. "Wait a minute. I've got an idea. I still have a sandwich in the car."

"I'm starved," Bill said, trailing after him. "Don't give it to the dog, give it to *me*."

Steve paid no attention. He dug into a brown paper bag below the front seat of the squad car and pulled out a thick, homemade sandwich wrapped in greaseproof paper. "If I catch him, can you take him home?" he asked.

"Are you serious? You know how tough my cat is," Bill said. "Besides, you're the one who likes him so much."

"Yeah," Steve agreed, "but I can't keep him. Not with Emily due any day now. I don't want to do anything to upset her. Besides, she's *already* bugged about me not getting the lights on the Christmas tree yet."

"You'd better get moving," Bill said, laughing. "There's only a week to go."

Steve nodded wryly. "I know, I know. I'm going to do it tomorrow, before my shift – I swear."

As he crossed the yard, carrying the sandwich, the dog shrank away from him. After all, it *could* be some kind of trick. His mother always helped him decide who they could trust, and who they couldn't. He didn't know *how* to take care of himself.

"Hey, what about your brother?" Bill suggested. "Didn't he have to have that old collie of his put to sleep recently?"

"Yeah, a few weeks ago," Steve said, and held the sandwich out in the dog's direction. "My niece and nephew are still heartbroken."

Bill shrugged. "So, bring the dog to them."

Steve thought about that, then shook his head. "I don't know, you can't force a thing like that. They might not be ready yet."

Just then, the police radio in their squad car crackled. They both straightened up and listened, as the dispatcher called in a burglar alarm in their sector.

"Looks like the dog is going to have to wait," Bill said. He hurried over to the car and picked up the radio to report in.

Steve gazed across the dark yard at the shivering little dog. "I'm sorry, pal," he said. "We'll send Charlie out after you tomorrow. Try to stay warm tonight." Gently, he set the meatloaf sandwich down in the snow. "Enjoy your supper now." Then he walked quickly back to the car.

The dog waited right where he was, even after the police car was gone. Then, tentatively, he took a couple of steps out of the woods. He hesitated, sniffed the air, and hesitated some more. Finally, he got up his nerve and bolted across the yard. He was so hungry that he gobbled each sandwich half in two huge bites, and then licked the surrounding snow for any crumbs he might have missed.

It was the best meal he had had for a long time.

Once he was finished, he ran back to the shed and wiggled inside through the hole in the back. If he waited all night, maybe his family would come back. No matter what, he would stay on guard until they did. He was very tired, but he would *make* himself stay awake.

The night before, he and his family had slept in a tangle of leaves and an old musty tarpaulin. The shed had felt crowded, but very warm and safe.

Tonight, all the dog felt was afraid, and very, very alone.

Chapter 2

It was a long cold night, and even though he tried as hard as he could to remain on guard, the dog finally fell asleep. When he woke up in the grey dawn light, he was still alone. His family really *had* left him!

He crept over to the jagged wooden hole in the back of the shed and peeked outside. Even more snow had fallen during the night, and the whole world looked white and scary. Just as he started to put his front paws through the hole, he heard a small truck parking on the street. Instantly, he retreated.

It was Charlie Norris, who was the animal control officer for the small town of Ocean-port. He climbed out of his truck, with some dog biscuits in one hand, and a specially designed noose-like leash in the other.

Inside the shed, the dog could hear the man trampling around through the snow, whistling and calling out, "Here, boy!" But the dog didn't move, afraid of what the man might do to him. The biscuits smelled good, but the leash looked dangerous. He *wanted* to go outside, but if the man tried to take him away, he would miss his family when they came back to get him.

"Don't see any footprints," the man mumbled to himself as he wandered around the snowy yard. "Guess the poor little thing took off last night." He looked around some more, then finally gave up and went back to his truck.

After the truck had driven away, the dog ventured outside. Today, he was going to go and *look* for his family. No more waiting. First, he lifted his leg to mark a couple of spots near the shed. That way, if they came back, they would know that he hadn't gone far.

He stuck his muzzle in the wind, and then down in the snow. With the new drifts, it was hard to pick up a scent. But he found a faint whiff and began following it.

The trail led him through the woods, in the opposite direction from the frozen stream. A couple of times, he lost the scent and had to snuffle around in circles to pick it up again.

Then, he came to a wide road and lost the trail completely. He ran back and forth, sniffing frantically. The smells of exhaust fumes and motor oil were so strong that they covered up everything else. He whined in frustration and widened his search, but the trail was gone.

He galloped across the street, and sharp crystals of road salt and gravel cut into his paws. He limped the rest of the way and plunged into the mammoth drifts on the other side. Again, he ran in wide circles, trying to pick up the trail.

It was no use. His family was *gone*.

He was on his own.

He ran back to where he had first lost the scent, his paws stinging again from the road salt. He searched some more, but the trail just plain disappeared. Finally, he gave up and lay down in the spot where his family had last been.

He stayed there, curled into an unhappy ball, for a very long time. Cars drove by, now and then, but no one noticed him huddled up behind the huge bank of snow.

Finally, he rose stiffly to his feet. His joints felt achy and frozen from the cold. He had tried to lick the salt from his paws to stop the burning, but the terrible taste only made him more thirsty. He needed food, and water, and a warm place to sleep.

If he couldn't find his family he was going to have to find a way to survive by himself.

He limped slowly down the side of the icy road. Cars would zip by, and each time he did his best to duck out of the way so he wouldn't get hit. None of the cars stopped, or even slowed down. A couple of them beeped their horns at him, and the sound was so loud that he would scramble to safety, his heart pounding wildly.

By the time he got to the centre of town, it was almost dark. Even though there were lots of people around, no one seemed to notice him. One building seemed to be full of good smells, and he trotted around behind it.

There was a tall dustbin back there, and the delicious smells coming from inside it made him so hungry that his stomach hurt. He jumped as high as he could, his claws scrabbling against the rusty metal. He fell far short and landed in a deep pile of snow.

Determined to get some of that food, he picked himself up, shook off the snow and tried again. He still couldn't reach the opening, so he took a running start. This time, he made it a little higher, but he didn't even get close to the top. He fell down into the same drift, panting and frustrated.

The back door of the building opened and a skinny young man about sixteen years old came out. He was wearing a stained white apron and carrying a bulging plastic sack of rubbish. Just as he was about to heave it into the dustbin, he paused.

"Hey!" he said.

The dog was going to run, but he was so hungry that he just stood there and wagged his tail, instead.

"What are you doing here?" the young man asked. Then, he reached out to pat him.

The dog almost bolted, but he made himself stay and let the boy pat him. It felt so good that he wagged his tail even harder.

"Where's your collar?" the boy asked.

The dog just wagged his tail, hoping that he would get patted some more.

"Do you have a name?" the boy asked. "I'm Dominic."

The dog leaned against the boy's leg, still wagging his tail.

Dominic looked him over and then stood up. "*Stay*," he said in a firm voice.

The dog wasn't quite sure what that meant, so he wagged his tail more tentatively. He was very disappointed when he saw the boy turn to go.

Dominic went back inside the building and the door closed after him. He had left the rubbish bag behind and the dog eagerly sniffed it. There was *food* in there. *Lots* of food. He nosed around, looking for an opening, but the bag seemed to be sealed. He nudged at the heavy plastic with an experimental paw, but nothing happened.

He was about to use his teeth when the back door opened again.

Dominic was holding a plate of meatballs and pasta, and glancing back over his shoulder. "Shhh," he said in a low voice as he set the plate down. "My boss'll flip if he sees me doing this."

The dog tore into the meal, gobbling it down so quickly that he practically ate the plastic plate, too. After licking away every last morsel, he wagged his tail at the boy.

"Good dog," Dominic said, and patted him. "Go home now, OK? Your owners must be worried about you."

Patting was *nice*. Patting was very *nice*. Dogs who got to live with people and get patted all the time were *really* lucky. Maybe this boy would take him home. The dog wagged his tail harder, hoping that the boy liked him enough to want to keep him.

"Hey, Dominic!" a voice bellowed. "Get in here! We've got tables to wait on!"

"Be right there!" Dominic called back. He gave the dog one last pat and then stood up.

With one quick heave, he tossed the rubbish bag into the bin. "I have to go. Go home now. Good dog," he said, and went back inside.

The dog watched him leave and slowly lowered his tail. He waited for a while, but the boy didn't come back. He gave the already clean plate a few more licks, waited another few minutes, and then went on his way again.

Oceanport was a small town. Most of the restaurants and shops were clustered together on a few main streets. The town was always quaint, but it looked its best at Christmas time. Brightly coloured lights were strung along the old-fashioned lampposts, and fresh wreaths with red ribbons hung everywhere.

The town square was a beautiful park, where the local orchestra played concerts on the bandstand in the summer. The park also held events like the annual art festival, occasional craft shows and a yearly small carnival. During the holiday season, the various decorations in the park celebrated lots of different cultures and religions. The town council had always described the exhibit of lights and models as "The Festival of Many

Lands". Oceanport was the kind of town that wanted everyone to feel included.

Unfortunately, the dog felt anything *but* included. He wandered sadly through the back alley that ran behind the shops on Main Street. All of the dustbins were too high for him to reach, and the only rubbish bin he managed to tip over was empty. The spaghetti and meatballs had been good, but he was still hungry.

There was water dripping steadily out of a pipe behind a family-owned grocery shop. The drip was too fast to freeze right away and the dog stopped to drink as much of the water as he could. The ice that had formed underneath the drip was very slippery and it was hard to keep his balance. But he managed, licking desperately at the water. Until he started drinking, he hadn't realized how thirsty he really *was*. He licked the water until his stomach was full and he was no longer panting. Then, even though he was alone, he wagged his tail.

Now that he had eaten, and had something to drink, he felt much better. He trotted into the snowy park to look for a place to sleep.

After food, naps were his favourite. The wind was blowing hard, and his short brown fur suddenly felt very thin. He lowered his head and ears as gusts of snow whipped into him.

The most likely shelter in the park was the bandstand and he forced himself through the uneven drifts towards it. The bandstand was an old wooden frame shaped in a circle, with a peaked roof built above it. The steps were buried in snow, and the floor up above them was too exposed to the wind. He could try sleeping on the side facing away from the wind, but that would mean curling up in deep snow. It would be much warmer and more comfortable if he could find a way in underneath it.

The bandstand was set above the ground, with lattice-like boards running around the entire structure. The slats were set fairly far apart and he tried to squeeze between them. Even when he pushed with all of his might, he still couldn't fit. He circled the bandstand several times, looking for a spot where the slats might be broken, but they were in perfect repair.

He was too cold to face lying down in the snow yet, so he decided to keep moving. There was a small white church at the very edge of the park. Its path and steps had been neatly shovelled clear of snow, and when he passed the building, he saw that the front door was ajar.

Heat seemed to be wafting out through the opening and the dog was drawn towards it. Shivering too much to think about being scared, he slipped through the open door.

It was *much* warmer than it had been out-side. He gave himself a good, happy shake to get rid of any lingering snow. Then he looked around for a place to rest.

It was a big room, with high, arched ceil-ings. There were rows of hard wooden benches, separated by a long empty aisle. The church was absolutely silent, and felt very safe. Not sure where to lie down, the dog stood in the centre aisle and looked around curiously. What kind of place was it? Did people *live* here? Would they chase him away, or yell at him? Should he run out now, or just take a chance and hope for the best?

He was so cold and tired that all he wanted to do was lie down. Just as he was about to go and sleep in a back corner, he sniffed the air and then stiffened. There *was* a person in here somewhere! He stood stock-still, his ears up in their full alert position. Instinctively, he lifted one paw, pointing without being sure why he was doing it.

All he knew for certain was that he wasn't alone in here – and he might be in danger!

Chapter 3

He sniffed cautiously and finally located where the scent was. A person was sitting alone in one of the front pews, staring up at the altar. Her shoulders were slouched, and she wasn't moving, or talking. She also didn't seem threatening in any way. In fact, the only thing she seemed to be was unhappy.

The dog hesitated, and then walked up the aisle to investigate. He paused nervously every few steps and sniffed again, but then he would make himself keep going.

It was a young woman in her late twenties, all bundled up in a winter hat, coat and scarf. Her name was Margaret Saunders, and she had lived in Oceanport her whole life. She was sitting absolutely still in the pew, with her hands knotted in her lap. She wasn't making a sound, but there were tears on her cheeks.

The dog stopped at the end of her pew and waved his tail gently back and forth. She seemed very sad, and maybe he could make her feel better.

At first, Margaret didn't see him, and then she flinched.

"You scared me!" she said, with her voice shaking.

The dog wagged his tail harder. She was a nice person; he was *sure* of it.

"You shouldn't be in here," Margaret said sternly.

He cocked his head, still wagging his tail.

"Go on now, before Father Reilly comes out and sees you," she said, and waved him away. "Leave me alone. *Please*." Then she let out a heavy sigh and stared up at the dark altar.

The dog hesitated, and then made his way clumsily into the pew. He wasn't sure how, but maybe he could help her. He rested his head on her knee, and looked up at her with worried brown eyes.

Margaret sighed again. "I thought I said to go away. Where did you come from, anyway? Your owner's probably out looking for you, worried sick."

The dog pushed his muzzle against her folded hands. Automatically, she patted him, and his tail thumped against the side of the pew.

"I hope you're not lost," she said quietly. "It's a bad time of year to feel lost."

The dog put his front paws on the pew. Then, since she didn't seem to mind, he climbed all the way up. He curled into a ball next to her, putting his head on her lap.

"I really don't think you should be up here," she said, but she patted him anyway. She was feeling so lonely that even a scruffy little dog seemed like nice company. She had never had a pet before. In fact, she had never even *wanted* one. Dogs were noisy, and needed to be walked constantly, and shed fur all over the place. As far as she was concerned, they were just more trouble than they were worth. But this dog was so friendly and sweet that she couldn't help liking him.

So they sat there for a while. Sometimes she patted him, and when she didn't, the dog would paw her leg lightly. She would sigh, and then pat him some more. He was getting fur all over her wool coat, but maybe it didn't matter.

"I don't like dogs," she said to him. "Really, I don't. I never have."

The dog thumped his tail.

"*Really*," she insisted, but she put her arm around him. He was pretty cute. If it *was* a he. "Are you a boy dog, or a girl dog?"

The dog just wagged his tail again, looking up at her.

"You know, you have very compassionate eyes," she said, and then shook her head. "What am I, crazy? Talking to a *dog*? As if you're going to *answer* me?" She sighed again. "I don't know, though. I guess I have to talk to *someone*. It's been a long time."

The dog snuggled closer to her. He had never sat like this with a person before, but somehow, it felt very natural. Normal. Almost like cuddling with his brother and sisters.

"My husband died," the woman told him. Then she blinked a few times as her eyes filled with more tears. "We hadn't even been married for two years, and one night –" She stopped and swallowed hard. "He was in a terrible accident," she said finally. "And now – I don't know what to do. It's been almost a year, and – I just feel so alone. And *Christmas* makes it worse." She wiped one hand across her eyes. "We didn't even have time to start a family. And we wanted to have a *big* family."

The dog wanted to make her feel better, but he wasn't sure what to do. He tilted his head, listening intently to words he couldn't understand. Then, for lack of a better idea, he put his paw on her arm. She didn't seem to mind, so he left it there.

"People around here are trying to be really nice to me, especially my parents, but I just can't – I don't know," Margaret said. "I can't handle it. I feel like I can't handle *anything* any more."

The dog cocked his head attentively.

"That's why I only come here at night," she explained, "so I won't have to run into anyone. I used to go to church all the time, but now I don't know how to feel, or what to believe, or – everything's *so hard*. You know?"

The dog watched her with great concentration.

"I can't believe I'm talking to a dog. I must really be losing it." Tentatively, the woman touched his head, and then rubbed his ears. "Is that how I'm supposed to do it? I mean, I've never really patted a dog before."

He wagged his tail.

"What kind of dog are you, anyway?" she asked. "Sort of like one of those police dogs? Except, you're pretty little."

The dog thumped his tail cooperatively.

"Your owners shouldn't let you run around without a collar and licence tag," she said. "They should be more careful."

He lifted his paw towards her, and she laughed. The laugh sounded hesitant, as though she hadn't used it for a very long time.

"OK," she said, and shook his paw. "Why not. Like I told you, I'm not much for dogs, but – that's pretty cute. You seem *smart*."

When she dropped his paw, he lifted it again – and she laughed again.

"Hello?" a voice called from the front of the church. "Is anyone there?"

Now Margaret stiffened. She reached for her purse, getting ready to leave.

Not sure what was wrong, the dog sat up uneasily, too.

An older man wearing black trousers and a black shirt with a white collar came out of a small room near the altar. He was also wearing a thick, handknitted grey cardigan over his shirt. When he saw the woman, he looked surprised.

"I'm sorry, Margaret, I didn't realize you were here," he said. "I was going to lock up for the night."

Margaret nodded, already on her feet. "Excuse me. I was just leaving, Father."

"There's no need for that," he said, and then came part way down the aisle. He paused, leaning against the side of an empty pew. "I haven't seen you for a long time. How have you been?"

Margaret avoided his eyes as she buttoned

her coat and retied her scarf. "Fine, Father Reilly. Everything's just fine. Just – super."

"I saw your parents at eleven o'clock Mass last Sunday," he said conversationally. "They looked well."

Margaret nodded, her head down.

Slowly, Father Reilly let out his breath. "This time of year can be difficult for *anyone*, Margaret. I hope you know that if you ever want to talk, my door is always open."

Margaret started to shake her head, but then she looked down at the dog and hesitated. Maybe it would be nice to talk to someone who could talk *back*. Maybe the dog had been good practice for the real thing.

"I was just going to make myself some tea," Father Reilly said, "if you'd like to come for a few minutes. Maybe we could talk about things, a little. How you're doing."

Margaret looked down at the dog, then back at Father Reilly. She had known Father Reilly since she was a child, and he had always been very sympathetic and understanding. The kind of priest who was so nice that even people who weren't Catholic would come and talk to him about their problems. "I think I'd like that," she said, her voice hesitant. "Or, anyway, I'd like to try."

"OK, then," Father Reilly said with a kind smile. "It's a place to start, right?" Then his eyebrows went up as he noticed the dog standing in the pew. "Wait a minute. Is that a dog?"

Margaret nodded and patted him again. He wagged his tail in response, but kept his attention on Father Reilly. Was this stranger safe – or someone who was going to chase him away? Would the stranger be nice to his new friend?

"*Your* dog?" Father Reilly asked. "I don't think I've ever seen him around before."

Margaret shook her head. "Oh, no. I really don't even like dogs." Well, maybe she did *now*. A little. "He was just – here."

"Well, maybe we'd better call the police," Father Reilly suggested. "See if anyone has reported him missing. He shouldn't be running around alone in weather like this." He reached his hand out. "Come here, puppy."

Seeing the outstretched hand, the dog

panicked. His mother had taught him that a raised hand usually meant something *bad*. He squirmed out of the pew and bolted down the aisle.

"No, it's OK," Margaret said, hurrying after him. "Come back, dog! You don't have to run away."

The dog stayed uncertainly by the door. Then, as Father Reilly headed down the aisle, too, he made up his mind and raced outside. The winter wind immediately bit into his skin, but he made himself keep running.

The strange man *might* be OK – but he couldn't take that chance.

He ran for what seemed like a long time. When he was exhausted, and quivering from the cold, he finally stopped. He was in an empty car park. There was a long, low red brick building beyond the car park and he followed a shovelled path over to the main entrance. There was some sand on the path, but it didn't hurt his paws the way the road salt had.

The wind was still whipping around and he

ducked his head to avoid it. He couldn't remember *ever* being this cold. Cautiously, he circled the big building until he found a small, sheltered corner. He climbed through a deep drift and then used his front paws to dig some of the snow away.

Once he had cleared away enough snow to make a small nest for himself, he turned around three times and then curled up in a tight ball. The icy temperature of his bed made him shiver, but gradually, his body heat began to fill the space and he felt warmer.

His snow nest wasn't the best bed he had ever had – but, for tonight, it would have to do.

It was going to be another long, lonely night.

Chapter 4

He woke up when he heard children's voices. In fact, there were children *everywhere*. His joints felt frozen, and he had a hard time standing up. He had *never* been cold like this when he slept with his family. He stood there for a minute, in the snow, missing them. In fact, he missed them so much that he didn't even notice how hungry he was. Would he ever find them? Would they ever find *him*?

There were lots of children running around in the snow, yelling and throwing snowballs at each other. Some of them were playing a game with a round red rubber ball, and he *wanted* to bound over and join them.

He ventured out of the sheltered alcove a few steps, then paused. Could he play with them? Would they mind? The game looked like fun.

While he was still making up his mind, the big red ball came rolling in his direction and he barked happily. Then he galloped after it, leaping through the broken snow.

Two boys who were running after the ball stopped when they saw him.

"Where did he come from?" one of the boys, whose name was Gregory Callahan, asked.

The other boy, Oscar Wilson, laughed. "He *looks* like Rudolph!"

Gregory laughed, too. "Oh, so he came from the North Pole?"

"Yep," Oscar said solemnly. "He flew down early. Wanted to beat the holiday traffic."

Gregory laughed again. In a lot of ways, the dog *did* look like Rudolph. Since he was still a puppy, his nose and muzzle were too big for his face. His short fur had the same reddish tint a deer's coat might have, and his legs were very skinny compared to his body. If his nose was red, instead of black, it would be a perfect match.

"Hurry up, you guys!" a girl yelled from the football field. "Break is almost over."

Gregory and Oscar looked at each other, and then chased after the ball.

It was too large to fit in the dog's mouth, so he was pushing it playfully with his paws. Each time the ball veered in a new direction, the dog would lope after it, barking. The whole time, he kept it under control, almost as if he was playing football.

"Check it out," Oscar said, and pushed his glasses up to see better. "We can put him in centre field."

Gregory shook his head, watching the dog chase the ball in circles. "On Charlie Brown's team, maybe. Or, I don't know, the *Cubs*."

Gregory and Oscar were in the fifth grade, and they had been best friends since kindergarten. Although they both loved break more than anything else, Gregory's favourite class was maths, while Oscar liked reading.

Harriet, the girl who had been playing on the wing, ran over to join them. "While you guys were standing here, they scored three goals," she said, with a very critical expression on her face.

Oscar sighed, pretending to be extremely sad. "Downer," he said.

"Big-time," Gregory agreed.

"So go and get the ball," Harriet said.

The boys both shrugged, and watched the dog play.

Harriet put her hands on her hips. "You guys aren't *afraid* of that dumb puppy, are you?"

"Yep," Oscar said, sadly.

Gregory nodded. "*Way* scared."

Harriet was much too caught up in the game to be amused. Instead, she ran after the dog and tried to get the ball away from him.

A game! The dog barked happily and nudged the ball just out of her reach. He would wait until she could almost touch it, and then bat it out of her range again.

Harriet stamped one of her boots in frustration. "Bad dog!" she scolded him. "You bring that ball to me right now!"

The dog barked and promptly knocked the ball further away.

"*That* worked," Gregory said.

"Good effort," Oscar agreed.

Harriet glared at them. "You could *help* me, you know."

Gregory and Oscar thought that over.

"We could," Oscar admitted.

Gregory nodded. "We most definitely could."

"Totally," Oscar said.

But then, of course, they just stayed right where they were and grinned at her. Since she lost her sense of humour pretty easily, Harriet was a lot of fun to tease.

She stamped her foot again. "You're just immature babies! *Both* of you!" Then she ran after the dog as fast as she could.

In the spirit of the game, the dog dodged out of her way. Harriet dived for the ball, missed, and dived again. Then she slipped, landing face-first in a deep mound of snow.

Oscar and Gregory clapped loudly.

"It's not funny," Harriet grumbled as she picked herself up.

Gregory reached behind his back and pretended to hold up a large card. "I don't know about you folks judging at home," he said, "but I have to give that one a nine."

Oscar shook his head and held up his own imaginary scoring card. "A seven-point-five is as high as I can go."

"But her compulsories were *beautiful*," Gregory pointed out.

"Well, that's true," Oscar conceded, "but – I'm sorry. The degree of difficulty *just wasn't there*."

"Babies," Harriet said under her breath as she brushed the snow off her down jacket and jeans. "Stupid, immature *babies*."

By now, the rest of the football players had given up on continuing the game and started a wild snowball fight instead. It was so rowdy that at least two teachers had already run over to try and break it up.

Gregory took his gloves off, and then put his fingers in his mouth. It had taken his big sister, Patricia, a long time, but she had finally managed to teach him how to whistle that way. Patricia was convinced that, to have any hope of being cool in life, a person *had* to be able to let out a sharp, traffic-stopping whistle. And, hey, she was in the sixth grade – as far as Gregory was concerned, she *knew* these things.

His hands were a little cold, so his first whistle came out as a wimpy burst of air.

"That's good," Oscar said. "Patty taught you *great*."

Gregory ignored that, and tried again. This time, his whistle was strong and piercing, and half of the kids on the playground looked up from whatever they were doing.

Hearing the sound, the dog froze. His ears went up, and his tail stopped wagging.

"*Stay*," Gregory ordered, and walked over to him.

The dog tilted his head in confusion. Then he gave the ball a tiny, experimental nudge with his nose. Was this part of the game?

"*No*," Gregory said.

The dog stopped.

Gregory patted him on the head. "Good dog," he said. He picked up the ball and tossed it to Harriet.

She caught the ball, and then made a face. "Gross. There's drool all over it."

"Greg can't help it," Oscar said. "He *always* drools. They take him to doctors, but…"

"I almost have it licked," Gregory insisted. "All I have to do is sellotape my mouth shut – and I'm fine."

"*So* immature," Harriet said in disgust, and trotted back to the football field.

A bell rang, signalling the end of break. All over the playground, kids groaned and stopped whatever games they were playing. They headed for the school entrance, where they were supposed to line up in classes before going inside.

"We'd better go, Greg," Oscar said.

Gregory nodded, but he kept patting the dog. His family's collie, Marty, had died recently, and this was the first dog he had patted since then. Marty had been really old – his parents had had him since before he and Patricia were *born* – and life without him was lonely. All of them had cried about it, more than once. His parents had said that they would get another dog sometime soon, but none of them could really face the idea yet, since they still missed Marty so much.

"He doesn't have a collar," Gregory said aloud. "Do you think he's lost?"

Oscar shook his head. "I doubt it. He probably just got out of his garden or something."

Gregory nodded, but he *liked* this dog. If he thought his parents wouldn't get upset, he would bring him home.

Mr Hastings, their teacher, strode over to them. "Come on, boys," he said sternly. "Leave the dog alone. Break is over now."

Gregory would *much* rather have stayed and played with the dog. All afternoon, if possible. But he nodded, and gave the dog one last pat on the head.

"Good dog," he said. "Go home now, boy."

Then he and Oscar followed Mr Hastings towards the school. The dog watched them go, very disappointed. The playground was completely empty now. Slowly, his tail drooped and he lowered his ears. He didn't know why, but for some reason, the game was over.

He was on his own again.

Chapter 5

The dog waited in the playground for a while, but none of the children came back. He was *especially* waiting for the boy who had patted him for so long. He wished that he could *live* with that boy and play with him all the time.

When it was finally obvious that they had gone inside for good, he decided to move on. He walked slowly, with his head down, and his tail between his legs. He was so hungry that his stomach was growling. He ate some snow, but it only made his stomach hurt more.

There were some bins behind the school, overflowing with rubbish bags. Smelling all sorts of wonderful food, he stopped short. He sniffed harder, then started wagging his tail in anticipation. Lunchtime!

The bins were taller than he was, but he climbed on to a pile of snow so he could reach. Then he leaned forward and grabbed one of the bags with his teeth. Using his legs for leverage, he was able to pull the bag free. It fell on to the ground and broke open, spilling half-eaten school lunches everywhere.

It was like a vision of dog heaven. Food, food, and *more* food!

In fact, there was so much food that he really wasn't sure where to start. Lots of sandwich crusts, carrot sticks and apples with one bite out of them. He ate until he was full, switching from leftover peanut butter and jelly to cream cheese and olives to ham. So far, the ham was his favourite. He sniffed the crumpled brown paper bags, hoping to find more.

American cheese, part of a pie, some tuna fish, pudding cartons with some left inside, hard granary rolls, a couple of drumsticks. He ate everything he could find, although he spat all of the lettuce out. He *definitely* didn't like lettuce. Or apples. The rubbish bin smelled more strongly of rotting apples than anything else, although he wasn't sure why.

Some of the milk cartons were still full, and he tore the cardboard containers open. Milk would spurt out on to the snow, and he would quickly lick it up before it drained away. Now his thirst was satisfied, too.

There was so much leftover food that even though he had been starving, he couldn't finish it all. Carefully, he used his front paws to cover the bag with snow. That way, he could come back later and eat some more. And there were other bags he hadn't even opened yet!

He trotted on his way in a much better mood, letting his tail sway jauntily. It didn't even seem as cold any more. He didn't have anywhere special to go, so he decided to wander around town and look for his family. Could they have gone to live with some nice people? Maybe if he went down every street he could find, he would come across them.

The streets were busy with cars full of people doing last-minute holiday shopping.

So, he was very cautious each time he had to cross one. Cars scared him. He would wait by the side of the road until they all seemed to be gone, take a deep breath, and dash across. When he got to the other side, his heart would be beating loudly and he could hear himself panting. No matter how many times he did it, it never got any easier.

He looked and looked, but found no signs that his family had ever existed. He even went back to the old abandoned house to check. The only thing he could find was faint whiffs of his own scent. If they hadn't come back for him by now, he knew they never would.

Tired and discouraged by his long search, it was an effort to keep walking. The sun was going down, and the temperature was dropping again. He wandered morosely through a quiet neighbourhood, looking for a good place to take a nap. When in doubt, he always napped.

He could smell dogs inside some of the warmly lit houses he passed and felt very envious of them. They would bark when he went by, so they must smell him, too. A couple of dogs were outside in fenced yards, and they barked so fiercely at him that he would end up crossing to the other side of the street.

There were tantalizing smells of meat cooking and wood smoke from winter fires wafting out of many of the houses. He would stop on the pavement in front of the best-smelling houses and inhale over and over again. Beef, chicken, pork chops – all *kinds* of good things. He whimpered a little each time he caught a new scent, feeling very sorry for himself.

He was going by a small, unlit white house when he heard a tiny sound. A frail sound. He stopped, his ears flicking up. What was it? A bad sound. A *sad* sound.

He raised his nose into the wind to see if he smelled anything. A person, somewhere nearby. In the snow. He followed his nose – and the low moaning – around to the side of the little house.

There was a car parked in the driveway, and he could still smell petrol and feel the warmth of the engine. Was it going to start up and run over him? He gave the car a wide berth, just in case, but kept tracking the sound.

Suddenly, he saw an old woman crumpled in the snow. She was so limp and still that he had almost stepped on her. There was a sheen of ice on the driveway, and she was lying at the bottom of a flight of steps leading to the back door. Two bags of groceries were strewn haphazardly around her.

She moaned weakly, and he went rigid. He backed away a few steps, and then circled around her a few times. Why didn't she move? When she didn't get up, he let out a small woof.

Her eyes fluttered open and she looked up at him dully. "Help," she whispered. "Please help me."

The dog put a tentative paw on her arm, and she moaned again. He jumped back, afraid. What was wrong? Why was she lying on the ground like that?

Unsure of himself, he ran up the back steps. They were covered with fresh ice and his paws skidded. He barked more loudly, standing up on his hind legs. He scratched at the door with his front paws, still barking.

"No one's there," the old woman gasped. "I live alone."

He barked some more, then ran back down the steps. Why didn't anyone come? Should he bark more?

"*Go*," she said, lifting one arm enough to give him a weak push. "Go and get your owner."

He nosed at her sleeve, and she pushed him harder.

"*Go home*," she ordered, her teeth chattering from the cold. "Get some help!"

The dog didn't know what to do, and he circled her again. There *was* something wrong; he just wasn't sure exactly what it was. Should he curl up with her to keep her warm, or just run away?

At the house across the street, an estate car was pulling into the driveway. He could hear people getting out of the car. There were at least three children, two of whom were bickering.

"Help!" the elderly woman called, but her voice was barely above a whisper. "Help me!"

There was so much urgency in her voice that the dog barked. Then he barked again and again, running back and forth in the driveway. The people noticed him, but still seemed to be going into their house.

He barked more frantically, running part way across the street and then back to the driveway. He repeated the pattern, barking the entire time.

A teenage girl, who was holding a grocery bag and a rucksack full of schoolbooks, laughed. "Whose dog is that?" she asked, pointing over at him. "He's acting like he thinks he's Lassie."

The dog barked loudly, ran up the driveway, and ran out to the street.

"He sure doesn't *look* like Lassie," one of the girl's little brothers, Brett, scoffed. "He looks like a *mutt*."

Their mother, who was carrying her own bags of groceries, frowned. "Maybe something's wrong," she said. "Mrs Amory usually has her lights on by now."

The teenage girl, Lori, shrugged. "Her car's in the driveway. Maybe she's just taking a nap or something."

Her mother still looked worried. "Do me a

favour and go over there, will you, Lori? It can't hurt to check."

Lori shrugged, and gave her grocery bag to Brett and her rucksack to her other brother, Harold.

The dog kept barking and running back and forth as she walked over.

"Take it easy," she said to him. "You've been watching the Discovery Channel or something? Getting *dog ambitions?*"

The dog galloped over to the injured old woman and stood next to her, barking loudly.

Lori's mouth dropped open. "Oh, *whoa*," she said, and then ran over to join him. "Mum!" she yelled over her shoulder. "Call 911! Quick! Mrs Amory's hurt!"

After that, things moved fast. Lori's mother, who was Mrs Goldstein, dashed over to help. Brett went inside to call an ambulance and Harold hurried to get a blanket.

Hearing all the commotion, other neighbours in the area came outside. By the time the police and the ambulance had arrived, a small, concerned crowd had gathered.

Since it was the northwest sector of town,

two of the police officers were Steve and Bill. They worked with the other cops to move the neighbours aside so that the two ambulance attendants could get through with a stretcher.

The whole time, the dog hung back nervously in the shadows of Mrs Amory's garage, not sure if he was in trouble. There were so many people around that he might have done something bad. They all seemed very upset, and it might be his fault.

"What happened, Officer Callahan?" one of the neighbours asked Steve. "Is Mrs Amory going to be OK?"

Steve nodded. "Looks like a broken hip, but the Goldsteins found her in time. She might have a little hypothermia, but she should be just fine."

The ambulance attendants shifted Mrs Amory very gently on to the stretcher, and covered her with two more blankets. She was weak from pain, and shivering from the cold.

"Thank you," she whispered. "Thank you so much."

"Don't worry about a thing," one of the attendants assured her. "We'll have you over at the emergency room in a jiffy."

"He saved me," she said weakly. "I don't know where he came from, but he saved me."

"Well, don't worry, you're going to be fine," the attendant said comfortingly.

As she was lifted into the back of the ambulance, Steve and Bill and the other officers moved the onlookers aside.

"Let's clear away now," Bill said authoritatively. "Give them room to pull out."

The ambulance backed slowly out of the driveway, with its lights flashing and its siren beginning to wail. Everyone watched as the emergency vehicle drove away with Mrs Amory safely inside.

"OK, folks, show's over," Steve announced. "Thanks a lot for all of your help. You can head in for supper now."

Although there was still an eager buzz of conversation, most of the neighbours started drifting towards their houses.

Bill pulled out his notebook and went over to the Goldsteins. "We just need a few things for our report," he said to Mrs Goldstein. "You and your daughter found her?"

"It was Lassie!" Lori's little brother Harold chirped. "He was totally cool!"

Bill looked sceptical. "What do you mean by that, son?"

Brett pointed at the dog crouching by the garage. "It was that dog!" he said, sounding just as excited as Harold. "He was barking and barking, and Lori followed him. It was just like TV!"

Bill's expression became even more doubtful. "You're saying that a *dog* came over to get help?"

"Exactly," Mrs Goldstein answered for her sons. "I know it must sound strange – but he was very insistent, and that's when I sent Lori over. I was afraid that something might be wrong."

Bill digested that, his pen still poised over the empty notebook page. "So, wait, let me get this straight. It was *your* dog who alerted you?" he asked.

"We don't have a dog," Brett told him.

Harold nodded, looking sheepish. "On account of, I'm allergic," he said, and sniffed a little to prove it.

Bill considered all of that, and then squinted over towards the garage. "You sure the dog didn't knock her down in the first place?"

"I don't think so," Lori said doubtfully. "He was trying to help."

It was completely dark now, except for the headlights on the two remaining squad cars. Bill unclipped his torch from his equipment belt. He turned it on and flashed the light around the yard.

Seeing it, the dog instinctively shied away from the beam. But it was too late – Bill had already seen him.

"Hey!" Bill said, and nudged his partner. "It's that same stray dog you were so hot about catching the other night."

"What about him?" Steve asked, in the middle of taking a statement from one of the other neighbours.

"He's over there," Bill said, and gestured with the torch. "The Goldsteins say he sounded the alarm."

Steve's eyebrows went up. "Really? Hey, all right! I *told* you he was a great dog." He shoved his notebook in his jacket pocket. "Let's see if we can get him this time. Find him a good home."

All of the neighbours wanted to help capture the hero dog. So everyone fanned out and moved forward. Some of them shouted, "Here, boy!" while others whistled or snapped their fingers.

Seeing so many people coming towards him, the dog slipped deeper into the bushes. He *was* in trouble! They had taken the poor old lady away, and now they were *blaming* him. He squirmed towards the woods crouched down on all fours, trying to stay out of sight. Then, he gathered all of his energy and started running as fast as he could.

Lately, escaping to safety had become one of his best tricks!

Chapter 6

The dog hid in the woods until he was *sure* that no one was coming after him any more. It had been a very long day, and all he wanted to do now was *sleep*. He could walk back to the school and sleep in that little alcove, but it seemed too far.

There was a pile of boulders to his right and he crept over to explore them. Most of the rocks were jammed close together and buried in snow. But a few had openings that looked like little caves. He chose the one that seemed to be the most private and wiggled inside.

He fitted easily, and there was even room to stand up and turn around, if he wanted.

Almost no snow had blown in, and there were lots of dry leaves to lie on. He could smell the musty, ancient odour of other animals who had used this cave for a shelter – squirrels, mostly, and maybe a skunk or two. But, as far as he could tell, no other animal had been in here for a long time.

As always, he turned around three times before lying down. The cave was so warm, compared to being outside, that he slept for a long time.

When he woke up and poked his head out through the rock opening, it was snowing hard. He retreated back inside. He wanted to go over to the school and find some more discarded lunches to eat, but the storm was just too bad. No matter how much his stomach started growling, he would be much better off in here, out of the blizzard. The wind was howling, and he was glad to be in a place where he could avoid it.

So, he went back to sleep. Every so often, he would be startled by a noise and leap to his feet. Then, when it turned out to be nothing out of the ordinary, he would curl up again.

It snowed all day, and most of the night. He only went outside to go to the toilet, and then he would return to his little rock cave. The snow was so deep now that his legs were completely buried when he tried to walk, and mostly he had to leap. Leaping was hard work, and made him tired after a while. He liked it better when there wasn't any snow at all. Grass and dirt were *easy* to walk on.

Once, he saw a chipmunk chattering away on a low tree branch. He was hungry, and thought about trying to catch the little animal. But before he could even *try* to lunge in that direction, the chipmunk had sensed danger and scampered further up the tree. He ducked back into his cave, not terribly disappointed. The poor little chipmunk was trying to survive the harsh winter, the same way he was. He would just go hungry today, that's all.

By the next morning, the storm had finally stopped. The temperature was higher than it had been, and the top layer of snow was already softening into slush.

He hadn't eaten for such a long time that he headed straight for the school rubbish bins.

When he got to the school, he stopped in the car park and shook out each front paw, since he had snow caked between his toes. Now, it was time to eat some breakfast.

He ran around behind the building, but the rubbish bins were empty! Now what? He had been so sure that he would find more ham, pies, and other treats.

He sank back on to his haunches and whimpered a couple of times. Where had all the food gone? The rubbish bins were closed now and piled high with snow. All he could smell was the lingering stench of rotten apples and sour milk. They weren't very nice smells, but his stomach still rumbled.

He prowled around the back of the school for a while. Then he came to a door where he could smell food. He barked a couple of times, then sat down to see what would happen. The *last* time he had smelled food behind a door, that teenage boy had given him those great meatballs. Maybe he would get lucky again.

The door opened and a very stout woman in a big white apron looked out. She was Mrs Gustave, the school cook.

"What?" she asked in a loud, raspy voice.

The dog barked again and held up one paw.

"Hmmm," Mrs Gustave said, and folded her arms across her huge stomach. "Is that the best you can do?"

She seemed to be waiting for something, so he sat back and lifted both paws in the air.

"That's better," she decided, and disappeared into the kitchen.

Even though she was gone, the dog stayed in the same position. Maybe if she came back, she would like it more the second time. Then he lost his balance and fell over on his side.

"*My* dog can do much better than that," Mrs Gustave said. She had come outside just in time to see him tumble into the snow.

He quickly scrambled up and held out one paw. One paw was *definitely* safer than two.

"You're going to have to work on that," she said. With a grunt of effort, she bent over and set a steaming plate on top of the snow.

It was crumbled hamburger with gravy, served over mashed potatoes. He wagged his tail enthusiastically and started eating.

"Now, remember," Mrs Gustave said.

"From now on, you should eat at *home* and not go around begging like a fool." Then she closed the door so she could go back to cooking the students' hot lunch.

He enjoyed his meal very much, and licked the plate over and over when he was done. It had been a hefty serving, but he still could have eaten five or six more. Still, the one big portion made him feel much better.

Cheerfully, he wandered around to the playground. Maybe his friends from the other day would come out again! Then he might get patted some more.

He waited for a long time, and then he got bored. He scratched a little, dug a couple of holes in the snow, and then rolled over a few times.

But he was still bored. He yawned, and scratched again. Still bored. It was time for a nap.

He trudged over to the sheltered area where he had slept that one night. He dug himself a new nest, stamping down the snow with all four feet. Then he lay down and went right to sleep. He slept very soundly, and even snored a little. The day passed swiftly.

"Hey, look!" a voice said. "He *did* come back!"

The dog opened his eyes to see Gregory and his friend Oscar standing above him. He wagged his tail and sprang to his feet.

"Where've you been?" Gregory asked, patting him. "We looked all over for you yesterday."

The dog wagged his tail harder and let them take turns patting him.

"You know, he's kind of scraggly," Oscar said. "Maybe he really *is* a stray."

Gregory shrugged. "Of course he is. Why else would he sleep here?"

Oscar bent down and sniffed slightly. Then he made a face and straightened up. "I think he needs a *bath*, too."

Gregory thought about that. "My father's always home writing, so I can't sneak him into my house. What about your house?"

Oscar shook his head. "Not today. Delia and Todd have the flu, so Mum had to stay home with them."

The dog tried to sit up with both paws in

the air again, but fell over this time, too.

Both boys laughed.

"What a goofball," Oscar said.

Gregory nodded. "He's funny, though. I really like him."

"Why don't you just say you want a dog for Christmas?" Oscar suggested. "Then you can show up with him like it's a big surprise."

Gregory was very tempted by that idea, but he was pretty sure it wouldn't work. "I don't know," he said doubtfully. "My parents said we could maybe go and pick one out together in a month or two."

Oscar packed together a hard snowball and flipped it idly from one hand to the other. "What does Patricia say?" he asked.

Gregory's big sister. Her advice was advice Gregory always took seriously. Gregory sighed. "That they're still much too sad to even *look* at other dogs right now."

Oscar nodded, then threw the snowball a few feet away. The dog promptly chased after it, and brought it back.

Gregory looked pleased. "He fetches! He's really smart!"

Oscar laughed and threw the snowball even further. "How smart is a dog who fetches *snow?*" he asked as the dog returned with the snowball, his tail beating wildly from side to side.

"*Extra*-smart," Gregory said.

Oscar shrugged and tossed the snowball twenty feet away. "If you say so."

The dog galloped happily after it.

"Boys!" a sharp voice yelled. "What are you doing over there?" It was Ms Hennessey, one of their teachers. She was always *very* strict.

Gregory and Oscar looked guilty, even though they weren't really doing anything wrong at all.

"Science," Oscar said. "We were just standing here, talking a whole lot about science."

Gregory nodded. "Like, gravity and stuff." He made his own snowball and flicked it straight up into the air.

They both watched it come down, shook their heads, and exchanged admiring glances.

"Gravity again," Oscar observed solemnly. "*Cool.*"

The dog picked up that snowball instead

and offered it to Gregory.

Ms Hennessey marched over, her face tight with concern. She was tall and extremely skinny, with lots of bright red hair. She liked to wear wide, billowy skirts, big sunglasses and ponchos. "Don't you boys know better than to go up to a stray animal! It's *dangerous*!"

This little dog might be many things, but "dangerous" didn't seem to be one of them. Gregory and Oscar looked at each other, and shrugged.

"Get away from him right now!" Ms Hennessey said with her hands on her hips. "He might have rabies!"

Gregory looked at the dog, who wagged his tail in a very charming way. "I don't think so, ma'am. He seems –"

"Look at him!" Ms Hennessey interrupted, and pulled both of the boys away. "There's *foam* in his mouth!"

"That's just drool, ma'am," Oscar explained. "Because he's sort of panting."

Gregory gave him a small shove. "Saliva, Oscar. Us science types like to call it saliva."

"Well, I'm going to call the dog officer," Ms

Hennessey said grimly. "We can't have a dangerous dog roaming around near children. I just won't have it!"

For years, Gregory's parents had always explained to him that it was important to be *careful* around strange animals – but that it was *also* important to help any animal who might be in trouble. "Please don't call the dog officer, Ms Hennessey," he said desperately. If the dog went to the pound, he would never get to see him again. "It's OK, he's –" Gregory tried to come up with a good excuse – "he's *my* dog! He just – followed me to school, that's all."

Ms Hennessey narrowed her eyes. "Where's his collar?"

Gregory thought fast. "He lost it, when we were walking on the beach last weekend."

"A seagull probably took it," Oscar put in helpfully. "They like shiny things."

"*Racoons* like shiny objects," Gregory told him. "Not seagulls."

"Oh." Oscar shrugged. "That's right, it was a racoon. I heard it was a big old *family* of racoons."

Ms Hennessey wasn't buying any of this. "What's his name?" she asked.

Gregory and Oscar looked at each other.

"Sparky," Gregory said, just as Oscar said, "Rover."

Ms Hennessey nodded, her suspicions confirmed. "I see."

"His, um, his *other* nickname is Spot," Gregory said, rather lamely.

"I don't appreciate having you two tell me fibs," Ms Hennessey said without a hint of a smile on her face. "I think you'd just better come along down to the office with me, and you can talk to Dr Garcia about all of this."

Dr Garcia was the vice principal – and she made Ms Hennessey seem *laid-back*. Being sent to the office at Oceanport Middle School was always a major disaster, dreaded by one and all.

"But –" Gregory started to protest.

"Come along now," Ms Hennessey ordered, taking each of them by the sleeve. She turned towards Ms Keise, one of the other teachers. "Cheryl, chase this dog away from here! He's a threat to the children!"

"He's not," Gregory insisted. "He's a really *good* —"

"That will be quite enough of that," Ms Hennessey said sharply, and led the two of them away.

The dog let the snowball fall out of his mouth. Where were his friends going? Then he saw a tall woman in a leather coat hurrying towards him. She was frowning and shaking her finger at him. Before the woman could get any closer, the dog started running.

He would much rather run away – than be *chased*.

Chapter 7

The dog ended up hiding behind the rubbish bins. When he no longer heard any voices, he slogged back to his little alcove to sleep some more. Who knew when his friends might come back? He wanted to be here waiting when they did.

This time, though, the voice that woke him up was female. He opened one eye and saw a thin girl, with her hair tied back in a neat brown ponytail. She had the same very blue eyes Gregory had, and she was wearing a red, white and blue New England Patriots jacket. It was Patricia, Gregory's big sister.

"So, you must be the dog my brother won't shut up about," she said aloud.

The dog cocked his head.

Patricia frowned at him. "He got *detention* because of you. So even though it's Christmas, Mum and Dad are probably going to have to ground him."

He wagged his tail tentatively. She didn't exactly sound mad, but she didn't sound friendly, either.

"Well," she said, and tossed her ponytail back. "The way he was going on and on, I figured you could *talk* or something. Tap dance and sing, maybe. But you just look normal. Even a little silly, if you want to know the truth."

Maybe she would like it if he rolled in the snow. Like *him*. So, he rolled over a couple of times.

"*A lot* silly," she corrected herself.

The dog scrambled up and shook vigorously. Snow sprayed out in all directions.

"Thanks a lot, dog," Patricia said, and wiped the soggy flakes from her face and jacket. "I enjoyed that."

He wagged his tail.

"We could still maybe talk Mum and Dad

into it. I mean, it *is* almost Christmas," she said. "Although we really like *collies*." She studied him carefully. "It would be easier if you had a limp, or your ear was chewed up, or something. Then my parents would feel sorry for you."

The dog barked. Then he sat down and held up his right paw.

Patricia nodded. "Not bad. If you could *walk* with your paw up like that, they could *never* say no. Here, try it." She clapped her hands to be sure she had his full attention. "*Come*."

Obediently, the dog walked over to her. "Come" was an easy one.

"No, *limp*," she said, and demonstrated. "I want you to limp. Like this, see?" She hopped around on one red cowboy-booted foot. Cowboy boots might not be warm in the winter, but they *were* cool. Always. "Can you do that?"

The dog barked, and rolled over in the snow. Then he bounded to his feet and looked at her hopefully.

"Well, that's not right at all," she said, and

then sighed. "If I tell you to play dead, you'll probably *sit*, right?" She shook her head in dismay. "I really don't know about this. I thought he said you were smart."

The dog barked and wagged his tail heartily.

"Right," Patricia said, and shook her head again. "And if I tell you to 'Speak', you're going to look for a hoop to jump through – I can see it now."

Perplexed by all of this, the dog just sat down and looked at her blankly.

"Well, this is just a waste," Patricia said, and then straightened the tilt of her beret. "Until we can get you home and I have some serious training time with you, you're clearly *beyond* my help." She unzipped her rucksack and took out some crackers and cheese and two chicken sandwiches. "Here, we saved most of our lunches for you. The crackers are from Oscar." She placed the food down in the snow. "Don't ever say I didn't do anything for you."

The dog wagged his tail, and then gobbled up the food in several gulping bites.

"We'll bring more tomorrow, even though it's Saturday," Patricia promised. "Greg can't come back this afternoon because Dad's going to have to pick him up after detention and yell at him for a while. You know, for appearances."

The dog licked the napkin for any remaining crumbs. Then he stuck his nose underneath it, just in case. But he had polished off every last scrap.

"See you later then," she said, and jabbed her finger at him. "Stay. OK? *Stay*."

The dog lifted his paw.

"Ridiculous," Patricia said, and walked away, shaking her head the entire time. "Just ridiculous."

The dog hung around the school until all the lights were out, and even the janitors had gone home. Then he decided to roam around town for a while. He took what had become his regular route, heading first to the abandoned house. There was no sign of his family – which didn't surprise him, but *did* disappoint him.

Again.

After that, he wandered through the various neighbourhoods, looking longingly at all of the families inside their houses. He explored the back alleys behind Main Street. The drainpipe near the pizza place was still leaking, and he had a nice, long drink.

Visiting the park was the next stop on his route. There were lots of townspeople strolling down the winding paths and admiring the holiday exhibits. He was careful to stay out of sight, but he enjoyed being around all of the activity. It was almost like being *part* of it.

There was a traditional Nativity scene, complete with a manger and plastic models of barnyard animals and the Three Wise Men. Further along, there were displays honouring Chanukah, Kwanzaa, and various other ways of celebrating the holiday season.

There was also, of course, a big, wooden sleigh. A fat model Santa Claus sat inside it, surrounded by presents, and the sleigh was being pulled by eight tiny plastic reindeer. Coloured lights decorated all of the trees, and the little model of Main Street had been built perfectly to scale, right down to the miniature people cluttering its pavements.

Christmas carols and other traditional songs played from the loudspeaker above the bandstand, every night from six to ten. On Christmas Eve, live carollers would gather there and hold an early evening concert for everyone to enjoy. Oceanport took the holiday season *seriously*.

He found a nice vantage point underneath a mulberry bush, and settled down for a short nap. When he opened his eyes, the park had cleared out and all of the holiday lights had been turned off for the night. The place *seemed* to be deserted.

He wasn't sure what had woken him up, but somewhere, he heard a suspicious noise. Laughter. Low male voices. Banging and crunching sounds. He stood up, the fur slowly rising on his back. Something wasn't right. He should go and investigate the situation.

The voices were coming from over near the crèche. The dog loped silently through the snow, approaching the Nativity scene from behind. The laughter was louder and he could hear people hissing "Shhh!" to one another.

Whatever they were doing, it didn't feel right. There was a crash, and then more laughter. The dog walked around to the front of the crèche, growling low in his throat.

Inside the Nativity scene, a group of boys from the high school were moving the plastic figures around. They had always been bullies, and vandalism was one of their favourite destructive pranks. They were especially active during the holidays.

One of them was just bending down to steal the baby Jesus figure from the manger. Two other boys were walking over to the Chanukah exhibit, holding cans of spray paint. The fourth boy was knocking over the Three Wise Men, one at a time.

The dog growled the most threatening growl he knew how to make, and all of the boys froze.

"Whose dog?" one of them, Luke, asked uneasily.

The other three shrugged.

"Dunno," the biggest one, Guillermo, said. "Never seen him before."

The dog growled and took a stiff-legged step forward.

"Hey, *chill*, dog!" Michael, the leader of the group, said impatiently. "We're only fooling around." He turned to his friends. "Ignore him – it's just a dumb puppy. Let's hurry up before someone sees us."

"Hey, he looks kind of like those reindeer," another boy, Rich, said, sniggering. "Let's tie him up front there."

Luke held up his can of red spray paint. "If you guys hold him, I'll spray his nose!"

They all laughed.

"Let's do it!" Michael decided.

As they crept towards him, the dog growled, his lips curling away from his teeth.

"Oh, yeah," Guillermo said. "He thinks he's *tough*."

"Let's leave *him* in the manger," Rich suggested. "That'd be pretty funny!"

As Luke and Michael lunged for him, the dog snarled and leaped forward. With his teeth bared, he slashed at Michael's jacket.

The sleeve tore, and Michael stopped short. He looked down at the jagged rip and started swearing.

"That's *Gore-Tex*, man," he protested. "You stupid dog!" He aimed a kick at the dog's head, but missed. "It was really expensive! How'm I going to *explain* this?" He tried another kick, but the dog darted out of the way.

Guillermo packed together a ball of ice and snow. Then he threw it as hard as he could. The chunk hit the dog square in the ribs and he yelped.

"Yeah, all right!" Guillermo shouted, and bent down to find some more ice. "Let's get 'im!"

The dog growled at them, and then started barking as loudly as he could. He barked over and over, the sound echoing through the still night.

"If he doesn't shut up, everyone in town's going to hear him," Luke said uneasily.

"We mess up these dumb exhibits *every* year," Rich complained. "We can't let some stupid dog ruin this – it's a *tradition*."

During all of the commotion, none of them had noticed the police squad car patrolling past the park. The car stopped and Officers Kathy Bronkowski and Tommy Lee got out. They had been two of the other cops at Mrs Amory's house the night before, when she had broken her hip on the ice.

Officer Lee turned on his torch, while Officer Bronkowski reached for her night-stick. When the beam passed over them, the boys were exposed in the bright light and they all stood stock-still for a few seconds.

"Hey!" Officer Bronkowski yelled. "What do you think you're doing over there!"

The boys started running, stumbling over one another in their hurry to get away.

"Get back here, you punks!" Officer Lee shouted. "You think we don't recognize you?"

Still furious, the dog raced after them. He snapped at their heels, just to scare them a little. It *worked*. He kept chasing them all the way to the end of the park. Then he trotted back to the crèche, barely panting at all.

The two police officers were carefully reassembling the exhibit. They brushed snow off the tipped-over figures, and then set each one in its proper place.

Officer Bronkowski picked up the two discarded cans of spray paint. "Those little creeps," she said under her breath. "Who do they think they are?"

Officer Lee put the baby Jesus figure gently in the manger. "I saw Michael Smith and Guillermo Jereda. Did you get a good look at the other two?"

Officer Bronkowski shook her head. She had long blonde hair, but when she was on duty, she kept it pinned up in a bun. "No, but it was probably the Crandall twins, Luke and Rich. Those four are always together."

"So let's cruise by their houses," Officer Lee suggested. "See what their parents have to say about this."

Officer Bronkowski nodded. "Good idea. It's about time we caught them in the act."

"The dog gave them away," Officer Lee said, with a shrug. He yawned, opened a pack of gum, and offered a piece to his partner before taking one for himself. "They shouldn't have brought him along."

Officer Bronkowski started to answer, but then she noticed the dog lurking around behind the scale model of the Oceanport town hall. "You know what? I don't think they did," she said slowly.

Officer Lee glanced up from the plastic donkey he was setting upright. "What do you mean?"

She pointed at the dog. "Unless I'm crazy, that's the same dog who found Mrs Amory yesterday."

Officer Lee looked dubious. "Oh, come on. You mean you think there's some dog *patrolling* Oceanport? You're starting to sound like Steve Callahan." Steve Callahan was, of course, the police officer who had been trying to catch the dog ever since he saw him at the abandoned house. Steve Callahan was also, as it happened, Gregory and Patricia's uncle.

Officer Bronkowski nodded. "That's exactly what I'm saying. Would we have pulled over just now if we hadn't heard him barking?"

"Well, no," Officer Lee admitted, "but—"

Officer Bronkowski cut him off. "And if Gail Amory had been out much longer last night, the doctors say she might have frozen to death. She owes her *life* to that dog."

Officer Lee grinned at her. "So let's put him on the payroll. Maybe even arrange a Christmas bonus." He gave the dog a big thumbs-up. "Good dog! Way to go!"

The dog barked once, and then trotted off.

"Wait!" Officer Bronkowski called after him. "Come back!"

The dog kept going. It was time to be on his way again.

Chapter 8

Remembering how warm it had been inside, the dog went back to the church. Unfortunately, tonight, the door was firmly closed. He leaned his shoulder against it and pushed, but the heavy wood wouldn't even budge.

OK. New plan. He would go back to the school, maybe. In the morning, his friends might come back. Gregory, especially, although he liked Oscar and Patricia, too. Maybe they would even have more food for him! Those chicken sandwiches were *good*.

He was cutting across a car park, when he heard – crying. A child, crying. It might even be a baby. He stopped to listen, lifting his paw. The sound was coming from a car parked at the farthest end of the car park.

He ran right over, stopping every few feet to sniff the air. There were several people in the car – he could smell them – but the crying was coming from a small child. A small, miserable child. A sick child.

All of the car windows were rolled up, except for the one on the driver's side, which was cracked slightly. The car was a beat-up old estate car, and it was *crammed* with people and possessions. He could hear a soothing female voice trying to calm the crying child. The baby would cry, and then cough, and then cry some more. There were two other children in the back seat, and he could hear them coughing and sneezing, too.

He barked one little bark.

Instantly, everyone inside the car, except for the baby, was silent. They were maybe even holding their breaths.

He barked again.

One of the doors opened partway, and a tow-headed little boy peeked out.

"Mummy, it's a dog!" he said. "Can we let

him in?"

"No," his mother answered, sounding very tired. "Close the door, Ned. It's cold out there."

"*Please?*" Ned asked. "He won't eat much – I promise! He can have my share."

His mother, Jane Yates, just sighed. They had been homeless since the first of the month, and she could barely afford to feed her *children*. She, personally, had been living on one tiny meal a day for almost two weeks now. For a while, after the divorce, she had been able to keep things going fine. But then, her ex-husband left the state and right after Thanksgiving, she got laid off. Since then, their lives had been a nightmare. And now, all three of the children were sick with colds. The baby, Sabrina, was running a fever, and her cough was so bad that she was probably coming down with bronchitis. They didn't have any money to pay a doctor, so the baby was just getting sicker and sicker.

"I'm sorry, Ned," Jane said. "We just can't. I'm really sorry."

Now Ned started crying, too. His sister,

Brenda, joined in – and the baby, Sabrina, had yet to stop.

"Go away," Jane said to the dog, sounding pretty close to tears herself. "Please just leave us alone." She reached over the front seat and yanked the back door closed.

The door slammed in the dog's face and he jumped away, startled. Now *all* he could hear was crying and coughing. What was going on here? It was bad, whatever it was.

He pawed insistently at the door, and barked again. No matter what he did, the crying wouldn't stop.

"Bad dog! Go away!" Jane shouted from inside the car. "Stop bothering us!"

The dog backed off, his ears flattening down against his head. He circled the car a couple of times, but none of the doors opened. These people needed help! With one final bark, he trotted uncertainly back towards the church.

When he got there, Margaret Saunders, the young widow he had met earlier that week, was just coming out with her mother. If they didn't exactly look overjoyed, at least they seemed to be at peace.

"Well, hi there," Margaret said, her face lighting up when she saw him. She reached down one gloved hand to pat him. "Mum, it's the dog I was telling you about. He's pretty cute, isn't he?"

Her mother nodded.

"Maybe I should *get* a dog, sometime," Margaret mused. "To keep me company."

"Sounds like a great idea," her mother agreed. Since Saunders had been Margaret's husband's last name, her mother was Mrs Talbot.

Margaret patted the dog again. "I think so, too. Whoever owns *this* dog is pretty lucky."

"No doubt. But I can't help wondering if maybe someone *sent* him to you that night," her mother said softly, and smiled at her daughter.

Margaret smiled back. Her mother had a point. The dog *had* appeared out of nowhere. "Stranger things have happened, I guess."

Margaret might be patting his head, but otherwise, they didn't seem to be paying much attention to him. He could still, faintly, hear the sound of crying, and he barked loudly. One thing the dog had learned, was that if he barked a lot, he could get people to follow him. He just *knew* that baby shouldn't be crying like that. He dashed off a few steps, barked, and ran back to them.

Margaret grinned. She had been feeling a little happier over the last couple of days. Hopeful, for the first time in many months. "What do you think, Mum? *I* think he's telling us that Timmy fell down the mine shaft, and we're supposed to bring rope."

Her mother laughed. "It certainly looks that way." Of course, neither of them was used to dogs. But *this* one seemed to have come straight out of a movie.

The dog barked again, and ran a few steps away. He barked more urgently, trying to make them understand.

Father Reilly came outside to see what all the commotion was. "What's going on?" he asked, buttoning his cardigan to block out some of the wind.

"Look, Father," Margaret said, and gestured towards the street. "That nice dog is back."

Father Reilly nodded, and then shivered a

little. "So he is. But – what's wrong with him?"

The dog barked, and ran away three more steps.

"I don't know," Margaret's mother answered. "I don't know much about animals, but he really seems to want us to follow him."

Father Reilly shrugged. "Well, he strikes me as a pretty smart dog. Let's do it."

So, with that, they all followed him. The dog led them straight to the car park. He checked over his shoulder every so often to make sure that they were still behind him. If he got too far ahead, he would stop and wait. Then, when they caught up, he would set forth again.

He stopped right next to the sagging estate car and barked. The baby was still coughing and wailing.

The driver's door flew open and Jane Yates got out.

"I told you to go away!" she shouted, clearly at the end of her tether.

Father Reilly stared at her. "Jane, is that you? What are you doing here?"

Realizing that the dog was no longer alone, Jane blushed. "Oh," she said, and avoided their eyes. She hadn't expected company. "Hi." Sabrina coughed and she automatically picked her up, wrapping a tattered blanket more tightly around her so she would be warm.

"You have the children in there with you?" Margaret's mother asked, sounding horrified.

"I couldn't help it," Jane said defensively. "We didn't have any other place to go. Not that it's anyone else's business. Besides, they're *fine*. We're all fine."

Since it was obvious to everyone that the family *wasn't* fine, nobody responded to that. Sometimes it was easy to forget that even in nice, small towns like Oceanport, people could still be homeless.

"Why didn't you come to the church?" Father Reilly asked. "Or the shelter? We would have helped you."

Jane scuffed a well-worn rubber boot against the snow. "I was too embarrassed," she muttered.

Again, no one knew what to say. The baby sneezed noisily, and clung to her mother.

Father Reilly broke the silence. "Still, you must know that you could *always* come to the church," he said. "No matter what."

"I'm not even *Catholic*," Jane reminded him.

Ned, and his sister Brenda, had climbed out of the car and were patting the dog. They got him to sit in the snow, and took turns shaking hands with him. Each time, they would laugh and the dog would wag his tail. Then, they would start the game all over again.

"It's not about religion, it's about community," Father Reilly answered. "About *neighbours*."

Jane's shoulders were slumped, but she nodded.

"Look," Margaret's mother said, sounding very matter-of-fact. "The important thing here is to get these poor children in out of the cold. And the baby needs to see a doctor, right away."

"I don't have any—" Jane started.

"We'll take her to the emergency room," Mrs Talbot said. "Before she gets pneumonia."

Father Reilly checked his watch. "We won't be able to get into the shelter tonight, but after that, why don't I take you over to the convent and see if the sisters can put you up for the night. Then, tomorrow, we can come up with a better plan."

Jane hesitated, even though her teeth were chattering. "I'm not sure. I mean, I'd rather—"

"You have to do *something*," Margaret's mother said. "Once you're all inside, and get a hot meal, you'll be able to think more clearly."

"Come on," Father Reilly said. "I'll drive everyone in my car."

Throughout all of this, Margaret stayed quiet. Although Jane had been two years ahead of her, they had actually gone to high school together. Since then, their lives had moved in very different – if equally difficult – directions. It wouldn't have seemed possible that things could turn out this way, all those years ago, playing together on the softball team. The team had even been undefeated that year. In those days, they *all* felt un-defeated. She shook her head and stuffed her hands into her pockets. Little had they known back then how easily – and quickly – things could go wrong.

Now, Jane looked at her for the first time. "Margaret, I, uh, I was really sorry to hear about what happened. I know I should have written you a note, but – I'm sorry."

Margaret nodded. When a person's husband was killed suddenly, it was hard for other people to know how to react. What to say, or do. "I guess we've both had some bad luck," she answered.

Jane managed a weak smile, and hefted Sabrina in her arms. "Looks that way, yeah."

They both nodded.

"So it's settled," Father Reilly said. "We'll lock up here, and then I'll run you all over to the hospital, and we can go to the convent from there."

Margaret's mother nodded. "Yes. I think that's the best plan, under the circumstances."

Seeing the shame and discomfort on Jane's face, Margaret felt sad. Then she thought of something. "I – I have an idea," she ventured.

They all looked at her.

Margaret turned to direct her remarks to Jane. "Dennis and I bought a big house, because –" Because they had wanted to have a *big* family. "Well, we just did," she said, and had to blink hard. "Anyway, I –" She stopped, suddenly feeling shy. "I have *lots* of room, and maybe – for a while, we could – I don't know. I'd like it if you came to stay with me, until you can get back on your feet again. What do you think?"

Jane looked shy, too. "We couldn't impose like that. It wouldn't be –"

"It *would* be," Margaret said with great confidence. "I think it would be *just* the right thing – for both of us." She bent down to smile at Ned and Brenda. "What do you think? Do you all want to come home with me and help me – deck my halls?" This would give her a reason to buy a Christmas tree. Even to celebrate a little.

"Can we, Mum?" Brenda pleaded.

Jane hesitated.

"I think it's a wonderful idea," Father Reilly said, and Margaret's mother nodded.

"Please," Margaret said quietly. "You may not believe this, but it would probably help *me* out, more than it's going to help you."

Jane grinned wryly and gestured towards the possessions-stuffed car. "You're right," she agreed. "I don't believe it."

Margaret grinned, too. "But you'll come?"

"If you'll have us," Jane said, looking shy.

"Actually, I think it's going to be great," Margaret said.

Standing alone, off to the side, the dog wagged his tail. Everyone seemed happy now. Even the baby wasn't really crying any more, although she was still coughing and sneezing. He could go somewhere and get some much-needed sleep. In fact, he was *long* overdue for a nap.

"Can we bring the dog with us, too, Mummy?" Ned asked. "Please?"

"Well –" Jane glanced at Margaret, who nodded. "Sure. I think we should."

They all looked around to see where the dog was.

Margaret frowned as she scanned the empty car park. The dog was nowhere in sight. "That's funny," she said. "I'm sure he was here just a minute ago."

They all called and whistled, but there was no response.

The dog was gone.

Chapter 9

Walking along the dark streets, the dog was just plain exhausted. The park was much closer than the school, so he went there to find a place to sleep. He was going to go back underneath his mulberry bush, but it was a little bit too windy. So he took a couple of minutes to scout out another place instead.

There was lots of straw piled up in the Nativity scene, but it felt scratchy against his skin. None of the other models were big enough for him to squeeze inside. He was about to give up and go under the bush, when he saw the sleigh. It was stuffed tight with the Santa model and the make-believe gifts, but maybe there would be room for him, too.

Wool blankets were piled around the gifts to make it look as though they were spilling out of large sacks. He took a running start, and leaped right into Santa's lap. Then he squirmed out of sight underneath the blankets. The blankets were almost as scratchy as the hay had been, but they were much warmer. This would do just fine.

He let out a wide, squeaky yawn. Then he twisted around until he found a comfortable position. This was an even better place to sleep than his rock cave had been. Snuggling against the thick blankets was – almost – like being with his family again.

He yawned again and rested his head on his front paws. Then, almost before he had time to close his eyes, he was sound asleep.

It had been a very eventful day.

The blankets were so comfortable that he slept well into the morning. When he opened his eyes, he felt too lazy to get up. He stretched out all four paws and gave himself a little "good morning" woof.

Food would be nice. He crawled out from

underneath the heavy blankets. The sun was shining and the sky was bright and clear. The ocean was only a couple of blocks away, and he could smell the fresh, salty air. Oceanport was at its best on days like this.

Instead of jumping down, he kept sitting in the sleigh for a while. Being up so high was fun. He could see lots of cars driving by, and people walking around to do their errands. He kept his nose in the wind, smelling all sorts of intriguing smells.

A sanitation worker named Joseph Robinson, who was emptying the corner litter basket, was the first person to notice him.

"Hey, check it out!" he said to his colleague. "It's Santa Paws!"

His colleague, Maria, followed his gaze and laughed. "I wish I had a camera," she said.

The town postman, Rasheed, who was passing by on his morning delivery route, overheard them. "Santa Paws?" he repeated, not sure if he had heard right.

Joseph and Maria pointed at the dog sitting up in the sleigh.

Rasheed shook his head in amusement.

"That *is* pretty goofy." He shook his head again. "Santa Paws. I like that."

Then they all went back to work, still smiling.

Unaware of that whole conversation, the dog enjoyed his high perch for a while longer before jumping down. It was time to find something good to eat.

There was a doughnut shop at the corner of Tidewater Road and Main Street. The dog nosed through the rubbish bins in the back. Finally, he unearthed a box of biscuits that had been discarded because they were past the freshness deadline. To him, they tasted just fine. A little dry, maybe.

From there, he went to the ever-leaking drainpipe behind the pizza place and drank his fill. There was so much ice now that the flow was slowing down, but he was still able to satisfy his thirst. He cut his tongue slightly on the jagged edge of the pipe and had to whimper a few times. But then, he went straight back to drinking.

With breakfast out of the way, he decided to make the rounds. The middle school would be his last stop. He visited all of his usual places, neither seeing – nor smelling – anything terribly interesting. It was three days before Christmas, and everything in Oceanport seemed to be just fine.

He was ambling down Meadowlark Way when he noticed something unusual in the road. To be precise, there were cows *everywhere*. Lots and lots of *cows*.

He stopped, his ears moving straight up. He had seen cows before, but never up close. They were *big*. Their hooves looked sharp, too. Dangerous.

The cows belonged to the Jorgensens, who owned a small family farm. They sold milk, and eggs, and tomatoes, in season. The weight of all of the snow had been too much for one section of their fence, and the cows had wandered through the opening. Now they were all standing in the middle of the street, mooing pensively and looking rather lost.

The dog's first instinct was to bark, so he did. Most of the cows looked up, and then shuffled a few feet down the road. Then they all stood around some more.

OK. If he kept barking, they would probably

keep moving, but he wasn't sure if that's what he wanted them to do. Except they were in the middle of the road. They were *in his way*. And what if scary cars came? That would be bad.

He barked again, experimentally, and the cows clustered closer together. They looked at him; he looked at them.

Now what? The dog barked a very fierce bark and the cows started shuffling down the lane. The more he barked, the faster they went. In fact it was sort of fun.

The cows seemed to know where they were going, and the dog followed along behind. If they slowed down, he would bark. Once, they sped up too much, and he had to race up ahead. Then he skidded to a stop and barked loudly at them.

The cows stopped, and turned to go back the other way. That didn't seem right at all, so the dog ran back behind them. He barked a rough, tough bark, and even threw in a couple of growls for good measure.

With a certain amount of confusion, the cows faced forward again. Relieved, the dog barked more pleasantly, and they all resumed their journey down the road. He didn't know where they were going, but at least they were making progress.

When they came to a long driveway, the cows all turned into it. The dog was a little perplexed by this, but the cows seemed pretty sure of themselves. He barked until they got to the end of the driveway where there was a sprawling old farmhouse and a big wooden barn.

The cows all clustered up by the side of the barn, and mooed plaintively. The dog ran back and forth in a semicircle around them, trying to keep all of them in place. If he barked some more, who knew *where* they might go next.

A skinny woman wearing overalls and a hooded parka came out of the barn. She stared at the scene, and then leaned inside the barn. "Mortimer," she bellowed in a voice that sounded too big for someone so slim. "Come here! Something very strange has happened."

Her husband, who had a big blond beard, appeared in the doorway, holding a pitchfork.

"What is it, Yolanda?" he asked vaguely. "Did I leave the iron on again?"

"Look, Morty," she said, and pointed. "*The cows came home.*"

He thought about that, and then frowned. "Weird," he said, and went back into the barn.

Yolanda rolled her eyes in annoyance. There was a fenced-in paddock outside the barn and she went over to unlatch the gate. "Come on, you silly cows," she said, swinging the gate open. "You've caused more than enough trouble for one day. Let's go."

The cows didn't budge.

"Great," she said. She turned and whistled in the direction of the barn.

After a minute, a very plump Border collie loped obediently outside.

"Good girl," Yolanda praised her. "Herd, girl!"

The Border collie snapped into action. She darted over to the cows, her body low to the ground. She barked sharply, and herded them into a compact group.

Wanting to help, the dog barked, too. The

Border collie didn't seem to want any interference and even snapped at him once, but when she drove the cows towards the open gate, he ran along behind her. It was almost like being with his mother again. *She* liked him to stay out of the way when she was busy, too.

One cow veered away from the others, and the Border collie moved more swiftly than seemed to be physically possible for such a fat dog. She nipped lightly at the cow's hooves and nudged it back into the group.

Imitating her, the dog kept the cows on the other side in line. Whatever the Border collie did, he would promptly mimic. In no time, the cows were safely in the paddock.

"Good girl, Daffodil," Yolanda said, and handed the Border collie a biscuit from her coat pocket. "That's my little buttercup."

The Border collie wagged her tail and waddled off to eat her treat.

The biscuit smelled wonderful. The dog sat down and politely lifted his paw. Maybe he would get one, too.

"Yeah, I think you've earned one," Yolanda

said, and tossed him a Milk-Bone. "Whoever you are."

He had never had a Milk-Bone before, but he liked it a lot. Nice and crunchy. When he was finished, he barked.

"No, just one," Yolanda told him. "Run along now. I have work to do."

The dog barked, trotted partway down the driveway, and trotted back.

"Oh." Yolanda suddenly understood what he was trying to tell her. "The cows had to come from *somewhere*, didn't they? I bet there's a big hole in the fence." She turned towards the barn. "Mortimer! The fence is down again! We have to go and fix it!"

"OK. You do that, honey," he called back.

"It doesn't sound like he's going to *help* me, now does it," she said to the dog.

The dog cocked his head.

"*Men*," Yolanda pronounced with great disgust, and went to get her tools.

The dog led her down the road to the broken spot.

"Well, how about that," she said. She bent down and lifted the fallen fence post. Then she pounded it back in place. "I don't suppose you want to stay," she said conversationally. "Our Daffodil would probably like some help herding."

Stay. He had heard "Stay" before. It meant *something*, but he wasn't sure what. He rolled over a couple of times, to be cooperative, but she didn't even notice. So he just sat down to wait for her to finish. Maybe she would give him another one of those good biscuits.

Yolanda hefted the two wooden bars that had collapsed and slid them into place. "There we go!" she said, and brushed her hands off triumphantly. She reached into her pocket for another Milk-Bone and held it out. "Here's your reward."

The dog barked happily and took the biscuit. Then he headed down the road, carrying it in his mouth. He had places to go, things to do – and a school to visit!

"Well, wait a minute," Yolanda protested. "You don't have to go, you can –"

The dog had already disappeared around the curve and out of sight.

Chapter 10

It was fun to walk along carrying his biscuit, like he was a *real* dog, with a *real* owner, who loved him. But soon, he couldn't resist stopping and eating it.

When he got to the middle school, the building was deserted. No cars, no buses, no teachers, no students, no Mrs Gustave.

No Patricia, no Oscar, no *Gregory*.

Where was everyone? They should be here!

He slumped down right where he was and lay in a miserable heap. Maybe they had gone away for ever, the way his family had. Why did everyone keep leaving him?

He stayed there on the icy front walk until his body was stiff from the cold. Then he got up and slunk around to the back of the building. Maybe he would be able to find some rubbish to eat.

When he passed his little sleeping alcove by the playground, he caught a fresh scent. Gregory and Oscar had been here! Not too long ago! He ran into the alcove and found a big red dish full of some dark meaty food. What was it? There were lots of chunks and different flavours. It tasted soft and delicious, like a *special* food, made just for dogs. It was *great*.

Next to the red dish, there was a yellow dish full of water. The top had frozen, but he slapped his paw against it, and the ice shattered. He broke a hole big enough for his muzzle to fit through. Then he drank at least half of the water in the bowl in one fell swoop.

What a nice surprise! Food *and* water! They hadn't forgotten him, after all.

If he waited long enough, maybe they would come again. He lay down next to the dishes and watched the empty playground with his alert brown eyes.

Several hours passed, but no one came. He

still lay where he was, on full-alert, without moving. A couple of birds flew by. A squirrel climbed from one tree to another, and then disappeared inside a hole. A big chunk of ice fell off the school roof, landing nearby.

That was it.

Maybe they had just come back *once*, and never would again. Maybe he was doomed to be alone for ever.

Discouraged, the dog dragged himself to his feet. His back itched, but he was too sad to bother scratching. It would take too much energy.

He wandered off in a new direction, exploring a different part of town. Soon, he came upon the largest car park he had ever seen. There were only a few cars in it, but the smell of exhaust fumes was so strong that there must have been many other cars here, not too long ago. He marked several places, just to cover up the ugly stench of petrol and oil.

The car park went on and on and on. It seemed endless. In the middle, there were a lot of low buildings. They were different sizes, but they seemed to be attached.

He walked closer, sniffing the air curiously. *Many* people had been walking around here. Recently. There were food smells, too. His feet touched a rubber mat, and to his amazement, two glass doors swung open in front of him.

Alarmed, he backed away. Why did the doors open like that? For no good reason?

Gingerly, he stepped on the mat again – and the doors opened again! Since it seemed to be all right, he walked cautiously through the doors and inside.

It was a very strange place. There was a wide open space in the centre, with lots of benches scattered around. Water bubbled inside a big fountain, and the lights were very dim. He could smell the sharp odour of industrial cleaner, and hear people talking about a hundred feet away. A radio was playing somewhere, too.

He wasn't sure if he liked this place, but then he saw a sleigh. It was just like the one in the park! He wagged his tail, and happily leaped inside. Mounds of soft cloth were tucked around the cardboard presents in the back. He wiggled around until he had made enough room to sleep among the boxes. This was even *better* than the sleigh in the park!

He yawned and rolled on to his back. Sometimes he liked to sleep with his feet up in the air. It was restful.

Off to the side of the Santa Claus display, two cleaners walked by with mops and pails. Hearing them, the dog crouched down in the sleigh. This was *such* a nice place to sleep that he didn't want them to see him. In the dark, they probably wouldn't, but he wanted to be sure.

"You two about finished?" a woman called to the two men.

"Yeah!" one of the cleaners answered. "The food court was a real mess, though."

The woman, who was their supervisor, walked down the mall with a clipboard in her hand. "Well, let's lock up those last two electric doors, and get out of here. We open at nine tomorrow, and this place is going to be *packed* with all the last-minute shoppers."

The other cleaner groaned. "I'm glad Christmas only comes once a year."

"Wait until the after-Christmas sales," his partner said glumly. "That's even crazier."

Their supervisor shrugged, making ticking marks on her clipboard. "Hey, with this economy, we should just be *glad* to have the business." She tucked the clipboard under her arm. "Come on. We'll go and check in with the security people, and then you two can take off."

As they walked away, the dog relaxed. It looked like he was safe. He yawned again, shut his eyes, and went to sleep with no trouble whatsoever.

During the night, he would hear someone walk by every so often, along with the sound of keys clanking. But he just stayed low, and the guards would pass right by without noticing him. He got up a couple of times to lift his leg against a big, weird plant, but then went back to bed each time. It was morning now, but he was happy to sleep late.

Then, a lot of people came, and he could hear metal gates sliding up all over the place. Different kinds of food started cooking somewhere nearby, and Christmas music began to play loudly.

He started to venture out, but he was afraid. What would happen if the people saw him? Maybe he *shouldn't* have come in here, after all. It might have been bad.

Suddenly, the weight of the sleigh shifted as a hefty man sat down on the wide vinyl bench in the front. He was wearing a big red suit with a broad black belt, and he smelled strongly of coffee and bacon.

The dog scrunched further back into the presents. He wanted to panic and run away, but for now, he decided to stay hidden. There were just too many people around.

"Ready for another long day of dandling tots on your lap, Chet?" a man standing next to the sleigh said.

All decked out in his Santa Claus costume, Chet looked tired already. "Oh, yeah," he said. "I *love* being Santa."

"Rather you than me," the man said, and moved on to open up his sporting goods store.

Soon, there were people *everywhere*. So many people that the dog quivered with fear as he hid under the soft layers of red and green felt. All of the voices, and music, and twinkling lights were too much for him to take. Too many sounds. Too many *smells*. He closed his eyes, and tried to sleep some more. For once in his life, it was *difficult*.

Tiny children kept getting in and out of the sleigh. They would talk and talk, and Chet would bounce them on his big red knee. Sometimes, they cried, and every so often, a bright light would flash.

It was *horrible*. And – he had to go to the toilet again. Could he go on the presents, or would that be bad? He would try to wait.

Unknown to the dog, Gregory and Patricia Callahan had come to the mall with their mother. They still had some presents to buy, and the next day was Christmas Eve. Mrs Callahan had told them that they could each bring along a friend. So Gregory invited Oscar, and Patricia called up *her* best friend, Rachel. Mrs Callahan was going to buy all of them lunch and then, if they behaved, they would get to go to a movie later.

"I'm going to have a burrito," Gregory decided as they walked along.

His mother looked up from her lengthy

Christmas list. Mrs Callahan taught physics at the high school, so she had had to do most of her shopping on the weekends. She had been doing her best, but she was still very far behind. She was a woman of *science*, but not necessarily one of precision.

"We've just had breakfast, Greg," she said. "Besides, I thought you wanted sweet and sour chicken."

"Dad said we could order in Chinese tonight," Gregory reminded her. "So he could finish his chapter, instead of cooking."

"Pizza," Patricia said flatly. "Pizza's *much* better."

Hearing that, their mother stopped walking. "If you two start fighting..."

They gave her angelic smiles.

"Never, *ever*, Mummy," Gregory promised, trying to sound sweet.

"We *love* each other," Patricia agreed.

Then, when their mother turned her back, Gregory gave his sister a shove. Patricia retaliated with a quick kick to his right shin. Gregory bit back a groan, and hopped for a few feet until it stopped hurting.

"Do you think the dog ever came back?" Oscar asked him, as they paused to admire the window of the computer shop.

Gregory shrugged. "I hope so. If we keep leaving food, he'll know he can trust us. Then we'll be able to catch him."

"What did your parents say?" Rachel asked, tapping the floor just ahead of her with her cane. She had been blind since she was four, but she got around so well that they all usually forgot about it. Her eyes hadn't been physically scarred, but she still *always* wore sunglasses. If people asked, she would explain that it was "a coolness thing". No one who knew the two of them was surprised that she and Patricia had been best friends since kindergarten. "Do you think they'll let you bring him home?" she asked.

"Well – we're working on them," Patricia assured her. "They still really miss Marty, so I think they want to wait a while before we get another dog." Then she touched her friend's arm lightly. "Rubbish bin, at nine o'clock."

Rachel nodded and moved to avoid the obstacle.

"Next year, you're old enough to get a dog, right?" Gregory said, meaning a guide dog.

Rachel nodded. "I can't wait. Except I have to *stay* at that school for a while, to learn how. Live away from home."

Patricia shrugged. "It's not so far. We can come and visit you."

Rachel pretended to be disgusted by that idea. "And that would be a *good* thing?"

"For *you*," Patricia said, and they both laughed.

"Those guide dogs are really smart," Gregory said, and paused. "Although not as smart as *my* new dog is going to be. He's the best dog *ever*."

Oscar snorted. "Oh, yeah. He's a whiz, all right." He turned towards Patricia and Rachel. "Fetches *snowballs*, that dog."

The girls laughed again.

"Well, that makes him about Gregory's speed," Rachel said.

"Absolutely," Patricia agreed. "He doesn't even know how to *sit* right." She glanced a few feet ahead. "Baby carriage, two o'clock," she said, and then went on without pausing.

"Rachel, you're going to have to help me train him, so he won't *embarrass* us."

Rachel grinned, tapping her cane and deftly avoiding the baby carriage. "You mean, Gregory, or the dog?"

"*Gregory*, of course," Patricia said.

"What if he never comes back?" Oscar said. "I mean, he might belong to someone, or – I don't know. He could be really far away by now."

Gregory looked worried. He was so excited about the dog that he had forgotten that he might not even see him again. Someone else might find him, or he might get hurt, or – all sorts of terrible things could happen! The worst part would be that he would never even *know* why the dog hadn't come back. He would just be – gone.

"Cheer up, Greg," Patricia said. "He's probably still hanging around the school. I mean, he didn't exactly seem like, you know, a dog with a lot of *resources*."

Gregory just looked worried.

"Are you kids coming or not?" Mrs Callahan asked, about ten feet ahead of them.

124

"We have a lot of stops to make."

They all nodded, and hurried to catch up.

Down in front of the Thom McAn shoe shop, a young father was trying to balance a bunch of bulging shopping bags and a push-chair, which held his two-year-old son, Kyle. At the same time, he was trying to keep track of his other three children, who were four, six and seven. His wife was down in the Walden book shop, and they were all supposed to meet in the food court in half an hour.

"Lucy, watch it," he said to his six-year-old as she bounced up and down in place, croaking. She was pretending to be a frog. His four-year-old, Marc, was singing to himself, while the seven-year-old, Wanda, was trying to peek inside the Toys R Us bags. "Wanda, put that down! Marc, will you –" He stopped, realizing that the push-chair was empty. "Kyle? Where's Kyle?"

The other three children stopped what they were doing.

"I haven't seen him, Daddy," Wanda said. "Honest."

The other two just looked scared.

Their father spun around, searching the crowd frantically. "Kyle?" he shouted. "Where are you? Kyle, come back here!"

His two-year-old was missing!

Chapter 11

Immediately, a crowd gathered around the family. Everyone was very concerned, and spread out to look for the lost little boy. The mall security guards showed up, and quickly ran to block of all of the exits. Children got lost at the mall all the time, and the guards just wanted to make sure that when it happened, they didn't *leave* the mall.

"What's going on?" Mrs Callahan asked, as they came out of the Sharper Image shop. One of her contact lenses had fogged up a little, and she blinked to clear it.

"Oh, no!" Patricia said, with great drama. "Maybe it's a run on the bank!"

"You mean, a run on the cash machines," Rachel corrected her.

"Maybe there's a movie star here or something," Oscar guessed. "Someone *famous*."

That idea appealed to Gregory, and he looked around in every direction. "What if it was someone like Michael Jordan," he said. "That'd be great!"

"*Shaquille*," Oscar said, and they bumped chests in the same dumb-jock way basketball players did.

Mrs Callahan reached out to stop a woman in a pink hat who was rushing by. "Excuse me," she said. "What's going on?"

"A little boy is lost," the woman told her. "Curly hair, two years old, wearing a Red Sox jacket. They can't find him anywhere!"

"Can we look, Mum?" Gregory asked.

"We'll look *together*," Mrs Callahan said firmly. "I don't want us to get separated in this crowd."

Up in the sleigh, the dog had heard all of the sudden chaos, too. The noise had woken him up. What was going on? Why was everyone so upset? He couldn't resist poking his head up and looking around. People were running around all over the place, and shouting, "Kyle! Kyle! Where are you, Kyle?"

The dog didn't know what to think. But, once again, he was sure that something was very wrong. Then, amidst all of the uproar, he heard a distinct little sound. A strange sound. He stood up in the sleigh and pricked his ears forward, listening intently.

It had been a *splash*. Now, he could hear a tiny *gurgle*. Where was it coming from? The fountain. Something – some*one*? – must have fallen into the huge, bubbling fountain in the middle of the mall. The dog stood there indecisively. What should he do? Run away? Run to the *fountain*? Stay here?

A man searching for Kyle right near the sleigh stared at him. It was Rasheed, the postman, who had seen the dog in the park the day before – sitting up in Santa's sleigh. The dog that Joseph, the sanitation worker, had called Santa Paws.

Rasheed had come to the mall on his day off to buy some presents for his colleagues. This was certainly the *last* place he would have expected to see that dog.

"Look at that!" he gasped to his wife, who

was standing next to him. "It's Santa Paws!"

She looked confused. "What?"

"Santa Paws!" he said, pointing up at the sleigh.

The dog had his full concentration on the distant fountain. There was something *in* there. Under the water. Movement. It was – a child! A drowning child!

He sailed off the sleigh in one great leap. Then he galloped through the crowded mall as fast as he could. The top of the fountain was very high, but he gathered his legs beneath him and sprang off the ground.

He landed in the fountain with a huge splash and water splattered everywhere. He dug frantically through the water with his paws, searching for the child.

By now, Kyle had sunk lifelessly to the bottom of the fountain. The dog dived underneath the churning water and grabbed the boy's jacket between his teeth. Then he swam furiously to the surface, using all of his strength to pull the boy along behind him.

All at once, both of their heads popped up. Kyle started choking weakly, and the dog dragged him to the edge of the fountain. He tried to pull him over the side, but the little boy was too heavy, and the dog was too small. He tightened his jaws on the boy's jacket, and tried again. But it was no use. The edge of the fountain was just too high.

The dog used his body to keep the little boy pressed safely against the side of the fountain. Then he started barking, as he dog-paddled to try and keep them both afloat.

"I hear a dog barking," one of the security guards yelled. "Where's it coming from? Someone find that dog!"

In the meantime, Rasheed was running down the mall towards the fountain.

"In there!" he panted, gesturing towards the fountain. "The little boy's in there! Don't worry, Santa Paws has him!"

Even in the midst of all the excitement, people stared at him when they heard the name, "Santa Paws".

"Santa *Paws*?" the security guard repeated. "Well. Hmmm. I think you mean –"

Rasheed ignored him, climbing over the side of the fountain. He plucked Kyle out of the water and lifted him to safety. Everyone nearby began to clap.

"Is he all right?" Kyle's father asked, frantic with worry. "Oh, please, tell me he's all right?"

Kyle was coughing and choking, but fully conscious. He would be just fine. Very carefully, Rasheed climbed back over the side of the fountain, holding the little boy in his arms.

Kyle's sisters and brother promptly burst into tears.

"Oh, *thank you*, sir," Kyle's father said, picking up his wet son in a big hug. Kyle started crying, too, and hung on to him tightly. "I don't know how I can ever thank you," his father went on.

"It wasn't me," Rasheed said. "It was Santa Paws."

All of the people who had gathered by the fountain to watch stared at him.

"Are you new to this country?" one of them asked tentatively. "Here, in America, we call him Santa *Claus*."

Rasheed looked irritated. "Oh, give me a break," he said, sounding impatient. "I'm *third-generation.*"

Now, the dog struggled over the edge of the fountain. He jumped down to the wet pavement and shook thoroughly. Water sprayed all over the place.

"*There's* your hero," Rasheed proclaimed proudly. "It's Santa Paws!"

Everyone clapped again.

Several stores away, still trying to get through the crowd, Gregory saw the dog. Instantly, he grabbed his mother's arm.

"Mum, that's him!" he said eagerly. "My dog! Isn't he great? Can we keep him? Please?"

His mother shook her head, not sure if she could believe the coincidence. "What? Are you sure?" she asked. "Here, in the *mall*?"

"That's the dog!" Gregory insisted. "The one we want to come and live with us!"

"That's no dog," a woman next to them said solemnly. "That's *Santa Paws*!"

"He just saved that little boy," one of the workers from the taco stand agreed. "He's a hero!"

Patricia looked disgusted. "*Santa Paws?*" she said. "What a *completely* dumb name."

Rachel nodded. "It's embarrassing. It's…" – she paused for effect – "not cool."

Patricia nodded, too. It wasn't cool *at all*.

"I have to get him!" Gregory said, and started trying to push his way through the crowd.

Down by the fountain, the dog was shrinking away from all of the people and attention. Everyone was trying to touch him and pat him at once. There were too many people. Too much noise. Too much *everything*.

So unexpectedly that everyone was startled, the dog raced away from them.

"Someone catch him!" Kyle's father shouted. "He saved my little boy!"

People started chasing the dog, but he was much too fast. He ran until he found one of the rubber mats and then jumped on it. The doors opened and he tore out of the mall. He raced through the car park, dodging cars and customers.

It was a scary place, and he was never going back!

Inside the mall, Gregory got to the fountain only seconds after the dog had left.

"Where's my dog?" he asked urgently. "I mean – where's Santa Paws!"

Everyone turned and pointed to the exit.

"Thanks!" Gregory said, and ran in that direction. But when he got outside, the dog was already long gone.

Disappointed, he walked slowly back inside. He had *almost* got him, this time. What if he never got another chance?

Oscar caught up with him. "Where'd he go? Is he still here?"

Gregory shook his head unhappily. "Lost him again. What if he disappears for good, this time?"

"I'm sorry," Oscar said. Then he threw a comforting arm around his friend's shoulders. "Don't worry. We'll find him again. Count on it."

"I sure *hope* so," Gregory said glumly.

Just then, Kyle's mother came walking up to the fountain. She was carrying lots of bags and whistling a little. She gave her husband and children a big smile.

"Well, *there* you are," she said. "I've been waiting in the food court *for ever* – I was

135

starting to worry."

Then, seeing the large crowd around her family, she frowned.

"Did I miss something?" she asked.

Everyone just groaned.

Chapter 12

The name "Santa Paws" caught on, and news of the hero dog spread quickly all over Oceanport. People began coming forward with tales about *their* experiences with Santa Paws. Some of these stories were more plausible than others. There were people who thought that a stray dog on his own might be wild – and possibly dangerous. They thought that he should be caught, and taken to the pound as soon as possible. One man even claimed that Santa Paws had growled viciously at him on Hawthorne Street, but since he was a Yankees fan living in the middle of New England, nobody took him very seriously.

Most of the town was behind Santa Paws

one hundred per cent. Officers Bronkowski and Lee told how the dog had scared the vandals away from the Nativity scene. Mrs Amory spoke from her hospital bed about how he had saved her life when she fell on the ice and broke her hip. Yolanda's husband Mortimer said, vaguely, "Oh, yeah, that was the weird dog who brought the cows home." One woman said that Santa Paws had magically cleared the snow from her front walk and driveway earlier that week. Another family claimed that he had been up on the roof and suddenly their television reception was much better. A little girl in the first grade was *sure* that he had come into her room while she was asleep and chased the monsters from her closet.

By now, the dog's brother and sisters and mother had all been adopted. Seeing the strong resemblance, their new owners were boasting that they owned dogs who might be *related* to the great Santa Paws. Although they had originally just gone to the pound to adopt nice stray dogs, these owners now felt very lucky, indeed.

In short, Santa Paws was the talk of the town. There was even a group who hung out at Sally's Diner & Sundries Shop taking bets on when, and where, Santa Paws might show up next. What heroic acts he would perform. Everyone who came into the diner had an enthusiastic prediction.

The newscasters on television had set up a Santa Paws hotline so people could phone in sightings. He was described as being small, and brown, and very, very wise.

In the meantime, the poor dog had barely stopped running since he had left the mall. He ran and ran and ran. He had got so wet from diving into the fountain that his fur froze. No matter what he did, he couldn't get warm. He ended up huddling against a tree in some waste ground as his body shook uncontrollably from the cold. He was glad that the little boy hadn't drowned, but it had still been a bad, scary day.

He was so tired and cold that he felt like giving up. He didn't *like* being on his own. It was too hard. He wanted a home. He wanted a family. He wanted to feel *safe*.

Instead, he sat in the waste ground all by himself and shivered. Every few minutes, he whimpered a little, too.

He was just plain *miserable*.

The same afternoon, Mrs Callahan let Gregory and Oscar skip going to the movies and leave the mall early. As long as they got home before dark, they had permission to go over to the school and leave some more food and water for the dog. If they could catch him, she said, Gregory could bring him home.

Gregory was overjoyed. Getting to keep the dog would be the best Christmas present he ever had! He just prayed that the dog would be there waiting for him. If not – well, he didn't want to think about the possibility of never finding him again. His parents would probably take him to the pound in a couple of weeks to get a different dog – but the *only* dog he wanted was Santa Paws. He had to be over at the school, he *just* had to be.

So, he and Oscar gathered up some supplies. Then Gregory's father left his word processor long enough to drive them over to the school. Gregory and Oscar were in such good moods that they didn't even complain when Mr Callahan made them listen to Frank Sinatra on the radio. They also didn't laugh when Mr Callahan sang along. Much.

Just as the chorus from "New York, New York" was over, Mr Callahan pulled up in front of the school. When he was in the middle of a new book, he was sometimes very absentminded. Today, he still had on his bunny slippers. Gregory and Oscar were afraid that they would laugh more, so they pretended not to notice.

"OK, guys," Mr Callahan said, as he parked the car. "You want me to wait, or would you rather walk home?"

Gregory and Oscar looked at each other.

"Would we have to listen to more Sinatra, Mr Callahan?" Oscar asked politely.

Gregory's father nodded. He was tall and a little bit pudgy, with greying hair and thick horn-rimmed glasses. "I'm afraid so," he said.

"Well, then," Oscar answered, very politely, "maybe it would be very good exercise for us to walk."

"Thanks for driving us, though," Gregory added.

Mr Callahan grinned, raised the volume on the radio, and drove away. He beeped the horn twice, waved, and then turned on to the main road to head home.

"For Christmas, you should give him a CD of *good* music," Oscar said. "So he'll know what it sounds like."

Gregory laughed. His father's idea of modern music was the Eagles. Mr Callahan liked the Doobie Brothers, too.

He and Oscar had brought more dog food, some biscuits, a couple of thick beach towels, and a new collar and leash. Gregory was also carrying a big cardboard box the dog could use for shelter, in case they missed him again. He hoped that as long as they kept leaving things, the dog would keep coming back.

When they got to the little alcove, they saw that all of the food was gone. Most of the water was, too.

"Good!" Gregory said happily. "He found it!" He would have been very sad if the bowls hadn't been touched.

Oscar nodded, bending down to refill the water dish. "I hope so. I mean, I wouldn't want *other* dogs to be eating his food."

Now, Gregory frowned. "Whoa. I didn't even think of that."

Oscar shrugged. "Don't worry. It was probably him, anyway." Then he took out a big can of dog food. To open it, he used a special little can opener his father had had in Vietnam. Oscar was very proud that his father had given it to him, and he always carried it on his key chain.

Gregory set up the cardboard box in the most protected corner. It had come from some catalogue when his mother ordered new duvets, so it was pretty big. Then he packed some snow against the side, so it wouldn't blow away. Right now, the wind wasn't blowing very hard, but it might pick up later.

"On the top, too," Oscar advised. "Just in case."

Gregory considered that, and then frowned. The box was *only* made of cardboard. "Maybe a little. I don't want it to collapse."

"It might be good insulation, though,"

Oscar said.

That made sense, so Gregory did it. Then he folded the beach towels and put them neatly inside. One was yellow, and the other had a faded Bugs Bunny on it. He arranged them until they formed a nice, warm bed. He had also brought three dog biscuits, and he laid them out in a row on the top towel. That way, the dog could have a bedtime snack.

"Think he'll like this?" he asked.

Oscar nodded. "Totally." He put his key chain back in his pocket and dumped the dog food into the big red dish. "I think he'll be really happy."

"Me, too," Gregory agreed. What he wanted more than anything was for the dog to feel *special*. Loved.

Once they had set everything up, they sat down in the snow to wait for a while. If they were lucky, maybe the dog would show up. If not, tomorrow was Christmas Eve, and they had a whole week of holiday vacation ahead. They could come here and wait around all day, every day, if they wanted. He would have to come back at some point – wouldn't he?

It was pretty cold, sitting there in the snow, but they stayed for over an hour. The dog was probably busy saving people somewhere. Oscar searched his jacket pockets and found a deck of cards. To pass the time, they played Hearts, and Go Fish, and Old Maid.

The sun was starting to go down, and shadows were creeping across the playground.

Gregory sighed. "We'd better go. We promised we'd get home before dark."

Oscar nodded and stood up. He put his cards in the pocket of his Bruins jacket, and brushed the snow off his jeans. "Don't worry, Greg. We'll just keep coming back until we find him."

"What if someone *else* finds him?" Gregory asked. Now that Santa Paws was famous, *everyone* was going to want him.

"*Nobody* is going to think to look here," Oscar pointed out. "Nobody."

Gregory sure hoped not.

The dog quivered against the tree in the waste ground for a long time. The ice particles in his fur felt sharp. He couldn't remember ever feeling so uncomfortable. He was very hungry, too. He was *always* hungry.

He was also still scared from having been in the big place with all those people. He didn't like the noise, or all the unfamiliar faces staring at him. He *never* wanted to go to a place like that again.

He was very hungry. If he started walking around again, he might find some more food. Maybe it would also seem warmer if he kept moving.

He was afraid of running into strangers, so he waited until it was dark. Then he waited until he didn't hear any cars going by. Finally, he got up enough nerve to leave the waste ground.

He decided to travel along side roads and back alleys. It might be safer. He took a route that went along the ocean, so that he could avoid the centre of town.

The dog walked very slowly along Overlook Drive. His paws hurt. He was hungry and thirsty. There was still lots of ice on his coat. Instead of carrying his tail up jauntily, the way he usually did, he let it drag behind him.

He just wasn't feeling very happy right now.

He wandered unhappily off the road and down to the beach in the dark. The cold sand felt strange under his paws, but he kind of liked it. He kept slipping and sliding.

The water was very noisy. It was almost high tide, and big waves were rolling in and out. The dog trotted down to the edge of the water to drink some.

Just as he put his head down, foamy water came rushing towards him. He yelped in surprise and jumped out of the way. Why did the water *move* like that?

He waited for a minute, and then tried again. The water rushed in his direction, almost knocking him off his feet. And it was cold!

He ran back on to the dry sand and shook himself vigorously. It was like the water was *playing* with him. He decided that it would be fun to join the game. A lot more fun than feeling sad. So he chased the waves back and forth until he got tired.

A flock of seagulls flew past him in the night sky and he barked happily at them.

This was a nice place, even though the water smelled sort of funny. He tasted some and then made gagging noises. It was awful!

The taste in his mouth was so sour and salty that he lost interest in chasing the waves. It was too cold, anyway.

He trotted along the sand until he came to a big stone seawall. It took him three tries, but he finally managed to scramble over it. He landed hard on the icy pavement on the other side with his legs all splayed out. It hurt. But he picked himself up and only limped for about three metres. Then he forgot that he had hurt himself at all, and went back to trotting.

Fifteen minutes later, the dog found himself at the middle school. He paused at the rubbish bins and lifted his nose in the air for a hopeful sniff. Even if he could have reached the rubbish, what little there was smelled rotten.

Even so, his stomach churned with hunger. When had he eaten last? That nice meaty food yesterday? It had been so good that he could *still* almost taste it.

He ran behind the school to the playground. He stopped before he got to the alcove, and whined a little. If there wasn't any food there, he was going to be very disappointed. What if they had forgotten him?

He took his time walking over, pausing every few steps and whining softly. Then he caught a little whiff of that special meaty smell. There *was* food waiting for him!

He raced into the alcove so swiftly that he almost knocked the dishes over. Food and water! All for him! He *loved* Gregory and Oscar. There was another familiar smell, too. He sniffed a few more times and then barked with delight.

Milk-Bones!

The dog was very happy when he went to sleep that night.

Chapter 13

The next day was Christmas Eve. The sky was overcast and the temperature was just above freezing. But the dog had been warm and comfortable inside his cardboard box. The thick towels felt very soft and clean next to his body.

He had eaten one of the biscuits right before he went to sleep. His plan was to save the other two for the morning. But they smelled so good that he woke up in the middle of the night and crunched down one more.

When he woke up just before dawn, he yawned and stretched out all four paws. He liked his box-home a whole lot! There was still one biscuit left and he held it between his front paws. It was so nice to have his own bone that he just looked at it, wagging his tail.

Then he couldn't stand it any more, and he started crunching. It tasted just as good as the other two! He was so happy!

It was time to go outside. Feeling full of energy, he rolled to his feet. He hit his head against the top of the box, but that was OK. He *liked* that it was cosy. He yawned again and ambled outside.

His water bowl had frozen again. He jumped on the ice with his front paws, and it broke easily. He lapped up a few mouthfuls and then licked his chops. He could still taste the Milk-Bone, a little. It still tasted delicious!

He galloped around the playground twice to stretch his legs. Because he was happy, he barked a lot, too.

Would his friends come back soon? He sat down to wait. Then he got bored. So he rolled on his back for a while. But that got boring, too.

Next, he took a little nap until the sun rose. When he woke up, Gregory and Oscar still hadn't come. He was very restless, so he decided to go for a walk. Maybe he would go back to the beach and play with the moving water some more.

After about an hour of wandering, he walked up Prospect Street, near a little parade of shops. A girl was standing on the pavement without moving. She was holding a funny-looking stick, and she seemed worried.

It was Patricia's best friend Rachel. She was on her way to the 7-Eleven to pick up some milk and rye bread for her mother. Unfortunately, her wallet had fallen out of her pocket on the way, and now she couldn't find it.

She hated to ask people for help. So she was retracing her steps and using her red and white cane to feel for the missing object. She could go home and tell her mother what happened, but she would rather not. It wasn't that she was afraid someone would *steal* the wallet if she left. She just liked to do things by herself.

The dog cocked his head. Why was she moving *so slowly*? Why was she swinging the little stick around? He didn't want the stick to hit him, so he kept his distance.

"Now, where is it?" Rachel muttered. She bent down and felt the snow with her gloved hands. This was so frustrating! "Why can't I find the stupid thing?" she asked aloud.

The dog woofed softly.

Rachel stiffened. "Who's there?" she said, and got ready to use her cane as a weapon. She knew that it was a dog, but how could she be sure that it was friendly? Sometimes, dogs weren't.

The dog walked closer, wagging his tail.

Rachel felt something brush against her arm. The dog? She reached out and felt a wagging tail, and then a furry back.

"Are you a dog I know?" she asked.

Naturally, the dog didn't answer.

She took off her left glove and felt for the dog's collar. Her fingertips were so sensitive from reading Braille that she could usually read the inscriptions on licence tags. But this dog wasn't wearing a collar at all.

Could he be – Santa Paws? She ran her hand along his side and felt sharp ribs. He was *very* skinny. His fur felt rough and unbrushed, too. This dog had been outside for a very long time.

The dog liked the way she was patting him, so he licked her face.

"You're that dog Gregory's trying to catch, aren't you," Rachel said. "You must be."

The dog licked her face again.

It felt pretty slobbery, but Rachel didn't really mind. "Can you fetch?" she asked. "Or find? Do you know 'find'?"

The dog lifted his paw.

"I lost my wallet," she said. "I have to find it."

The dog barked and pawed at her arm.

"OK, OK." Rachel shook her head. Patricia was right – this dog needed some *serious* training. "Stay. I have to keep looking for it."

Stay. "Stay" meant something, but right now, the dog couldn't remember what. He barked uncertainly.

"*Stay*," she said over her shoulder.

He followed her as she kept retracing her steps. She would take a step, bend down and feel the snow and then take another step.

Was she looking for something? The dog sniffed around. The girl was walking so slowly that he leaped over a big drift to pass her. He could cover more ground that way.

He could smell that she had already walked on this part of the pavement. There were little bootsteps in the snow. He followed them until he smelled something else. He wasn't sure what it was, but the object had her scent on it. It was square and made of some kind of sturdy material.

So he picked the object up in his mouth and romped back up the street to where she was.

"I really can't play with you now," Rachel said, pushing him away. "I have to keep searching."

He pressed his muzzle against her arm, and then dropped the object in front of her.

Rachel heard it hit the ground and reached out to feel – her wallet!

"Good dog!" she said, and picked it up. "No wonder they call you Santa Paws. Good boy!"

The dog wagged his tail and woofed again.

Rachel couldn't help wondering what he

looked like. She had vague memories of things like colours and shapes. Mostly, though, she had to use her hands to picture things.

"Is it OK if I see what you look like?" she asked, surprised to find herself feeling shy. He was only a *dog*, even if he was a particularly good one.

The dog wagged his tail.

She put her hand out and felt the sharp ribs again. His fur was short and fairly dense. His winter undercoat, probably. The fur wasn't silky at all. Her family had a cocker spaniel named Trudy and she was very silky. This dog's fur was much more coarse.

The dog's hips were narrow, but his chest was pretty broad. Gregory had said that he wasn't full grown yet, but he was already at least forty or fifty pounds. He felt bony and athletic, not solid and stocky. That was the way her friend Gary's Labrador retriever felt. This dog was built differently.

She ran her hand down the dog's legs. They were very thin. His paws were surprisingly *big*. That meant Gregory was right, and the dog was going to grow a lot more.

She left his head for last. His ears seemed to be pointy, although they were a little crooked right at the very tip. His head and muzzle were long and slim. His mouth was open, but he was so gentle that she knew he wouldn't bite her.

"Thank you," she said, and removed her hands. She always felt better when she could *picture* something in her mind. She had a very clear picture, now, of this dog. A nice picture.

She was almost sure that the 7-Eleven was only about half a block away. There was a pay phone there. She should call Patricia's house right away and tell them to come and pick up the dog.

"Come here, Santa Paws," she said. "Just follow me down to this telephone, OK?"

There was no answering bark.

"Santa Paws?" she called. "Are you still here?"

She listened carefully, trying to hear him panting or the sound of his tail beating against the air. She could almost always sense it when any living being was near her.

The only thing she could sense right now was that the dog had gone away.

Rachel sighed. Oh, well. She could still call Patricia and tell her that the dog *had* been here. Briefly.

She wasn't sure if that would make Gregory feel better – or worse.

The dog's next stop was behind the doughnut shop. He checked the rubbish bins, but all he found were coffee grindings and crumpled napkins. He was more lucky at the pizza place, because he found a box full of discarded crusts. They were a little hard, but they tasted fine.

Now it was time to go to the beach. A couple of people shouted and pointed when they saw him, but he just picked up his pace. They sounded very excited to see him, but he had no idea why. So he kept running along until he outdistanced them.

Trotting down Harbour Cove Road, he heard several dogs barking and growling. They sounded like they were just around the next corner. He could also hear an elderly man shouting, "No, no! Bad dogs!" There was definitely trouble up ahead!

More alarmed than curious, he broke into a full run. He stretched his legs out as far as they would go, feeling the wind blow his ears back.

Just up ahead, at the base of an old oak tree, a big Irish setter, a Dalmatian and a husky-mix were all barking viciously. They had chased a kitten up the tree and were still yapping wildly at her from the bottom.

The elderly man, Mr Corcoran, was brandishing a stick and trying to make the dogs run away. The kitten belonged to him, and he loved her very much.

"Bad dogs!" he shouted. "Go home!"

The little kitten trembled up on the icy tree branch. Even though she was tiny, the branch was swaying under her weight and might break at any second.

The dog growled a warning, and then ran straight into the fray. He butted the Dalmatian in the side, and then shoved past the husky-mix, still growling.

At first, since he was obviously a puppy, the other dogs ignored him. They were having too much fun tormenting the kitten. The

Irish setter seemed to be the leader of the pack, so the puppy confronted him with a fierce bark.

This got the Irish setter's attention, but the puppy refused to back down. He showed his teeth and the Irish setter returned the favour. The Dalmatian and the husky-mix decided to join in, and the odds were three against one.

The dog was ready to fight *all* of them! He would probably lose, but he wasn't afraid. He stood his ground, trying to keep all three dogs in sight at once and not let any of them sneak up on him from behind. It was much harder than herding cows! And this time, Daffodil wasn't here to help him!

"Bad dogs!" Mr Corcoran yelled. "Leave him alone!"

Just as the husky-mix lunged towards the puppy, with her teeth bared, the kitten fell out of the tree with a shrieking meow. She landed in a clumsy heap in the snow, mewing pitifully.

Before the other dogs could hurt her, the puppy jumped past them, ready to protect her with his body. The other three dogs circled him slowly, planning their next moves. The puppy kept his teeth bared and growled steadily.

Swiftly and silently, the husky-mix leaped forward and bit his shoulder. The puppy yelped in pain, but snapped at one of the husky's back legs and heard the husky yelp, too.

Now the Irish setter moved in. At the last second, the puppy ducked and the setter sailed right over him. While the setter was trying to recover his balance, the puppy whirled around to face the Dalmatian.

The Dalmatian didn't like to fight, and he took one nervous step forward. Then he backed up, whining uneasily. The puppy made a short, fierce move towards him and the Dalmatian hesitated for a second. Then he tucked his tail between his legs and started running home.

Before the puppy had time to enjoy that victory, the Irish setter and the husky had already jumped on him. The puppy fought back, trying not to let them get between him and the mewing kitten.

He was ready to fight for his life – and the
kitten's life!

Chapter 14

The fight was fast, confusing and brutal. "Stop it!" Mr Corcoran kept yelling helplessly. "Stop it right now!" He tried to break the fight up, using a stick he had found on the ground. It took a while, but he finally managed to knock the snarling husky away.

The husky growled at him, but then just limped off towards his owner's house. He had had enough fighting for one day.

Mrs Quigley, who lived across the street, came tearing outside in her bathrobe. "Pumpkin!" she shouted. "Bad dog, Pumpkin! You come here *right now*!"

Hearing the voice of authority, the Irish setter instantly cringed. Mrs Quigley grabbed him by the collar and hauled him away a few feet. "Bad, bad dog! You, *sit*!"

The Irish setter sat down, looking guilty.

"I'm so sorry, Carl," she said to Mr Corcoran, out of breath. "I don't know what could have got into him."

"*Eggnog*, probably," Mr Corcoran grumbled.

Mrs Quigley sniffed her dog's breath and then glared down at him. "Pumpkin! How could you? You bad, bad dog!" She looked up at Mr Corcoran. "I am so sorry. Are Matilda and your puppy all right?"

Mr Corcoran reached down and gently lifted his terrified kitten out of the snow. She was a calico cat, and her name was Matilda. He checked her all over, but except for being very frightened, she wasn't hurt.

"Oh, thank God," he said gratefully. "She's OK. I don't know what I would have done if they'd hurt her."

"I'm sorry," Mrs Quigley said, wringing her hands. "I promise I won't let Pumpkin get out like that again."

Hearing his name – and his owner's

disappointment – the Irish setter cringed lower. He was very ashamed.

In the meantime, feeling dazed, the puppy dragged himself to his feet. He hurt in a lot of places. He could feel blood on his left shoulder and his right ear was dripping blood, too. He had lots of other small cuts and slashes, but his ear and shoulder hurt the most. He shook his head from side to side, trying to clear away the dizziness.

Suddenly, Mrs Quigley looked horrified. "That isn't Santa Paws, is it?" she asked.

Mr Corcoran's eyes widened. "I don't know. I guess it could be. Who else would come to save Matilda?" He studied the dog more carefully. "The TV *did* say that he was small, and brown, and wise."

At that moment, the dog mainly looked *small*.

"Well, we're going to have to take him straight to the vet," Mrs Quigley said decisively. She aimed a stern finger at her Irish setter. "You are *very bad*, Pumpkin! You're going to have to go back to obedience school!"

The Irish setter wagged his tail tentatively

at the puppy. Now that the heat of the battle was over, he couldn't remember how, or why, the fight had started.

The puppy ignored him and tried to put weight on his injured shoulder. It hurt so much that he whimpered.

"Oh, you poor thing," Mrs Quigley cooed. "You just come here, snook'ums, and I'll take you to the vet."

The puppy veered away from her. He was in so much pain that he just wanted to be alone. Mrs Quigley and Mr Corcoran both tried to stop him, but he staggered off down the street. Then he forced himself into a limping run.

He wanted to get as far away from Harbour Cove Road as possible!

The dog only managed to run a couple of blocks before he had to stop. He lurched over to the side of the road and into the woods. His injured leg didn't want to work at all.

He collapsed next to an old tree stump. He rested on his bad side, and the snow numbed the pain a little. But it still hurt. A lot.

The dog whimpered and tried to lick the blood away from his wounds. He had never been in a fight with other dogs before. Dog fights were terrible! Especially when it was three against one!

His ear was stinging badly. He rubbed it against the snow to try and get rid of the pain. Instead, it started bleeding even more.

The dog whimpered pitifully and then closed his eyes. Right now, he was too weak to do anything else. Then, before he had a chance to fall asleep, he passed out.

It would be a long time before he woke up again.

Gregory and Oscar met on the school playground at ten-thirty. Patricia had insisted on coming along, too. Since the food was gone and the towels in the cardboard box were rumpled, they knew that the dog had been there. But he was gone now — and they had no way of knowing if he would ever come back.

"Where does he *go* every day?" Gregory asked, frustrated. "Doesn't he want us to find him?"

Oscar shrugged as he opened a brand-new can of dog food. "He's off doing hero stuff, probably."

Patricia didn't like to see the towels looking so messy. She bent down to refold them. "You know, that was really something at the mall," she remarked. "I've never seen a dog do anything like that before."

"He's not just any dog," Gregory said proudly.

Patricia nodded. For once, her brother was right. "I have to say, it was pretty cool." She reached into the open Milk-Bone box. "How many should I leave him?"

"Three," Gregory told her. "In a nice, neat row."

"Since it's Christmas Eve, let's give him four," Oscar suggested.

"Sounds good," Patricia said, and took out four biscuits.

When they were done, they sat down on a woollen blanket Oscar had brought. It was much more pleasant than sitting in the cold snow. Mrs Callahan had packed them a picnic lunch, too.

So they spent the next couple of hours eating sandwiches, drinking out of juice cartons, and playing cards. Patricia hated Hearts, so mostly they played inept poker.

"Is this going to get any more interesting?" Patricia asked at one point.

Gregory and Oscar shook their heads.

"Great," Patricia said grumpily. Then she slouched down to deal another hand of cards. "Aces wild, boys. Place your bets."

They waited and waited, but the dog never showed up. They had stayed so long that the batteries in Gregory's portable tape deck were running down.

"Is it OK if we go now?" Patricia asked. "I'm *really* tired of playing cards."

"Me, too," Oscar confessed.

"We might as well," Gregory said with a sigh. He was pretty sick of cards, too. "I don't think he's coming." He reached for a small plastic bag and started collecting all of their rubbish. "Do you think Mum and Dad would let us come here at night? Maybe we'd find him here, asleep."

"They wouldn't let us come *alone*," Patricia

said. "But if we asked really nicely, they might come with us. I mean, they're the ones who are always telling us to be kind to animals, right?"

Gregory nodded. His parents had always *stressed* the importance of being kind to animals.

"You should write down what you're going to say first," Oscar advised them. He never really liked to leave things to chance. In the Cub Scouts, he had learned a lot about being prepared. "That way, you can practise how you're going to do it. Work out all the problems."

"Let me write it," Patricia told her brother. "I have a bigger vocabulary."

Gregory just shrugged. All he wanted to do was find the dog – one way or another.

He was beginning to be afraid that the dog didn't *want* to be found.

Hours passed before the dog regained consciousness. It was well past midnight, and the woods were pitch-black. His shoulder had stiffened so much that at first, he couldn't get up. But finally, he staggered to his feet. He wanted to lie right back down, but he made himself stay up.

He stood there, swaying. He felt dizzy and sick. What he wanted right now, more than anything, was to be inside that warm cardboard box, sleeping on those soft towels that smelled so clean and fresh.

He limped out to the road, whimpering every time his bad leg hit the ground. The bleeding had stopped, but now that he was moving around, it started up again.

The only way he was going to make it back to the school was if he put one foot in front of the other. He limped painfully up the road, staring down at his front paws the whole way. One step. Two. Three. Four. It was hard work.

Whenever possible, he took shortcuts. He cut through alleys, and car parks, and backyards. The lights were off all over town. People were sound asleep, dreaming about Christmas morning. The dog just staggered along, putting one foot in front of the other. Over and over.

He was plodding through someone's front

yard when he felt the hair on his back rise. Oh, now what? He was *too tired*. But – he smelled smoke! Even though he was dizzy, he lifted his head to sniff the air. Where was it coming from?

He followed the trail across several yards and up to a yellow two-storey house. Smoke was billowing out through a crack in the living room window. Someone had left the Christmas tree lights on, and the tree had ignited! The lights were snapping and popping, and the ornaments were bursting into flames. He could hear the crackle of electricity, and smell the smoke getting stronger.

The house was on fire!

He lurched up the front steps and on to the porch. He was too weak to paw on the door, but he *could* still bark. He threw his head back and howled into the silent night. He barked and barked until the other dogs in the neighbourhood woke up and started joining in. Soon, there were dogs howling and yapping everywhere.

After a few minutes of that, lights started going on in houses up and down the block.

The dog was losing strength, but he kept barking. Why didn't the people come outside? Didn't they know that their house was burning?

The living room windows were becoming black from the smoke, as the fire spread. Why wouldn't the people wake up? Maybe he was going to have to go in and *get* them. But, how?

He started throwing his body feebly against the front door, but it wouldn't budge. Why couldn't the people hear him barking? Where were they? If they didn't wake up soon, they might die from the smoke!

The dog limped to the farthest end of the porch, trying to gather up all of his strength. Then he raced towards the living room window and threw himself into the glass at full speed. The window shattered and he landed in the middle of the burning room. He was covered with little shards of glass, but he didn't have time to shake them off. He had to go and find the family! The floor was very hot, and he burned the bottom of his paws as he ran across the room. It was scary in here!

The doorway was blocked by fire, but he

launched himself up into the air and soared through the flames. He could smell burned fur where his coat had been singed, but he ignored that and limped up the stairs as fast as he could. He kept barking and howling the entire way, trying to sound the alarm. A burning ember had fallen on to his back and he yelped when he felt the pain, but then he just went back to barking.

A man came stumbling out of the master bedroom in a pair of flannel pyjamas. It was Mr Brown, who lived in the house with his wife and two daughters, and he was weak from smoke inhalation.

"Wh-what's going on?" Mr Brown mumbled. "It's the middle of the –"

The dog barked, and tugged at his pyjama leg with his teeth, trying to pull him down the stairs.

Mr Brown saw the flames downstairs and gasped. "Fire!" he yelled, and ran into his children's bedroom. "Wake up, everyone! The house is on fire!"

The dog ran into the master bedroom, barking as loudly as he could until Mrs

Brown groggily climbed out of bed. She was coughing from the smoke, and seemed very confused. The dog barked, and nudged her towards the door.

Mr Brown rushed down the stairs with his two sleepy children and a squirming Siamese cat, and then went back for his wife. By now, she was only steps behind him, carrying a cage full of gerbils.

The dog was exhausted, but he kept barking until they were all safely outside. Once he was sure the house was empty, he staggered out to the yard, his lungs and eyes hurting from the thick smoke. He sank down in the snow, coughing and gagging and quivering from fear.

One of the neighbours had called 911, and the first fire engine was just arriving. The firefighters leaped out, carrying various pieces of equipment and grabbing lengths of hose. By now, the fire had spread from the living room to the dining room.

"Is anyone still in there?" the engine company lieutenant yelled.

"No," Mrs Brown answered, coughing

from the smoke she had inhaled. "It's OK! We all got out."

Because they had been called only a minute or two after the fire started, the fire department was able to put the fire out quickly. Although the living room and dining room were destroyed, the rest of the house had been saved. Instead of losing everything, including their lives, the Browns would still have a place to live.

During all of this, the dog had limped over to the nearest bush. He crawled underneath it as far as he could go. Then he collapsed in exhaustion. His injured shoulder was throbbing, he was still gagging, and all he could smell was smoke. His paws hurt, and he licked at the pads, trying to get rid of the burning sensation. They hurt so much that he couldn't stop whimpering. His back was stinging from where the ember had hit it, and he had lots of new cuts from leaping through the glass. He huddled into a small ball, whimpering to himself. He had never been in so much pain in his life.

While the other firefighters checked to

make sure that the fire was completely out, the chief went over to interview Mr and Mrs Brown. The Oceanport Fire Department was staffed by volunteers, and Fire Chief Jefferson had run the department for many years.

"How did you get out?" Chief Jefferson asked, holding an incident report form and a ballpoint pen. "Did your smoke detector wake you up?"

Mr and Mrs Brown exchanged embarrassed glances.

"We, um, kind of took the battery out a few days ago," Mr Brown mumbled. "See, the remote control went dead, and…" His voice trailed off.

"We were going to get another battery for the smoke detector," Mrs Brown said, coming to his defence. "But, with the holidays and all, we just –"

"Hadn't got round to it yet," Chief Jefferson finished the sentence for her.

The Browns nodded, and looked embarrassed.

Chief Jefferson sighed. "Well, then, all I

can say is that you were very lucky. On a windy night like tonight, a fire can get out of control in no time."

Mr and Mrs Brown and their daughters nodded solemnly. They knew that they had had a very close call.

"So, what happened?" Chief Jefferson asked. "Did you smell the smoke?"

The Browns shook their heads.

"We were all asleep," Mrs Brown said.

Chief Jefferson frowned. "Then I don't understand what happened. Who woke you up?"

The Browns looked at one another.

"It was Santa Paws!" they all said in unison. "Who else?"

Chapter 15

It was Christmas morning, and the Callahans were getting ready to go to church. On Christmas Eve they had gone over to the Oceanport Hospital maternity ward to visit their brand-new niece. Mr Callahan's brother Steve and his wife Emily had had a beautiful baby girl named Miranda. Gregory and Patricia thought she was kind of red and wrinkly, but on the whole, pretty cute.

On the way home, they talked their parents into stopping at the middle school. But when they went to the little alcove, the food and water dishes hadn't been touched. The towels were still neatly folded, too. For some reason, the dog had never returned. Maybe he was gone for good.

Gregory knew that something terrible must have happened to him, but right now, there wasn't anything he could do about it. As far as he knew, no one had seen the dog since he had found Rachel's wallet that morning. And that was *hours* ago. Now, for all Gregory knew, the dog could be lying somewhere, alone, and scared, and *hurt*.

His father put his hand on his shoulder. "Come on, Greg," he said gently. "It'll be OK. We'll come back again tomorrow."

Gregory nodded, and followed his family back to the car.

They went home and ate cookies and listened to Christmas carols. Mrs Callahan made popcorn. Mr Callahan read *The Night Before Christmas* aloud. Patricia told complicated jokes, and Gregory pretended that he thought they were funny. Then they all went to bed.

Gregory didn't get much sleep. He was too upset. Deep inside, he knew that the dog was gone for good. He was sure that he would never see him again – and the thought of that made him feel like crying.

When he got up, even though it was Christmas Day, he was more sad than excited. He and his father both put on suits and ties to wear to church. His mother and Patricia wore long skirts and festive blouses. Patricia also braided red and green ribbons into her hair.

Every year, on Christmas morning, there was a special, non-religious, interdenominational service in Oceanport. No matter what holiday they celebrated, everyone in town was invited. This year, the Mass was being held at the Catholic church, but Rabbi Gladstone was going to be the main speaker. Next year, the service would be at the Baptist church, and the Methodist minister would lead the ceremony. As Father Reilly always said, it wasn't about religion, it was about *community*. It was about *neighbours*.

"Come on, Gregory," Mrs Callahan said as they got into the car. "Cheer up. It's Christmas."

Gregory nodded, and did his best to smile. Inside, though, he was miserable.

"When we get home, we have all those

presents to open," Patricia reminded him. "And I spent *a lot* of money on yours."

Gregory smiled again, feebly.

The church was very crowded. Almost the entire town had shown up. People were smiling, and waving, and shaking hands with each other. There was a definite feeling of goodwill in the air. Oceanport was *always* a friendly and tolerant town, but the holiday season was special.

Gregory sat in his family's pew with his eyes closed and his hands tightly folded. He was wishing with all of his heart that the dog was OK. No matter how hard he tried, he couldn't seem to feel *any* Christmas spirit. How could he believe in the magic of Christmas, if he couldn't even save one little stray dog?

Rabbi Gladstone stepped up to the podium in the front of the church. "Welcome, everyone," he said. "Season's greetings to all of you!"

Then, the service began.

After the fire had been put out and the Browns had gone across the street to stay with neighbours, the dog was alone underneath his bush. He dragged himself deeper into the woods, whimpering softly. He knew he was badly hurt, and that he needed help.

He crawled through the woods until he couldn't make it any further. Then he lay down on his side in the snow. He stayed in that same position all night long. By now, he was too exhausted even to *whimper*.

In the morning, he made himself get up. If he stayed here by himself, he might die. Somehow he had to make it back to the school. If he could do that, maybe his friends Gregory and Oscar would come and help him. He *needed* help, desperately.

Each limping step was harder than the one before, and the dog had to force himself to keep going. The town seemed to be deserted. He limped down Main Street, undisturbed.

The park was empty, too. The dog staggered across the wide expanse, falling down more than once. He was cold, he was in pain and he was *exhausted*.

Naturally, he was also hungry.

When he tottered past the church, he paused at the bottom of the stairs. The doors were open and welcoming, warm air rushed out at him. For days, he had been trying to *give* help. Maybe now it was time to *get* some.

He dragged himself up the steps. His shoulder throbbed and burned with pain the entire way. When he got to the top, he was panting heavily. Could he make it any further, or should he just fall down right here?

He could smell lots of people. Too many people. Too many different scents. Some of the scents were familiar, but he was too confused to sort them all out. *Walking* took up all of his energy.

He hobbled into the church, weaving from sided to side. He started down the centre aisle, and then his bad leg gave out under his weight. He fell on the floor and then couldn't get up again. He let his head slump forward against his front paws and then closed his eyes.

A hush fell over the church.

"I don't believe it," someone said, sounding stunned. "It's Santa Paws!"

Now that the silence had been broken, everyone started talking at once.

Hearing the name "Santa Paws", Gregory

sat up straight in his pew. Then he stood up so he could see better.

"That's my dog," he whispered, so excited that he was barely able to breathe. "Look at my poor dog!" Then he put his fingers in his mouth, and let out – noisy *air*.

Sitting next to him, Patricia sighed deeply. "*Really*, Greg," she said, and shook her head with grave disappointment. "Is that the best you can do?" She sighed again. Then she stuck her fingers in her mouth, and sent out a sharp, clear, and *earsplitting* whistle.

Instantly, the dog lifted his head. His ears shot up, and his tail began to rise.

"That's my dog!" Gregory shouted. He climbed past his parents and stumbled out into the aisle.

The dog was still too weak to get up, but he waved his tail as Gregory ran over to him.

"Are you all right?" Gregory asked, fighting back tears. "Don't worry, I'll take care of you. You're safe now."

Everyone in the church started yelling at once, and trying to crowd around the injured dog.

Patricia lifted her party skirt up a few inches so that she wouldn't trip on it. Then she stepped delicately into the aisle on her bright red holiday high heels.

"Quiet, please," she said in her most commanding voice. Then she raised her hands for silence. "Is there a vet in the house?"

A man and a woman sitting in different sections of the church each stood up.

"Good." Patricia motioned for them both to come forward. "Step aside, please, everyone, and let them through."

A few people did as she said, but there was still a large, concerned group hovering around Gregory and the dog. The vets were trying to get through, but the aisle was jammed.

Patricia's whistle was even more piercing this time. "I *said*," she repeated herself in a no-nonsense voice, "please step aside, in an orderly fashion."

The people standing in the aisle meekly did as they were told.

Watching all of this from their pew, Mr Callahan leaned over to his wife.

"Do you get the sudden, sinking feeling

that someday, we're going to have another cop in the family?" he asked.

Mrs Callahan laughed. "I've had that feeling since she was *two*," she answered.

Gregory waited nervously as the two vets examined the dog.

"Don't worry," the female vet announced after a couple of minutes. "He's going to be just fine."

Her colleague nodded. "Once we get him cleaned up and bandaged, and put in a few stitches, he'll be as good as new!"

Everyone in the church started clapping.

"Hooray for Santa Paws!" someone yelled.

"Merry Christmas, and God bless us every-one!" a little boy in the front row contributed.

Mr Callahan leaned over to his wife again. "If that kid is holding a crutch, I'm *out* of here."

Mrs Callahan grinned. "That's just Nathanial Haversham. His parents are *actors*."

"Oh." Mr Callahan looked relieved. "Good."

Up in the front of the church, Rabbi Gladstone tapped on the microphone to get everyone's attention. Gradually, the church quietened down.

"Thank you," he said. "I think that this week, we've all seen proof that there *can* be holiday miracles. Even when it's hard to believe in magic, wonderful, unexplained things can still happen. That dog – an ordinary dog – has been saving lives and helping people throughout this season." He smiled in the dog's direction. "Thank you, and welcome to Oceanport, Santa Paws!"

Gregory didn't want to be rude, but he had to speak up. "Um, I'm sorry, Rabbi, but that's not his name," he said shyly.

"Whew," Patricia said, and pretended to wipe her arm across her forehead. "Promise me you're not going to call him Brownie, or Muffin, or anything else *cute*."

Gregory nodded. If he came up with a cute name, his sister would never let him live it down. Somehow, the name would have to be *cool*.

"What *is* his name, son?" Rabbi Gladstone asked kindly from the podium.

Gregory blinked a few times. His mind was

a complete blank. "Well, uh, it's uh –"

"Sparky!" Oscar shouted, sitting with his family several rows away.

Everyone laughed.

"It's *not* Sparky," Gregory assured them. "It's, uh –"

"Solomon's a very nice name," Rabbi Gladstone suggested. "Isaiah has a nice ring to it, too."

Now, everyone in the church started shouting out different ideas. Names like Hero, and Rex, and Buttons.

"Oh, yeah, *Buttons*," Patricia said under her breath. "Like we wouldn't be totally humiliated to have a dog named *Buttons*."

Other names were suggested. Champ, and Sport, and Dasher, and Dancer. Frank, and Foxy, and Bud.

Bud?

Gregory looked at his dog for a long time. The dog wagged his tail and then lifted his paw into his new owner's lap. Gregory thought some more, and then, out of nowhere, it came to him. After all, what was another name for Santa Claus?

"His name's Nicholas," he told everyone. Then he smiled proudly and shook his dog's paw. "We call him *Nick*."

The dog barked and wagged his tail.

Then, Gregory stood up. "Come on, Nicky," he said. "It's time to go home."

The dog got up, too, balancing on three legs. He wagged his tail as hard as he could, and pressed his muzzle into Gregory's hand. He had a new owner, he had a new home, and he was going to have a whole new life.

He could hardly wait to get started!

One Moment

about the author

Kristina McBride is a former English teacher
and yearbook advisor. She lives in Ohio with
her husband and two children. *One Moment* is her
first novel to be published in the UK.

One Moment

KRISTINA MCBRIDE

USBORNE

To my parents, who have spent many moments listening to,
supporting, encouraging, and loving me.

First published in the UK in 2013 by Usborne Publishing Ltd., Usborne House,
83-85 Saffron Hill, London EC1N 8RT, England. www.usborne.com

Copyright © 2012 by Kristina McBride

Published by arrangement with Trident Media Group, LLC.

Cover photo © Jenna Citrus/Flicker/Getty Images

A CIP catalogue record for this book is available from the British Library.

ISBN 9781409557463 FMAMJJASOND/14 02902/06.

Printed in Chatham, Kent, UK.

1 so close to flying

"SO YOU'RE GONNA DO IT?" Adam looked at me, his sun-blazed cheeks aglow with a daring smile.

I was sitting on Joey's damp towel near the lower bank of the gorge, squinting at the large rock wall ten or so metres away, my hands propped behind me on a cool patch of grassy ground. Light sparkled off the rippling water swirling in a deep pool before us, flashing me a warning I would never decode. Joey was there, tangled in the message, floating on his back and squirting water up from his mouth like he was some lazy fountain.

"I said I'd do it." My eyes trailed up the wall, stopping at a tangle of trees and vines. Bright patches of azure sky peeked through fluttering leaves, like a child searching for a long-lost promise. My head was heavy from the beer I'd drunk, the heat of the sun, and the twang of Kid Rock's "All Summer Long" coming from the iPod dock beside me. My body practically screamed with the twining fear that had curled itself into every space within me.

"You sure?" Adam playfully swiped my damp fringe into my face.

"No freaking way she's gonna do it," Shannon said. She was lying on a fuzzy yellow towel, lazily running her fingers through her thick brown waves, her sunglasses propped on the bridge of her nose.

"Maggie's full of surprises." Tanna stood up from her towel and drifted towards the edge of the water. Her long blonde hair, tied loosely in two braids, fell forwards as she turned. "Isn't she, Joey?"

"What's that?" he asked, standing. I imagined mud squishing through his toes.

"Maggie." Tanna smiled, scrunching up her tiny nose. "She's a wild one."

Joey laughed. "My Maggie?"

"She's gonna do it this time." Adam offered me a hand and pulled me up. "You'll love it. Total free fall. It's like you're flying."

"Last time all she did was stand up there and hyperventilate," Shannon said. "You don't have to do it, Mags. We'll love you anyway."

"Of course we will." Joey stumbled as he made his way up the bank, water dripping off his tanned skin with bright sparkles. "But if you jump, we'll think you're a rock star."

Tanna laughed. "Maggie's already a rock star."

"I know exactly what Joey's thinking," Shannon said. "If she jumps off the cliff, he might finally get her to jump into his bed."

"Shannon!" I leaned down and smacked her bare thigh, dying to tell both Shannon and Tanna to shut up before they ruined the plan I'd been working on for weeks.

"What?" Shannon asked, sitting up and adjusting the strap of her bikini top. "It's not like we don't all know that you two haven't sealed the deal."

"You have nothing to be ashamed of." Tanna twirled one of her braids between two fingers.

"Of course not." Shannon tipped her head back, turning her face to the sun. "I'm just being honest that's all."

"Because you're always so honest?" Joey snorted.

Shannon didn't respond. Just whipped her hair from one shoulder to the other like she couldn't care less what anyone thought of her.

Joey rolled his eyes, then looked towards me with a wide grin. I tried to focus on the shimmering droplets of water falling from his longish brown hair, instead of the ball of panic that was coming to life in my chest. But it was difficult.

"Ready?" he asked, reaching his hand out and snagging my arm in his. It felt nice, his warm skin sliding against mine.

I nodded, unable to speak. I wasn't sure if I would ever be ready. But I knew I had to do it.

"Clear?" A deep voice echoed off the walls of the gorge, tumbling down the rocks.

We all looked up, Joey and me, Tanna, Adam. Shannon, too, though it seemed as if she was focused on something beyond the cliff top, her eyes sparking in the rays of light cascading from the blue, blue sky.

"All clear." Adam cupped his hands around his mouth to shout the familiar go-ahead. "Jump on!"

Pete, who was standing at the edge of the cliff looking down, gave us a thumbs up before turning away, his thick dreadlocks swaying with his head. He disappeared after only a few steps, the height and angle of the cliff hiding him from our view. And all we could do was wait.

I held my breath as I stood there, watching in silence as he flung himself out into open air, spun around a few times, and dropped through the plane of the water with a glittering splash.

When Pete surfaced, his laughter pinged around us in a crazy dance. That was one of the things I loved most about the gorge. The way it took sound and distorted it, flung it around like it was something tangible but as light as air.

"*That*," Pete shouted with a laugh, "is the best rush in the world."

"Maggie's going up," Shannon said. Her voice was tinged with vicious energy, making me more determined to follow through with the jump that had started out as a simple dare. Shannon had pulled the same thing the first time Tanna decided to jump. It was like she needed to be the only girl bold enough to take the ten-metre plunge, but she'd just have to get over it.

Joey, Adam, and Pete had found the cliff one day during the summer before eighth grade. After a long upstream hike along the creek that bordered our sleepy nothing-ever-happens-here neighbourhood in Blue Springs, Ohio, they came to the top of the cliff. Once Joey, the oldest of us all, had his driver's licence, he'd found an easier route, starting with a parking lot and two-kilometre trail. I loved the gorge, especially our Jumping Hole, even if Shannon was acting bitchy. Besides, I had more important things to worry about. Like survival.

"Rock on," Pete said, pumping a fist in the air, flinging water everywhere.

"I'd prefer if you didn't use phrases that include the word *rock* right now, seeing as how my main goal in the next twenty minutes will be to *avoid* all rocks," I said, glaring at him.

"You'll be fine," Joey said, one hand rubbing my back, the other pointing to a spot halfway up the steep wall. Or halfway down, depending on how you viewed things. "All you have to do is miss that ledge and you're golden."

"Right." I twisted my hair up into a messy bun and secured it in place with a hairband. "Miss the ledge.

Golden. Does that mean I can have a swig of that tequila once this is over?"

"You can have anything you'd like," Joey said, pinching my butt.

I squealed and jumped away from him, swatting at his hand. "Will you stop it? This is serious."

Joey shrugged. "Made you laugh, didn't I?"

"I'm too nervous to laugh." I attempted to smile, but I wasn't sure if it worked. "Let's just go."

Joey and I made our way down the trail, towards what we'd always called the Jumping Rocks, a natural bridge that crossed the creek and led to the cliff-top trail. I stumbled the first few steps but fell into pace beside him quickly, almost melting into his warm, reassuring body.

"It's no scarier than The Beast," Joey said. "That's your favourite roller coaster at Kings Island, isn't it?"

"The Beast has a harness to strap me in. Doesn't compare."

The trail twisted to our right just downstream from the Jumping Hole, and Joey hopped across several boulders bridging the narrower section of water. When he reached the middle and largest rock, he stopped and held out his hand. I leaped towards him, crashing into his lean body, almost toppling him over.

We laughed and bowed our heads together. He kissed me lightly on the lips. "You can do it," he whispered, the tart smell of the beer he'd drunk invading me.

"Sometimes, when I'm with you, I feel like I can do just about anything." I almost told him that I loved him. It would have been the perfect moment. But whenever I thought about saying those three words, I remembered what Joey had said when we'd first started dating.

We'd been driving – to Shannon's for one of her infamous, my-parents-are-out-of-town-again parties – and I was talking about how, even though it's totally cliché, I'd had that butterfly feeling in my stomach while I was waiting for him to pick me up. He'd looked at me then, maybe sensing where I was headed after three months of dating, and said, "Can we make a deal?" I'd been a little nervous but nodded my head anyway. I remember the taste of my Razzy-Tazzy lip gloss, how it turned bitter with my fear of what he was about to say. "Let's never pull the *I Love You* card. It's like a curse. And I like you too much to let it ruin things." He'd actually held his hand out. I thought he'd wanted to hold mine for the rest of the ride, but when my palm met his, his fingers curled upwards like a Venus flytrap, and he gave my hand three short shakes before letting go. "It's a deal," I'd said with one of the fakest smiles I'd ever worn.

That had been about a year and a half ago. I wondered if the statute of limitations on our deal had passed. But standing there on the rock with Joey, with the steady flow of water rushing towards us and then away, with the steep dirt trail calling to me, I did not have the focus to wonder such things for long. I could deal with that later. After the last day of school, when we would officially be seniors. After our first time, which I'd secretly planned for the first week of summer when Joey's parents were heading out of town for an entire week.

I took a deep breath, tasting the honeysuckle that saturated the air around the rock bridge, and swallowed my words. He knew I loved him. I didn't need to say it.

My chest was heaving, my thighs screaming, but I pushed myself forwards. I hadn't climbed the narrow dirt trail leading to the top of the cliff since the previous fall, when I'd chickened out of the jump and had to scurry back down again. The light-headed feeling I'd experienced that day was threatening to take over again, so I tried to focus on my feet, the steps, anything but the reason that I was steadily moving away from solid ground.

"You're lookin' pretty good from this angle," Joey said from behind me, swatting the butt of my black bikini bottoms. "Is it terrible that I'm hoping you lose your top on impact?"

"Joey, sometimes you border on pervert."

"I'm a seventeen-year-old guy. Whaddo you expect?"

I turned, propping my hands on my hips. "Let's switch places and see how you like being objectified." Waving a hand in the air, I indicated that he should take the lead.

"Oh, baby!" Joey held on to my shoulders as he passed, leaning in to nip at my neck with his teeth. That's when I noticed something different about him.

It was a bracelet. A small and totally insignificant accessory. But something about it bothered me.

I studied it as we climbed, the way the leather strap tied around his wrist slid up and down with the swing of his arm. The way the sun glistened off the three turquoise-coloured glass beads threaded onto the leather.

"Where'd you get that?" I asked when we'd reached the flat part of the climb.

"Where'd I get what? My fine ass? My rippling muscles?"

"Your bracelet."

Joey swung his arm up, as if he'd forgotten he was even wearing a bracelet. He paused for a beat. "Found it in the laundry room. I thought it was cool, so I snagged it. Rylan's probably gonna be pissed off."

Something was off, but I couldn't wrap my mind around it. And then I wasn't sure if my stomach had bottomed out because of Joey and that bracelet, or because I was standing at the top of the cliff looking down at my friends, getting ready to jump. A breeze stirred and I swayed with the treetops, the prickly feeling of terror spreading through my body.

"You can do it, Maggie," Tanna yelled up to me.

"Don't stand there looking down for too long," Adam called. "Just figure out how far right you need to be to avoid the ledge."

Shannon must have said something, because I saw Tanna smack her arm.

"What's her problem, anyway?" I asked, trying to focus on anything but the wide open space before me that was causing my vision to blur.

"Who?" Joey looked at me, his blue eyes eerily alive in the sunlight.

"Umm, Shannon," I said, like he was clueless. "She's being such a bitch."

"Isn't she kind of always a bitch?"

I shrugged.

"I thought that's part of what we all love about her." Joey wrapped his arm around my waist and pulled me to him. "Focus."

I nodded once, feeling a little dizzy.

"You can do this."

I nodded again, sure that the world was tumbling through space at super-warp speed with gravity pressing me forwards and the universe itself daring me to leap over the edge of the cliff.

"I'm going to jump left, so you don't have to worry about the ledge."

"Can we hold hands?" I felt like a little kid, but I needed a connection to something real and stable if I was going to do this.

Joey smiled and bumped his nose against mine. "Of course."

"How far back do we have to go?"

Joey took ten or fifteen steps away from the edge of the cliff, turned, and held out his hand. "We just need to get a running start."

"Why does there need to be any running?"

"Momentum. We need to jump as far from the wall as we can."

"Oh. Duh."

I walked towards Joey and took his hand. He squeezed mine. I squeezed his in return. From where we stood, I could only see the edge of the cliff and a leafy batch of swaying treetops beyond. It was as if our friends didn't exist.

"We're gonna go on three," he said. "You ready?"

I shook my head. "No."

"You trust me?"

I looked at him then. Took in his freckled nose, the wisps of damp hair clinging to his forehead, the way his smile always tilted to the left.

I nodded. "I trust you."

He squeezed my hand again. "Everything's gonna be fine."

I ran my thumb up the inside of his wrist, feeling the pulse of blood, his life, ebbing through his body.

"One."

The cool shock of those turquoise beads zapped my skin like I'd been electrocuted.

"Two."

What was it about those beads?

"Three!"

Running.

We were running.

Almost there.

But the thunder of my feet crashed through something in my consciousness.

And I knew.

It was like I hit an invisible wall. One that did not exist for Joey.

I had been so close to flying.

Then, suddenly – I stopped.

2 the ripple of my fear

SCREAMING. SOMEONE WAS SCREAMING. Maybe more than one someone.

Or was that a trick?

The sound bouncing – bouncing – bouncing off the walls of the gorge.

I was on my knees. Sharp rocks biting into my bare skin. Little, prickly teeth.

What was going on?

I remembered climbing. Joey smacking my butt. But that was it.

Splashing. There was splashing, too.

And I remembered where I was.

At. The. Top.

But I wouldn't look.

Couldn't.

Then the screams broke open.

Turned into words.

One word – bouncing – bouncing – bouncing.

"No! No! No!"

And then I was running. Shades of green racing past me. Bright flashes of light.

Claws tearing at my legs, my arms, my face, slicing me open.

Everything in my mind had flung itself into the air, splintered into a million tiny pieces, and rearranged itself into a jumbled mess.

I had to figure it out. Something. There was something I needed to understand. But I knew I didn't want to. Whatever it was – back there.

Hide.

I could hide.

There, in the underbrush of that tree. The slender sprouts creeping up from the ground leaning against it like a leafy tent.

Perfect.

I slid under the waxy shelter, pulling my knees to my chest. My breath coming in short bursts, exploding out of me.

Tipping my head back was bad. It made me dizzy.

But forwards was worse.

That made me throw up. The sticky mess covered my right thigh. I didn't even bother to wipe it away.

There was something I had to understand.

I tried. Really I did. I'm not sure how much time passed

as I sat there riffling through the disconnected bursts that whipped through my mind – one minute – or a million. And I still couldn't figure it out. Didn't know if I would ever understand. Regardless, I kept trying. It was the only thing I could do.

But the footsteps interfered – heavy, clomping footsteps that made the earth vibrate beneath me.

I tried to hold my breath, to keep from shaking, so the ripple of my fear wouldn't strike the person coming down the trail, so they wouldn't know where I'd folded up and hidden myself.

It didn't work. He felt me. And he stopped.

"Maggie?" he was out of breath. Like me. Huffing and puffing, sucking in the air like there wasn't enough. "Maggie, I can see your feet."

Feet. I looked at my feet, at the Totally Teal polish I'd painted on my nails last night. Just last night. For the party.

"I—" I tried to speak, but my throat was crackle dry, on fire.

Adam leaned down, crawled towards me, and put his hand on my knee. I saw blood and didn't know if it was his or mine. "Are you hurt?"

Hurt?

I thought about that for a second. Shook my head.

Adam looked at me, the green of his eyes reminding me of sea glass. I could smell something rancid, and I wondered if it was me. Or him. Or something dead, rotting and seeping into the ground beneath us. Then I remembered I'd thrown up.

"Maggie," Adam said, his voice slow and cautious, "what happened?"

I closed my eyes. Squeezed them tight. And I tried to remember.

"Screaming," I said. "I heard screaming."

"Yeah." Adam ran a hand through his hair, tugging plastered strands of golden blond away from his forehead. "I meant before the screaming. What happened before the screaming?"

"The music," I said. "Kid Rock. I remember singing 'All Summer Long' with Tanna and Shannon."

"Right. I remember that, too."

"And the Jumping Rocks. Standing on the rocks with Joey, the water all around. He kissed me." I smiled, practically feeling the flutter of his lips against mine. But when I opened my eyes, he wasn't there. It was Adam, his eyes wild, his lips pressed tight. "He kissed me."

Adam nodded. "What happened after that?" he asked. "After you reached the top of the trail?"

The sky had been there. Leaves hushing and shushing.

"I don't know."

"What do you mean, you don't know?" Adam asked. "Mags, it just happened, like—"

"I don't know!" I yanked away from Adam, pressing myself into the tree, trying to find my way through it and to the other side. "I-don't-know-I-don't-know-I-don't-know-I-don't—"

"Okay, okay," Adam pulled me to him. His chest was sticky and warm, and he smelled like summer. "It's okay. You don't have to tell me anything."

"I can't," I said. "I can't remember. Just the kiss. And the screaming."

Adam grabbed my hands as I jerked away. He looked me in the eyes again. "Mags. You have to pull it together, okay?"

I nodded.

"We have to go back down."

"I'm not jumping," I said, tasting the terror in my words. "I can't jump."

"We'll take the trail down. Pete went to get help, so when we—"

"Help?" I asked.

"For Joey."

"Why does Joey need help?" I asked, feeling something inside me coil up tight.

"Oh, Mags." Adam pulled me to him again, squishing my nose against his shoulder. It hurt. Everything hurt.

"I want to leave," I said. "I want to go home."

He rocked me, back and forth.

I wrapped my arms around his shoulders. "What's going on, Adam?"

"Let's go down. We'll figure everything out."

"Did I— I mean, I didn't—"

"How about this," Adam pulled me up, shoving the leafy arms of the brush away, and tugged me to the trail, "you just keep quiet. Let me do all the talking."

I nodded. Wiped my nose and realized my whole face was wet. Was I crying?

And then we were moving through the woods, back to the top of the cliff. Towards the screaming, which was softer now, but not gone like I needed it to be.

"I can't," I said, pulling away, wanting to run again. "I can't go down there."

Adam grabbed my arm, his fingers wrapping around my skin like a vine from one of the trees surrounding us, and wouldn't let me go. "We have to."

"I'm taking her to the car," Adam said as we stepped from the bridge of rocks to the other side of the bank.

Shannon's eyes were wide, glossy, and Tanna's arm, which was wrapped around her waist, looked to be the only thing holding her up.

"Are you okay, Maggie?" Tanna's braids dripped. Trembled with her body.

Shannon scraped her hands through her hair. She looked around, her eyes searching for something that wasn't there.

"I don't under—"

"She's not hurt." Adam squeezed my arm. He hadn't let go. Not once the whole way down. "But I'm getting her out of here. Pete can lead the paramedics back. Okay?"

"Go through the grove," Tanna said, her eyes darting towards the circle of trees behind her. "Not past the…"

Adam nodded.

I looked at them all, the way their eyes had turned dark, their faces shadowed with something that had nothing to do with sunlight.

With one swift breath, I pulled away, yanking my arm from Adam's grip so quickly that he didn't have time to respond. And then I was running again. But this time, not away.

At first I looked at the water, expecting to see Joey floating on his back, spitting a glittering fountain up into the air the way he had earlier. I thought of him popping up, winking, and yelling, *Gotcha!* Because that's the kind of guy he was. Always joking. Playing. Trying to make someone laugh.

But he wasn't there. Not in the water.

The towels were still laid out. The one Joey and I had shared. Tanna's. Adam's.

I found Joey, too.

That stopped me.

He was lying there.

Motionless.

One arm flung wide.

I was confused, trying to figure out what had happened to Shannon's yellow towel. Because it was gone. Replaced by another that I had never seen.

Or was it?

No. Just different, soaked in something dark and sticky.

"Joey?"

As the word escaped my mouth, I felt Adam yanking me back, twisting me around and pulling me tight against him so that the only thing I could see was the sway of the treetops.

"We have to go, Maggie. You can't be here."

"But, Joey—"

"He's gone, Mags." Adam's voice was hoarse. Broken. "I'm so sorry, but he's gone."

"You're lying!" I tried to push Adam away, to break free of him, but he was too strong. And my body wasn't working right. I was shaky, and unstable, and dizzy all at the same time. "He's right there!"

Adam spun me around and I jumped up on him, digging my elbows into his shoulders and neck. It was the only thing I could think to do. And it worked. From over his head, I caught one last glimpse of Joey.

That's all it took.

I might not have understood everything at that point. But Joey's head didn't look right. It was misshapen. Concave at the temple.

And I knew Adam was telling the truth.

A shriek hit the rock wall, bouncing around several times before I realized it had come from my mouth. Adam yanked me down, jerking me towards the trail. Swiping our backpacks from their perch against a tree, he flung them both over his shoulder.

"They're coming. We have to go."

"Who's coming?" I asked, trying frantically to string everything together so it would make sense while, at the same time, trying to push it all away. It felt like I was swimming through the scene, like I was in an underwater movie that I couldn't control. But then I heard them.

Sirens.

They were getting closer.

"You're not ready to talk to anyone, Mags," Adam said firmly.

My hip bumped hard against a large tree as I tried to twist out of his grasp again, the rough bark scraping at my skin.

"You have to come with me." Adam turned back, flashing me a frenzied look. "Please."

There was something in his face, his eyes, that kept me from resisting. It was like Adam was the only real thing left in my world. And I trusted him. I had since second grade when he helped me up after I'd fallen from a swing in the playground. Everyone was laughing at me because they'd seen my Hello Kitty underwear, but Adam, who was way cool even for a second grader, had told them to stop, and they'd listened. He had, after all, just beaten every fifth grader in the school-wide hula-hoop contest.

If he wanted to take control now and tell me what to do, I needed to listen.

We moved through the trees, silent but for our frenzied breathing and the soft crunch of our footsteps on the trail.

The sirens got louder. Closer.

We reached the end of the trail at the same time that the ambulance pulled into the parking lot. Adam stopped, backing into me, the zip from my purple backpack biting into the skin of my arm.

"What're you doing?" I asked. "We have to—"

"Shh!" In one swift movement, Adam turned, wrapped his hand over my mouth, and pulled me into the line of trees, ducking us behind the largest, which only stood a metre from the trail.

Pete yelled over the cries of the siren. I heard words like *cliff*, *jump*, and *ledge*. There were steady shouts back and forth as the paramedics realized they'd have to hike into the woods to reach the injured person they were there to help.

And then I heard the worst thing of all. The word I'd been trying to claw from my mind since the moment I'd seen Joey lying still on that towel.

"We tried CPR," Pete called out as he started down the trail, racing just ahead of two uniformed men who were carrying a backboard and large bags filled with medical supplies. "I think he's dead."

3 the whole spinning world

THE QUILT MY GRANDMOTHER MADE for my parents when they were first married covered my legs. I sat on the plush couch in my living room, imagining all the things that could be damaging the fabric her fingers had lovingly sewn together: greasy sunscreen, algae from the water at the gorge, cigarette ash, beer I'd spilled on myself when Tanna cracked a joke and made me laugh too hard. But those were the easy things.

There was also sweat, vomit and blood. Rubbing off my skin. Soaking into the blanket to for ever become part of its make-up. Tainting the patch of yellow flowered fabric from the dress my mother wore on her first day of school, sullying the blue-striped swatch that came from my grandfather's favourite flannel, contaminating the oldest square, a piece of scratchy grey wool from my great-grandmother's fanciest Sunday dress.

"What are you saying?" My mother's voice came from the hall, her words high-pitched and staccato quick, stabbing at every part of me.

Adam answered, but his voice was so hushed I couldn't make out his reply.

A choked sound escaped my mother.

And I knew that she knew.

I squeezed my eyes shut, gripping the fabric of the blanket in my hands as if it had the magical power to transport me back in time. Not far. Just to late last night. After Dutton's party. When Joey stood on my doorstep, glowing in the faint light of the moon, his brown hair mussed, his thick hands engulfing mine.

"Tomorrow's gonna be awesome," he'd said with a grin. "And Monday night at Shan's, even better."

If only I had known then as I'd stood there with him. Joey was all out of Monday nights.

I sucked in a shaky breath and tried to remember every detail of our last moments alone – the crickets crying out to the cool spring air, a gentle breeze that carried the tangy scent of the earth, the feel of Joey's cotton shirt, soft against my cheek as we wrapped our arms around each other.

He'd stopped me as I pulled away, looking right into my eyes, placing a finger under my chin and tipping my head back slightly. He smiled in that crooked way of his.

"You happy?" he'd asked. "With me, I mean?"

An easy laugh worked its way from my lips. "Couldn't be happier," I'd said. And then I had leaned in, closing my eyes, tasting him before our lips even met. It was lazy and sweet, our last real kiss. So unlike our very first. I felt safe and sure, because I knew everything that mattered, I felt it deep inside. Joey was mine.

Joey tugged his favourite Adidas baseball cap from his back pocket, pulling it on as he walked back to his black truck, which he'd parked cockeyed in the street. He stopped and looked at me one last time, tossing his hand in the air before hopping into the driver's seat. I stood watching as he drove away.

Shannon, who sat in the passenger seat, tipped her head against the glass of the window, her silver hairslide straining for release. Joey turned the radio on, and Pete, in the truck's bed, nodded his head to the beat of a sleepy song that I couldn't quite make out. The music streamed through the back windows like strands of thick velvet ribbon, trailing into the deep blue-black of the night. I watched until the tail lights turned the corner at the end of my street, wishing for nothing in particular. Because I didn't know that I needed to.

If only there had been some kind of sign. If only *something* had made me insist we change our plans. If only I'd kept Joey away from the gorge. He would be safe.

With me.

But now he was gone.

My whole body ached with the thought that I would never see him again.

Never. Again.

"So you just *left*?" my father asked.

Adam's muffled answer rushed from his lips.

Something inside me broke open and a sob shot from my lips. I bent forwards, bringing the blanket to my face, burying myself into its history, smothering the awful sounds that poured from my body.

It's not real. It's not real. It's not real. It can't be real.

I squeezed harder. My eyes. My fingers on the blanket.

I shoved my mind out of the room, away from the moment.

Taking a deep breath, I thought of towering trees, the way they swayed in the breeze. But that took me right back to the gorge. Next I saw a flash of toy windmills, multicoloured, spinning and spinning and spinning in the front garden of the house on the corner, the last turn before the gorge entrance. But that made me wonder if Joey had seen them, if those twirling colours had been one of the last things his eyes took in. So I envisioned a night sky, so big it could swallow any problem, whisk it away. But then I remembered the evening Joey and I lay on our backs in the bed of his truck, staring up as shooting stars streaked across the dusky canvas above us.

That was the first night.

I couldn't believe we'd just had our last.

But more than anything, I couldn't believe I'd just left

him at the gorge. He'd been hurt. And I'd abandoned him.

I had to go back.

I swung my legs over the side of the couch, yanking at the quilt, tearing it off my body. But my bare feet were caught in the fabric, tripped up by all the history it contained, and I slid to the ground in a shivering heap.

"Joey," I said, my voice a hoarse whisper. "Joey?"

My hands were frantic, shaky and numb as I clawed at the fabric that trapped me. I kicked my legs out, flinging the little squares of the past into the air. I heard a loud ripping sound and couldn't understand enough to care. I needed to be free. To go back. To be with him.

I pulled myself upright just as my mother, my father, and Adam rushed from the hallway into the living room.

"Maggie." My mother's voice shook.

"You're okay," my father said, walking to me and kissing the top of my head. He lingered, his hand gripping my shoulder like he was afraid to let go.

"No," I said. "I'm not." I pulled away from him, stumbling into the coffee table. Adam grabbed my elbow, steadying me so I didn't tumble back to the floor.

My father's eyes blinked furiously as he ran his hand along his stubbled chin. "Honey, I think you need to sit down."

"Maggie." My mother dropped to the couch, patting the cushion beside her, her brown eyes glistening with so much emotion, I had to look away. The quilt lay in a messy heap at her feet. "Please have a seat. We need to talk."

"I'm not talking." I shook my head, my hair whipping around my shoulders. "I have to go back." I looked at Adam, whose hands were clasped together in one giant fist. His eyes glimmered with tears, the kind that didn't spill over. The kind that let you know something still didn't feel quite real. "You have to take me back."

"Mags, we can't just—"

"What if we were wrong? What if he's still alive? I don't want him to wake up and wonder where I am. What if he's—" I choked then, on my words, on the heaviness twisting through me. I looked at Adam and saw the way he'd squeezed his eyes shut, trying to block me from his mind. "What if he's *scared*?" I asked, my voice streaking through the room, trying to find a place to hide.

"Sweetie." My mother stood, placing her hands on my shoulders. "You need to sit down."

I yanked away from her. My feet tangled in the blanket again, and I crashed to the floor. Adam's hands were on me before I even registered what had happened, and he pulled me up. He'd always been steady and strong. So very alive.

I didn't want to be there. Not any more. Not with any of them.

I pushed my way past Adam, through the hall, and

bounced off the door jamb as I made my way out the front door, stumbling down the porch steps to the walkway.

This time I didn't make it far. Adam, again. He caught me.

I was spinning. The whole world was spinning. And I wondered if that's how it had felt for Joey.

My breath exploded out of me as I hit the ground, Adam on top of me. Sticky prickles of grass and blinding sunlight invaded my senses, bringing me back to reality, sucking me under waves of pain.

Adam pressed his heaving chest into mine. Tears streamed from his eyes onto my cheeks, chin and neck.

"Maggie," he whispered, "he's gone."

I shook my head, straining against the tears that burned my own eyes.

Adam buried his face in my neck, his hot, heavy sobs drowning me.

I looked straight at the sun, the burning, spiralling sun, and hated every wave of its energy. If only it had hidden behind a thick batch of storm clouds today, we never would have gone to the gorge. If not for that faraway star, Joey would still be alive.

My father peeled Adam and me from the sticky ground, balancing us as we shuffled to the house. My mother was waiting with the quilt, and she draped it over me when I sat on the couch next to Adam. I watched my father go for the phone, pick it up and dial. Then he disappeared into his office, his voice trailing behind him as someone answered on the other end of the line. I looked down and saw my knee poking through a gaping hole that sliced through the patches of fabric.

"Mom," I said, sucking in a deep breath. "I ruined Grandma's quilt."

My mother patted the bare skin of my knee. "That can be fixed."

Adam's parents arrived less than fifteen minutes after my father called them. Twelve, to be exact. I knew because I'd been staring at the clock like it was the only tether still tying me to Joey, even if each second ticked me further and further away from the last moment I had had with him. My last moment with Joey. Nothing about that thought felt real.

"Adam! Oh, dear God, thank you." Mrs. Meacham rushed to the couch and wrapped her arms around Adam, pulling him close. Mr. Meacham stepped in front of them, straddling their legs, and hugged them together. "You're okay?" Adam's mother leaned back and looked Adam up and down.

"There's blood," Mr. Meacham said, gently gripping Adam's arm and inspecting his skin.

"It's not mine." Adam rubbed at the spot and then quickly pulled his hand away.

"Oh, God." Mrs. Meacham melted into the couch cushion, holding her hand to her heart, her brown curls quivering. "Joey. I feel like that boy is one of my own, you two have been friends for so long. I have no idea how Trisha and Mike are going to handle the news."

I closed my eyes at the thought of Joey's parents. I saw them in a hundred different ways all at once: playing cards at the dining room table, sitting together on the porch swing, reading on the back patio. Smiling. They were always smiling. Pressing my fingertips into my eyes, I erased their happy faces, groaning at the thought of them hearing the news. Would the police just knock on their door and tell them that their son had died?

"Mom." Adam gripped my hand in his, pulling my fingers away from my eyes. "Can you *not* do that right now?"

"Oh." Mrs. Meacham wiped tears from her face and sucked in a deep breath. "I'm sorry. I just… Do they know yet? Has anyone called them?"

"We figured it would be best if we let the police handle that," my father said. "Since we don't know exactly what's going on."

"You told us they left the scene," Mr. Meacham said. "Is that true?" Mr. Meacham looked from Adam to me and back again.

"Yeah," Adam nodded, looking to the ground. "I had to... Maggie couldn't stay, Dad. I had to get her out of there."

"I just don't understand how you could leave Joey—"

"I didn't *leave* Joey, Dad." Adam's voice shook with anger. "There was nothing I could do for him. But Maggie needed my help."

"Maggie was the only person on top of the cliff with Joey when it happened," my father said. "She doesn't remember anything. At least nothing significant. I think Adam was focused on getting her away as fast as he could, to keep her from seeing...anything."

"It's like I was losing her, too," Adam whispered, squeezing my hand. I squeezed back and tugged away quickly, unsure why the action sent an electric jolt up my arm. "It scared me when she couldn't remember, how she couldn't answer any of my questions. I was afraid of what might happen if she stayed with him. Joey was so...still. And I knew he wouldn't want her there."

Adam's words tripped me up. I remembered when he first found me in the woods. The vision was a quick flash, but his eyes came back to me, how the swirling currents of green were wild with something that ran much deeper than fear. Everything else had faded into a dark, shadowy nothing.

"Thank you," I said, my voice soft. "For taking care of me."

A silence that felt like a heavy weight blanketed the room, and I wished I'd just kept my mouth shut. I wondered if we were all thinking the same thing: *Why didn't anyone take care of Joey?*

"You can't recall anything, dear?" Mrs. Meacham's voice was tinged with a pleading that made me want to scream.

I shook my head.

"She can remember some of the stuff that happened right before they climbed up the trail," Adam said. "But nothing else."

"I'm sure it's the shock." Mrs. Meacham looked at my mom and shook her head. "Nothing to worry about."

"What about you?" Mr. Meacham tilted his head towards Adam. "What do you remember?"

Adam's eyes flitted to me, and then quickly away. "Dad, now's not the time to—"

"It's fine." I wasn't sure if that was true or not, but I needed to find out. "I want to know, too."

Adam sighed and leaned forwards, propping his elbows on his knees. He didn't look at anyone, just the ground, as he started talking.

"We all saw Joey and Maggie when they got to the top of the cliff. They walked out to the edge, like always, to make sure the water was clear. Maggie looked a little pale, kind of freaked, and Joey was talking to her."

I strained, trying to remember. What had Joey said? What had happened in those last minutes? No matter how hard I tried, I couldn't see Joey. Couldn't remember one single word he had said.

"They turned, and we waited. Just like always. Then, a minute or two later, Joey flew over the edge. But that part wasn't like always. He was kind of twisted, his fall was awkward."

"What do you mean by awkward?" Mr. Meacham asked.

"Off balance. His arms were spread out. Like he was trying to steady himself. But he couldn't do it in time. And he hit the ledge."

I pulled my legs to my chest and wrapped my arms around them, burying my face in the patches of old fabric that I'd pulled over my knees. Joey hit the ledge?

"His head." Adam's words were hoarse. Strained. "He hit the ledge with the side of his head. And then he was in the water. We all raced out to get him – everyone except Shannon, who grabbed a phone – and got him to the bank as fast as we could."

What had I been doing? I asked myself. *While my friends were trying to save my boyfriend's life, where was I? Why hadn't I scrambled down to help?*

"When we realized there was nothing we could do, I climbed up to find Maggie. We'd been calling to her, but she hadn't answered. I found her a good way from the cliff, hiding just off the trail. And when she said she didn't remember anything, I panicked."

As I listened to Adam's shaking voice, I wasn't so sure if I ever wanted to remember. Remembering might make everything feel worse than it already did. And I wasn't sure I could handle that.

"Were you drinking?" Adam's father asked, his eyes tight.

"I don't think now is the time to delve into all of that," my father said.

"There is no better time." Mr. Meacham shoved a hand in the pocket of his tan golf shorts. "The police will be asking the kids all kinds of questions in the very near future."

My stomach dropped and the room started to spin. "I don't want to talk to the police," I said, tilting my head up from my knees even though I felt as if I might be sick.

"I don't mean to sound harsh, Maggie, but you're not going to have a choice." Mr. Meacham pinched the bridge of his nose. "And the first thing they're going to ask is why you two left the scene."

Adam looked at me. "I'm sorry," he said. "I thought I was doing the right thing."

"We appreciate you taking care of our daughter," my mother said to Adam, her voice soft, reassuring. "Don't you two worry about anything. The police will ask a few questions and leave. They have to follow procedure. Nothing will come of it."

I took a deep breath, hoping she was right. Hoping they would accept the fact that I didn't remember anything. Because after hearing Adam's version of what happened, I decided that I didn't want to recall my own memories. No matter who wanted to know, I wasn't about to try to sort through the jumble of flashes and put it all back together again. If it were up to me, I would erase every moment that happened after Joey kissed me on those rocks. If I could, I might even erase myself.

"If it's all right with you, I'm going to take Maggie upstairs," my mother said. "A nice warm shower and—"

"No!" I sat forwards, looking right at Adam. "I want to stay with Adam."

"I think it's best if we take Adam home," Mr. Meacham said.

"I'm not going anywhere," Adam said.

My father cleared his throat. "What if we call the police? Making the first contact might be the smartest choice, letting them know we're willing to help in any way we can. We could tell them they can stop by and speak to the kids together."

I nodded. Anything to keep Adam from leaving. I felt like he was the only thing holding me together, and I was scared that if he was gone everything left of me would crumble into a fine dust.

"It might be a good idea." Mrs. Meacham looked at her husband. "We don't want them to think we're hiding anything."

"They're not going to come here," Mr. Meacham said. "They'll want to question the kids at the station."

"You watch too much television, dear," Mrs. Meacham said. "I'm sure, under the circumstances, they'll be happy to come to the house."

"I'll call them now," my father said.

I looked up at Adam's face, at his shimmering eyes, and had an overwhelming need to touch him. To make sure he was real. Because nothing in my world felt real any more. It all seemed like a dirty trick someone was playing to get back at me for something. Trouble was, I couldn't figure out what.

I reached out and grabbed onto Adam's wrist and felt the pulse of blood flowing through his body. He looked at my hand and then covered it with his own.

Holding on to him, staring at the frayed edges of the ripped quilt, I focused all of my fading energy on keeping that moment from turning into the next.

4 hands clasped tight

"WHAT ARE WE GONNA SAY?" I whispered as two uniformed police officers walked past the chairs where Adam and I were seated. It was a wide hall in the entrance of the police station, the tiled floor a marbled grey and white that looked like it would be cold against the bottoms of my feet if I kicked off my flip-flops.

"What do you mean?" Adam looked at me, his eyes scrunched tight. The officers' footsteps slammed against the walls, echoing like the gorge, vibrating my entire body, threatening to explode my pounding head. "We're gonna tell the truth."

I pressed myself against the straight back of the chair, trying to mould my body to the hard surface. "Right."

"We don't have anything to hide." Adam's foot, which had been tap-tap-tapping the floor nervously, suddenly stopped. He swivelled in his seat and leaned towards me, his eyes searching mine. "Do we?"

Adam's hand gripped my knee, and I placed my hand

over his, soaking in the warmth of his skin, reassured that he was sitting there next to me. Alive.

"Mags." Adam ran a hand through the dried clumps of his sun-streaked hair. "If I should know something, *now* is the time to tell me. They're gonna be done talking to our parents any minute, and—"

"There's nothing more to say." My fringe fell forwards and I swiped it out of my eyes, blinking away the fear that had taken hold of me, and settled even deeper into the raw pain of Joey's sudden absence. "I can't remember anything."

"You really can't?" Adam pressed his lips together so tightly they disappeared. He quivered a little, and for a moment, he looked like the kindergarten version of himself, lost and alone, like he had when his mother dropped him off for his first day of school. I squeezed his hand, the way I had all those years ago when I'd led him to the reading corner to distract him from being left behind.

I closed my eyes, playing the day's events along the backs of my lids like a silent movie. Driving in Tanna's car, windows down, music blaring, watching Shannon's hair whip, and dip, and flip all around her head in the crazy, rushing wind as she giggled about how Ronnie Booker had puked all over Gina Hanlon's purse at the party we'd gone to the night before. Hiking up the trail from the parking lot to the Jumping Hole, the rush of a cool breeze against my skin. Feet running, pounding, crashing.

My eyes snapped open and I sucked in a deep breath. It felt like I was underwater, struggling to find my way to the surface.

"What?" Adam asked, his eyes wide. "Did you remember something?"

"Feet," I said. "Running and—"

The door to the room where the detectives had taken our parents swung open with a loud *click-swoosh*, and the gruff voice of the detective, who reminded me of a gorilla, chased my found memory back into hiding.

All that was left was the fear. And the comfort of not knowing.

They filed out of the room in pairs, the two detectives, my mom and dad, Mr. and Mrs. Meacham. Our parents looked like deflated shells of their usual selves. I saw it in their eyes, the way their heads hung low, how their shoulders slumped with exhaustion, like two hours of this news was already too much for them to bear. If there was hope there, masked by the emotion that threatened to suck them under, I couldn't find it.

When they saw us, their feet stuttered. Stopped.

The long, flowy skirt my mother wore swayed around her legs as if a strong wind had just drifted through. I heard a slight grunt escape Adam's father's lips.

The detectives just stared, taking us in.

Me.

Adam.

Our heads bowed together.

Hands clasped tight.

And the way we practically clung to each other like our individual survival depended on the connection.

It was as if they'd been able to forget reality for a moment, to place it in the dark corner of a high shelf while they dealt with the formalities. But seeing Adam and me shifted things, brought it all spilling down, nearly knocking them to the ground.

"We're very sorry for your loss, Maggie." Detective Wallace looked at me, creases wrinkling the loose skin on his face. "Your parents told us that you and Joey had been dating for the last two years."

"*Almost* two years." I pressed my fingers into my eyes, realizing they were leaking again. "Would have been two years this fall."

My mother handed me a tissue, then placed a hand on my knee.

"We asked you here so you can help us piece together the events of the day. We need you to tell us everything you can about what led to Joey's accident." Detective Meyer shifted in his seat. His large body strained the chair beneath him, causing it to moan in protest.

I took in a shaky breath. "I can't remember much," I said, wishing they'd allowed Adam and me to be questioned together, wondering what they'd asked him while he was sitting at this very table with his own parents just ten minutes ago. We'd passed one another as he exited the interrogation room and I entered, his eyes saying a thousand things at once: be calm; that was brutal; you can do this; I hate these men. He'd grabbed my hand and given it a quick squeeze before the detectives rushed him along with a firm reminder that we were to be questioned separately. And now, without Adam by my side, I felt lost.

My father cleared his throat, and I realized I hadn't really answered. "After the climb up the trail, everything kind of disappears."

Detective Wallace's mouth twitched, the thick grey moustache on his upper lip looking like a caterpillar wriggling to free itself from a prison. "Your parents explained that already, Maggie. Occasionally, in the case of a trauma, a person will suffer from memory loss. You'll probably begin to recall the day in bits and pieces. You can give us more information as it returns to you. For now, we would like for you to tell us what you *do* remember."

I looked from one detective to the other, hating the way their eyes pierced my skin. "Okay."

"Let's start with the easy stuff." Detective Meyer flipped through a small spiral notebook and tugged a pen from the inside pocket of his suit jacket. "When did you arrive at the gorge?"

I looked at my father whose face somehow seemed ten years older than it had when he'd sat across the table from me earlier in the morning as we ate a blueberry pancake and bacon breakfast.

"It was a little after eleven," I said. "We wanted to be all set up by noon, to get the best sun."

"And when you say 'we', who are you referring to?" Detective Wallace asked.

"Me, Tanna, Shannon, Pete, Adam and…Joey." My voice broke when I said his name.

"What would you say Joey's demeanour was when you arrived?"

"He was just Joey." I closed my eyes and remembered the way the sunlight framed him after his first jump. He'd stood above me, shaking water from his hair all over me as I lay on the towel. I'd giggled. Kicked him away. I wanted to scream at myself for that. I should have pulled him closer and never let go.

I took in a deep slicing breath as I remembered his smile. The sound of his laughter. "He was joking. Laughing. Like always."

"So you wouldn't say he seemed depressed. Or angry about anything? Maybe a fight with his parents? His brother? Or…anyone else?"

"No." I blinked several times, something else in my memory shifting just out of reach. "Summer's about to start… We're almost seniors. He was as far from depressed as a person can get."

"Can you walk us through the events leading to Joey's accident?" Detective Wallace asked. "Tell us everything you remember?"

"We were just hanging out," I said. "Listening to music. Tanna, Shannon and I were lying out on our towels, getting into the water when we were too hot. The guys went up and made several jumps. Tanna and Shannon jumped, too. Once each, I think."

"But not you?" Detective Meyer asked, his eyebrows pulling inward.

I shook my head. "I've never jumped off the cliff."

Detective Meyer jotted something down on the paper in front of him, then looked me directly in the eyes. "Why not?"

I shrugged. "Too afraid."

"I see," Detective Wallace said. "So what made you go up with Joey? We were told that you intended to jump together. Is this true?"

Shannon's face flashed in front of me. *I dare you*, she'd taunted, a giggle escaping her lips as she grabbed the bottle of tequila planted at the head of the towels and took a long swig.

"It was a dare," I said. "I've tried to jump before. It's like a running joke. That I'm too afraid."

"Who dared you?" Detective Wallace asked.

"Shannon."

Detective Meyer wrote the name in his notebook.

"And what made you decide to try again? What made you feel like you could do it today?"

"I dunno," I said, remembering Joey's smile, the feel of his skin sliding against mine as he tucked my arm against his body and we began walking towards the bridge of rocks.

"Was it the alcohol?" Detective Meyer asked. "We found a bottle of tequila at the scene."

The scene? I cringed at the word. Blue Springs Gorge, our most sacred hangout, had become a crime scene.

"How much did Joey have to drink?" Detective Wallace asked.

My eyes stuttered between the two men's faces, their features blurring into a shadowy puzzle.

"We'll find out for ourselves when the results from the autopsy come back," Detective Meyer said.

"Autopsy?" The word whirred through my brain, flipping around and around. That meant they were going to cut Joey open.

"Yes." Detective Wallace's lip twitched again and I had an urge to pluck the hairs from his face. "In the case of an accidental death we always order an autopsy. And we run through a complete investigation."

"He'd had a little to drink," I said, recalling the way Joey had stumbled as he walked out of the water the last time.

"Would you say he was intoxicated?" Detective Wallace asked.

I shook my head. "I don't know."

"You're aware that we just finished interviewing your friend Adam. He told us that Joey was a daredevil," Detective Wallace said with a sad smile. "That he often showed off, performing stunts when he jumped off the cliff."

I pictured Joey at the top of the cliff, smiling down at us, his arms spread wide. *Watch this,* he'd yelled just before disappearing. Seconds later, he reappeared, soaring out from the lip of the cliff, his body circling over itself in a flip before he slipped into the water with barely a splash. Had that been his second or third jump of the day?

"Yeah," I said. "Joey liked attention."

"Can you describe your relationship with Joey?" Detective Meyer asked. "Would you say that the two of you were happy?"

I closed my eyes, remembering my plan to spend the night with him in just a few weeks. "We were very happy," I said, opening my eyes.

"What about your relationship with the rest of your

friends?" Detective Meyer asked. "It seems as if you are all very close."

My father cleared his throat. "These kids have all grown up together, Detective. They've known one another since kindergarten."

"That's a lot of history." Detective Wallace scrunched his lips in a sympathetic pout.

Detective Meyer scribbled more words on the paper in front of him. I wanted to rip the notepad out of his hand, to tear the flimsy paper from the wire spiral. How could my life – and Joey's death – be whittled down to just a few words?

"We're trying to figure something out," Detective Wallace said. "And we'd like your help, Maggie."

"Okay," I said, drawing the word out so it sounded more like a question.

"We don't understand why you and Adam left the scene." Detective Meyer's voice suddenly sounded very official. Almost demanding.

My heart started beating more rapidly. I felt hot. Stifling hot. I shifted in my seat, and my mother's hand squeezed my knee again.

"Maggie?" Detective Meyer said. "Can you explain that for us?"

I shook my head. "I don't know."

"You don't know why you left?" Detective Meyer's voice

was tight with something I couldn't place. Anger. Maybe irritation. "Or you don't know if you can explain it?"

"Adam was looking out for our daughter," my mother said. "He was the one to find her after Joey's fall. Maggie was in shock, and it scared him when she claimed to have no memory of what had happened. He thought it was best to bring her straight home."

The detectives looked at each other. Then they stared at me.

"Can you tell us the first thing you remember?" Detective Wallace asked. "*After* Joey's fall?"

I looked at the table in front of me, my eyes following the swirls in the wood, shuffling through the memories I had, trying to categorize them into *before* and *after*.

"The seat belt clicking into place," I said. "Adam's hand."

"Adam put your seat belt on?" Detective Meyer asked. "Good. That's very good. What else?"

"The quilt my grandmother made. Spread across my lap. And whispering."

"That was right after she came home," my mother said. "She sat on the couch while Adam told us what happened."

"You must be grateful that Adam is such a caring young man," Detective Meyer said, looking at my parents.

"Yes." My mother straightened herself in her chair and smoothed one hand down the side of her brown hair.

"We feel very fortunate that our daughter had someone looking out for her best interests today."

Detective Meyer leaned forwards, his hulking chest creating a shadow on the table in front of him, blanketing the words he'd written on the paper.

I looked at my dad. He steepled his fingers under his chin. "Can you explain what happens from here? You said something about an autopsy?"

The detectives exchanged a glance and then turned to my father. "Yes. Though this appears, in all respects, to be an accidental death, it's standard to open an official investigation. It is our job to learn everything we can about exactly what happened today so we can consider *everything* that might have led to the accident." Detective Wallace spread his hands in the air.

Detective Meyer agreed with a curt nod. "We will be searching Joey's car and bedroom, looking over his phone records, and cross-referencing the statements from all of our interviews, which will also include friends who were not at the scene, to get the most detailed picture of his last twenty-four hours. Only then can we close the investigation."

"So—" I said, trying to think of anything but the words that were ringing through my head: death, accident, autopsy. "This is, like, a full-on investigation?"

"Yes," Detective Wallace said. "It is."

My mother's fingers dug into my knee.

"And we have one more very important question for you at this time." Detective Meyer looked directly into my eyes. "Where was Joey last night?"

"A party," I said with a sigh. "We were all at the party."

"Yes." Detective Wallace nodded. "Jimmy Dutton's. We're aware of the party."

"We'd like to know where Joey was *after* the party," Detective Meyer said.

"He took me home," I said. "And then dropped off Shannon and Pete. He was probably home by twelve thirty."

The two detectives stared at me. Hard. And then they looked at each other. I was almost certain that Detective Wallace shrugged his shoulders, but the movement was so slight I couldn't be sure.

Something inside me started to back-pedal, like I was mentally trying to escape. But I didn't move fast enough.

"No –" Detective Meyer cleared his throat and turned his eyes to me again – "Joey did not make it home last night."

My thoughts stretched back to the previous evening, which now felt like it had happened in some alternate lifetime. I went back to the kiss on my front porch. Watching Joey drive away. Hearing the music stream from the windows of his truck. What would have kept him from going home?

"I'm not sure that I understand why this is important." My mother sat forwards in her seat, tipping her head sideways. "What does last night have to do with today's accident?"

"As I already explained, Mrs. Reynolds, we're trying to construct a detailed timeline of Joey's last twenty-four hours of life." Detective Meyer watched me closely as he spoke. "It's standard procedure, I assure you. We simply need to know where Joey was during the overnight hours."

"There's a mistake, or something." I shook my head. "I already told you. Joey dropped me off a little after midnight. He took Shannon and Pete home. And then he went home."

Detective Wallace shook his head slowly. "No, Maggie. He did not go home."

"He said…" Everything in my head jumbled together. I wasn't sure if I knew anything any more. If Joey was out all night, why hadn't he said anything? We'd hung out at the gorge for hours; Joey had plenty of opportunity to share if he'd been out all night doing something crazy. It's the kind of thing he'd usually brag about… But he hadn't mentioned a thing. "He had to have been at home."

Detective Meyer leaned towards me, lowering his voice. "We've spoken with his parents. They are certain that he spent the night out, and that he wasn't where he said he would be."

"Maggie, do you have any idea where he might have gone?" Detective Wallace asked. "Or who he might have been with?"

I opened my mouth, trying to think of words that might answer the very same questions that had started to spin around in my own mind. But I had no answers, so all that came out was a choppy, stuttering sound that hardly reminded me of my own voice.

"This is an awful lot to take in," my mother said, squeezing my knee again. "If Maggie remembers anything, we'll be sure to call you." From my mother's tone, it was obvious that the conversation was over. But I suddenly didn't want it to be.

"You're *sure* he didn't go home?" I asked, focusing on the sound of the words tumbling out of me instead of the fact that, if they were true, it meant Joey had been keeping some kind of secret.

Both detectives nodded, eyes trained on me. "Positive," Detective Wallace answered.

I looked down at my hands, squeezing them together so tightly they turned a sickly whitish-blue. I wasn't sure if I was angry with Joey for keeping a secret or glad to realize that maybe he could go on living through all the little things I didn't yet know. Things that I could easily find out.

"I assume it is standard, in cases like this, for people to obtain lawyers," my father said, placing a hand on my shoulder. "If you believe you may need to question Margaret again, we will certainly call our attorney."

"That would be fine with us." Detective Wallace met my father's eyes.

"Just so you know," Detective Meyer said, "we will be requesting that Maggie undergo a medical and psychological exam in the next week or so."

"I'm not hurt." I pushed my chair back, standing, wavering a little, and placed my hand on the table for balance. "I don't need to see a doctor."

"But, Maggie, you *are* suffering from memory loss," Detective Wallace said. "This might actually help you."

"We will have our lawyer contact you for any further directions." My father stood, his chair scraping along the tiles of the floor.

My mother grabbed her purse from the floor and flung it onto her arm before she got to her feet.

Placing a hand on my back, my father led me towards the door. But I was still shaky and moved slowly as I tried to figure out what Joey could have been doing all night without me.

The detectives stood before I'd rounded the corner of the table. My fingers trailed the looping grain of the wood, and for some reason I didn't want to lose my connection with that cool surface.

But then I saw something that made me feel like racing

from the room. As the detectives buttoned their suit jackets, like men always do when they stand, I sneaked a peek at their full uniforms, which hadn't really seemed like uniforms at all, since they were dressed like businessmen. But businessmen don't have handcuffs strapped to their waists, badges making their pockets bulge, or guns stuffed into holsters at their hips.

Suddenly, every fuzzy quality that had made the day feel like a dream slipped away from my consciousness. It was like I broke the surface of the water, my sight and hearing clearing in an instant. And for the first time since the accident, everything felt excruciatingly real.

Especially the thought of myself, alone in bed, while Joey was out in the dark night doing things without me. Things he obviously didn't want me to know about. And the gaping emptiness where my memories ought to be – memories of Joey's last moments on this earth, of our last moments together. There was so much that I suddenly needed to uncover, no matter the cost. Because learning all the things I didn't already know, finding a few more slices of life when Joey was with us, even if it only helped for a little while, was the only way I could cheat my way out of his death.

5 waiting for his touch

BE THERE IN TEN, the text said. *T.*

I wasn't ready. Didn't know if I ever would be, but that wasn't what mattered.

I'd spent the last few hours sitting on the floor in my dark closet, knees pulled to my chest, remembering Saturday by sifting through the parts that hadn't disappeared. It had only been two days, but it felt more like for ever.

After the police station, my parents called in a lawyer – a friend of a friend of my father's. With his stiffly combed hair and red-striped tie, I felt like Mr. Fontane had just stepped out of an 80's movie. I'd sat there in our living room as my parents spoke for me, silent except when I was asked a question, and then I only offered a *yes* or *no*.

My moment of clarity at the police station hadn't brought back any memories, hadn't answered any of the questions spinning around in my mind, spiralling out to the air around me. All I knew for sure was that the day's events were real. Something had happened. And Joey was gone.

To make matters worse, I had a feeling. A creeping feeling that slithered through the shadows of my heart, whispering to me when I was quiet – what if something I had done had killed Joey? What if something I didn't do could have saved him? And when I zoned out on the carpet or at the drone of someone's voice, I saw flashes – treetops and tears and rippling water. I was afraid that if everything came flooding back, I'd face a realization that might be too much for me to handle. But even with all that fear, I wanted to pull the pieces together. The memories that had escaped me – I had to find them.

During a few quiet moments that first day, I'd wondered if it was real. The part where Joey had died. The part where I didn't. Maybe, in some parallel universe, Joey had survived and I was gone. Maybe my mom knew all about it, and that was why she had one hand on me every second she could. She thought I was fragile and wanted me by her side so she could keep me from imploding or exploding or whatever she was afraid might happen next.

My little secret: I was glad. It felt like she was keeping me from floating away. I was scared to death to leave the house without her. But this night, it was something I had to do. Something we all had to do. Together.

So I took a deep breath and slid out of the cocoon my

closet had become, yanking my fingers through my tangled hair. As I pulled on a pair of jeans, I glanced in the mirror and saw the dark smearing shadows under my eyes. I ran a finger over the stitching on the front of Joey's baseball shirt: JOEY. It still smelled like him, and I pulled it on to feel like he was closer. Still with me.

I'd found the shirt in my car and remembered how he'd flung it into the back seat after school Friday (was that three days ago, or another lifetime?), claiming he was *hot-hot-hot*. With a smirk, I'd agreed. He'd flexed his arms dramatically before leaning towards me, nuzzling his face into my neck, knowing that tickle zone was the easiest way to make me laugh. My giggles mixed with his words, twined around them. *We're gonna have a kick-ass Memorial Day weekend,* he'd said. *Two parties and the gorge to kick off the best summer ever.* And then he'd kissed me, long and insistent, like he knew what I'd secretly planned for us when his parents left town in a few short weeks, and wanted to give me a prelude so I wouldn't back out.

When he pulled away, he cranked the dial on my radio until "Dynamite" by Taio Cruz pumped out the open windows and collided with everyone walking past. I reversed out of my parking space unaware that it would be the last time Joey would ever ride in my car.

*   *   *

When Joey's brother opened the front door of the Walthers' house I wanted to run. But I ignored that urge, because this night wasn't about me. My second impulse was to push past Rylan and rush up the staircase, to lock myself in Joey's room and bury myself in his blankets so I could feel him all around me one last time. But I didn't do that, either. Instead, I stepped into the hall and wrapped my arms around Rylan's shoulders, pulling him close as everyone filed in behind me.

I breathed him in and held tight, not wanting to let go.

"This is one suck-ass Memorial Day, huh?" Pete asked, stepping around us and clapping Rylan on the shoulder.

As I pulled away, Rylan's lips turned up in an attempt at a smile. But it faded before it had the chance to form. Just two years younger, he reminded me so much of Joey – his sizzling blue eyes, his freckled nose, the curve of his chin – I had to look away, to search for something that might not hurt as much. But it didn't work. Joey was everywhere.

Resting on the hallway table was a copy of *A Prayer for Owen Meany*, which Joey had been reading for English class. It sat as if he'd be back soon to pick it up and make his way through the last chapters. Perched on the staircase were his favourite Converse shoes, faded black with holes threatening the seams, one on its side, the laces flung loose. As if Joey would bound down the steps any minute to tug them on his feet before rushing out the door. They, too, seemed to be waiting for the touch of his hands.

"How are your parents?" Tanna asked, placing a hand on Rylan's back.

Rylan shook his head. "They're in the family room. I gotta warn you," he said, looking over his shoulder, towards the kitchen, "they're asking a lot of questions."

"Really?" Adam asked, looking up from the wood floor of the hall.

"Yeah, dude. They keep asking me where he was Friday night." Rylan's voice was a whisper. "Do any of you know—"

"Are they here, Rylan?" Joey's father asked, his voice deep and raw, his words pulsing towards us from the family room. "We need some help with this."

"Look, if you know anything, just tell them," Rylan said. "And thanks for coming, guys. You have no idea how much it means to them... To us."

"Bro," Pete said, wrapping an arm around Rylan's shoulders as we all moved towards the kitchen and living room, "where else would we be?"

"Yeah," Shannon said. "We're all family, Ry."

I imagined Joey by my side as we filed down the hallway and into the kitchen, rounding the bend into the cosy but enormous space of the Walthers' family room. It all looked so normal, it nearly killed me. Until I saw that nothing was normal at all. That was even worse.

Mr. and Mrs. Walther sat on the carpeted floor in front of a huge fireplace with pictures spread around the hearth in rippling waves. I wasn't so sure I could face those memories. But when Joey's parents stood and opened their arms to us, I didn't have a choice. I lost myself in their deep, shaking warmth, knowing that they felt the same pain that I did. A wall closed in behind me and I knew we'd all come together, huddled in the centre of the room.

I'm not sure how long we stood like that, Shannon hugging my back, Pete tucked against my side, Tanna and Rylan pressed up against Mrs. Walther, Adam practically keeping Mr. Walther from collapsing to the floor. But I would have been okay if it had never ended. Really, it may have been better that way. But nothing stays the same in life.

"Imagine if he could see this." Adam broke the moment, somehow finding the most fitting thing to say. "All of us standing here like a bunch of babies."

"He'd have our asses," Rylan said.

"Rylan!" Mrs. Walther's voice was so hoarse it made me cringe.

"Sorry, Ma. He'd have our *butts*. Is that better?"

"Don't be such a smart-ass," Mr. Walther said, ruffling Rylan's hair like he was still five.

We were pulling apart by then, wiping our faces with the palms of our hands, swiping at our noses, and moving towards the closest seats. As I sat between Pete and

Shannon on the couch, I tried not to look down at the pictures. But that didn't work.

There was one of all of us from a football game sophomore year, faces painted with blue and black stripes, our arms up in the air as we screamed after a touchdown. A shot of Joey and me from prom. Another of him in his baseball uniform. Then there was one of Joey and Rylan from last year's family trip to Myrtle Beach, where just behind them, the sun plunged into the ocean.

"Those are just from the last few years," Mrs. Walther said, sitting cross-legged on the floor, wiping her raw nose with a tissue and clearing her throat. "Rylan's working on a slide show, but we'd also like to have several different posters for the funeral. I was thinking you guys could make a few."

"We can do whatever you need us to," Pete said, sliding off the couch and grabbing a picture. "These pictures are great. You guys remember this one?" He held the photo in the air, and there we were. All six of us, sitting on a floating dock in the middle of a wide, open lake. I stared at the way Joey had slung his arm lazily across my lap, wishing I could go back. The shot had been taken last summer, on the Fourth of July, when we'd gone to the lake with Pete's parents.

It all rushed back to me in a series of simple moments, the entire day speeding through my mind in an instant: lying out on the floating dock, the guys splashing us as they drove past on jet skis, Tanna's wild laughter, Shannon turning up the music when her favourite song came on the staticky radio. The smell of sunscreen and lake water, the salty taste of potato chips, and my fizzy, too-warm Coke. And later, the barbecue where Pete practically set all of our burgers on fire, and how Adam had saved the day by closing the lid, thick smoke drifting up towards the darkening sky. Tanna sitting on the steps to the deck, smiling about a new, secret boyfriend. And Joey, teasing her. His hands reaching for her phone, tugging at her hair, pulling her off the deck and throwing her over his shoulder, spinning her in circles, threatening that he wouldn't stop until he had a name. But he *had* stopped, his bare feet in the thick grass, as soon as she shouted that she was going to throw up all over him, and her secret had been saved. Shannon, watching everything as she walked under the trees, looking for the perfect marshmallow sticks to use for s'mores during the bonfire. And later still, the orange tint of the fire glowing as Joey pulled me away from the sounds of Pete's guitar and the singing voices of our friends as the first blasts of fireworks splashed through the sky.

"Remember the fireworks?" I asked. I could practically feel their thunderous booms hitting me deep in the chest. One after another. And Joey's arms wrapped around my waist as we leaned against a tree near the shore.

"They were insane," Shannon said, but her voice was flat, like she didn't really believe herself.

It was quiet for a moment, Shannon's words echoing through the air. I wondered if we were all thinking the same thing. That we had been so lucky. And we hadn't even known it.

"My mom told me the funeral will be this Thursday," Adam said. He was rocking in a recliner next to the couch, clutching an oatmeal-coloured pillow.

Mr. Walther took a deep breath. "Yes."

I couldn't believe they were talking about Joey's funeral. I wanted to press my hands to my ears to stifle the words, to scream so loud I would drown out the new reality that had taken over my life. But I knew I had to keep it together. At least until I was alone in my closet with Joey's sweatshirt pressed against my mouth, muffling my sobs.

"We've asked the baseball team to serve as pall-bearers," Mrs. Walther said. "And we'd like you all to sit up front with us. I was thinking that you could maybe choose something to read. As a group. Or however you think would be—" She bowed her head then, squeezing her eyes shut, and her body began to shake. Mr. Walther moved towards his wife, rubbing her shoulders.

"We thought you might like to make a few CDs for the viewing, too," Mr. Walther said. "I'm sure you'd know better than us what—"

"There's going to be a viewing?" I asked, my body stiff.

Mrs. Walther sniffled. "We thought it was important."

"Oh," I said, squeezing my hands tight. The thought of seeing my boyfriend's body laid out in a coffin made me feel like I was going to throw up. But the question that came next made me feel worse. Two words strung together on a rushed and frantic wave.

"What happened?" Joey's mother asked, her eyes trained on me.

"Trisha," Mr. Walther said. "We decided we weren't going to—"

"I know Joey is...*was* wild, and beautifully fearless. I'm not blaming anyone. And I'm so grateful that he wasn't alone, that your faces were the last ones he saw. But I *need* to understand," Mrs. Walther said, fisting her hands tight. "*What happened Saturday?*"

My heart exploded in my chest, every breath so tight I felt like I might pass out.

"I explained to you this afternoon," Adam said, "Maggie doesn't remember anything after climbing up the trail with Joey."

I looked at Adam, barely registering that he had been to speak with them already. That he'd talked to them about me.

"Maggie," Mrs. Walther said, "can't you tell me anything?"

My throat threatened to close up on me. It was the guilt of not remembering, of surviving when Joey hadn't. But I forced the words out. "I'm trying to see it, to remember, but—"

"You were with him, though? At the top?"

I closed my eyes, wanting to go back instead of facing what lay ahead, and saw the treetops, swooshing slowly from side to side. Then my eyes travelled down the length of several thick trunks, resting on my friends as they stood expectantly along the bank of the swimming hole.

Don't stand there looking down for too long, Adam called.

My eyes popped open. Found Adam. He leaned forwards in his seat, staring right back at me.

"Adam told me not to look down for too long," I said. That part had to be right. It was like a movie playing on some invisible screen, the way I could see his face, tipped up towards me, how I could hear his voice echoing off the walls of the gorge.

"Yeah," Adam whispered. "I did."

"Wait," Shannon said, her eyes flickering from me to Adam and back again. "You remember something? Something new?"

I stared at her, watching her long eyelashes beat time with the second hand of the clock on the mantlepiece, taking in the way her hair had gone stringy from not being washed, following the curve of her neck turning into her shoulder and sweeping down her tanned arm. And then I got another flash.

Tanna smacking Shannon's arm. The spark of a smirk on Shannon's face.

My voice, one word: *Bitch.*

And Joey's: *Part of what we love about her.*

The sounds echo-echo-echoed off the stone walls of my skull.

Still staring. Shannon's brown eyes, the smooth peachy skin of her cheeks, the strawberry pink of her lips.

"Maggie?" Tanna said, her voice tight, high-pitched. "Are you okay?"

"No, I—" I tried to steady my rushed breathing, knowing I had to lie. These new flashes, I needed to figure out how to find more, how to piece together the whole scene before I said anything. "I'm sorry. I don't remember anything new. Just walking up to the top. Standing there." I looked to Mrs. Walther, tears spilling from my eyes. "I don't know what happened. I wish I could tell you. But it's just…gone."

Adam stood from his chair, and everyone turned to look at him. I wanted to take the chance to sneak away, to duck into one of those photographs and slip right back into the past.

"I think he was trying one of his stupid stunts," Adam said, leaning down and plucking a few pictures from the pile, shuffling through them.

"He was always so crazy up there." Pete rubbed a hand on my knee, squeezing in a way that let me know they all had my back. Which was good, because I didn't think I could face any more questions. "At one point or another, I think we all told him to chill."

"Joey?" Rylan asked. "Chill? You think he even knew the definition of that word?"

Pete and Adam chuckled. From her spot on the floor, Tanna scooted closer to me, her warm eyes meeting mine as she stopped near my feet, her body practically shielding my own. And Shannon, she slumped beside me, practically melting into the cushions of the couch.

"We were told that he hit his head," Mr. Walther said. "And that you all went into the water to pull him to shore."

"Except Shannon," Pete said. "She went for the phone."

"I knew it was bad," Shannon whispered, "when he didn't pop up from the water and crack some stupid joke."

"And he was still breathing?" Mr. Walther asked.

"It was strained." Tanna pressed a hand to her chest and took a deep breath. Then reached out to me, wrapped her fingers around my ankle and squeezed.

"I didn't know that," I said, my chest feeling like it was caving in. I looked at everyone in the room, my eyes stopping on Shannon. "No one told me anything about him breathing. He was alive?"

"When they got him to the towel, he looked up at me." Shannon closed her eyes. Her whole face squeezed tight. "I know he saw me. He tried to say something. But I couldn't make it out. And then he squeezed my hand once." Shannon's voice broke open. With all the passion that I had ever felt in my life, I hated that the memory of Joey's last moments were hers instead of mine.

"We started CPR," Adam said, "when Shan noticed he wasn't breathing any more."

The room fell silent. It felt like a fog had fallen over us, trailing into our mouths so no more words could be spoken. I heard Shannon's soft, breathy cries. All I could think was that while I was glad Joey had someone with him in his last minutes, I despised that it wasn't me. For a moment, all that deep, dark hate was directed at her. And then I felt horrible. She'd lost Joey, too. We all had. So I pulled her against me, rubbed her back, and felt myself begin to suffocate under the weight of our sadness. Looking at the letters of Joey's name stitched on his baseball shirt, I tried not to think about how Shannon's breath, and perfume, and tears were evaporating the last scents Joey had left on the fabric enfolding me.

I tried not to think about Joey's parents, who were still on the floor, deflated and broken. I thought it was over then. But they had one more question. The one that I'd been asking myself since the police station.

"Where was Joey Friday night?" Mrs. Walther held her breath for a moment. "He told us he was staying at Adam's house."

"Wait, he didn't?" Shannon asked, pulling away from me. "Joey took us home – Maggie and me and Pete. Adam called right after we dropped Maggie off. I just thought…"

"Nope," Adam said, shaking his head. "I talked to him sometime after twelve, but that's it."

"None of you have any ideas?" Mrs. Walther asked.

We looked around at each other, shaking our heads. It seemed like a totally insignificant detail when you considered the whole mess, but it hit hard in that moment. We might not ever know where Joey went after Jimmy Dutton's party. Joey wasn't there to tell us any more.

His room felt like a bubble. A safe place that, when I closed my eyes, gave me the illusion that Joey was still alive. The air practically sizzled with his energy, so intense I could have believed he was standing next to me. I wasn't supposed to touch anything. I'd promised I wouldn't when I made my escape, using the excuse that I wanted to grab a few of his CDs for the mix we were going to make. But I had to.

I leaned down and pressed my face into his pillow, breathing him in. Imagined him lying there, perfectly alive. Then I crossed the room and opened his closet door as quietly as I could, running my fingers along the soft fabric of his clothes. I wished I could tuck myself into the thick shadows of the small space. To stay there for the rest of my life.

But nothing that I wanted could happen any more.

So I reached for the inside handle of the closet door and started to swing it shut. But my fingers brushed against something wrapped around the neck of the silver knob, stopping me.

I looked down. Smiled.

There, twisted and pulled tight, was a rainbow-coloured necklace, a pattern of tiny beaded flowers. Pete had won it for me at the Spring Carnival, just five weeks ago. Joey couldn't come because his father had scored some killer tickets for a Reds game in Cincinnati. Joey had been excited for the game, but he'd been pissed we were all doing something without him. He'd always hated missing out.

After the carnival, Tanna drove me home, both of us singing to loud music as the wind rushed at us through the open windows of her car. I'd been wishing Joey would call me; I wanted to hear the velvety tone of his voice before I slipped under my covers and fell asleep. But he'd been so late, I didn't talk to him until the next day. When he stopped by my house, we went up to my room, and I'd flung the necklace in the air, teasing him that another guy had given me jewellery, that he'd better be careful or someone might just steal me away. And then I shoved the bright flowers into the right-hand side of my dresser drawer, along with a messy collection of hairslides and bottles of nail polish, with Joey leaning into me, tugging at the waist of my shirt and whispering that he was the only one for me. I'd had no idea he'd taken the silly necklace, but somehow seeing it wrapped around the handle of his closet door, knowing he'd thought of me every time he'd seen it, made me happy.

I grabbed a stack of CDs from his dresser before making my way out into the darkened hallway. As I stepped to the top of the staircase, I was thinking that I would give anything for one more night with Joey, so I could tell him and show him and make him feel exactly how much he meant to me.

I was three or four steps down before I heard them. Hushed whispers, hurried and insistent. The first voice was Shannon's. The second, Adam's. The sharpness that punctuated the tone of the conversation stopped me. My hand gripped the railing and held tight.

"Adam, that's not fair. You have to think about—"

"It's *all* I'm thinking about, Shannon."

"Then you should understand that we can't—"

"No. You need to understand. I'm not going to do this. I won't."

"Is this about that phone call? The night of Dutton's party?"

"That's none of your business, Shannon."

"The hell it isn't. I know you were fighting. You have to tell me what—"

"The only thing I have to do right now is leave." Adam sounded so angry, nothing like himself. And that scared me. "I can't handle this. Not for one more second."

There were footsteps then. And the click of the front door.

I rushed down, my palm sliding across the railing, just in time to see Adam step through the open doorway. Shannon's back faced me, her body tense.

"She's right, Adam," I said.

Adam stopped. Stood there for a moment. And then turned to face me, tears welling in his red-rimmed eyes.

Shannon turned, too, her tears spilling over, running down her cheeks and dripping off her chin.

"Right about what?" Adam asked, his tone softening a bit.

"You can't just leave. We have to do this together."

Adam bit his lower lip and looked around the hall. "It's just too much," he said, tipping his head towards those black Converse shoes. "Being here. Doing this."

"This isn't about us," I said. "It's about Joey. And his family. It sucks and hurts and we hate it, but we're doing this because we love him." I wondered how I could feel so comfortable telling Adam that I loved Joey when I'd never had the guts to tell Joey himself. I felt like screaming, knowing I'd lost that chance, that I'd never have it again.

Adam shook his head.

"Shan said you and Joey were fighting?" I was dying to ask a thousand questions at once but forced myself to let it go until Adam and I were alone and he might actually tell me something. "Is that why you're so—"

"Nothing was going on." Adam looked at Shannon. Then me. "It was stupid."

Shannon reached out towards Adam, but he pulled away.

"He was a brother to you," Shannon said. "He wasn't perfect. He was more than a little crazy sometimes, but that's why we loved him. Right?"

Adam pressed his hands to his face. Sighed. "Right. It's just that… He *died*. And I'm so freaking pissed off, I swear I'd punch him in the face if he were standing right here."

"That's normal, right? I mean, I feel that way, too, sometimes," I said, trying to smile. "And then the next second, I'm a slobbering mess, just wanting to give him one more hug."

"We've all turned schizophrenic," Shannon said with a snort. "Joey would be proud he's had that effect on us."

Adam shook his head. "The sick thing is that you're right."

"So, you're staying?" I asked.

Adam closed the door, shutting out the dark night. "Yeah," he said. "I guess I don't have a choice."

"Thank you," Shannon said.

Adam looked at her, something unfamiliar crossing over his face, sending a ripple of fear through my chest. I tried to push the thought away, but it kept coming back. Adam seemed different somehow. A shade darker. And I was suddenly afraid that Joey, and all those memories, weren't the only things I'd lost at the cliff top.

6 a punched-up shade of blue

IT HAD HIT ME THE night before, after coming home from Joey's house. The memory crashed into me as I was falling asleep, and I couldn't get it out of my mind. The image of Joey lying on the ground. Unmoving.

It's like my brain had taken a snapshot of the moment and seared the single frame to the insides of my eyelids so that every few seconds it would wash over me again. Pull me under. Drown me. Joey on the bank – just lying there – his legs bent awkwardly, head tipped back, mouth gaping open.

I squeezed my eyes tight and pressed my fingertips into the lids, turning the flash into a million pinpricks of light – erasing his death.

The vision made me feel this desperate need to hide in the vacuum of my closet. But I wasn't alone. And I didn't want anyone to know that I'd started to spend so much time backed into a corner, huddled beneath my clothes. So I stayed where I was, burrowed between Tanna and Shannon.

Earlier, when we'd finished the last of Joey's posters and CDs, after Pete left us sitting on my front lawn with the setting sun turning the sky a bruised shade of purplish blue, Tanna had insisted on spending the night, saying we should use pillows and blankets to make a bed on the floor of my room, like we used to do when we were kids. With only one day until the funeral, Shannon had agreed, saying that none of us should be alone.

I didn't tell her that, for me, *alone* was the only thing that felt right any more.

Lying on the floor, digging my toes into the carpet to give myself the reassurance that something beneath me was solid, I lied to myself. Told myself Joey had just been sleeping. Because that was easier. An escape. Lying took me to the times that were protected, indestructible.

Like the semester of freshman health class, when Joey and I would shuffle to the back of the classroom, duck behind Chris Grater's wiry Afro, and whisper back and forth until the interminable video of the day began. Then we'd nestle down in our seats, prop our heads on bunched-up fleece jackets, and close our eyes. I always opened mine again, watching Joey for a few minutes as the drone of the documentary voice-over began, counting the freckles dotting the slope of his nose, or thinking about braiding his chocolate-brown hair, imagining the feel of the silky strands sliding against the length of my fingers until the information about STIs or news of the latest super-virus trickled into my brain and I was swept away by the sleep that had overtaken Joey.

Just sleeping, I told myself, pressing my shoulders, my back, my butt against the bedroom floor – against solid ground. Pressing my mind forwards, tripping away from that horrible vision, and onto the next. Adam's face, his eyes, stricken with panic. But that only made me feel more alone. More unsteady and in need of balance. Why was everything making me feel like I was suspended in eternal free fall?

"You guys checked your phones again, right?" I asked the darkness, the steady sound of sleepy breathing coming from both of my friends. "When we turned off the light?"

"Yeah." Tanna flipped to her side, facing me. I could smell the soapy scent of the cleanser she'd slathered on her face earlier. "I did."

"Me, too." Shannon tossed an arm up and over her head.

"Nothing?" I asked.

"Nada," Shannon said. "It's official. Adam's ignoring us."

"I don't get it," I said. "Why wouldn't he show tonight? How could he miss helping with the posters and CDs for the funeral?"

"The important thing is that we know he's okay. I talked to his mom earlier, remember?" Tanna reached out and gave my hand a squeeze. "We're all having trouble with this, and we won't all deal with it in the same way."

"Yeah, but he's, like, completely shut us out," I said. "How many times did you text him?"

"Not as many as you," Shannon said with a yawn.

"I sent him *three* nine-one-one messages. And left him, like, a thousand voicemails." I flipped to my stomach, grabbing my phone and pressing the button to take it out of sleep mode.

"Maybe he just needs a little time," Tanna said. "To process—"

"Nothing," I said, scrolling through my texts. "Still nothing." Somehow, Adam's absence was making me feel twice as empty. Which didn't make any sense. I knew he was alive. He was out there, somewhere. And that should have made me feel relieved. But instead, his sudden disappearance left me twice as shaky, twice as unsure about the world that was suddenly closing in around me.

"Where do you guys think he is?" Shannon asked, her voice trailing into the darkness, tripping across Tanna and me.

"Hell if I know," I said, tossing my phone on the floor near my pillow, close enough for me to grab in a flash if Adam finally decided to respond. "All we know for sure is what Pete said after he left here and drove past Adam's house – that his car wasn't in the driveway. Trust me, if I knew where to go, I'd leave right now and tell him exactly what I think about him ignoring us."

"I meant *Joey*," Shannon said, her soft words tumbling after mine. There was a pause then, a silence that seeped into our bones as the truth of Joey's death washed over us again. "I keep thinking he's on the moon. I've been picturing him up there in that purplish-white glow. I see him watching us. Listening in."

My chest tightened with the thought of him being so very far away. I bit at my lip, trying to keep all sound trapped inside.

"I see him in a field," Tanna said. "The grass practically glows, it's so green, and the sky above him is this punched-up shade of blue. He's running, his arms pumping with his steps. And he looks strong. Healthy. But most important, he's smiling."

I was jealous and ashamed, and I didn't want to tell them that my vision of Joey was so unlike theirs. That what I mostly saw was him lying on the ground at the Jumping Hole. Dead. Where he was now, that was something I hadn't yet dared to face. And I didn't want to. So I said the first thing that came to my mind, needing to escape before I became locked in the grip of yet something else that would drown me.

"I just want to rewind everything," I said. "To take it all back."

"Take what back?" Tanna's voice was stronger, more awake.

"*Everything!* Planning the day at the gorge, driving with you guys instead of Joey, taking that stupid dare. What if one small thing changed? Would we all be hanging out right now, listening to music while Joey laughed at something stupid someone said, instead of making posters and planning the music for his—"

"Maggie," Tanna said, "you can't do that."

"But I can't stop myself." I sat up and pulled my knees to my chest. "What if it's as simple as one moment? One tiny thing, like that kiss on the rocks? What if I'd kissed him a little longer? Would he be alive right now? Or what if I'd stayed with him Friday night, what if I'd been with him... wherever he was?"

"You've got to let that go," Shannon said. "It's going to drive you crazy. And none of us know, so—"

"Besides," Tanna's hand fluttered against my back, her fingers pressing into the cotton of my shirt, "it doesn't work like that."

"And then I think all kinds of stupid shit, right? Like, what if I'd just had sex with him at prom? Could something as far back as a few weeks ago have made a difference?"

"No way, Mags." Tanna's voice was a whisper. Like she wasn't sure if she was right or not.

"But if we'd done it that night, like he'd wanted to, instead of me holding out for the week his parents were going out of town... If I hadn't been so against becoming a total cliché, he wouldn't have died a virgin."

"Oh, God, Maggie, you think…" Shannon's voice fell, dropped away with her thought. Then it came back, even stronger. "You can't blame yourself for anything like that."

"Who else is to blame?" My question strung out in the air between us like a thread, ready to break.

Tanna and Shannon were silent in the darkness.

"No one." I tipped my forehead against my knees and tried to hold back my tears.

"Maggie," Tanna said, rubbing my back in slow circles. "You have to stop this."

I choked on a sob, then let it all the way out. Sitting there between them, clutching tight to the edge of my blanket, watching the clock tick me from the-first-Tuesday-without-Joey into the-first-Wednesday-without-Joey, I needed an escape.

So I focused on the calming memories of what had been, scrolling through the years, the stages, the people we once were and had come to be.

But somehow, that made everything feel worse.

"I'm just really tired," I said. "I don't want to talk any more."

"Are you sure?" Tanna asked, her hand slipping away from my back.

"Yeah," I said, the word shaking out into the darkness. "Please."

I lay back then, closed my eyes, and did the one thing that always helped me when I was feeling alone.

I remembered my favourite night with Joey.

The most important night of all.

The night *we* became *us*.

I'd always loved the sky. The night sky, though, was the best. The purplish-blue blanket that folded itself over my little town, it promised me things. Whispered to me when I was in that hazy state of almost sleep where anything seemed possible.

Like Joey and me.

Together.

After so many years of my secret longing, it was quite fitting that it all started under the veiled and sparkling shelter only a night sky could offer.

"Favourite midnight snack?" Joey lay next to me in the bed of his new black truck, which was actually quite used, his shoulder bumping mine as we played Twenty Questions in the middle of an abandoned back field on the outskirts of town.

"Bozie's Doughnuts."

Joey's head tipped towards me, his hair falling across his forehead. "No way."

I smiled and bit my lower lip to keep myself from looking

as excited as I felt to be so close to him. He smelled good. Like cut grass and honeysuckle. And I wanted to taste him.

"I mean, *seriously*, no way." As Joey shook his head, his eyes remained plastered to mine. "That's too creepy."

"Last time I checked," I said, "there's nothing creepy about Bozie's Doughnuts."

Joey chuckled. "Wait until you see this."

He sat up and slid across the open tailgate of his truck, disappearing in the thick blackness that blanketed the night around us. I readjusted myself on the inflatable camping mattress Joey had unrolled in the truck's bed and scooted closer to the centre, listening to the swooshing sound of Joey's footsteps as they mingled with the crooning chirp of the crickets. He got into the truck, and I heard rustling, then the soft sound of music before the slam of his driver's side door rippled across the open field. He hopped into the truck's bed, a white bag swinging in his hand.

"Check it out." He held the bag in the air.

I laughed, surprised to see the Bozie's Doughnuts logo. "That is a little creepy."

"I thought we'd get hungry while we waited." Joey opened the bag and took a deep whiff.

"You ever gonna tell me what we're waiting for?" I raised myself on my elbows, feeling the shiver of my hair against my neck.

"It's a surprise." Joey held the bag towards me. "You like devil's food?"

"Are you kidding?" I sat up and reached into the bag, feeling my way around some frosted doughnuts and a twisted pretzel doughnut before finally finding the perfect specimen. "They're only the best."

"Creepy."

I laughed, wishing he would sit right next to me again. That he would lie down, turn to me, and flip this thing between us into full speed.

After taking a few bites of the sweet chocolate doughnut, I looked at Joey. He tipped his head back, staring up at the sky as he wiped crumbs off his hands and swallowed his last bite.

"You have to give me a hint." I decided to lie down again, hoping the action would lure him closer. "Is everyone meeting us out here? Is that what we're waiting on?"

"Nope." Joey slid towards me. "Tonight's just for you and me."

I smiled. Then pinched my lips together. Tight. It had been awkward, this thing between us. Whatever *it* was. Joey and I had hung out alone a zillion times. I mean, we'd grown up together, the six of us, and we'd all spent time in small groups or pairs while the others were busy. But when Joey had stopped me after school exactly one week earlier and said he had a surprise planned, that he wanted me to be his first passenger after passing his driving test, he was nervous. And *nothing* made Joey nervous. I knew from the way his voice wavered, how his eyes looked everywhere but right into mine. And that had gotten me excited. I'd never told anyone about my long-standing, secret crush on Joey. Ever. Because I knew what feelings like mine could do to a friendship. And I couldn't lose him.

"Joey, look!" I flung my hand into the air, pointing at a brilliant trail of light streaking across the sky.

"There we go," he said, lying down and scooting his body right up against mine.

"Should we make a wish?" I stared at the fading light. "Shooting star, and all?"

Joey's hand reached out, his fingers twining into mine. "We're going to have plenty of wishes to make tonight."

As soon as he spoke, another star flashed across the sky. "Did you see that?"

"It's a meteor shower," Joey said. "And the show is just starting."

"No way!" I wriggled a little with my excitement, causing the truck to sway beneath us. "I've never seen a meteor shower. I've always wanted to."

"Same here," Joey said. "I thought it would be the perfect way to show you...well, how I'm feeling."

I turned towards him, but not all the way. You never want to go all the way. "How you're feeling?"

Joey rolled his eyes. "You really gonna make me work for it?"

"I just want to hear you say it."

"I'm having feelings. Different than normal." Joey traced his thumb along my lower lip. "For you."

"Good feelings?" I licked my lips, tasting the sugary coating left over from my doughnuts. The song on the stereo changed, and I recognized the beginning beats of Dave Matthews Band's "You and Me".

Joey leaned forwards, his breath a sweet, delicious heat that had me spinning under another leaping star.

"Definitely." His voice was a whisper, but it washed through me.

And then he kissed me.

It was insistent from the beginning. That kiss, there was nothing soft about it. Like he'd been waiting his whole life to finally make it happen. And it swept me away, carried me further than anything ever had. I rode the wave as long as I could, feeling his fingers twisting through my hair, the way his body pressed against mine, how his eyelashes brushed against the upper part of my cheek. I'm not sure how long it lasted, our first kiss. All I know is that it was long enough to flip the earth inside out. To turn everything around for ever. I no longer cared about the beauty of the plunging stars. All I wanted was to kiss him again. And again. And again.

Joey stopped before I was even close to ready. All kinds

of things raced through my mind – *Did the kiss not measure up? Did his feelings vanish as quickly as they had appeared?* – until he smiled, his fingers stroking my chin, trailing slowly down my neck, lighting my entire body on fire.

"That was nice," he said.

I nodded, unable to find my voice.

"I want to gulp you down."

I loved the smoky sound of his voice as he whispered to me.

"But I have to take sips. Or else this thing could be dangerous."

I took a deep breath. And I finally understood. He felt the same way I did. And everything was going to be fine. Slow. But good. I could handle that.

After bumping his nose against mine and giving me one last small kiss, he looked up. I tipped my forehead against his and stared at the dancing sky.

I wanted the night to last for ever. It killed me, knowing that each moment ticked me closer to the time we would have to part from the magic of the field. I looked at Joey, traced the dip of his nose with my eyes. And I got an idea.

"You have to be quiet," I said as I pulled my phone from my pocket.

"Why?" Joey looked at me with curious eyes.

I had already punched in the number and was listening to the third ring. "Shh."

"Honey, what is it? Are you okay?" My mom's voice was heavy, and I knew that I'd woken her. I wondered if she was in bed or still on the couch with the quilt draped over her legs while late night television flickered light across the living room.

"I'm fine, Mom," I said with a yawn. "Just tired. Is it okay if I sleep over at Tanna's tonight?"

My mom caught my yawn. "That's fine," she said. "Just call me in the morning."

"Okay." I grinned at Joey. "Night."

When I closed my phone and slid it back into my pocket, Joey turned to his side, propping himself on an elbow. "You," he said, "are trouble."

I laughed, the sound of my voice skipping across the empty field. "You gonna call home, too?" My heart was beating fast, in time with the rapid melody of the crickets that surrounded us. I wasn't sure what Joey would think about what I'd just done. I knew that call had been the final step, crossing a line that meant our friendship was now something much more complicated. And I was excited to see what lay ahead. "Or do I have to spend a night in this field *alone*?"

Joey leaned forwards, his lips brushing mine, lingering, his breath an intoxicating sugary mist. "You think I'd miss out on this opportunity?" Joey asked, shaking his head. "Not. On. Your. Life."

7 crashing onto me

I HELD MY BREATH BECAUSE of the smell. It was stale, and musty, and wrong.

My feet stepped slowly, skidding every so often on the thick carpet, a deep maroon pool that sucked me under with its circular pattern, pulling me forwards to the last place I ever wanted to be. The last place I ever thought I would be.

"There she is," someone just ahead of me whispered. I did not look up.

"Do you think it's true?" another voice asked.

Shannon's grasp on my hand tightened. "Ignore them."

"You got this," Tanna said. I wasn't sure if she was speaking to herself or me.

The dark box was just ahead, its shiny surface glinting, even in the dim lighting of the room. One glance and I squeezed my eyes so tight I saw starbursts. I wished I could squeeze so hard I'd pass out and miss this entire thing.

The faint sound of "You and Me" by Dave Matthews

Band caught in my ears. At first, I thought I had imagined it. But then I remembered the CDs Pete, Tanna, Shannon, and I had made. I could hardly recall sitting on my front lawn as we made the playlists on Pete's iPod, or going inside to burn the songs to discs. What I remembered most was all of us wondering why Adam had refused to join, worrying about why he was pulling away, and hoping that we would get him back.

When I opened my eyes, I saw it again. The long box. But I saw something else, too. Joey's profile peeking just above the side. It looked like he was sleeping.

Those long-ago memories rushed me again. Joey in health class. Joey lying under the shooting stars. Joey – just sleeping.

But then my eyes skittered around the room, and all illusion vanished.

The terrible sadness that had overtaken me, the truth of Joey's death, shadowed everyone in darkness. I looked at the crowd of varsity cheerleaders, sports lovers, drama clubbers and overall party freaks hovering around the pocket of easels on the right side of the church, their backs facing the hundreds of pictures we'd taped to the poster boards. It felt as if each person in the room was staring directly at me. Then my eyes jumped left, found Joey's baseball team clamouring around a seating area, all in white Oxford shirts and black ties, their faces so melted by sadness I could hardly recognize them as they waited for me to break open.

I bobbed through the centre aisle of the church, Tanna and Shannon at my sides, focusing on one thing: Joey's mother's shoes. They were tan, flat, and ugly. *Joey would have been embarrassed*, I thought, then scolded myself. The poor woman had just lost her son. It was a wonder she had found the sanity to put on any shoes at all.

Five steps later, I was in front of her, standing on two shaky legs. I put my hand on her shoulder and kissed her tear-stained cheek, trying to keep my eyes from darting to the body lying next to her husband. As I stood back from Mrs. Walther, Joey's father reached out and folded me against him. He whispered something across the top of my head, but all I caught was the vibration coming from his chest. I wanted to stop time, to stay there in his arms for ever, because his shirt smelled like Joey. And he was the last stop before my final goodbye.

Mr. Walther pulled away from me, holding me at arm's length as his eyes wandered the planes of my face. "Doesn't he look peaceful?" Mr. Walther asked, tilting his head.

And I turned.

Faced him for the last time.

My Joey.

*   *   *

Tanna uncurled my fingers from the side of the coffin and tucked my hand into hers, squeezing. "It's okay," she said. "Just say goodbye."

I sucked in a deep breath and looked from Joey's cheeks to his nose to his chin, wanting with everything I was to see one more of his radiant smiles light up his face. Wanting to see his eyes flash out at the world around him.

His blue, blue eyes. They matched his favourite T-shirt almost perfectly. I was glad Rylan had talked his parents out of burying Joey in a suit; I knew they'd had several arguments over the matter. Rylan had insisted on Joey's sky-blue, HullabaLOU T-shirt, which he had picked up last summer when the six of us spent the entire day at the music festival. It was crisp and pulled tight across Joey's still chest and was actually tucked into his favourite Abercrombie jeans, which was so not how he did things, but whatever. At least he would be comfortable.

"How'm I supposed to say goodbye?" I asked.

"You just do it," Shannon said. "You gotta."

I shook my head. Tears fell from my chin onto Joey's face. I wanted to wipe them away. But I was afraid to touch him.

Terrified.

And that nearly made me collapse. Because *this* was Joey.

"Okay," I said. "I can do this."

"Yeah," Shannon said. "You can."

I nodded. More tears fell.

"Do you want us to stay?" Tanna asked. "Or leave you alone?"

I didn't know how to answer. And then I forgot the question, because I heard him. *Right* behind me. A huge wave of relief surged through me as I turned, a smile daring to form on my lips, and said his name.

"Joey?" It's crazy, I know, but I really believed. The waxy version of him lying so still did *not* seem real, so it felt right, the hope that blossomed through my chest.

But then his mother crumpled in her chair, and I realized my mistake.

It wasn't him at all. No. It had been Rylan.

"Oh, God," I said, my hand slamming to my mouth.

Rylan looked at me, his blue eyes pinched tight, and blew a burst of air from his lips.

"I'm sorry," I whispered.

Rylan's shoulders slumped as he slid into the chair next to his mother. He leaned forwards, propping his elbows on his knees, and buried his face in his hands. It was the first moment I wondered what it might be like to live in the Walthers' house, so quiet with Joey gone. It must be so much harder for Rylan to be left behind, a reminder to everyone just by being himself, because he looked and sounded *so* much like Joey.

I turned then, back to my goodbye, and leaned towards Joey's still face.

My lips were so close to his ear that I would have felt the heat of him if he'd been alive.

"I love you, Joey," I whispered for the first and last time in my life.

Then I pressed two fingers to my mouth, placing my final kiss for him there, and settled my fingers on his lips.

But his lips were all wrong.

They were cold and hard. The exact way I did *not* want to remember Joey.

The moment the touch registered in my brain, I realized that I never should have done it. The seconds my fingers rested on his stony lips would never be erased. Not in all my life. No matter what I did to scrape them away.

I turned and ran then, through the throngs of hushed people trying not to stare, past my mother, who had held out her arms to stop me. I shoved myself through the back door of the church and out into the bright light of the last May of Joey's life.

My knees dug into the soft soil, the grass prickling my skin.

My body heaved, stomach tight as I threw up a wave of acidic bile, the only thing left in me.

I curled my fingers into the ground, ripping up a handful

of the earth beneath me, hurling it into the bushes that lined the side of the church.

Tanna's feet, her black-painted toes and black strappy sandals, appeared at my side. "You okay?"

"No." If I'd had the energy, I would have screamed it loud enough for everyone in the world to hear.

Tanna knelt beside me, gently pulling my hair out of my face, tugging it into a ponytail, and securing it with an elastic band.

"I want to be alone." I curled into myself, a tight ball, and rested my cheek on the cool grass, closing my eyes and feeling a ghostly breeze attempt to dry the tears on my cheeks.

"Your mom was chasing after you," Tanna said. "I convinced her to let me come out instead. You sure you want me to go?"

I nodded, the fresh scent of cut grass mingling with the sour smell of my vomit. "Just tell her I need some space."

"Pete and Adam are over by the koi pond," Tanna said. "I'm going to tell them to wait for you."

I didn't say anything. Just focused on my breathing.

Tanna rubbed her fingernails along my back, giving me goosebumps. "You're still alive, Mags. You might not feel like it. But you have to keep going."

"I love you, Tan, but I need you to leave," I said. "Please."

"You have all of us here to help you through this," Tanna said. "When you're ready. Don't forget that."

She stood then, without another word, and walked away. When the vibration of her footsteps stopped buzzing the ground beneath me, I turned onto my back and stared up at the too-bright, too-blue sky, wishing it would come crashing down onto me.

"What're you playing?" I asked as I sat on the large rock between Pete and Adam. When Tanna left me, I had planned to lie there in the grass until my body failed and I no longer had to force myself to remember to breathe. But then I thought of the shrink they were making me see next week and imagined myself being wheeled down a dim corridor in some far-off mental hospital. I couldn't lose it completely. At least not in a way that was so obvious to others.

Pete's fingers kept moving, plucking invisible strings on the imaginary guitar propped on his lap. He did it often, the whole air guitar thing. Especially when he was bored or angry. Once I'd even caught his fingers playing after he fell asleep during a movie.

"Skynard," he said. "'Freebird'."

I stretched my legs forwards, kicking out of the high-heeled sandals Tanna had yanked from my closet the night before. "It should be raining," I said, tipping my face to the clear blue sky. "Angry, thrashing rain with streaks of lightning and crashing thunder."

Adam looked up, too, squinting at the sun. "That would make more sense."

"It should rain for ever," I said. "Now that we're stuck without him."

Pete rocked forwards a bit, looking down at the koi swimming in the little rock-lined pond. "Sucks inside," he said. "Hard. We had to get away."

I stared into the glimmering water, focusing on the largest fish in the group. It was silver and black and almost disappeared as it whipped around the others, a streak of shimmering lightning. It seemed like everything I saw or thought of brought me right back to Joey. The fish was no exception with his fearless, unstoppable energy.

"I think he looks good," Pete said, tilting his face towards me without looking into my eyes.

"You do?" I asked, my voice shaking.

"Not really." Pete scrunched his eyes, like he was in pain just thinking about the vision of Joey lying there in his coffin. "They did a good job on his head, where he hit the ledge, which is surprising. Other than that, he looks like some kind of wax version of himself. But I wasn't about to say that to *you*."

"You just did." I chuckled. The sound felt scratchy and

raw as it travelled up my throat. "And I agree." My fingers were still tingling from the icy feel of Joey's lips. I wondered if I would go through the rest of my life with my skin crawling as if I was still touching his death.

"I'm just glad they put him in that HullabaLOU T-shirt." Adam's voice was small, like he was very far away.

I sucked in a deep breath, remembering our day at the crazy-huge music festival. Pete had scored us the tickets through someone his dad knew, and all six of us had spent ten hours in the crowd, sweating in the summer sun, drinking what we could get our hands on, and dancing to the coolest bands. It was almost dark when the Steve Miller Band hit the main stage, and the rain began to fall. It came in a huge rush, like the clouds above knew how hot and sticky we were, and drenched us in an instant. The six of us danced, and laughed, and sang all at the same time, spinning on the slippery, muddy ground. It was at the very end of "Fly Like an Eagle", when they were singing about time slippin' forwards, that Joey swept me against his body and pressed his lips to my ears. "This is the best night of my life," he'd said with a laugh. "And you're the best thing that's ever happened to me."

It was the closest Joey had ever come to telling me that he loved me. Then he spun me away and whipped his hands into the air, bumping into Adam and Pete as they pulled Tanna up from the muddy ground. Shannon slung

an arm around my shoulders and sang along with the band, droplets of water rushing down her face, drip-drip-dripping off the wavy strands of her darkened hair.

If only we could go back. When Joey leaned in, his warm breath tickling my neck, that would be the one moment of my life I'd choose to relive. Over, and over, and over again.

"You guys want to get together later?" Pete asked, his voice low, like he knew he was pushing when he wasn't sure if he should. "Hang out and...I don't know, just be together or something? All of us? I feel like he'd like that. Joey, I mean."

I looked at Adam, the way his eyes had fallen down to the ground, not looking at either of us, not responding at all.

"Yeah," I said. "We should. Adam, you in?"

"I dunno," Adam said. "My mom's kind of clingy right now, you know? And I have some shit for school—"

"Dude," Pete said. "School? What about *Joey*?"

Adam looked up then, his eyes flaring. "Just call me when you figure it out. I'll come if I can."

"Right," Pete said, standing. "I gotta go in. My parents should be here by now."

"We'll be there in a few," I said, looking at Adam, wondering how the person sitting beside me was the same guy I'd considered one of my best friends for most of my life. Because, suddenly, he seemed like someone I barely

knew. I was dying to touch him, to feel that he wasn't so far away. I missed him like crazy, had thought of a thousand things I'd wanted to say to him over the last few days while he ignored us, but I didn't know how to cross the expanse that all the questions had created between us.

Pete walked away, and I tried to think of the right way to start. Of how I could get the answers I needed without pushing Adam into an even darker place.

"I've tried calling you," I said, deciding to talk to him as if nothing had changed, saying exactly what was on my mind instead of dancing around all the feelings. "Like, a hundred times."

Adam nodded. "Haven't felt much like talking."

"You can't push us all away, Adam. We're still here."

Adam buried his face in his hands. "I know."

"I don't want to make things worse. But there's stuff I need to ask."

Adam sighed. "Like?"

"Why were you and Joey fighting?" The question tumbled out of me before I could stop it. I knew it was the wrong way to approach this new version of Adam, but I didn't take it back. I just stared at the glinting back of the silver fish, hoping it was the moment I would finally get some answers.

"I already told you." Adam's voice was tinged with a shaky kind of anger. "It was nothing."

I closed my eyes and pictured Joey standing on Jimmy Dutton's back deck, a wave of something powerful rolling off him and dashing across the lawn, right towards Adam. But I'd been standing there, too. Right next to Adam. A little more than drunk, my head spinning from dancing in circles. And I couldn't be sure some of that anger hadn't been directed at me. If that's why Joey hadn't told me where he'd spent Friday night.

"I don't believe that it was nothing." I swiped a few strands of hair from my eyes. "When I think back to Dutton's party, the part where Joey came outside and first saw that you were there, something seemed off. Like, really off. I want to know what was going on."

Adam stared off to the batch of trees that separated the back area of the church from a line of houses that had been converted into a dentist's office, an insurance agency, and a picture-framing store.

"It's complicated." Adam clasped his hands together.

"Was he mad at me?" I asked. "Did he say anything about me that night, when you called him after the party?"

"Maggie," Adam said, turning to look at me. "What reason could Joey possibly have had to be angry with you?"

I shrugged. Felt tears welling up in my eyes. "I don't know. But everything's so mixed up. I just need to—"

Adam grabbed my hands and slipped closer to my side, looking right into my eyes. Relief flooded me. *This* was the

Adam I knew. The crease of his eyebrows, the tremble of his lips, the way he looked at me like he knew all of me – these things showed that he actually cared, that he hadn't forgotten what we meant to each other.

"Don't for one second doubt yourself, Maggie," he said, his words shaky. "Joey was *not* mad at you. This…thing, it was between us. And I have to figure it out before I can say anything, okay? You and Shan are the only ones who know, and I need to trust that you'll keep this quiet."

"I don't know," I said. "You're really scaring me, Adam."

I readjusted myself on the rock, pressed my feet into the prickly grass, and looked down at my toes. The paint was chipped, almost gone, but the colour was the same. Totally Teal.

And that's all it took.

Whirl. Swirl. Twirl.

Back to the woods.

Adam's sea-glass eyes, his crinkled lips, his damp hair. Clinging. I was clinging. His hand, tight as a vine. The scramble down the trail. Tanna's wet braids. Trembling. And Shannon. Her eyes darting everywhere, crazy with pain.

"Oh, my God."

"What?"

"I remember. You. Finding me. My bare toes in the leaves. The climb down. Seeing Tanna. And Shannon."

Adam's hands squeezed mine. "It's not your first memory, is it?"

I shook my head. "I've had a few others."

"I knew it. That night at the Walthers' you were so off balance when you mentioned being at the top of the cliff, when you talked about me telling you not to look down for too long. I thought maybe it was because Joey's mom was asking so many questions. But I wondered if the memory was new." Adam let go of my hands and looked down to the rippling water. "And you haven't told anyone yet?"

"The memories, they're just pieces," I said, rubbing my palm across my forehead. "I need more time, to see how many I can get back. To put all the fragments together again before I can talk about it."

"That's *exactly* how I feel, Mags." Adam sighed. "I need more time before I can talk about the stuff that was going down between me and Joey."

I breathed in the damp, muddy scent of the fish pond, wishing I could make sense of everything that had happened. "I was glad the memories were gone. At first. But now...I want to remember everything."

Adam stood up then. "Don't pressure yourself, Maggie. The memories'll come back when they're ready." He held a hand out between us.

"I hope so," I said, grabbing his hand and letting him

pull me from the rock. I shoved my feet back into my shoes. "Can we make a deal?"

Adam held a hand over his eyes, blocking the sun. "What kind of deal?"

"We're gonna tell each other everything. *Everything*. When we're ready."

Adam closed his eyes and sucked in a deep breath.

"Please, Adam."

"Just give me a little time, okay? For now, we gotta go in there," Adam said, turning towards the back of the church. "You ready?"

I shook my head. "I don't think I could ever be ready for this."

"The viewing's over soon. I don't want to walk in late for the service."

I clutched Adam's hand and followed him across slick blades of grass, lit so brightly by the sunlight they almost glowed, and into the dark chamber of the hushed church.

My legs went numb as Adam led me down the centre aisle, and I was glad he was there to lean on. I tried to block out the sea of heads, the sets of shoulders cloaked in black (frilly, sheer, lacy, cotton). Some people from school turned to stare as Adam and I made our way to the reserved seats in the front row, to our places with Shannon, Pete and Tanna. Others did their best to give us the privacy we needed. I tried not to notice. Tried to ignore everything. Especially Joey.

As I dropped onto my cold, hard seat, I focused instead on Shannon. I stared intently at her jittery feet, her black ballet flats tap-tap-tapping each other in the quiet hush that had fallen over the room. I watched her long fingers, wrestling with two tattered tissues. And I listened to the stuttered sound of her breath as she struggled to keep her composure.

When the pastor stepped onto the podium in a swooshing flutter and spoke with a reverent tone saved for especially devastating occasions, I closed my eyes and blocked out everything. Everything except my curiosity about Joey and Adam's argument, because that was the one thing that I *knew* I could figure out. And maybe, if I started with the things that I knew for certain, the rest would fall into place without me having to try so damn hard.

8 a whole new normal

"THEY'RE MAKING ME SEE A SHRINK," I said, stuffing a cracker into my mouth and crunching down. "Tomorrow."

"Really?" Shannon pulled the top off her strawberry yoghurt and dropped it into her lunch bag. "That sucks."

"It's because of the memory loss." I sighed. "Among other things."

Tanna looked at me, her silver hairslide blinking in the bright light of the early-June day. A June that Joey would never see. "Talking to someone could be really good for you, Maggie."

"I guess," I said. "It might help me remember."

"Mags, it just happened," Tanna said. "You need to give yourself a little time."

I leaned my head back against the trunk of the tulip tree that we had claimed as our lunch spot the first day of sophomore year. This was my favourite place on the campus of Blue Springs High School, and had been since I'd spent freshman year staring out the window of my geometry classroom watching the tree change through the seasons. Bright yellow and red leaves during the fall gave way to a slender, snow-covered frame through the winter. Then, in the spring, waxy tulip-shaped leaves filled out the branches just before these crazy bright yellow and orange flowers popped open to decorate my view, celebrating the end of geometry and the fast-approaching summer.

"Hey, Maggie," a voice called from behind us.

I turned to see Jimmy Dutton standing there, his hands stuffed in the front pockets of his droopy cargo shorts, a backpack slung over one shoulder. His hair was all messy, sticking up in places, and he looked so much like the last time I'd seen him when Joey had been alive and standing right by my side that my chest started to ache.

"I didn't get the chance to talk to you last week at the, um, funeral," he said. "I just wanted to tell you how sorry I am about Joey."

I tried not to react to his name, but my breathing hitched a beat and caught in my throat. I forced myself to stare at the lingering petals that had fallen from the tulip tree, fluttering on the ground near my feet.

"Thanks, Jimmy," Shannon said.

"No problem," Jimmy said. "I keep thinking about the party. Seeing him for the last time, racing down that driveway. I can't believe he's— Oh, God, I'm sorry. I sound like an asshole." Jimmy slapped a hand to his forehead and yanked his fingers through his hair. "Really, though, Maggie, you were out for a week, and exams are in a few days, so I just wanted to let you know that if you need my notes from English or wanna talk about the test, I've got everything you need."

I looked up, squinting at the bright blue backdrop behind him. "Thanks, Jimmy. I'll let you know."

He stood there for a minute, awkward, like there was something else he wanted to say. And then he turned and walked away.

"I feel like I'm under a microscope," I said. "You guys getting this, too?"

Tanna shrugged. "Not like you, with it being your first day back," she said. "I see the way everyone's watching you. Like you're going to shatter, or scream, or something else that'd be text-worthy."

Shannon grunted. "He was closest to you," she said. "I mean, everyone knew it. And you were the one with him when...well, when it happened."

I detected something strange in her voice. Something I couldn't quite put my finger on. For one horrible moment, I wondered if she blamed me. I wanted to ask, but I was afraid of her answer.

"People are just clueless," Tanna said. "They have no idea what to do."

Shannon tossed her empty yoghurt container and

plastic spoon into her lunch bag and pulled her knees to her chest.

Across the quad, Adam and Pete pushed their way through the back doors of the cafeteria. Adam looked at the ground, his body slumping, like he was caving in on himself. It was the first time I'd seen him since the funeral, since he'd chosen to ignore all of us when we'd hung out Saturday night. Pete had been worried when Adam didn't show – I could tell by the way he chewed on his lip – but he kept it to himself, trying to cheer us up by playing songs on his guitar and making us guess which memory the music had come from. Every single one he'd chosen had been a perfect Joey moment, and Pete had actually gotten us laughing.

Missing Adam that night, I had thought seeing him would make me feel better. But he'd walked the other way when I'd called out to him in the parking lot earlier in the morning, and in the classes we shared, he seemed to be avoiding me, his eyes focused downwards at all times. Surprisingly, seeing him had only made me feel worse.

"How do you guys think Adam is doing?" I asked.

Shannon looked out over the quad, her eyes stopping on Adam and Pete. "Not good," she said.

I looked at her, at the slope of her freckled nose, how wild strands of her hair waved in the breeze, wondering exactly how much she knew about the fight between Joey and Adam. I felt floaty. In a very bad way. Like nothing around me actually existed. I pressed my hands into the ground, digging my fingers into the dirt.

"All of this avoidance, it's because of whatever happened the night of Dutton's party, right? What do you think was going on?" I asked.

Shannon tossed her hair from one side to the other, like she was trying to shake off the conversation. "Dunno," she said. "And I think we should leave it alone until Adam's ready to talk."

"But he's totally blowing us off," Tanna said. "Even Pete hasn't talked to Adam since the funeral. He told me this morning."

Shannon pointed. "They're talking now."

I looked up and saw Adam and Pete passing over the brick path that criss-crossed the quad. They stopped about thirty metres from the tulip tree, fist bumped, and then Adam turned and started to walk towards the parking lot.

"Where's he going?" I asked.

"You haven't been here," Shannon said. "He hasn't exactly been eating with us."

"That's putting it mildly," Tanna said.

"Then, where's he been eating?"

"Adam's been ditching," Tanna said. "Like, every day."

"Well, I'm sure his parents—"

"They have no idea," Shannon said. "I talked to his mom yesterday when she called my mom about some fundraiser they're doing for the library, and she said something about how school seems to be helping Adam keep his mind off things. Whatever the hell that's supposed to mean."

I watched Adam's backpack disappear around the corner of the gym, wondering where he was going and what he would do when he got there.

"Did you say anything?" I asked.

"To his mom?" Shannon asked. "Um. No. We took that oath, like, a thousand years ago. We don't rat each other out."

"Unless," I said, "one of us is in trouble. And Adam is starting to show some signs of serious trouble, Shan."

"Why?" she asked. "Because he's skipping a few classes and not eating lunch with us? Because he needs a little space? Think about it, Maggie, he just watched his best friend die. You can't expect him to act normal. These days, we're dealing with a whole new normal."

"I don't know," I said, imagining Adam walking straight to the creek in our neighbourhood and following the twisting trail of the stream until it swirled out into our Jumping Hole. All alone.

"You haven't exactly been normal yourself, there, Miss Memory Loss," Shannon said, scrunching up her nose. "Should we go talk to *your* parents?"

"That's not fair," I said. "I'm trying here. But Adam…it seems like he's just gone, somehow."

"I see what you're saying," Tanna said. "But I think we need to give him some space. Let's just get through the end of the week and see how he seems after summer break starts."

"You think?" I asked.

"I do," Tanna said. "We're all dealing with this differently. He deserves a mourning period, and we should offer him a little peace."

"She's totally right," Shannon said.

"Fine," I said. "If you guys think he's okay. But it won't be long before I insist on a full-scale intervention."

And I was serious. If Joey could die and Adam could slip away, what would stop the rest of my world from disintegrating into nothing?

I stared down at the lined notebook paper in front of me. At the thick black ink staining the page, the scientific terms and definitions I was trying to memorize all blurring together. I wished with everything in me that I could slide full speed down the neck of the *J* I'd drawn in the bottom corner of the page, fling myself off the hooked end, and flip into another existence.

But there was no other existence. My life consisted of quick glances, open arms, hushed whispers, pointing fingers, tear-soaked cheeks – all of which were about two seconds away from causing me to lose it.

I wanted out.

A free pass out of my body and mind.

During the last nine days, I'd been continuously hoping for some escape.

A way to release everything.

If only I'd known that the wish might backfire, bring me more pain, I might have taken it back. But I didn't know. Not as I sat there pressing the tip of my pen into the groove of the J, not as the door behind me opened and another person stepped into the small conference room of the guidance office, not as Nolan Holiday plopped his backpack next to me and sat on the wheely chair to my left.

"Glad you're back," he said, running a hand through his longish brown hair. "This whole office assistant gig has been lame without you." He ducked his head, meeting my eyes for a split second before deciding it would be better to stare at the floor.

"Can't say I've missed it," I said, looking through the large windowed wall as a skinny freshman boy juggling a load of books walked in from the hall and up to the secretary's desk.

"You missed a lot of drama," Nolan said, his eyes sparkling with deviousness before turning dark. "Oh. I didn't mean... God, that was stupid."

"I coulda guessed that about the drama part."

"I was talking about our favourite budding romance. The one that was cut short." He grinned, slicing a finger across his throat. Then his eyes dimmed again. "Shit, man. Should I just shut my mouth?"

"Awkward is my new normal," I said, knowing how to put on a well-rehearsed, I'm-just-fine face. It was worth it just to avoid everyone's strings of questions (*How are you holding up? Are you taking care of yourself? Can I do anything?*) and the general awkwardness that Joey's death had left behind.

"That blows," he said. "The whole thing just bl—"

"It's okay," I said, leaning back in my swivel chair and facing Nolan Holiday head-on. "I know you're talking about Mr. and Mrs. Sophomore Suck Face, and I'd love a distraction, so please fill me in."

"Sweet. I've been dying to tell you." Nolan clapped his hands and rubbed them together, leaning forwards. "Mrs. Suck Face's father came in, demanding to know how a picture of his daughter being, and I quote, *felt up* in the school hallway managed to be taken and posted on Facebook."

"No way," I said. "Did you see the picture?"

"Hell, no," Nolan rolled his eyes. "As if I have any interest in a flat-chested sophomore? But Mrs. Suck Face's father was quite entertaining as he met with the guidance counsellors and Principal Edwards, demanding to know how such behaviour could possibly occur in an educational environment."

"What'd they say to that?" I asked, grabbing my purse and riffling through the contents.

"The wall interfered." Nolan tipped his head towards the wall separating the small conference room, where we were, from the larger one. "All I heard after that first part was mumbling. Until the end, when Mrs. Suck Face's father stormed out, saying that the administration had better make it more of a priority to monitor the students in the building."

"Oh, God," I said, plucking a pack of gum from under my iPod. "That's pathetic. He'd rather blame someone else than face the problem that's right in front of him."

"Thought you'd enjoy a detailed description." Nolan smiled, his eyes catching mine as I unwrapped my piece of gum and popped it into my mouth.

"Thanks. Nice three-minute distraction." I smiled and held the pack of gum between us. "Want one?"

Nolan grabbed a piece, his fingers grazing mine and pulling back as though he'd been shocked, like he was afraid he could catch death from me. The thought of electricity running between us sent a shiver of something familiar through my body. I shook it off, though, forcing myself to stay in the moment.

"You okay, then?" Nolan asked as he slowly pulled the

silver wrapper off his piece of gum.

"I'm not gonna freak out or anything," I said, hoping that would remain true. Somehow, over the past week, I had gone from being on the brink of freak-out ninety-nine per cent of the time to about...seventy-five per cent of the time. Until, of course, some random thing brought Joey rushing back. At first, I never thought I'd get used to the idea of Joey's death, but it had settled over me like a fine mist. It had started to feel like reality instead of a bad dream. "It sucks. But I'm dealing."

Nolan looked up at me, his head still tilted down a bit, his brown eyes searching mine for any hint of truth or lie. "Yeah?"

I shrugged.

Nolan shoved his gum into his mouth and crushed the wrapper up into a tiny ball, staring down at one of the blue tile squares on the floor. "It's just weird," Nolan said. "The whole death thing. Everyone's talking about the last time they saw him or talked to him."

I scooted forwards on the seat of my wheely chair, inching towards him, longing for one more slice of Joey's life to add to the patchwork of memories I had begun to assemble. Wishing I had access to my last seconds with him, hoping I would remember soon, that I would finally find the full truth and have my own story to tell in moments like these.

Nolan looked at me, his eyes watery and reddening. "Sorry. That's probably the last place you wanna go."

"No!" My voice bounced off the walls, too loud for the room. "I want to know as much as I can. Any new memory, even if it's not mine... They all seem to help, you know?"

"Yeah?"

I nodded. "Will you tell me? Everything you remember from the last time you saw him?"

Nolan shook his head. "It's really nothing, though."

"Please," I said, something desperate flaring, and surging, and spreading through my body. "It's crazy, I know, but it helps keep him alive just a little longer when I hear other people's stories."

Nolan swung his head to the side and wiped his eyes.

"Did you see him the night of Dutton's party?" I asked, hope blossoming in my chest. Maybe Nolan was the key to finding out what Joey had been doing after he had taken me, Shannon, and Pete home.

"No, I was out of town that weekend with my parents, picking my brother up from college. Heard the party was a blast, though." Nolan leaned back in his seat and propped his hands behind his head, elbows splayed outwards. "Last time I saw Joey, actually talked to him, I mean, was at the Spring Carnival."

I shook my head, trying to jar the words loose before they took root. "Joey wasn't at the carnival."

Nolan's eyes creased. "Yeah. He was."

"You must have mistaken someone else for him," I said with a forced laugh, feeling a nervous tingle flash through my body. "He went to a Reds game with his father that night. Killer tickets, or something like that."

"Oh." Nolan's entire face crinkled up and he looked away, dropping his hands into his lap. "Okay. I must've been wrong." He pulled himself up to the desk and grabbed his backpack, opening the front pouch and plucking up a blue pen like he was ready to end the conversation and start his homework. As if he *ever* did homework during our office assistant period.

I reached for his hand, stopping him. "Well, maybe Joey came late." I glanced up at the ceiling, trying to look confused or thoughtful or something that would keep Nolan talking. "I was kinda drunk." I giggled, as if what I said had been funny.

Nolan squinted, looking unsure. "It *was* late."

"God," I said, smacking Nolan on the arm, needing that memory. "You're acting so weird. Just tell me already."

"Right. Okay." Nolan sat back in his chair, click-click-clicking the top of his blue pen. "I had to work that night, so I got to the carnival late. It was dark already, and there were about a zillion cars in the parking lot, all lit up from the flashing lights on the rides."

I flipped back to that night in an instant – it had been

several weeks ago, one of the last days in April. Tanna, Shannon, and I had vowed to ride every ride before we left. Pete and Adam had laughed at us, saying we were acting like we were ten again. And then Shannon almost puked while we all were on one of those spinning things where the floor drops away from your feet. So we abandoned our plan, laughing as we passed a stick of pink cotton candy between us, leaving Pete and Adam behind.

"I had to park in the back of the lot, where it was super dark and shadowed," Nolan continued. "That's where I saw his truck."

I wanted to stop Nolan there. To tell him that all kinds of people drove black trucks and it would have been easy to mistake Joey's for someone else's. Especially in the dark. But I was afraid that if I spoke again, I'd ruin my chance to hear the story. A story I was certain was wrong. A story I wanted to deconstruct so I could prove that Joey was exactly where he had said he'd been. Because one thing I knew for certain was that Joey was *not* at that carnival.

"I didn't see him at first," Nolan said, "but when I walked by the truck, Joey shot his arm out of the driver's side window and grabbed my shoulder. Scared the living shit out of me."

"So, you actually *did* see him? *Talked* to him?" I sucked in a deep breath and held it. I couldn't keep breathing. Not with this in the air.

"Yeah…I mean, it was only for a few minutes. He gave me some shit about how I squealed like a little girl. I made fun of him for hiding in the shadows. Then I promised I'd get him back when he wasn't looking. That kind of thing. I told him he'd had a good game the night before. I remember that part. I also remember how, the whole time we were talking, he kept looking in his rear-view and checking his phone. I just figured he was…"

"What?" I asked, holding a shaky hand in the air.

"I figured he was in trouble with you over something." Nolan shrugged. "I didn't want any drama, so I said *later* and walked away."

My heart was about to explode. Joey really was at the carnival? Why hadn't he told me?

"He was, wasn't he?" Nolan asked. "In the doghouse?"

"No." I shook my head. I felt as if it might swim away from my body.

"Oh, shit, I knew I shoulda kept my mouth shut."

"No. It's okay. I asked. I just wish I knew what had him so bothered, that's all."

"Don't know." Nolan chewed his gum so hard it seemed like he wanted to pulverize it.

"Strange." I tugged at a strand of my hair and wrapped it around my finger, pulling harder and harder until I felt pain. "That's all?" I asked. "You don't remember anything else?"

Nolan shook his head. "I'm sorry, Maggie. I never woulda—"

"Nolan, it's fine. Totally fine." I shrugged. "He must have been waiting to surprise me. Give me a ride or something. But Tanna took me home, and her car was, like, right up front. We got a great spot. So he wouldn't have seen me." I sounded pathetic, more pathetic than Mrs. Suck Face's father, the king of avoiding what's right before your eyes, and we both knew it. Whatever had brought Joey to the carnival that night had been something he'd intentionally kept to himself. Just like whatever he'd been doing after he dropped me off the night of Dutton's party.

"Right." Nolan slid his chair forwards and tugged a notebook from his backpack, flipping it open without looking at me. He clicked his pen one last time. "Makes complete sense."

But it didn't.

It made no sense at all.

Not unless Joey was keeping major secrets.

As I sat there hearing echoes of the carnival music, feeling the breeze drift across the heat of my cheeks, tasting the sweet fire of the raspberry vodka we had poured into our sodas, I wondered... What else had Joey been hiding from me?

And more importantly, why?

9 forget you

"I CAN'T BELIEVE YOU'RE MAKING ME DO THIS." I tipped my head against the cool glass of the passenger-side window, closing my eyes against the bright sunlight that was trying to convince me it was a happy kind of day. "It's just weird."

"Maggie, the police said you have to be evaluated." My mother sighed.

"You're taking the easy way out, blaming them," I said, looking right at her.

"You want me to tell you that I think it's a good idea?" My mother slowed our black Hyundai Tucson to a stop at a red light in downtown Blue Springs. "You suffered a major trauma, Maggie. And you're dealing with memory loss. I think this is the best—"

"Really?" I asked. "Did you even look at those intake forms? The questions are for someone who's really messed up, Mom. Not me."

My mother sighed. "No one's saying you're messed up, hon. Just that you need a little help with all that's happened."

"What I need," I said, "is *Joey*."

I swivelled my head so I wouldn't have to look at my mother. I couldn't get a handle on my emotions. Part of me felt relieved that I might be a few hours away from some answers. *If* this woman could help me access my memories, which was a big *if*. I'd been trying non-stop on my own when I was alone in my room, focusing on what I knew for certain. But I had yet to uncover anything new. The other part of me was just plain scared. What if talking about everything made it all feel worse? I wasn't sure I could handle worse. It might break me all the way.

"I know this is scary for you. I'm still asking you to give it a try."

"Asking?" I tilted my head towards the window again. "As if I have a choice?"

We spent the rest of the ride in silence, moving beyond the centre of Blue Springs, with a McDonald's on one corner and a 7-Eleven on the other, through fields and fields of corn and soybean.

The ride relaxed me, put me in a trance-like state. I focused on the things that didn't hurt. The trees, how they were so thick they looked stronger than I ever expected to feel. The wide fields, so green they almost shimmered. The deep blue sky, so vast and open, it felt like I could dive right through its surface and disappear.

After about thirty minutes, we hit the town just south

of ours, Bradyville, which was smaller than where I had grown up. The first houses we encountered were older, and a few leaned, almost like they were drunk. Bradyville is a farm town, and as soon as we crossed over the county line, I lowered my window. I had always loved that Bradyville seemed to be drowning in the scent of hay, so I focused on the sweet, comfortable feeling it brought me. When we passed by a park, I stared at the kids hanging off the playground equipment, their laughter filling the air, chasing the silence out of our car.

I was okay for those few moments, while my mind drifted from one thing to the next, because none of it had to do with Joey. Or the cliff top.

But then I saw the high school. And I remembered my last trip here, less than two months ago, when I'd had to take the ACTs – the tests that would go on my college applications and decide my future – in a musty-smelling science room because I'd been sick the day they had them in town.

I'd stood against the wall next to the double doors of the high school's entrance, rain falling all around me, slamming into me with sweeping gusts of wind. Trying to avoid being soaked, I pressed my back against the scratchy red bricks but still ended up looking like a drowned and droopy version of myself. Which was the last thing I wanted, because Joey would pull up and see mascara running down my face, like I'd been standing there crying over him.

I was tempted to jump out into the rain, to look up at the sky and scream. But the sky hadn't deserved my rage. Neither did the little red Ford Taurus my grandmother had sold me for one hundred dollars, which was in the garage getting a new transmission.

My anger was all directed at Joey, who was late-squared picking me up.

Since my cell phone died during the first break in testing, I didn't have a way to check my messages. I used another girl's phone, calling Joey three times as the sky darkened overhead and rain began to fall. But the connection just rolled me over to his voicemail. When the girl's father came to pick her up, I was left completely alone.

I stood in the rain, shivering, feeling like a fool, wondering what to do.

I was seconds from walking three kilometres to the nearest convenience store to call my mom for a ride when Adam's light blue Oldsmobile pulled into the front lot of Bradyville High School. I was as surprised to see him as I was grateful that he had come. I hopped into the front seat, shaking from the cold and my anger at Joey. Adam threw a towel at me, and I wrapped it around my shoulders to warm up.

"Where is he?" I asked.

Adam just shook his head, his lips pinched tight. "Dunno."

"Whaddo you mean, you don't know?" My teeth chattered as I looked at Adam. "You're here instead of him, so I know you guys talked. Is he still fighting with his mom? Did she take his phone?"

Adam's body was tense, rigid. "Something like that."

"Well, I don't see why she wouldn't let him at least answer his phone to make sure I'd get home okay. I almost walked three kilometres in this shit to use a payphone because my cell phone died and—"

"He's just a guy, you know?" Adam looked at me, his eyes sparking in the dim light.

"What's that supposed to mean?"

"You put him up on a pedestal, like he can do no wrong. Trust me," Adam said, "he can."

"I know he's not perfect."

"Coulda fooled me."

"This isn't his fault," I said. "His mom's a freak about his curfew. He was, like, three minutes late and she totally flipped her shit. Joey has never done anything like this before."

Adam grunted.

"What?" I asked. "What's that supposed to mean?"

"He's never done *anything* like this before? What about homecoming?"

I snorted, flinging my hand in the air, dismissing the long-ago memory, which I had shoved from my mind as soon as Joey had explained himself. "That wasn't his fault. His mother made him go to his grandparents' that night, and—"

"Right. I remember." Adam shook his head. "And Joey forgot his phone in the rush to leave, so he couldn't call you to explain anything."

"His grandfather had a *stroke*, Adam. I was probably the last thing on his mind." I slid lower in my seat. "Besides, he did call me."

"Yeah. At, like, eleven o'clock. When the dance was almost over and you were still sitting in your house waiting for him." Adam looked out the windshield, his eyes squinting as he tried to focus on the road through the thick wash of rain that the wipers couldn't keep up with.

"If I recall correctly, we had the best pizza of our lives that night." I poked Adam in the arm. He elbowed my hand away.

"It was okay."

"Okay?" I asked. "It was the best. Really."

"Just because it was hand-delivered by the biggest stud in town."

I laughed, the sound rushing out of me.

Adam looked at me and grinned. "The studliest stud."

"M-hmm." I poked Adam again, glad that a smile had lit

his face. "If you're such a stud, why'd you drop your date off before midnight, huh? Most studs would have been getting it on until dawn."

Adam shrugged. "I felt bad for you."

"Liar."

"I did." Adam looked at me, his eyes tight. "I felt awful when you called looking for him. You'd spent the whole night all dressed up alone in your basement, wondering where he was."

"Well, it was still nice of you." I twisted my wet hair behind me and tucked it into a bun so it would stop dripping down my back.

"Yeah. It was." Adam looked at me and rolled his eyes. "It was also nice of me to stop and get your favourite treat to make you feel better after waiting so long today. Three devil's food from Bozie's Doughnuts. I even grabbed you a hot chocolate. Thought you might be cold." Adam passed me a steamy cup of hot chocolate, and I sipped from the plastic lid. The foamy top was sugary sweet, and the drink was the perfect temperature after Adam's long ride into Bradyville, warming me from the inside out.

"Well," I said, "if anyone's in the running for perfect, I'd say it's you."

Adam finally smiled. "You just remember that, girl. You hear?"

"Only if we can blast a song of my choice."

Adam threw his head back and groaned. "No. *Please*, no."

"I deserve it," I said. "I stood there for almost an hour not knowing what the hell was going on."

"Fine," Adam said, leaning towards the windshield as several gusts of wind rocked the car. "Blast your crappy music. Scream at the top of your lungs. See if I care."

"You rock, Adam." I leaned forwards then, ruffling Adam's rain-stained hair. From the corner of my eye, I caught him watching as I hooked my iPod into his system and twisted the dial. I wondered what he was thinking. But just for a moment. Then the fearless sound of "Forget You" by Cee Lo Green surged through the car and carried me away.

"So, Maggie, today's session will be for us to get acquainted, and to formulate some goals for your treatment." Dr. Guest sat back in her swivel chair and tipped her head towards me, strands of auburn hair escaping her loose bun and falling to frame her face. Her legs were uncrossed, and her hands lay still on top of the open notebook on her lap.

I looked around the office, reading the framed degrees that certified Dr. Patricia Guest as a licensed professional clinical counsellor and a doctor of psychology.

"You're just about to finish up your junior year of high school, right?" Dr. Guest asked.

I nodded, sliding down the seat of the brown leather couch.

"And I hear that you have a very tight-knit group of friends." Dr. Guest smiled. My eyes flitted from hers to the tray of snacks on the coffee table between us. Did people really have the stomach to *eat* during these sessions? I couldn't believe that a handful of peanuts and M&M's made a person feel safe enough to open up.

"Let's start by going over some of the forms you completed for me." Dr. Guest lowered her voice. She suddenly sounded like a real person. "You mentioned that you don't really want to be here, Maggie. Can you tell me a little more about that?"

"Don't take it personally," I said as she stared at me, her eyes searching every flicker of movement that my body made. "I don't really want to be anywhere any more."

"What about your friends? Does spending time with them give you any sense of security?"

I sighed. Tried not to think of Adam, all the voice messages and texts he had ignored over the last week. But he was there, mixed in with everything else, and the thought of his absence, once again, sparked a feeling of uncertainty in my chest.

"We're all just trying to deal," I said.

Dr. Guest pressed her lips together and gave me a slow nod. "It can be very difficult, finding balance at a time like this."

I looked up at her, wondering how, after spending only five minutes with me, she'd hit on my biggest fear in life – never being able to balance everything out. Finding my lost memories and dealing with what had happened on the cliff. Living this new life without ever seeing or talking to Joey again. Blending the old version of Adam with this new, out-of-reach person he had suddenly become. None of it seemed possible. And that scared me more than anything ever had.

"You described your feelings, here, Maggie." Dr. Guest looked down at her notebook, shuffling through a few loose papers, and I caught a glimpse of my handwriting, the teal pen I'd used to scribble answers to all of those questions. "Shock is definitely a normal reaction to losing a person you love. And this fear you mention? Can you explain that for me?"

"Aren't you the one who's supposed to do the explaining?"

Dr. Guest smiled. "I'm here to guide you, Maggie. But I can't do that if we don't have a dialogue."

"Right," I said, taking in a deep breath. "So, the fear? It's just there –" I placed a hand on my chest and pressed it against my cotton shirt – "all the time."

"Fear about what, exactly?"

"Everything," I said. "But mostly just the realization that all it takes is one moment for your entire world to turn upside down. One wrong decision, and it's over."

"I understand, Maggie. This must be a terribly difficult thing for you to process. The trauma of losing someone you love, being there to witness the event, it can—"

"But I don't remember anything," I said. "So it's not like I actually *witnessed* it."

Dr. Guest sat forwards, her elbows propped on her knees, keeping the notebook in place. "Yes, Maggie, it is. You might be repressing the memory, but you were there. Everyone places you at the top of the cliff. You, yourself, even say that you remember climbing the trail with Joey."

I flinched at his name. I wanted to stand up and run. For ever.

"So, what, I have a classic case of memory repression?"

"That's what we're here to figure out." Dr. Guest smiled. "You're not alone, Maggie. I'm here to help you through this."

"What if I don't want your help?"

Dr. Guest shrugged. "The police requested that you be evaluated. It might take some time, but I'll determine your diagnosis, and we'll go from there. I'm here for the long haul if you need me."

"Diagnosis? Like I'm sick?"

"Why don't we stop trying to label everything and just

talk?" Dr. Guest flipped through the forms again, my words swimming together to create a teal puddle in her lap. "You say here that your main goal is to remember what really happened on the cliff top. Is that still the case?"

I sucked in a deep breath and looked her right in her blue-grey eyes. I was shaking. My hands. My legs. I wanted to find my lost memories, but I didn't want to do it this way. I just wanted to be in my room, shoved deep in the cave of my closet.

"How do you…you know, do that with someone? Find memories that have slipped away?"

Dr. Guest leaned back in her chair, her hands falling over the paper that was dripping with my words. "There are several methods, and we can discuss them to see which you might be most comfortable with."

Sitting there, talking about my memories, wondering what we would do with them once they were found, I was suddenly hit with a question. One that had been bouncing around in my mind since I'd stood up from the table in the police station and walked away from the two detectives. And I had to know the answer.

"Do the cops think I'm faking or something?"

Dr. Guest's eyes pulled tight. But it was only for a second. And then she picked up her pen. "Why would you ask that?"

I shrugged. "They're calling this an official investigation.

Questioning all of us. Searching through Joey's private stuff. And they sent me here to be evaluated. I just wondered, that's all."

"Now is not the time to worry about any of that." Dr. Guest scratched something on the page of her notebook without looking down. "Today, let's just get comfortable with each other."

I sighed. Wove my fingers together and squeezed tight.

Dr. Guest straightened herself and looked me right in the eyes. "You said that you don't want to be anywhere any more. Does that mean that you're thinking of hurting yourself?"

I squeezed my eyes shut. If only it were that easy. "No."

"Good. That's very good." I heard the pen scratching on the paper again and opened my eyes. "Why don't you tell me a little about Joey."

I smiled. I couldn't help it. But then the prickly feeling came back. The one that had been lurking beneath the surface of my skin since that day at the cliff. I closed my eyes for a beat, shoving that awful feeling away, and focused on Joey. My Joey.

"He was amazing," I said. "Beautiful. And a little crazy."

Dr. Guest grinned.

"He loved music, and his truck, and being outside. Oh, and baseball. But he could play any sport. He was a natural athlete. Actually, when I think about it, he was kind of a natural at everything. Life – it just seemed to come easy for Joey."

As soon the words were out, I wanted to capture them. Shove them back inside. Because thinking about his life brought me right back around to his death.

"What, Maggie? What about saying those things made you catch yourself?"

"I think about it all the time," I said, looking down at my hands again. "That day. Focusing on what I remember, trying to find the rest. But I don't get anything new."

"That's very brave of you." Dr. Guest sat back in her chair and nodded. "Many people in your situation would probably prefer to keep it all buried. But I believe that finding those memories and dealing with your emotions will help you move on more successfully. Facing what happened is the best way to keep this from weighing you down for the rest of your life."

I squeezed my hands tighter. Looking down, I saw that my fingers were white. "Even if I remember everything, it's going to weigh me down," I said. "I feel like it's pulling me under."

"I'm on your side, Maggie." Dr. Guest leaned forwards again, wearing those pleading eyes. "I need you to trust me."

And that was all it took.

Flip. Dip. Trip.

I was back on the cliff top. Looking into Joey's eyes. There, right in front of me, I could see his freckled nose, the wisps of damp hair clinging to his forehead, the way his smile tilted to the left.

I wanted to reach out and grab him. But I blinked, and he was gone.

It was just Dr. Guest and me in the too-cool office with the whistling sound of the air conditioning drowning out the heavy cadence of my breathing.

Dr. Guest stood and stepped around the table. She sat next to me slowly, as if I was a wild animal that she might scare off. "Maggie. Can you tell me what just happened?"

"I was back. At the cliff top."

"And how were you feeling?"

"Scared. Terrified."

"Of what?"

"Jumping. I'm afraid of heights. Like, pass-out afraid."

"Okay. This is good, Maggie. What did you see? Hear? Smell? Tell me everything."

"It was just a flash." I blinked and saw him again.

"Can you try to describe what you saw?"

"Joey." I could barely hear my own voice. Dr. Guest moved closer. She smelled like peaches. "Joey's face. He was smiling."

"Do you remember anything else? Even if it doesn't seem to fit, did anything else come with that vision of Joey?"

I shook my head. But I was lying. I heard him loud and clear. His voice washed through me like a warm and tingly wave.

You trust me? he'd asked.

I had.

Oh, I really always had.

"HAVE YOU HEARD ABOUT THE CLIFF?" Shannon asked, rocking slowly back and forth on the recliner in her basement. "I saw on Facebook that a bunch of people went out there the other night, and—"

"I don't want to talk about the cliff," Adam said, leaning back on his bar stool, running his fingers along the stubble of his chin. I wondered when he'd shaved last. If he'd even bothered since the funeral, two weeks ago. The usual golden shimmers had turned a dark brown with the length. Somehow, in the last three weeks, he'd aged about ten years. I felt like I didn't even know him any more.

Shannon slid her legs down the front of the chair and leaned forwards, looking right at Adam. "I was just going to say that people have been taking flowers and notes, and stuff there. I saw a picture."

"That's kinda creepy," Pete said.

"It's nice, though." I leaned back on the couch. "In a slightly creepy way."

Pete sat on the floor in front of me, crossing his legs and pulling his dreads back with an elastic band. He tucked his caramel-coloured acoustic guitar against his body, strumming his fingers slowly across the strings, spilling a calming melody into the air around us. "It doesn't feel real yet. I half expect him to rush down the steps and laugh at us for being so freaked out."

Tanna looked up from the vodka and pink lemonade she was mixing at the bar. "It'd be nice if this was just one of his pranks."

"Can we *not* talk about Joey?" Adam asked. "For one freaking night?"

I stared at the looping strands of carpet, so soft on my bare feet that I felt like I could melt into the ground. Pressed myself further into the back of the couch, gripping my hands in tight fists. I started counting: seconds without Joey, the ways Adam seemed to be changing, all the things Joey would never have the chance to do. I allowed the simple *one, two, three* to take over, to crowd out everything else.

"You okay, Adam?" Tanna asked as she rounded the corner of the bar holding two glasses filled with her special, pink-tinted drink. She crossed the room, handing one of the glasses to Shannon and the other to me, her hair spilling over her shoulder.

"I'd be better if we could just move on," Adam snapped.

"I don't get it," Pete said. "You just want to erase him? Like he never existed?"

Adam snorted. "Something like that."

"That's cold, man." Pete gripped the neck of his guitar, his fingers tight across the strings. "We're talking about a guy who has been like a brother to you most of your life, you know?"

Adam looked at Pete, but didn't say one word.

"This is the kid who traded his favourite baseball card to get you a video game for your birthday in sixth grade," Pete said. "The same guy we've played basketball tournaments with every Friday during the summer since middle school. And let's not forget Independence Day."

"Aw, man," Adam ran a hand through his hair and squeezed his eyes shut, "why the hell are you bringing that shit up?"

"Because, for some reason, it's like you've forgotten who he is."

"What's so important about the Fourth of July?" Shannon asked, looking from Pete to Adam. "Haven't we spent all of those together since, like, birth or something?"

Adam and Pete exchanged a glance, and I thought I saw the shadow of a smile creep across Adam's lips. Tanna slid a glass across the granite countertop into Adam's open hand, the pinkish liquid sloshing over the side, and then grabbed the remaining two. She sipped one as she took the other to Pete and sat cross-legged next to him on the floor.

"I'm talking about a different kind of Independence Day," Pete said. "It's been our secret since the year we found the Jumping Hole."

"Care to share?" Tanna asked with a laugh. "I mean, you can't just tease us with something like that."

"You do the honours." Pete tipped his head towards Adam.

"It's not that big a deal," Adam said with a shrug. He'd seemed to soften a little with the memories Pete had brought up, and I hoped that our plan was working.

"Must've been kind of a big deal," Tanna said. "I thought there were no secrets with us."

Adam sighed and looked up, focusing on each of us before he spoke. When his eyes met mine, I felt something crack open in my chest, and the full weight of everything we'd lost hit me again. It happened like that – a song or a scent, the sad look in someone's eyes – something simple and seemingly innocent brought the feelings rushing in, like that day at the cliff was happening all over again. Then the fear sliced through me, the terrible fear that nothing would ever be the same again. Not just with Joey, which had obviously changed for ever, but with all of us.

I took a deep breath, focusing on Adam's lips, waiting for his voice to wash away the sting of my fear.

"We found the Jumping Hole that summer between seventh and eighth grades," Adam said, his voice soft. "It was me, Pete, and Joey, remember? Being there, so far from everything, just gave us this sense of total freedom, so we decided to claim July thirteenth – the day of discovery – as *our* Independence Day."

"There's a tradition, too," Pete said with a smirk, "but that's top secret. We took an oath, swearing we'd never tell."

Adam shook his head. "I don't see why it matters now."

"Don't you get it?" Pete asked, leaning towards Adam. "It's up to us to keep him alive."

"I'm just not into it." Adam shook his head. "I don't think I can, bro."

"Why?" I asked, anger flaring through every fibre of me. I'd felt like we were getting somewhere, and then Adam trampled all of my hope in the same moment that he trashed Joey's memory. "It's not like he ever did anything to you." My voice was cold, my words sharp.

"You're right, Maggie," Adam said. "He never did anything to me."

"So why are you so pissed at—"

"This," Adam said, hopping up from his bar stool and twirling a finger in the air, "was a bad idea. I'm gonna hit it." He turned then, starting for the steps towards the main floor.

"Wait," Tanna said, throwing a hand in the air. "Just sit, okay? We need to talk to you."

Adam looked around the room. I wondered if he knew what was coming. That we'd planned tonight just so we could ask him about why he was suddenly too busy to hang out with us. That we weren't going to let him go until he talked to us. That we were here trying to pull him back. And even though he'd pissed me off, even with all my fear that he'd push us even further away, I still hoped he would actually let us in.

"You guys need to talk," Adam said, sitting down again, placing his hand on the bar. "Talk. But do it fast, because I'm not hanging around for long."

"Fine," Pete said. "We're worried. You seem so pissed off all the time. And you're avoiding us."

Adam took a swig from his glass. "I'm not avoiding you," he said with a shrug. "I'm just doing my own thing."

"It seems like a hell of a lot more than that," I said. "You never return my calls."

"Mine, either," Tanna said.

"We're a week into summer, and you haven't even stopped by to play basketball in my driveway," Pete said. "Doing stuff without him isn't wrong, it's a way to honour his memory."

Shannon tucked herself into a ball on the recliner in the corner near the fireplace, rocking slowly back and forth.

She sipped the pink drink and rested it on her knee. "I practically had to threaten you to come over tonight."

"You, threaten me?" Adam took another gulp, leaving his glass almost empty. "That's funny, Shan."

Shannon looked up to the ceiling, scraping her nails down the legs of her blue striped pyjamas.

"Dude," Pete said, strumming a few chords on the guitar. "Not cool. She's trying to help."

"I don't know what the hell you guys want from me," Adam said, tossing his hands in the air.

"We want to know what's going on," Tanna said. "Why you're so angry. And why you're acting like you hardly know us."

"*We* are not *us* any more," Adam said. "It's like all we have in common right now is the most fucked-up thing that's ever happened in any of our lives."

I couldn't handle it, couldn't keep quiet for one more second. Even though I didn't know the specifics, everyone needed to understand that Adam's issues were a lot more complicated than he was letting on.

"Tell them, Adam," I said.

"What?" he asked, his eyes snapping to me.

"Tell them. Or I will."

Adam took the final sip from his glass and plunked it down on the bar, shaking his head.

"Adam and Joey were fighting," I said. "The night of

Dutton's party. And if he would just tell us about it, so we could all help him understand—"

"What will you help me understand?" Adam asked. "That Joey was all kinds of perfect and we should bow down to his memory? Well, Maggie, he wasn't perfect. Truth is, he wasn't even that—"

"Shut *up*, Adam!" Shannon jerked forwards in her chair. "Stop trying to make it seem like Joey was the bad guy. I saw what happened at Dutton's. And Joey did, too."

"What are you talking about?" I asked, looking from Shannon to Adam and back again. "Since this whole phone call thing came up, you've sworn you didn't know why they were fighting."

"Please, Maggie. Like you don't know?" Shannon snorted and sat back in her chair, rocking back and forth with her movement.

"Wait," I said, "what am I missing? I have to be missing something because I feel like I just slipped into an alternate universe."

"I'm talking about *you two*," Shannon said, pointing to me and then Adam. "The way you were dancing that night. Joey might have been across the yard, but he saw you. And from my perspective, it sure as hell looked like something sketchy was going on."

"You can't be serious," I said. "You were dancing *with us*."

"No," Shannon said. "I definitely wasn't."

"Oh, my God," I said. "I can't believe this is—"

"Shannon, don't do this." Adam's voice ripped through the air.

I shot up from the couch, staring Shannon right in the eyes, hating her.

"Are you seriously accusing me and Adam of—"

"Look," Shannon said, "I'm just calling it like I saw it. You two seemed pretty close that night. And since Adam isn't sharing specifics with us, I'm simply taking a wild guess."

"Well, you guessed wrong," I said. "Way wrong."

"Whatever you say." Shannon's lips turned up in a little smile that I wanted to scrape right off her face. In that moment, I might even have scraped her out of my life for good. But angry as I was, it was still Shannon. And with Joey gone and Adam in some kind of crisis, we had to stick together. So I just turned away from her and pressed my lips together.

"This has been real," Adam said. "But I'm over it."

"Adam, you still haven't—"

"You expect me to spill my guts after that?" he asked, tossing a hand towards Shannon. "Don't count on it."

He turned and raced up the steps, taking them two at a time, disappearing before I could even begin to grasp what had just happened.

I stood there staring after him, tugging at the sleeves of my sweatshirt, Joey's favourite baseball hoodie. It was light grey and had deep front pockets that I used to love digging my hands into when Joey was wrapped in its warmth. I'd done it often: waiting in line for the haunted hayride last Halloween, hanging out and sipping hot chocolate after ice-skating in the centre of town last Christmas, and walking through the hall between classes when I tucked a note in the soft darkness as we kissed a quick goodbye.

And now, standing in Shannon's basement, with the last trace of Adam's energy quickly fading from the space around us, with his anger, Shannon's accusations, and Joey's secrets spiralling all around us, I shoved my hands deep into those pockets, feeling like I'd just said goodbye in a whole new way. To Joey, the only boy I had ever loved; to Adam, the guy who'd always been there, but suddenly wasn't; and to a lifetime of friendship that I never thought would fade.

11 secrets of my own

LIKE JOEY, I HAD SECRETS OF MY OWN. Plans that I'd never shared with him. Questions I'd never admit to. Things that gave me the rush of excitement and daring he probably felt on a daily basis, Joey being Joey and all. Most of them were good secrets. Secrets that, if he'd learned of them, would make Joey break out that lopsided grin that had been spinning my world on its axis for most of my life. And the rest – those secrets Joey might not like so much. But those ones didn't matter. Those were mine alone. Dreamy, private thoughts that would never exist outside the safety of my mind.

"Seriously?" Tanna's eyes widened and a smile spread across her face. She leaned forwards, the thick braid that she'd twisted her hair into slapping against my arm as she pulled me into a hug. "You're gonna be all grown up, Mags."

Shannon made a sound that was between a snort and a

snigger and took a swig from the can of Budweiser in her hand. "You're sure you're ready?"

I looked over my shoulder, catching a quick glimpse of Joey as he bounded through a crowd of people who were all cheering as Jimmy Dutton kicked his feet up in the air for a keg stand. Joey took the back patio steps of the Duttons' enormous house two at a time, his hand breezing across the wooden railing. Light spilled out of every window causing Joey to practically glow as he opened the screen door and stepped into the kitchen. I could still feel the kiss he'd planted on my forehead when he ran by, telling me he had to pee and then he'd be back with drinks.

"It's the little things," I said, staring through the bay window of the dining room so I could watch Joey stand in line for the bathroom, bouncing from one foot to the other, his baggy tan shorts swaying around his muscular legs. "All the little things make me sure it's right."

"For some reason, I'm guessing it's *not* very little." Shannon giggled and pressed her fingers to her lips.

"Shannon!" Tanna smacked her on the arm. "Maggie is confiding a secret of supreme importance. Have some respect."

Shannon raised her hand to her forehead, pulling her face into a tight mask, and saluted Tanna. "Yes, sir."

"She might be drunk, but she asked a good question." Tanna plopped down in the green lawn chair at the base of a large oak tree in Jimmy's backyard, ignoring the chaos of the party surrounding us. Three topsy-turvy seniors stumbled past in a blur of long arms and legs, rushing through the flickering shadows of the Duttons' backyard towards the sound of Pete's guitar, accompanied by a banjo and harmonica as he and two friends played some fast-paced bluegrass song near the fire pit. "You're sure you're ready?"

I listened to all the laughter. There was so much of it. Everywhere. I could almost see the looping strands of sound colouring the air around me.

"It's a good party," I said.

"I can't believe it's Memorial Day weekend. We're almost *seniors*." Shannon propped herself against the oak tree and looked up into the leafy branches.

"Mags," Tanna said, her eyebrows arched. "You're ignoring me."

"No." I shook my head, looking back through the bay window to find Joey standing right in front of the closed bathroom door. He was knocking on the dark wood and, from his profile, I could tell he was laughing. I knew the sound of his laughter so well, I felt like I could hear it pulsing through the walls of the house, carried by the bright light streaming through the windows. "I'm thinking."

"If you have to think about it," Shannon looked right at me, "you're *not* ready."

"That's not true." I could hear the defensive tone in my voice and wondered what colour it would be if it floated into the air, mixing in with all the happiness surrounding us. I pushed the thought away and looked at Joey again, finding the curve of his neck, where I planned to kiss him first when he returned with a fresh beer in his hand. "Thinking about it means I'm being responsible. And that's what makes me ready."

"Nope." Shannon shook her head. "What makes you ready is feeling that you might *explode* if you wait one more second to be with him."

"There is that." Tanna sighed and straightened the striped skirt she was wearing, tugging it up a tad to show off more of her tanned legs. "But thinking about it is good, too. Preparing. Knowing."

I laughed then, out loud, the sound rippling into the night and riding the air to far-off places. "I *totally* know."

Tanna looked at me and gave me the loudest *squee*. "This is huge," she said. "We'll have to go shopping. You need something *sexy* to wear."

My stomach did a little twist. "Sexy?"

Shannon pushed off the tree and walked over as I sank into the chair next to Tanna. "You gotta show Joey that you feel him," Shannon said as she leaned against the back of my chair.

When I looked for him again, Joey was gone. In his

place were four girls, giggling and red faced. I imagined that he'd said something to make them all flutter before he closed himself into the bathroom.

"Oh, he'll know I feel him," I said. "I'm just not a Victoria's Secret kind of girl."

Shannon kneeled down in front of me, draping her arm across my legs. "If you're planning to lose your virginity to the guy you've been dating for almost two years, you need something sexy. He deserves it for being so patient, right?" Shannon's eyes flickered between me and the bay window. I turned to find Joey exiting the bathroom, tugging up the zipper on his shorts and high-fiving the senior captain of the baseball team as he passed on his way to some deeper part of the house.

Joey's eyes sizzled with life. I could practically feel their heat.

Tanna kicked me, the heel of her sandal biting into my shin.

"Ouch!" I leaned over and tugged on her braid. "What'd you do that for?"

"We're discussing the details of your first time, and you can't focus long enough to commit to a shopping trip?"

"You said his parents are going out of town?" Shannon lifted her eyebrows and took another swig from her drink.

"His parents'll be gone for an entire week, just after school lets out. I've been planning it since I heard." I giggled at the way my insides went all shiver-shaky at the thought of Joey's naked body on top of mine. "You wanna go shopping next week, fine. Maybe you're right."

"Ladies." The deep voice came from behind us, and we all turned to face him.

"Adam, where have you been?" Tanna asked. "This party is in, like, full swing. You're gonna have to do at least five keg stands to catch up."

Adam chuckled, pushing his fringe away from his eyes with the palm of one hand. "Shan didn't tell you she saw me earlier?"

"No," Shannon said, something strange crossing over her face. "I forgot."

"Well, I've been in the crowd –" Adam nodded towards the ever-growing circle of people clamouring around the fire pit, most of them bouncing to the beat of the bluegrass – "listening to Pete jam with G and Rusty. They're rockin' it out."

I closed my eyes, tipped my head back on the chair, and focused on the sounds drifting across the backyard. I pictured bright reds and oranges spiralling through the air, a spiking strand of yellow thrown in here and there, all tumbling from the instruments, twisting around the people, and bleeding out to colour the night sky. It was one of those moments where everything in my life felt right. I had these awesome friends. And the best boyfriend, ever,

to whom I was about to give myself completely. Summer
was about to begin, and when it ended I'd run smack into
my senior year of high school, which I'd only been thinking
of reaching since sixth grade. I felt in sync with everything
around me. Even the drunk people stumbling around the
yard. But especially Joey.

I plucked my head from the back of the chair and sat up,
my brain swimming in all the beer I'd downed. "Where's
Joey?"

"Pee break, remember?" Shannon threw a thumb
towards the kitchen door.

I shook my head. "I saw him come out of the bathroom.
He should be back with the beer now." Not that I cared
about the beer. I wanted him to swing me out of my seat
and dance me, barefoot, across the cool carpet of grass.
The music, it was infectious, streaming into my body, and
I needed to get up and move to the bucking banjo and
taunting harmonica, to the threads of guitar pulling it all
together. It was the song, a twangy version of Snoop Dogg's
"Gin and Juice", that had done it to me.

"I want to dance," I said with a giggle. I knew I was
drunk, but it was a nice heavy feeling, like a warm blanket,
and not out of control.

Tanna looked at me with a smile. "Dance?" she asked,
placing her beer in the grass. "You want to dance?"

I laughed, nodded my heavy head. And then my hand

was in Tanna's. She pulled me from the chair and swung me around, my hair lifting off my shoulders and dancing right along with me. Shannon joined in, and the three of us sang along to the lyrics like it was our song and no one was there to watch us.

Soon, Adam's feet were in the mix, his brown sandals kicking up into the air with my bare feet, Tanna's heels, and Shannon's flip-flops. We twisted around one another, shouting the words, linking arms, trading places as our voices and happiness flew out into the night.

It was at the very end, when the song slowed down, that I found myself in Adam's arms. His grasp was tight around my waist, keeping me steady as I belted the lyrics out to the dark night that lay beyond the reach of the fire's light. I leaned into him, closing my eyes, focusing on nothing but the sounds Pete and the guys were flinging into the air. I breathed Adam in, the scent of him damp and hot, a spice so different from my Joey. But so familiar-good.

As the last notes sounded, I looked up at Adam, tugging a strand of hair from his eyes. He tilted his head down, gave me a wink. And right there, in the Duttons' backyard, with people dancing all around us, drunk on music and alcohol and summer, I started to wonder... If I kissed him, eyes closed tight, where would I feel his hands first? If his lips met mine, would it be soft and sweet? Or rushed and insistent?

Then Shan laughed and Tanna bumped into me, pushing me right up against Adam's chest. The way his eyes sparked when I pressed my hands against him made me wonder if all the stuff rushing around my head had invaded him, too. But then I let it go, tossed out all those questions until they disappeared. Because I had Joey, who was all kinds of amazing.

"I think you need to sit down," Adam whispered into the loose strands of hair tickling my face.

He squeezed me close as he guided me back towards the chairs. I just breathed. Focused on the in and out. Because if I focused on all the rest, guilt would come flooding in. And I hadn't done anything wrong.

"That was…" I started, but couldn't find the words to balance the thoughts that were still echoing through my mind.

"Nice," Adam said.

"Yeah," I said as Adam dropped me into the chair. "Very."

Adam took a step back, moving me from a pool of darkness to light in the space of one single breath. And that's when I saw him, staring out at me from the top step of the Duttons' back deck. His face was in shadow, but I could tell from the stiff slant of his shoulders that something was off.

I waved him over. But he just stood there watching. I wondered how long he'd been there. If he was upset that

I'd been dancing with Adam. But Joey wasn't like that. Never had been.

Then I wondered if my thoughts had been so loud that maybe he'd heard them. If he knew I'd pictured Adam kissing me, and me kissing Adam right back. I wanted to explain. To tell him that it was a simple moment of drunken curiosity. I wanted to assure Joey that I would never, ever do anything to answer the questions that had been spinning around in my mind. But that would have been crazy, spilling all that out into the space between us. So my only choice was to act normal.

"Joey," I yelled. "C'mere."

That's what got him moving. The sound of my voice. He jumped the five steps, pummelling the grass with his feet, and bounded across the space between us.

"Here you go." He handed me a beer and then passed one to Tanna and Shannon, too. "Didn't know you were here, man," Joey said to Adam.

"Got here a while ago." Adam's voice was tight.

"Mmm." Joey took a swig from his beer. "It's a wild one."

I looked up at both of them. They were standing next to each other, but they were stiff. Awkward. I felt like something was going on, and I hoped it didn't have anything to do with Joey knowing me so well he could read my thoughts. Then another song started, painting the irritation that drifted between them deep shades of dusty pink, indigo, and green, whisking it away after just a few notes.

Joey began to tap his hand on his knee. And then, without warning, his eyes flashed mischievously, and he started to speak. As always, he surprised me.

"I found something in there." He threw a hand towards the house. "Anyone up for a little excitement?"

"Way to be mysterious." Shannon hopped up from her spot on the ground, her wavy brown hair flying around her shoulders. "I'm totally in."

Adam shook his head, looking from Joey to Shannon. "You two," he said. His lips parted as if he were about to say more, but then he pressed them together, trapping the words.

"Leave it alone," Joey said, his eyes tight with irritation. "You don't wanna come along, fine by me. But don't spoil our fun, dude."

Adam grunted as Joey and Shannon turned and started towards the house. I squealed and jumped up, tugging Tanna with me. "Wonder if it's some secret passageway." I envisioned pressing Joey up against a curved wall, bound to him by total and complete darkness, and showing him with one single kiss how very much he meant to me.

"C'mon, Adam," Tanna called over her shoulder. "You need a beer, anyway."

I looked back and caught Adam as he took a few slow

steps after us. "Come on!" I shouted, tossing my head towards the house, throwing myself off balance, thinking it was a good thing that Tanna was there to keep me upright.

12 shaky fingertips

"YOU *DO* KNOW IT'S SUMMER, RIGHT?" Tanna asked from the other end of the line.

I pressed my phone against my cheek and slid off my bed, moving across the room to the mirror above my dresser. "I'm so pale, you can almost see through me."

"Exactly my point. And that, my friend, calls for a pool day."

"Tanna, I'm not sure." Guilt flared through my stomach. I felt like I shouldn't allow myself to go on doing all the stuff Joey couldn't. Like I'd be betraying him if I went to Gertie's Dairy Farm for ice cream or sat around laughing with our friends. But then Dr. Guest's voice trailed through my mind, a direct quote from our last session, asking me to list the worst things that could happen if I decided to go on living my life. And the worst thing I could come up with was the guilt, which Joey would have hated.

"A day in the sun will do you more good than you can imagine," she said. "Trust me."

"I don't know," I said, thinking of the other reason I didn't want to do much of anything any more. "Is Shannon going?"

"Yes. But don't let that—"

"I don't think I'm ready to see her after the other night."

"It's been four days, Mags. If you let this drag out for too long, it'll get to be like Adam. A total disconnect."

"I'm not so sure I care," I said. "She accused me of cheating, Tanna."

"It was a heated moment. She wasn't thinking."

"Still, she threw it out there."

"We all know Shan can be a bitch sometimes. And considering everything that's happened with Joey, maybe we should cut her a break."

"Yeah. But what she said was just stupid," I said.

"Right. But Joey drunk equals Joey crazy. Who the hell knows what went down between him and Adam the night of Dutton's party? Or what Shannon overheard from that phone call after Joey dropped you off? Bottom line is she's one of your best friends. You don't want to lose her, too, so we just need to move on. To take a day to focus on the basics: bikinis, sun and swimming."

I groaned and looked down at my feet.

"I'll need a few to get ready," I said, pulling the drawer on the right side of my dresser open.

"Well, make it snappy," Tanna said. "I'll be there in fifteen."

"I'm painting my toenails, at the very least. There's nothing uglier than winter-white feet."

"I promise this will make you feel better."

"I hope so. See you in a few."

I ended the call and placed my phone on the dresser, digging through my stash of nail polish, mentally cataloguing everything I'd need for a day in the sun: sunscreen, magazines, iPod—

And that's when I saw it.

When my hand danced closer to the back of the drawer, aiming for a bottle of Perfectly Pink. There, tucked between the Totally Teal and Raspberry Sorbet was my rainbow-coloured flower necklace. I was confused at first, and then I remembered. Stupid, stupid me. The Spring Carnival. Pete throwing coloured balls through the open mouth of a cardboard clown, tossing his arms up in the air once, twice, three times. He'd won *three* prizes. One for me, one for Tanna and one for Shannon. And the prizes he'd chosen had been identical.

I sat there, braiding the slippery beads through the fingers of my left hand, thinking that I'd been wrong. I wondered what it meant, that I was sitting there holding my necklace when Tanna's or Shannon's had been wrapped around the handle of Joey's closet door. But none of my conclusions made any sense.

And then I remembered Tanna pulling her hair off her

neck, twisting it into a bun for one of the wild spinning rides, the elastic thread of her necklace snapping. Then there were the flashing lights of the carnival's exit, and the trash can we'd passed on our way out, Tanna's hand flinging her broken flowers in the trash as we traipsed through the gates and into the parking lot on our way home. Tanna's necklace, it was in some landfill next to a dirty diaper or a soggy box of crackers. And mine was in my hands.

The necklace in Joey's room, it had belonged to Shannon.

As I laced the beaded flowers through my fingers, I saw her. Eyes wide. A smile splitting across her face.

"I'm going in," Shannon had said, her sandals clicking on the tarmac of the parking lot as the carnival lights tripped across her face, sparked in her eyes. She stood there, twisting the flower necklace around her thumb. "That Toby Miller is *hot-hot-hot*."

"You sure?" Tanna had asked. "Maybe wait until you're a little more…"

"Sober?" I'd asked with a laugh.

Shannon had burped then. Pressed a finger against her lips. Shook her head. "No way, guys. He'll take me home if he thinks I've been left behind."

She'd taken off then, a shaky half skip, half run. When she was a few cars away, Shannon turned, her yellow skirt fanning out around her legs, motioning for us to step back. "Duck," she'd whisper-shouted. "Don't let him see you!"

Tanna and I watched from the shadows as Shannon tapped Toby on a broad shoulder, as he turned, as they spoke. He smiled, laughed, and ran a hand through his hair (choice *I-want-you* body language, according to Shannon). When he turned and started towards the shadows of the back lot, Shannon threw us a high thumbs up.

Tanna tossed her head back and laughed in that wide-open way I loved so much.

"She gets anything she wants, doesn't she?" Tanna had asked as she slid into the driver's side of her blue Honda.

"It is amazing." I'd turned to watch Shannon disappear between two dark minivans. To where I now knew Joey had been sitting, waiting for something. Something that, for some reason, had nothing to do with me.

"You're still pissed off, aren't you?" Shannon leaned forwards in the green lawn chair situated between Tanna's and mine and reached into her beach bag for a bottle of sunscreen.

I didn't say anything. Instead, I focused on three middle schoolers with deep tans as they flip-flopped past our chairs, laughing and juggling hot dogs, Slushies and Twizzlers. My eyes followed them as they made their way to their towels, which were laid out on the large stretch of lawn in the back of Blue Springs Swim and Tennis Club, wishing I could jump out of my own life and into the simple happiness that seemed to enfold them.

"You *were* pretty harsh the other night," Tanna said, readjusting the straps of her bikini top.

"Yeah, whatever." Shannon rubbed white lotion into her shoulders and upper arms in quick little circles. "I'd had a little too much to drink; I started before you guys even got there. And Adam, he was pissing me off, acting like Joey means nothing to him."

I wanted to ask her if she really thought Adam felt that way. But there were more important questions. Like, what was her necklace doing in Joey's bedroom? And what else did she know that I didn't? But I wasn't sure where to start. Or where to end. So I decided to wait until I figured a few things out before I dived into the questions that were making me feel nauseous.

I bit my lip, grabbing a magazine from the foot of Shannon's lawn chair, wishing I'd trusted my first instinct and avoided this pool day altogether.

"So, Shan," Tanna said. "Isn't there something you wanted to say to Maggie?"

"Right," Shannon said, throwing the sunscreen into her bag as she leaned against the chair's back, propping one knee up in the air with the casual-sexy vibe that she always tried to emit. "I'm sorry if what I said upset you, Maggie. I know we're all just trying to deal, and calling you out wasn't fair."

"It wasn't fair to me or Adam," I said, flipping to the middle of the magazine, zoning in on an ad for hairspray where a girl with spiky hair walked into a nightclub. "I just hope you didn't push him even further away."

Shannon propped her sunglasses on her nose and tipped her face up to the sky. I could tell by the way her foot was shaking that she was agitated, close to leaping off her chair, even, but was trying to restrain herself.

"He'll come around," Shannon said. "We just need to give him a little more time."

I looked down at the magazine again, trying to escape through the doors of the nightclub with that spiky-haired girl. But before I could even read the stupid slogan, I was jolted as the five lifeguards blew their whistles simultaneously, ending the rest period. Peals of laughter rang through the humid air as kids dived into the water from all sides of the large pool. Three guys with long hair hopped into the crystalline water a little way from from our chairs, splashing us. I threw the splattered magazine back onto Shannon's chair. It was pointless, anyway, trying to distract myself.

"I'm burning up," Tanna said, standing and tossing a mess of damp hair over her shoulder. "I gotta jump in."

I looked up then, shielded my eyes from the sun that was positioned almost perfectly over Tanna's head.

"Anyone wanna join?" she asked.

Shannon grabbed the iPod sitting on her flowered towel, twirled the wires from the earphones around one finger. "Not yet," Shannon said. "I wanna listen to some tunes first."

"I'm game." I was glad to have an excuse to get away from Shannon and hoped the water might wash away all the uncertainty that had flooded me since finding my necklace.

I'd just swung my feet over the side of the lawn chair and was about to stand up when Toby walked by. I had about a millisecond to react, or I would have lost my chance altogether. It was his shoulders, broad and bare, tanned from his many days stationed at his lifeguard post, the same shoulders that I'd seen in the parking lot as we left the Spring Carnival. Those shoulders kicked my mouth into action. I wasn't sure exactly what I was after, or if I would find it, but if I didn't ask a few questions, I knew I'd never get rid of the uneasy feeling that had settled in my chest.

"Hey, Toby," I said, standing quickly, sure to speak over the steady roll of splashing and laughing coming from kids in the pool.

He stopped, turning only partially, the whistle hanging

from a red string around his neck swaying back and forth across his six-pack abs. "Oh. Hey, guys." He gave us a half wave.

"How's your summer?" I asked, willing him to step a little closer.

Those shoulders swivelled all the way towards us, and I knew I had him. "Okay, I guess." His voice was tight. A little unsure. He was confused about why I'd chosen to talk to him as though we were old friends when we'd only ever spoken once or twice before.

"You working a lot?" I asked, tipping my head towards the nearest lifeguard chair.

Toby shrugged. "Just about every day. But it doesn't feel like work."

"Shan," I said, looking down to see that her hands were frozen in the air, her skinny little iPod clutched in one, the earphone wires dangling from the fingers of the other. Her eyes were wide. Her mouth hanging open. And that made me feel good. "This job would be perfect for you. You'd get paid for working on your tan." I giggled then. All of them looked at me like I was crazy.

"But I'd have to wear a one-piece," Shannon said, her voice quiet. "I don't do one-pieces."

Toby laughed. So I did, too.

"Hey, I wanted to thank you," I said, an idea forming as the words tripped off my tongue.

"Me?" Toby pointed a finger at his chest.

I nodded. "I know it was almost two months ago, but Tanna and I feel awful about leaving Shannon behind at the Spring Carnival. Total miscommunication. It was awesome of you to take her home."

Toby's eyes creased then, and he looked from me to Shannon and back. "I don't have any idea—"

"Maybe Maggie's right," Shannon said, interrupting him, hopping up and grabbing his glistening forearm. "Is there an application or something? In the office? I mean, getting paid to sit in the sun sounds pretty nice. And my mom's been all over my ass to get a summer job."

"I think the schedule's full," Toby said. "But you can fill out an application, anyway. If you really want to."

Shannon turned and yanked the sundress off the back of her lawn chair, tossed it over her head, and grabbed Toby's arm again. "Let's do it," she said with a smile.

Toby started to turn away, but he stopped. Faced me once again. "Hey, Maggie. I'm really sorry about Joey. He was cool. A little insane, but cool."

I nodded. Smiled. But it was forced, so I had to look down.

Shannon tugged at his arm. "To the office?" she asked, urgency springing from each word.

"I gotta stop by the locker room. I'll meet you in a minute," Toby said. "Nice to see you guys." Toby nodded his head towards Tanna and me, and the two turned and started towards the clubhouse office.

"What's up with her?" Tanna asked, moving to stand next to me.

I watched the way Shannon's tiny little butt swayed from side to side, the wave of her sundress swooshing around her thighs. Her hand dropped from Toby's arm, and she moved away from him. Not much. But the distance was telling. I wondered if she'd ever had a thing for Toby Miller.

"What do you mean?" I asked.

"This thing with Toby. She's throwing herself at him. Totally against her rules."

"Maybe she's in love," I said. "Love makes you break all the rules, doesn't it?" My chest exploded, hot and heavy. The thought nearly knocked me down. But then I pushed it away. Because whatever had been going on between Shannon and Joey, it *couldn't* be that.

Tanna twirled her hair up on top of her head, tucking it into a makeshift bun. "I guess with Shannon, there really are no rules, huh?"

I shrugged. "Guess not."

"You coming in?" Tanna stepped towards the edge of the pool, the water sparkling, throwing diamonds of light across her tanned stomach.

"In a minute," I said, leaning down to reach into

Shannon's bag. "I gotta call my mom to tell her I'm here. She wants me to check in every five minutes these days."

Tanna gave me a pouty look. Then, with creased eyes, looked at the phone my fingers were clutching. Shannon's phone.

"Mine's almost dead," I said, tipping my head towards my purse. "Go on without me. I'll be there in a minute."

"I'm heading over to the deep end," Tanna said. "Those college guys are here. I want to position myself for when they start to practise their diving."

I laughed. "Being fully submerged in water does nothing to flatter your figure."

Tanna tipped her head to the side. "Maybe not. But if I get a cramp and need help, they'll get a great view when they pull me out of the water."

"Tanna, you're very creative," I said as she hopped into the water with a little splash and a giant squeal.

"It feels awesome," she said, flipping to her back and swimming away.

I looked to the office and could see through the large opening at the window counter that Shannon was twirling her hair around one finger as she talked to several guys. I had a few minutes at least. Even if she wasn't interested in them, she was interested in them being interested in her.

As I watched her, my mind flipped through several incidents I'd forgotten. Little things that seemed like nothing. Until now. The hairslide in Joey's car that she said she'd forgotten when he took her home after a football game. His shirt on the carpet in her bedroom, which he'd supposedly loaned her after she spilled pizza down hers at lunch one day.

I sat on my towel, turning my attention to that phone. Scrolling through her messages, my fingers and breathing and heart got all tripped up. I was scared of what I'd find. But I needed answers, and the only people who had them were either not talking, or acting like they didn't know anything.

I couldn't risk looking for too much. I was dying to. But there wasn't enough time. So I searched for the date. Friday, April 28th. The night of the Spring Carnival.

I had to figure it out. If he was with her. To know for sure what I only suspected.

But as I searched the history of messages between Shannon and Joey, I found a string of texts from another, more recent night.

The night of Jimmy Dutton's party.

An entire conversation.

Right at my shaky fingertips.

12:53 a.m.: *Shan, we nd 2 tlk.*

12:53 a.m.: *What did A say 2 u?*

12:53 a.m.: *Ur nt gng 2 b happy.*

12:54 a.m.: *He's nt making threats, is he?*

12:54 a.m.: *Something like that.*
12:54 a.m.: *U dropped P off?*
12:55 a.m.: *Yup. I'm abt 2 leave.*
12:55 a.m.: *Get over here.*
12:56 a.m.: *Be there in 10. Meet me outside.*

"So this is where you've been hiding out," I said, stepping from between two trees and into the moonlight. The creek was directly in front of me, bubbling its way through the back edge of the park that bordered our neighbourhood. Before the guys found the Jumping Hole, this clearing had been one of our favourite hangouts. Since Adam had started avoiding us, I'd imagined him here several times, wondering if he might be sitting with nothing but the rustling trees as his companions. But I hadn't been ready to investigate.

I stood there, still, trying not to think about where all this water had come from; that this creek was fed by the flow that came from the gorge – from our Jumping Hole – where Joey had spent his last moments alive.

Adam looked over his shoulder, as if he'd been expecting me.

"This is *one* of my hideouts," he said from his seat on a large rock at the edge of the water. I remembered a younger version of him, sitting in that exact place, his shoes tossed to the side, his bare feet plunged into the flow of the creek.

"I've texted you, like, a zillion times since yesterday." I'd been hoping I could find him alone so we could talk, just the two of us, to see if maybe I might be the one thing to bring him back.

"Been ignoring my phone," Adam said. "It's easier that way."

"Not for us." I stuffed my hands into the front pockets of my capris.

Adam patted the rock beneath him and scooted sideways to make room for me. I walked over and curled my legs underneath my body, bumping his shoulder as I sat.

"You okay?" he asked.

I took in a deep breath and shook my head slowly, side to side, tasting the moist scent of the earth, swallowing the ball of fear that had risen in my throat.

"Me, neither." The golden hues of Adam's blond hair practically shone in the night. Alcohol rode the wave of his words, a thick, syrupy scent that made my head swirl.

"You have something to drink?" I asked.

"M-hmm." Adam held a bottle in the air. The moonlight flickered through the leaves above us, playing with the curves of the glass, splashing light in all directions.

My fingers wrapped around the neck of the bottle,

pulled it towards my lips. I only intended to have a sip. To simply feel the stinging fire racing down my throat. But I kept going. After several gulps, Adam pulled the bottle from my mouth, yanked it from my clasped fingers.

"That's enough," he said.

I swiped my hand across my chin, flinging droplets of the liquid into the night. "Since when do you have a vote?"

Adam grunted. "I'm still your friend, Mags."

"Coulda fooled me." I swung towards him, my hair fanning out over my shoulder.

"Then why'd you call me?" Adam's voice was tired. He seemed totally drained of life.

"I need your help."

Adam turned to face me, raising both eyebrows.

"I figured out who Joey was with the night of Dutton's party." I swiped some hair from my eyes, blinking away the frustration that had settled into every molecule of my body.

Adam straightened his knee and dropped his foot over the side of the rock, swinging it slowly back and forth, just above the surface of the water. He didn't look at me. And he didn't say a thing.

"It was *Shannon*. They were all worried about some kind of threat you'd thrown down. And then there's something strange about the night of the carnival. Remember how Joey supposedly got home really late from the Reds game? Well, that's *not* how it happened. My mind is racing to all these terrible places, but I don't want to go to any of them – I just can't – not until I know something for sure. So I'm asking you, Adam. What the hell was going on?"

Adam stared at the rippling surface of the water, the way the moonlight danced across the silver channels, as if I wasn't even there.

I grabbed his arm, pulling him towards me. "You *have* to tell me."

"I'm sorry, Mags." Adam shook his head.

"Adam, *please*."

Adam shifted his weight, twisting on the rock so he could face me. He hesitated for a moment, his eyes focused on mine. "Where did you hear all this?" he asked. "What happened?"

And then, though he remained perfectly silent, I heard his voice continue, a distant echo in my head. *What happened before the screaming?*

I pulled back, sucking in a shaky breath.

Adam recoiled like I'd shocked him. "Maggie, I'm sorry. I didn't—"

"Screaming?" I clasped my hands together. Tight. "There was screaming?"

Adam leaned towards me again, holding my hands in his. Somehow, the touch warmed my entire shaking body.

"Why are you asking that?" Adam's lips were tight and his eyes looked frantic. Wild.

I kicked my legs out, clawing my feet at the rock, trying to gain my footing.

Adam put a hand on my knee, and I saw a flash of blood. Remembered not knowing if it had come from him or from me.

"There was blood on your arm," I said. "It was *Joey's?*"

"Just relax for a minute, okay?" Adam pressed the bottle into my hand.

I took another long swig. This time Adam didn't pull it away. When I stopped, the spicy liquid dribbled down my chin, but I didn't care. "You asked me what happened before the screaming. At the cliff. Right?"

Adam took a deep breath. "Yes," he said. "I did."

"What else?" I asked. "What else happened? Because I can't remember now. Not anything."

"You didn't remember then, either." Adam stared at me, his eyes turning a silvery green in the moonlight. He looked so much like his old self that I almost believed everything since Memorial Day weekend had been a bad dream, and that, even if it wasn't, Adam would suddenly snap back to normal and be the friend I'd always known.

"Adam, you have to help me. I feel like I'm losing my mind here. I mean, everything from the cliff top is gone. And then you, you're gone, too—"

"Maggie, I'm not gone."

"It sure feels like it. You're one of my best friends, Adam. And it's like you've died, too. And then I find out some shady shit was going down between you and Joey. And somehow Shannon's tied into it. I'm just walking around bumping into random things and hoping I find some answers. But at the same time I'm afraid. What if those answers just confirm my worst fears? What if the things I can't even say out loud are true?"

"You can handle this. The memories, they seem to be coming back in pieces," Adam said. "That's good, right? You've remembered a lot in the few times we've hung out."

"I've only remembered *one* thing without you, Adam. One. And it was a snapshot, not an actual memory, okay? You'd know that if you'd taken the time to be more available."

"Available?" Adam's voice changed then. It went from soft to charged with just one word. "To what? Help lead you through your feelings? Newsflash, Maggie, I lost Joey, too. And I'm dealing with my own feelings. Huge, suck-ass waves of feelings that are about to take me under. So, I'm sorry, but I can't carry you to the other side of this. I have to carry myself. And if that means there's a little distance, then you either deal with it or you don't. I can only take on what I can handle right now."

"I don't expect you to carry me, Adam. But I expect some honesty. I mean, this is *us* we're talking about."

Adam laughed. Stood from the rock and looked down at me. "Jesus, Maggie, do you ever stop?"

I wanted to kick his legs from under him so he would fall back down and have to face me. "Tell me what you know, Adam."

"You're asking the wrong person, Mags."

"What the hell is that supposed to mean? Why do you always talk in code now? Nothing you say makes one bit of—"

"I don't know how I can make it any clearer for you. There's nothing more I can say." He looked at me, his eyes filling with an emotion I couldn't read. "I'm sorry. I really am."

And then he turned and stepped off the rock, moved through the trees and into the darkest part of the shadows until he disappeared. It was in that moment that I finally understood I'd lost him, all the way. It hurt more than I'd expected it to, the pain crashing down on my chest until I felt like I could hardly breathe.

"I FOUND A PACKAGE ON the front porch for you," my mom said as I came down the steps the next morning. She was standing at the island, the newspaper spread in front of her as she munched on a piece of peanut butter toast.

"From whom?" I asked, not really caring. With Joey gone and Adam so totally disconnected, nothing seemed to matter any more.

My mother smiled, holding a small rectangular box in the air. It was wrapped in brown packaging paper, with my name written on the front. No address or shipping labels. Just my name, which was spelled in block letters with a dark blue marker.

"It's very mysterious," my mom said. "I think you have an admirer."

"Mom, please."

"I'm not saying that you have to jump into a new relationship right away," my mother said. "But you can't close yourself off for ever. It's not healthy."

"Why don't you leave the therapy to Dr. Guest?" I said. "She's a trained professional."

"Well, it's something you may want to discuss with her. There will naturally be some guilt. But it's something you need to—"

"Mom, really," I said, walking behind her and tugging on the belt of her robe, "leave it alone."

My mother sighed, then turned to face me, holding her coffee mug with both hands. "I'm heading upstairs to get ready for work."

"Have a good day," I said as my mother made her way through the kitchen and to the staircase.

"Maggie," my mother said, stopping, her robe swaying around her legs. "I meant what I said. I know you and Dr. Guest have been focusing on your memories because recovering them is so important to you, and I know that a month is too soon to expect you to move on, but everything that comes next is just as important as everything that's already happened. Okay?"

"Right."

"Don't do that," she said, shaking a finger in the air. "Say what I want to hear so I'll—"

"Mom. I get it. Okay?"

She sighed. "I made you some pancakes and bacon. They're in the microwave if you want to zap them for a warm-up."

I thumbed the buttons on the microwave and grabbed the bottle of maple syrup from the counter, turning to look down at that package. Part of me wanted to rip it open. But another part of me wanted to throw it in the trash. In my life, the concept of surprises had lost its appeal.

But as I poured the syrup on my pancakes, the package stared up at me, calling to me, and I had to know what was inside.

So as soon as I finished breakfast, I grabbed a pair of scissors and went back up to the privacy of my room, wishing the little brown-wrapped gift had the power to flip everything back to normal.

When I pulled the paper away, I was confused. Someone had left me a photo album, the front cover dotted with hand-drawn hearts. My first thought was that it was from Joey. That was the stutter my brain still suffered from, a misfire that made me instinctively believe that he was still alive. But even if he were still here, he'd never been the type to doodle pink hearts.

I reached out, expecting the book to send shock waves of emotion up my arm – love, loss, hope, regret.

Something inside me pulled tight with unease, but I told myself that was stupid. That none of my fears were justified. That there was a perfectly good explanation for all the things Joey had kept from me. And that this photo album was probably someone's way to honour the relationship I'd had with him, cataloguing our time together with photos I'd somehow never seen.

I held my breath, wondering if someone from the yearbook staff or the school newspaper had searched through old files for pictures that had once been unimportant. I visualized a shot of Joey and me walking through the locker-lined hall, clasped hands swinging between our bodies. But that vision was quickly erased.

As I flipped open the front cover of that album, I saw the worst thing ever.

A picture.

Of Joey.

And Shannon.

Kissing.

Shannon had taken the picture. I could tell by the way her outstretched arm reached towards me that she'd been holding the camera, turned it towards them, and pressed the button the instant Joey's lips had touched hers. How she'd gotten the picture so perfectly centred, I'd never know.

But she had.

And there they were.

Sitting in Shannon's basement. On her couch. *Exactly* where I had been sitting just a week ago, when we confronted Adam about blowing us off.

Shannon was laughing, her eyes squeezed tight.

Joey, too, his parted lips pressed against hers.

I slammed the album shut. Pressed my palm into all those hearts. Willing it away, away, away. But it didn't disappear like I needed it to. Instead, the album seemed to grow heavier, holding me down.

It flooded me in an instant. Understanding that all of Joey's secrets revolved around Shannon. That everything I'd feared most since finding that stupid necklace in my drawer was actually true.

His secrets. They weren't just his. Those secrets belonged to both of them. Together.

I wanted to know how big it was. How long it had been going on.

But the only way to find out was to face everything in that album.

I was nauseous from just one picture. I didn't want to go on.

But I had to. There was no other choice.

"You have to face this, Maggie," I told myself. "Just do it. Fast."

And so I did.

I flipped through the pages, finding more of the same.

Pictures of Joey and Shannon together in the woods surrounded by falling red, orange, and yellow leaves; eating ice cream while wearing wool caps and gloves; sitting lazily on a swing in the park in T-shirts and jeans. They were laughing, or kissing, or touching in almost all of them – through the seasons of at least one full year.

The others, the ones where it was obvious there was some special meaning even though I couldn't see either of them, those were creative, just like Shannon. A shot of their bare feet in the grass, her toenails painted a bright pink, his underneath, perfectly trimmed. One of a sunset melting into a bank of snow-covered trees. A picture of pebbles along the bank of a creek, gathered together to spell out their names.

Joey & Shannon.

So together.

And so very alone.

The last page was different. A folded piece of paper, creased and worn.

Joey's name written on the front flap in Shannon's loopy handwriting. In her favourite purple pen.

I yanked the note free, practically ripping it in my need to understand.

Maybe I had something wrong. Maybe this was old, whatever had been going on. I needed to believe it had all happened before Joey and I ever began.

As I started to read, I held onto that hope.

And quickly felt it all fade away on the tide of a new grief that somehow outweighed the darkness of Joey's death.

Joey,

I know what you're thinking. What you've been thinking since this all started last fall. That this is bad. All kinds of bad. But it's not, Joey. Nothing that feels this good can possibly be bad. It might hurt some people, Maggie most of all, but we have to figure this out. And we have to get it out in the open before the damage can't be undone.

School will be ending soon. Summer starting. And that gives everyone three months to deal. To understand. And to let go.

They will. You'll see. They have to.

I love you. And you say you love me. So this should be simple. I'll do it any way you want. So take the next few weeks to do what you need to do. And then the summer will be ours.

I'll be waiting.

Always.

Shannon

My hands were shaking so badly that I couldn't refold the note. So I balled it up tight and shoved it back under the thin plastic sleeve, flipped the album closed, and threw it on the floor. I scrambled to my feet, clawing my hands through my hair and wanting to scream so loud that everything around me would shatter to pieces. I was pissed. So very pissed I could practically see waves rippling from my body and out into the room.

But then I saw his face. His too blue eyes. And his smile. Staring right up at me from the frame on my nightstand. It was my favourite picture of us together, because we looked so at ease. Tanna had taken the shot after school one day just a few months ago, when we'd all gone to Getrie's Dairy Farm for ice cream. I was sitting on Joey's lap, one leg kicked up, with my head tipped back mid-laugh. Joey's arms were wrapped around me, his hands clasped around my waist. The hands that had touched Shannon. I didn't understand how the Joey in my picture could have been the same Joey that was tucked away in her photo album.

I slipped down onto my bed, curling up on the quilt my mother had mended with thread that didn't quite match the rest, feeling the pain well up fresh. Joey's death somehow hurt more in that moment, swelling inside me until I felt like I might burst.

THEY HAD ALWAYS BEEN SO ALIKE. Crazy and senseless, rushing into things without thinking. Plotting pranks together. Daring to dive down the most curvy sledging hill in town while I stood at the top trying to convince myself I'd be fine if I followed after.

She'd always looked at every boy but Joey.

And me, I was the opposite.

Cautious. Reserved. And Joey had always been my only interest.

When I thought about it, all of it, the years we'd spent growing up together, it made sense, Joey and Shannon together. More sense than Joey picking me.

And that thought nearly killed me.

But what sliced into me even more were all the things I should have picked up on. All the rushed glances I'd missed. All the spontaneous things they'd done together that essentially eliminated me from the picture.

How totally stupid I had been.

*   *   *

"Lookie there, lookie there," Joey said, running a hand along his chin as he stood in the middle of the Duttons' oversized, three-car garage. A metre or so in front of him was a shiny black and green motorbike, with paint that literally sparkled in the overhead fluorescent lighting.

"Joey," I said. "Please tell me you're not thinking what I think you're thinking."

Joey looked at me. His eyes sparking with the not-so-quiet kind of mischief he'd always been known for. "I promise I'll be good."

Tanna laughed out loud, the sound echoing off the white walls of the garage, the super-shined surface of the Duttons' black Jaguar, the riding mower, and the totally organized work space stuffed with every kind of tool imaginable.

"Good?" Shannon asked, poking Joey in the arm, and the back, and the gut like an annoying little sister. "I wasn't aware you knew the definition of that word."

Joey whipped around, grabbing Shannon's hand and twisting it behind her back. "What did you say?" He was smiling, and so was she, but Shannon was wriggling to pull away from his grasp.

"Let her go," Tanna said, jumping onto Joey's back, "or you'll wish you did."

"I can take you both." Joey's voice strained as he

struggled to upend Tanna while keeping his grip on Shannon's arm.

And then I saw it, the one thing that would stop him like nothing else. Tanna had a finger in her mouth and was juicing it up with fervour.

"Ears," I warned, "watch your ears."

But it was too late, Tanna had already plugged Joey's right ear with her slimy finger. Joey shuddered and yelped, releasing Shannon and flinging Tanna off his back as he jumped away.

"You are so disgusting," Joey said as he wiped Tanna's spit from the side of his face and the inside of his ear.

Tanna and Shannon practically collapsed in a heap of giggles, giving each other a smacking high five in celebration of their victory.

"You," Shannon said, "are a bully."

Joey propped his hands on his hips and shrugged. Then he turned to look at the motorbike again. I could practically see the thoughts flying from his perfectly beautiful head: *I want to ride, I need to ride, I will ride...*

"Joey," I warned. "You said you'd be good."

Joey nodded. "And I will."

I sighed. "Thank God. I thought you were about to steal this thing."

Joey shook his head, his deep brown hair falling down into his face. "Nope." He turned and walked towards the door that led to the Duttons' hallway. I stepped quickly behind him, my bare feet padding along the cool grey paint that covered the garage floor. Adam was right behind me. I could tell because he felt like a heavy load pressing against my back. Whatever had him so ticked off was going to be problematic with the three-day break ahead. Memorial Day weekend was full of tradition, and if the guys weren't speaking, the gorge the next day would be awful and stressful, the partying would feel disjointed, and the overall mood would—

"Wait," I said, scrunching my eyes as Joey stopped instead of placing his hand on the doorknob and making his way back into the house. I could feel Adam's tension rise a notch or two behind me. "What are you doing?"

"I said I'd be good." Joey grinned, his lips tilting to the side a little in that sexy way that always made me feel light-headed. He stared into my eyes, the blue of his own practically glowing with excitement of a promised rush. "And I swear I will. It's just…I can't not." With that, Joey turned and jabbed the little glowing button next to the door that led into the house, and the steady hum of the garage door invaded all the spaces around us, vibrating everything, including my beer-soaked brain.

I shook my head. "It's not a good idea," I said.

"Yeah, Joey." Tanna stepped around me then, tugging

at the braid that had come loose during her wild ride on Joey's back. "You've been drinking."

"But –" Joey crossed a finger over his chest, one way, and then the other – "I haven't had any of those Jell-O shots yet. And I haven't smoked a thing tonight."

"A crotch rocket, Joey?" Adam asked, the irritation in his voice bordering on outright anger.

I looked at the bike, my eyes skimming the words scrolled on its side – *Kawasaki, Racing Team, Ninja, ZX6* – which were a little fuzzy and out of focus. The full light of the garage made me realize I'd had more to drink than I thought.

"You've ridden a dirt bike at your uncle's, like, a coupla times," Tanna said. "You ready for this?" She pointed her finger at the motorbike.

When I stared at the thing too hard, it began to look like a large grasshopper. A very fast grasshopper that I didn't want Joey riding. But I knew what would happen if we pushed him, especially me, so I kept my mouth shut.

"I rode my uncle's Harley last month," Joey said, pulling his shoulders back. "That thing was a beast. I can handle this baby. She'll be smooth. Like buttah." Joey ran a hand across the green bump that sloped towards the black leather seat.

"Don't worry, guys," Adam said. "He'll never get it started."

Joey smirked.

I could have smacked Adam for challenging him. One thing about Joey, he *never* backed down from a challenge.

"Now we're screwed," Shannon said, sitting on the workbench and looking down at the smattering of stickers that covered the seat: John Deere, Carhartt, Harley Davidson.

"Oh," Joey laughed, "you guys were already screwed." Joey turned on his heels and walked to a metal box on the wall, flipped open the little door, and revealed a plethora of keys hanging off tiny hooks.

"Oh, shit." Tanna pulled her fingers through the waves her braid had created, shaking her head.

"Joey," I began, trying to think of the right thing to say to talk him out of it.

"Don't bother, Mag-Pie. I'm going."

"I hate it when you call me that," I said.

"I know. This might be easier if you're pissed off."

"No. Not so much. You can't just go around stealing people's—"

"What the fuck's going on here?" A red-faced and breathless Jimmy Dutton skidded to a stop on the tarmac driveway in the opening of the garage. "You guys shouldn't be in here."

Joey smiled then, a real beamer, and nodded his head towards the motorbike. He ran a hand through his hair and whistled. "She's a beaut."

"Yeah. And she's off-limits," Jimmy said, his voice shaking. I wondered if he knew he'd just thrown a double on top of Adam's challenge.

I sighed, resigning myself to the simple fact that before the night was over, Joey would find a way to ride that motorbike.

"Is she yours?" Joey asked, his voice as sweet and sticky as honey. Poor Jimmy didn't have a chance.

Jimmy shook his head. "My brother's. The brother that talked my parents into leaving me here instead of forcing me to go to the lake for the weekend. The brother who got us the keg. And the fireworks. The brother who would skewer me alive if he knew I'd let someone take his bike out for a joyride."

"Dude," Joey said with a chuckle. "I totally respect all that. And your brother's a cool guy. Graduated a few years ago, right? I remember the game where he dislocated his shoulder trying to keep the ball in bounds. He saved the team that night. We made it to state tournament because of him."

Jimmy's face loosened a bit, his eyes leaving Joey for the first time as he glanced at the bike. "My brother saved every dime for a coupla years to buy this thing, man. If someone breathes on it wrong, he knows."

"I'll be careful," Joey said. "I know how to ride. Have been for years."

Lie. Total lie. He'd ridden that Harley three times. On the dirt road at his uncle's farm so the bike would land on softer ground in case Joey keeled over.

Adam shifted his weight from one foot to the other behind me. Tanna looked at me and raised her eyebrows as she twisted her hair back into its braid. Shannon smacked her flip-flop against the bottom of her foot over, and over, and over.

"Dude, I dunno. I swore I'd keep everything locked up. Especially my brother's shit."

"He'll never know," Joey said. "I swear he'll never know a thing."

Just then a screeching sound tore through the night. Jimmy turned to look over his shoulder as someone flew through the front door and started puking in the bushes that lined the walkway. "Oh, man," he said, rubbing the top of his head. "Look, whatever, okay? Just so you know, if you get caught, I'll tell the cops, my brother, and God himself that you stole the thing. If you go down, you're not taking me with you."

I almost reminded Jimmy that he would probably be going down no matter what. The party was supposed to be low-key but had started to rage as people poured down the long driveway in a steady stream, holding six-packs and coolers, lit cigarettes and joints, shouting to one another and pumping fists in the air at the luck of having such a secluded place to hang for the night. No way Jimmy would be able to clean this up before his parents returned. An entire month wouldn't be enough time.

"You rock, man," Joey said, smiling. "I'll be careful. Don't worry."

Jimmy shook his head and turned quickly, jogging to the puker. When he reached her, he tugged on her shoulders, pulled her up, and half-walked, half-dragged her further from the house.

"Told ya." Joey turned towards us, a smirk planted on his face. "I'm gonna ride." He threw a key high up in the air, a key I couldn't recall him plucking from the metal box. I watched it loop and spiral, the overhead light glinting off its shiny surface. As Joey caught the key in one hand, I stood there wondering if it had been cupped in the darkness of his palm since he'd come out back to gather us for his mysterious adventure. An adventure that really had nothing to do with us.

Joey spun to face me, his eyes glinting with energy. "You comin' with?"

I looked at the motorcycle. Then back at him. "I dunno," I said, my legs feeling wobbly with the thought of trying to hold on. Wobbly good because my entire body would be wrapped tightly against Joey's, a prelude to the surprise I'd planned for the week his parents would be out of town. Wobbly bad because the thought of the bike's motion made me feel a little sick. "I'm kinda drunk."

Tanna giggled. "You," she said, "are a lot drunk. And I forbid you to risk your life on that death machine."

"Oh," Joey said, slapping a hand to his chest. "The confidence you have in me is overwhelming."

"Ask me if I care." Tanna stuck her tongue out at Joey.

"So I can assume that *you're* not interested in a ride?" he asked her.

"No freaking way."

Joey looked at Adam, then. They both smiled, and a fresh glimmer of their friendship sparked into the cool night air. "Dude," Adam said, "don't even ask."

Joey shrugged. "Your loss, bro."

Shannon stopped flipping and flopping her sandal and looked at the bike.

"You wanna?" Joey's voice cracked a little and he cleared his throat.

She shrugged. "I guess."

"You guess?" Joey's threw his head back and groaned. "That is not the kind of enthusiasm I was looking for, Shan."

Shannon giggled. "I've never ridden a motorbike before."

"Never?" Joey asked. "That's a tragedy. Stand up. Hop on."

Shannon jumped up from the workbench and fluttered her long arms in the air, clapping her hands and giggling.

Joey straddled the bike's seat and started the motor with a quick and easy turn of that little key. The sound was louder than I'd expected, flooding the large garage, vibrating my insides with an irritating tickle.

When Joey tipped his head at Shannon, she flung a long, tanned leg over the back of the leather seat, bouncing up and down as she slid onto its centre and sidled up to Joey's back. I was jealous. The feeling ripped through me. I wanted to be the one behind him, and I almost told them to forget it, that I was going instead. But Tanna was right. I'd had way too much to drink, and it wouldn't be safe for Joey or me if I rode with him.

"All you gotta do is hang on," Joey yelled back at Shannon as he tugged her arms around his waist. "And don't lean too far when we turn."

"Wait," I said stepping towards them, "aren't you guys gonna wear helmets?"

Joey shook his head. "We're not going far."

Shannon whisper-shouted something into Joey's ear. He grinned and looked at me, Tanna, and Adam.

"Shan wants a countdown," he said, blowing a strand of brown hair from his eyes.

I turned and grabbed Tanna's hand, Adam's, too, and squeezed.

"Three," we shouted in unison. "Two! One!"

We threw our hands into the air, shouting, Tanna and I

kicking our feet out in a little dance, and waited for them to take off.

Joey winked at me, smiled, and picked his feet off the ground, easing the shiny green bike out of the garage. A crowd had gathered, open-mouthed and gawking, and they watched with drinks raised, cheering, as Joey and Shannon peeled down the long strip of dark drive that led to the country roads twisting through the edge of town.

16 a slice of something beautiful

"DO YOU THINK YOU CAN ever really know a person?" I asked, shaking a handful of M&M's in my hand as I settled in for my fourth appointment with Dr. Guest.

"Are you referring to Joey?" Dr. Guest looked at me, raising her eyebrows.

"It's just a question," I lied, popping the M&M's into my mouth.

I hadn't told her about the cheating yet. I hadn't told anyone. I was afraid of saying the words, as though once they were out there, it would make the whole thing all the way true. I'd spent the four days since finding that album struggling with the idea that the real Joey was nothing like the Joey I thought I knew, trying to avoid facing the fact that the Joey I loved had never existed.

Dr. Guest flipped to a fresh page in her notepad, held it in the air, and turned it to face me. She started drawing squares on the paper. Little ones. Big ones. I listened to the scratch of her pen, wondering what insight she was about to share, enjoying the sweetness of the chocolate melting on my tongue.

When she'd filled about three quarters of the paper with different-sized squares, all linked together, she looked at me. "You've talked about that patchwork quilt your grandmother made, how you ripped it the day Joey died."

"I stole it from the living room," I said. "It's on my bed now."

"Your question made me think of how a person is just like a quilt."

I watched in silence as Dr. Guest filled in the rest of the empty space with small, medium and large squares. Then she swivelled in her chair, her knees bumping the table between us, and presented her patchwork piece of paper.

"I don't get it," I said.

"Think about your grandma's quilt. The whole thing, it's a work of art, a slice of something beautiful."

I looked at the paper, all the squares, imagining the blanket that I'd spread across my bed a few weeks ago. "Yeah."

"Like Joey. He was a slice of something beautiful."

I swallowed. Hard. Trying to keep the tears down. Because no matter how much he'd hurt me with all the shit he'd left behind, that was so true.

"A work of art," I said.

"But if you look closely at that quilt your grandmother

made, I bet there are pieces that you don't really care for. Small patches of fabric that you can handle when you look at the whole, but that you would never choose for yourself if you were making your own quilt."

I thought of the scratchy grey wool that had once been a part of my great-grandmother's Sunday dress.

"Just like Joey. If you look closely enough, there are pieces of him that you probably don't care for. Pieces of him that, since his death, you're seeing for the first time. Pieces that might be ripped or torn. Imperfections. Ugliness. And that's okay."

"But what if, when I look really close up, I realize those small pieces that I don't like, all the imperfections, are bigger than the whole of him that I thought I loved?"

"Then you do what you would do if he were still alive. You let go." Dr. Guest looked at me with very sad eyes. "And you move on."

"But I don't want to. Joey, he is –" I sucked in a deep breath – "*was* everything to me."

"That's how people get into trouble, Maggie." Dr. Guest pressed her lips together. Then she let out a big sigh. "I sense that something has changed since we last spoke. You want to fill me in?"

I thought about letting the words spill into the room. But I couldn't say them yet, so I just shook my head.

"It's important for you to allow yourself to feel whatever

you need to feel right now. Get angry. Cry. Scream if you have to. Move through this in the way that suits you best, and don't worry about Joey. He'll come back to you, even if it feels like you don't know him right now. You know, deep down, that you knew him very well."

But I didn't. I didn't know that at all. And that scared me more than anything.

"So, how do I remember?" I asked. "All the stuff that I left at the cliff. How do I go back and find it?"

"You reclaimed a memory the first time you were here. Have you remembered anything more?"

"I try every day," I said. "I sit by myself and concentrate on being there, on seeing and feeling and hearing everything that happened."

"And?"

I threw my hands in the air. "Nothing! All I get is the stuff I never lost, or the few flashes that have already come back."

Dr. Guest looked to the floor, shook her foot a few times, and then looked right at me. "I want you to think back to the times that the memories have returned. Tell me about what you were doing, where you were. We need to find your trigger."

I almost laughed. Adam had been tied to almost every single memory that had come back to me. And Adam was gone now. But I wasn't about to get into all of that.

"It's pretty random. They kind of flash into my head, like lightning. One second they're gone. And the next second they're back. But each time it's happened, someone has been there with me."

"You've had none when you were focusing alone? When you're actively trying to access those memories, they stay in the dark?"

"Right."

"Well, if what you want to do is to remember, and by the way, in my professional opinion that would be best, I have one question."

"Okay. Shoot."

"Do you think maybe you should stop trying so hard?"

I sat there speechless. Dr. Guest shrugged her shoulders.

"That's so simple," I said.

"It might just work."

"And you get paid *how much* for this?"

Dr. Guest tipped her head back and laughed. I realized that I'd never heard her happy, only concerned, and the change was nice.

"Okay, then." Dr. Guest plopped her pad on the table, the pen scooting across the page of squares. "Here's your homework. You're going to give yourself a break. Just relax and stop focusing so much on the memories. Live your life. Spend time with your friends. And just wait and see what happens."

I sat there thinking that her advice could be applied to many areas of my life. The missing memories, obviously. And Adam. Sweet Adam, who had changed so much. My pushing him was the worst idea I'd ever had. But Dr. Guest's homework might just help me handle my frustration over how to deal with Shannon. I'd been unsure how to confront her, trying to come up with some grand plan that would end with her explaining everything in a way that made all the pain disappear and that, at the same time, might bring us all back together again.

Since that would never happen, I figured I had nothing to lose. I deserved a break. And it just might be my turn to be unpredictable and go a little crazy for once.

17 the earth spinning beneath me

I STARED AT THE FLAMES of the bonfire, watching them leap and dive in front of me, my fingers wrapped tightly around a bumpy stick as the fire licked the sides of the marshmallow I was roasting. I felt hazy, like I was only half there. It had nothing to do with alcohol – I'd only had a few swigs from Tanna's special Fourth of July mug, just to keep her from asking questions about why I'd been so quiet lately. It had worked. She was sitting next to me on a knotted log, singing along with a bunch of people as Pete played Jason Mraz's "I'm Yours" on his guitar.

It had started thirty-eight days ago, the dreamy fog I'd been swimming through. Since Joey's death, life had been swirling by in swatches of colour, waves of sound, thunderous moments of truth. And it was all out of my control. I knew it was up to me to regain some kind of order. But I wasn't sure how. So I kept treading, ever so lightly, through each moment and into the next.

But then the marshmallow fell. Slid right off the end of

that stupid stick. And everything that I'd been trying to hold together leaped right after it, directly into those writhing flames.

"Maggie!" Shannon squealed from somewhere close. "I just told you we're almost out of marshmallows." I watched the marshmallow bubble and fizz from its place in the ashes, a blue flame melting it into a goopy mess.

"Here." Shannon stepped around the fire and plopped down beside me, holding out the near-empty bag of marshmallows. "*One* more chance."

People were all around, sitting on lawn chairs circling the fire, waiting for the fireworks to start as they roasted their own marshmallows to perfection. A shout came from a cluster of people bunched around the game of beer pong set up on Shannon's back porch. Everyone was at ease with Shannon's parents out of town, savouring the music, the fire, and the summer night.

Everyone except for me. I batted Shannon's hand away, nearly toppling the fresh marshmallow to the ground. "I'm good."

Tanna whipped her head around, her hair flicking me in the face. "What's wrong with you?"

"Whaddo you mean?" I asked, trying to tear my eyes away from the flames.

"You live for s'mores, Maggie. Don't try and tell me nothing's wrong."

"You really need to ask?" I flashed her a warning just-leave-me-alone look. She might have taken the hint. If it wasn't for Shannon.

"Yeah. Something's *definitely* up. I thought it was just me. But then I watched you totally blow off Pete earlier tonight."

"I didn't blow off Pete," I said, trying to keep my voice steady, my eyes away from her face, because I knew very well that I had. I'd been so surprised to see Adam round the corner of Shannon's house, I'd turned away from Pete and practically run. I hadn't seen Adam since the creek, more than a week ago, and I had no idea what I was supposed to say to him. Or anyone else, for that matter.

Pete stopped playing and turned to us, his lips parted like he wanted to say something, but he kept quiet.

"Pete was in the middle of a sentence and you just walked away." Shannon gave me a little snort. I wanted to claw at her perfect little throat. But that image made me think of Joey's lips, his warm breath, his tongue, all tracing their way up to her pretty pink lips. My whole body started to shake with a fresh rush of anger.

"You *have* been acting a little off lately," Tanna said, tipping her head to the side and gazing at me like she was thinking that if she stared long enough maybe the real me would come through.

I rolled my eyes. "You think?" I asked. "Not like there's a reason for me acting differently or anything."

From the corner of my eye, I saw Shannon looking at me with the same intensity. She leaned forwards, her hair falling over her shoulder. "Oh. My. God. You remembered, didn't you?"

I looked at her then, the way her eyes had lit up, glinting in the flickering light of the fire.

"You remembered what happened at the top of that cliff." Shannon's eyes locked on mine. "Tell me the truth, Maggie."

Her words made me laugh. It was a sick sound that burst from me before I could contain it. And it brought Adam over from the shadows of the trees, his face creased with concern.

"What's going on?" he asked.

I stood and swivelled around, facing him. "Shannon thinks I remembered something from the cliff top."

Then Shannon stood, shoulders pulled back, chin up, her face a tight mask of anger. "I'm telling you, I've felt it all along. *Something* happened up there."

"What happened between me and Joey at the top of that cliff is none of your business, Shannon."

"The hell it isn't." Shannon looked right at me, her eyes harder than I had ever seen them. Meaner and more accusing than when she called Nick Hadley out for stealing Pete's guitar back in eighth grade. "Why didn't you jump, too?" Shannon asked. "How come it was only him?"

"*I don't remember*," I said, my words shaking with a fresh wave of anger. How could she stand there and accuse me after everything she'd done?

"He was all twisted up, Maggie. Bent backwards," Shannon said, her voice dropping. "Like he didn't get the right start. Which makes no sense, because he's jumped that cliff about a thousand times since eighth grade."

"It was an *accident*." Pete shook his head. "He was crazy-stupid sometimes. We all know that. And no matter how much we talk through this, I don't think we're going to get the answers we're after."

"We might." Shannon shrugged, tucking a strand of hair behind her ear and tipping her head my way. "If only she would *remember* something."

"Shannon, that's enough!" Tanna stood and placed a hand on my shoulder. "We're all freaking out here. You can't blame Maggie any more than the rest of us. We were drinking. And Joey? He was the kind of guy who would take a walk in the park and find a way to make it reckless. This whole thing is a terrible tragedy, Shan. But the only person to blame is Joey."

"Guys," Pete said, "Joey would *not* like what's happening right now."

"But why aren't we asking more questions?" Shannon asked. "Why haven't we—"

"What, exactly, are you accusing me of?" I asked, my

entire body tingling. I felt disconnected from everything. The scene unfolding in front of me wasn't reality. It couldn't be.

"I think you have a secret – something you don't want *anyone* to know – about what happened up there on the cliff." Shannon's words sparked into the dark night.

"Oh, now here we go. Let's dig in, shall we?" I clapped my hands together and stepped closer to Shannon. "I find it ironic that *you're* accusing *me* of having a secret. You have one of your own, don't you, Shan?"

The anger in Shannon's eyes flared and then flashed into something that looked like fear. "What are you talking about?"

I swivelled, walked around the fire's edge, and yanked Shanon's purse from its perch under her lawn chair. I was pissed at myself for leaving the photo album at home. I'd thought about bringing it but was worried that having it close would make me want to attack Shannon. And earlier, I hadn't been ready to face her. Because facing her meant everything I'd had with Joey was all the way over. And everything we'd all had together, that was over, too.

When I turned, Adam was there. "You don't want to do this, Maggie," he said, his voice a shaky whisper.

"Yes," I said, "I do."

"Here?" Adam swept a hand in the air, indicating all Sthe people standing around, clutching beers and staring.

"With all these people watching?"

"Why the hell not? They're gonna find out anyway, the way rumours fly in this town. Some of 'em probably already know." I shrugged, turned, and pressed my way back to the fire before I lost my nerve. Shannon's mouth dropped open as I yanked at the zipper of her purse and turned the bag upside down, toppling nearly the entire contents on the grass before my fingers wrapped around her phone. Adam came up from behind and stood at my side. It felt good to have him there, almost normal, but I worried that he'd try to stop me before I was through.

"I was just wondering," I fumbled around, pressing buttons to find the messages, ducking away from Shannon as she leaped towards me, grabbing for her phone.

"Wait," she said. "You have no right—"

"*I* have no right?" I laughed, tipping my head back towards the heat of the flames. "Now that's funny. Almost as funny as you asking me to tell you the truth."

Pete rushed up from behind me and grabbed my arm. "Guys. Enough, okay?"

"No. I don't think so." I stared at Shannon, not even trying to wriggle loose from Pete's firm grip.

Tanna moved closer, trying to get between Shannon and me. "What the hell is going on here?"

Shannon's eyes flickered between me and Tanna and Pete and Adam.

"What's the matter, Shan? Wondering how much I know? Trying to figure out which parts to reveal?" I stepped towards her. Held the phone in the air between us, the string of text messages a wall that would divide us for the rest of time. "It's over, Shannon. I know everything."

Shannon swiped the phone from my hand and looked at the lines of text. "Fine," she said. "It was me."

"What was you?" Tanna asked. "Somebody tell me what's going on."

"I'd love a clue, too," Pete said, his hand dropping from my arm.

"The night of Dutton's party, when Joey didn't go home, that's because he spent the night with Shannon." I crossed my arms over my chest, looking right at Shannon. I wondered if she'd admit everything. The sick truth is that I almost wanted her to deny it, so I could still hold on to a tiny slice of hope that my Joey was the real Joey.

"What?" Tanna asked.

"Whoa," Pete looked from Shannon to me and back again. "Why didn't you just tell us?"

"Because, Pete," I said, "there was a lot more to it than that."

"Wait." Tanna threw a hand up in the air. "I'm sorry? What the hell?"

"Right. I know!" I giggled, this crazy sound that sparked in the super-charged air. "That's exactly what I was thinking when I found the pictures."

Shannon's entire body stiffened. Then she pulled her shoulders back and looked me right in the eyes. "You saw pictures?"

"Someone left them on my front porch. There were, like, twenty shots perfectly arranged in this cheesy little album. And the pictures, they told the story of a sweet little romance. One that had been going on for a year, if I had to guess."

"Almost." Shannon stared at me, a flicker of nervous excitement in her eyes. "It was *almost* one year."

I stepped forwards, my hand screaming to smack her pretty little face. It made me sick, looking at her, thinking of how many years I'd considered her one of my best friends. "You wanted me to find out, didn't you?"

"I left so many clues, you'd have to be blind or stupid not to have – wait a minute..." Shannon looked into the fire, her face glowing in the orange-tinted light, her brain stuttering over some new thought that I wasn't so sure I wanted to hear. "You already knew...*before* Memorial Day weekend, didn't you? That's what happened up there?"

"Shannon, let it go," Adam said.

Shannon looked to the ground, her fingers twisting, twisting, twisting a ring on her left hand. Then she looked up at me again. "Joey and I might have had some secrets. But yours, it's way worse, isn't it?"

"You were supposed to be one of my best friends," I said, "and this is what I get after finding out you and Joey had been together, hiding some twisted romance for a year?"

Shannon shrugged. "Afraid to be out of the spotlight, Mags? Afraid of what'll happen now that people know he loved me, too?"

"Are you serious? You think that I'm angry because of—"

"I kept it a secret, Maggie, after he was gone. *For you.* I stood there in your shadow and let everyone console you like you were the only one who mattered. So don't try to act like I didn't think about your feelings."

"I'm supposed to feel sorry for *you* now?"

"No," she said, tipping her head to the side. "And you don't have to feel sorry for Joey, either."

"What the hell is that supposed to mean?"

"Remember that night at your house? Before the funeral, when you told Tanna and me how guilty you felt that he was still a virgin? Well…" Shannon said, her lips curling up in a little smile.

That's all it took.

One simple string of words.

Our friendship, the one we'd taken a lifetime to form, it vanished into nothing during the exhalation of a single breath.

"Shannon!" Adam stepped into our circle, placing his

hands on my shoulders and squeezing tight. "That is enough!"

"Adam, get the hell off me," I said, trying to pull free as he twisted me towards him. I jerked sideways, but it did nothing. His grip was solid, and I wasn't getting away.

"Maggie, it's time to leave." Adam's voice was firm, forceful. But there was something else there, too. An undercurrent of fear that swelled into every syllable. Fear that, at first, didn't seem to make any sense at all. Until I realized the one thing that had been missing since I first confronted Shannon. Surprise.

It clicked into place when I looked into his eyes, the echo of his voice tumbling through my mind, crashing through the different levels of my awareness until I understood without question. "Oh, my God," I said. "You and Joey were fighting about *this*, weren't you? You knew everything this whole time?"

"Maggie, you have to let me explain."

I shook my head. "You've had plenty of time to do that, Adam."

"I couldn't just—"

"Adam, I don't want to listen to one thing that you have to say."

And that's when they started. With a triple bang, the first of the fireworks splashed into the sky, painting all of us a sparkling red, white, and blue.

All the energy that had been driving me suddenly drained away. I felt deflated, like someone had sucked the life out of me. And I had to sit down.

Right.

Then.

Right.

There.

I tucked my face into my hands and scrunched my eyes so tight I thought I might blink away the entire world.

But when I opened them, the world was still there.

I knew because of the feet circled around us.

The fireworks' erratic drumbeat in my chest, Adam's hand rubbing my back, his voice whispering in my ear, "Please, just talk to me Maggie. Please listen to what I have to say."

The lip gloss and purple pen and key chain that I'd dumped from Shannon's purse.

And the bracelet. Perched on a little tuft of grass.

The band was a thin leather strap.

I knew without thinking that it had once been tied around Joey's wrist.

Moved with him, sliding up and down with the swing of his arm.

And the three turquoise-coloured glass beads strung right in the centre.

The sun had once played with those beads, like the flash

from the fireworks did now, glistening off their smooth sides, spilling out to tint the world a bright shade of blue.

"Oh, Shannon." I pressed one hand into the cool grass, the earth spinning beneath me, and reached out with the other. "You didn't."

Then I had it. Laced between my fingers. Sending waves of memories through my already tormented mind.

Dash. Crash. Splash.

18 then suddenly I stopped

"WE'RE GONNA GO ON THREE," Joey said. "You ready?"

I shook my head. "No."

"You trust me?"

I looked at him then, took in his freckled nose, the wisps of damp hair clinging to his forehead, the way his smile always tilted to the left.

I nodded. "I trust you."

He squeezed my hand again. "Everything's gonna be fine."

I ran my thumb up the inside of his wrist, feeling his blood, his life, pulsing through his body.

"One."

The cool shock of those glass beads zapped my skin like I'd been electrocuted.

"Two."

What was it about those beads?

"Three!"

Running.

We were running.

Almost there.

But the thunder of my feet crashed through something in my consciousness.

And I knew.

Those beads, they were Shannon's.

A vision flashed into my mind – the dreamcatcher her grandmother had given her when she was little, broken, on the floor of her room, Tanna kneeling down, apologizing, while Rihanna's voice filled the air around us. Shannon plucking the beads from the spiralled web, stringing them on a necklace that she would wear only for special occasions.

And another flash – school-enforced, ninth-grade dance, when Joey chose Shannon for the final song, a waltz, and I'd been so jealous I thought I might burst. Until Adam stepped up to me, his eyes intense, hand extended, and asked if he could have the honour of one single dance. I'd accepted, trailing through the room with his arms tight around me, but I'd kept track of Joey and Shannon. It was easy, the way those beads caught the light from the chandelier and threw shimmering bubbles all through the room.

Those beads, she thought they were protective. Sacred.

No one was supposed to touch those beads but Shannon.

Ever.

Yet there they were, threaded on the leather strap that was tied around my boyfriend's wrist.

My momentum slowed, my arm tugging Joey's back.

His hand held tight. Pulled me on.

We were only a metre from the edge of the cliff.

And then, in a quick succession of broken images, I remembered. Her hairslide in his console, lying there like it had been flung aside in a rushed moment. His shirt balled up on her bedroom floor, and the flimsy excuse she'd given for it being there. The mix CD she burned for him for Christmas that I wasn't supposed to see. The times I'd smelled a hint of her perfume when she was nowhere near us. How their hands always lingered when they passed a bottle we were sharing. How, when we were all together and I was watching Joey, he was usually watching her. And how she was always watching me, a strange flicker of anger in her eyes.

It was like I hit an invisible wall, one that did not exist for Joey.

I had been so close to flying.

Then suddenly – I stopped.

Dug my feet into the dusty ground.

Yanked my hand from his.

And. Refused. To. Go. On.

He kept moving, though, slower, twisting back to face me, a question in his eyes.

"You and Shannon?" I asked breathlessly.

He tried to stop then, waved his arms in the air to catch his balance, the glass beads on the leather string clicking together.

"Mags, let me exp—"

And that's all I got from him. His shoulders pulled him backwards. There was too much momentum for him to stop. So he tried to twist forwards again, but the movement just tripped him up, angled him for more of a dive than a jump.

The last thing I remember of Joey alive was the fear in his eyes, their electric blue sparking like embers in a raging fire. There was regret there, too.

I understood the fear. He knew. Maybe not that he was going to die. But he knew he was in major trouble. With me. With the ledge. With the water sparkling below him.

But the regret. That's what I'd like to ask him about.

If I had one more moment with Joey, I'd ask what part of it all he regretted most in that last moment of his life. Was it lying to me? Crushing me into nothing? Or did it have more to do with the part where he'd been caught?

"EVER SINCE I FIGURED OUT they went behind my back, I've had this sick feeling in my stomach," I said as I weaved my way through the crowd at Gertie's Dairy Farm, a cone with a single scoop of mint chocolate chip in one hand, a wad of napkins in the other. "It's like I'm one second from puking all the time now."

"I still can't believe it," Tanna said from beside me. "Joey and Shannon. It's just *weird*."

"He had to feel awful," Pete said. He was right behind me, his guitar pressed between us as we made our way to the side door of the huge shop, which was packed wall-to-wall with people out for a country drive and afternoon on the farm.

"Not awful enough." I stepped on someone's foot, and when I turned to apologize was elbowed in my side, so I gave up. "And Shannon – keeping everything to herself after he died – she didn't feel a bit of remorse."

Pete pressed his lips together, silent as we separated from the main crowd.

"As twisted as it is, I think she was trying to protect you," Tanna said through a bite of her strawberry ice cream and waffle cone.

"Like Adam?" I asked with a snort. "Don't even get me started on him."

"Maggie," Pete said, "you have to understand—"

"No. I don't. Adam's worse than both of them. At least they had a reason to keep their twisted little secret."

I stopped to toss my gum in the trash can by the door to the side yard, which was peppered with picnic tables and old tractors for kids to climb on. Without thinking, my eyes grazed the cork board posted on the wall. It was supposed to hold seven pictures of Gertie's most daring patrons, who had taken on and conquered the Big Dipper Challenge. But now there were only six. In place of the seventh photograph, marking its former existence, was a dark square of cork board, the edges surrounding it faded by sunlight and age. My feet stopped, shoes planted to the sticky, pink tile floor.

I stood there, staring at the board, trying to remember every detail of that day from the previous summer. How Joey had accepted the challenge on a whim. How he'd let each of us pick two flavours for his ten-dipper sundae. How, when he held his stomach with a pained face, we'd all cheered him on, telling him to keep going.

"Shannon was sitting right next to him," I said, shaking my head.

"Maggie, what are you talking about?" Pete's face creased into that worried-about-Maggie look that was starting to make me feel crazy.

"The picture from Joey's Big Dipper Challenge," I said, pointing up at the empty space. "It's gone."

Tanna glanced over my head and sighed. "Wonder who did that?" she said, taking another bite of her ice-cream cone.

"His other girlfriend, maybe?" I asked sarcastically. "She was sitting right next to him that day. I remember her ring, glinting in the sunlight from the front window, as she handed him those tiny plastic cups of water."

Pete pushed the door open and Tanna and I followed him out into the bright light of another humid July day. In an instant, I felt like I'd been sucked away from the present, taken back to so many moments from the past in one burst of thought. I saw him everywhere. Joey feeding the goats a handful of pellets from the dispenser. Joey balancing on the top of the wooden fence to the pigs' pen. Joey leaning up against the silo, standing in the open door to the cow barn, leaping onto a tractor. Joey. Joey. Joey. How could he be everywhere and nowhere at the same time? How long would the realization continue to stab into me? And then, just as quickly, be followed by the slicing thought of Joey and Shannon together?

"Should we sit here?" Tanna asked. "Or do you want to

walk out to the trails?"

I was about to say that I wanted to get away from the crowd, to sit in a clearing deep in the woods while Pete played us a few songs, to simply hang out and not talk about all the stuff that hurt so much. But that's when we heard him. I knew we all did, because Pete's and Tanna's eyes looked as sad as I felt.

I looked over Pete's shoulder and found him, Joey's brother, along with several of his friends, pouring out the side door of Gertie's, ice-cream cones in hand.

"It's Rylan," I said softly. "Just Rylan."

The group walked right past us, over to the main tractor. From the corner of my eye, I saw a few of them climb the large front wheels to sit right on top of the worn tread, while three others fought for the driver's seat and steering wheel. But not Rylan. He'd stopped just a few steps short of Pete and Tanna and me. He was just staring. Like there was something important he wanted to say.

"Ry," I said. "How are you?"

Rylan shrugged and licked the top of his ice cream, moving a few steps closer. "Pretty sucky."

"Yeah," I said. "Me, too."

"We had people in town for the Fourth last weekend, relatives all up in my face. People crying, and sniffling, and snotting. They try to hide it. Take me out to do some random thing, but that only helps for a little while."

"Yeah." I moved my ice-cream cone from one hand to the other, feeling like one taste would make me sick. "Nothing helps for very long, does it?"

Rylan looked at me, his eyes creasing. "You're probably one of the only people who really gets it."

I sighed. "I don't know if that's true."

Rylan's mouth twitched. "I heard about what happened at Shannon's. I don't have a clue what I'm supposed to say." Rylan's eyes flicked to Pete and Tanna, then back to me.

"I don't think there's anything you can say."

"No. Probably not." Rylan shook his head. "He could be a real ass sometimes, that's for sure."

"Yeah," I said. "But the hard part is that he could also be pretty perfect."

Rylan moved closer, his eyes glinting in the sunlight, so much like Joey's that it hurt me in a deep place I hadn't even known existed. "My mom knows, too. She wants to talk to you, Maggie."

I closed my eyes, thinking of Shannon's accusations and how Mrs. Walther would have so many more questions now. "I don't think I'm ready for that yet."

"But you'll call her? When you are ready?"

"Sure," I forced out. "I'll call soon."

"Good," Rylan said. "I'll see you guys later."

I watched as Rylan ran towards his friends and the tractor, taking a giant leap and scrambling up to the top of the right front tire. I looked down, realizing both my hands were empty. My ice-cream cone lay splattered at my feet, a soupy mess. The wind tossed all the napkins I'd yanked from the dispenser, twirling them around in lazy circles.

"Maggie, are you okay?" Tanna asked.

"No," I said, thinking of facing Joey's mother. "What if she has the same questions Shannon does? What if she blames me for something? I don't know if I can—"

"Maggie, stop. Mrs. Walther wouldn't think that way. And Shannon, she doesn't, either. Not really."

"Yeah," Pete said. "Shan's just trying to cope, like we all are, and doing a pretty shitty job at it."

Tanna grabbed my hand then and pulled me away from the crowd, across the field of grazing cows, their crooning twining around the rays of sunlight that pierced the air. Through the back gate with the crooked door that only latched if you made it. Into the woods that stretched forever and ever, eventually dumping you out on the cliff top where everything had begun.

Or was that where it had ended?

I was no longer sure.

"You have to ignore it," Pete said, his fingers dancing across the guitar resting in his lap.

"Which *it*?" I asked, leaning back against the rough bark of a tree, staring through the clearing and towards the narrow trail nearby. I wanted to run to the end of the world. Jump off. And free-fall for the rest of time.

"The stuff with Joey and Shannon. All the lies. Focusing so much on all that is going to make everything worse."

"You make it sound so easy," I said with a snort.

"I don't mean to be like that," Pete said. "But you have to figure out a way to deal."

"I keep thinking that it couldn't have gone on for too much longer," Tanna said. "With everything you're finding out, I think it was about to all blow up in his face. But he died and left it all behind for you to untangle."

"I have to do this right." I clawed at my chest, wanting to rip away the anger. "If I don't, I might never get rid of this feeling."

"It's gonna hurt," Tanna said. "There's no way around it. You gotta find a way to go straight through the pain and get yourself to the other side."

"You sound like my shrink," I said with a chuckle. "She'd totally agree. The thing is, I was starting to handle Joey's death okay. I mean, as okay as I could. But this is way worse, because this kills him in a different way. The Joey I thought I knew, that Joey never existed, did he?"

Pete shrugged. "The Joey you loved, he was *real*, Mags. Don't let his thing with Shannon take that away. You have to figure out how to separate everything if you're gonna make it through this."

"How the hell am I supposed to separate anything at this point?"

"Maybe spend some time remembering special stuff you did, just the two of you." Pete strummed the guitar, spilling a chord out into the rays of sunlight trickling down through the leaves.

"Don't let this new person take his place in your mind, Maggie," Tanna said. "Joey would hate that."

"I keep wondering how he would feel," I said. "Wondering what he would say. You know, if he were here and he could."

"Me, too," Pete said. "And every time I think about him and you, and the whole thing with Shannon, this one song pops into my head."

"Oh, yeah?" I asked.

"Yup. It's kinda cheesy, but I feel like he's sending it to me. Just for you." Another chord poured from the guitar and tripped through the trees. "I can play it if you want."

"Yeah," I said, scooting away from the tree and lying on the grass, looking through the leaves at the too blue sky. "That would be nice."

As soon as Pete started, I knew the song – Nickelback's "Far Away". My eyes filled with tears as the lyrics streamed into my mind, and I wanted to tell Pete how perfect the song was. But I wasn't so sure I could get the words out. Tears slipped down the sides of my face, and I tried to swipe them away, but they kept coming, so I let them fall.

I felt so sad and alone, even with Tanna lying close by, even as Pete started humming the tune. I wondered if Joey had really loved me, if he missed me from wherever he was. He felt so far away, I held my breath and tried to remember something that would bring him back. Something that would make me feel all the right things instead of everything that was so very wrong.

As Pete hit the chorus and Tanna started singing the words, a ribbon of wind flowed through the treetops, pulling a leaf from its hold on a high branch. The waxy green teardrop tumbled and flipped towards me in slow motion. And that's all it took to bring him back.

My Joey.

We were almost two years in the past, lying on a blanket in the gorge, looking up at the trees, which were dressed in fancy reds, yellows, oranges and browns. We didn't talk or laugh or even kiss. We just lay there, my head on his chest, looking up-up-up the bodies of all those towering trees. They were almost silent, but when I listened really closely, I could hear them whispering reassurances into the air around us, speaking of trust and daring, of just letting go.

The amazing thing was when they did it, when those leaves simply freed themselves. Joey and I, we just watched as the reds, the yellows, the oranges and the browns released their grips from the tangled arms of those trees. We watched, and they took flight in a spiralling, swooshing ride that left me breathless.

20 surprises in the strangest moments

"Maggie, we called you in today because we'd like to know if you've remembered anything else from the day Joey died." Detective Wallace's moustache twitched around his words. His slender hands were perched on top of the same conference table from that terrible Saturday when I'd lost Joey for ever. I wondered how many questions had been hurled across its faux wood surface over the years.

"My client is still in therapy," Mr. Fontane said from his seat beside my father, who had insisted that I sit between him and my mother when we took our places around the table. "She is working with Dr. Guest to recall those lost memories. We have already told you that we'll offer anything of significance as soon as we can."

"Dr. Guest's original reports suggest that Maggie may be suffering from either post-traumatic stress disorder or dissociative amnesia, both of which may leave her unable to access her lost memories. With all due respect, our investigation can't just sit idle, waiting to discover the outcome of her therapy." Detective Meyer pressed his thick lips together.

"We have some new information," Detective Wallace said. "And we'd like to hear Maggie's side of the story."

Not ready to face whatever they were about to throw my way, I tried to sink back into my chair without being obvious. Detective Meyer, however, caught me and stared into my eyes. I tried to hold my head up, but the shaking in my hands had travelled up my arms and taken over most of my body. I felt like I had the shivers, but I was hot and a little sweaty. I looked at my lawyer, trying to focus everything on him, trying to drown out the detectives.

Mr. Fontane clicked his tongue on the top of his mouth. His hair was combed back tightly, stiffened by some kind of product. It looked exactly the same as it had the day Joey died, when I'd met with him for the first time. He'd sat on the recliner in our living room, asking all kinds of questions. Questions that I could not even think about answering, not even now that I did remember.

"What type of new information?" my mother asked from her seat beside me.

"Apparently, there was a party on the Fourth of July during which Maggie and another young woman had a confrontation." The words spilled out of Detective Meyer's mouth in a way that made me sure he had rehearsed them.

"Shannon," I said with a sigh. "She talked to you?" But then I wondered if it had been someone else. Like Joey's parents. That thought brought some of the old panic back, the nervous feeling of guilt that had taken over the day Joey died.

"We can't divulge that information." Detective Meyer sat back in his chair, placing both of his hands on his large belly. "What we can share is that while we had been ready to close the investigation, our final interviews raised some new questions."

I wanted to stand up and scream at the detectives. Scream so loud I melted the skin right off their smug faces, so hard I'd blast Shannon right off of this miserable earth, so long I might be able to bring Joey back so that he would have to face what he'd done.

"We've learned that there may have been some kind of altercation between you and Joey before the accident. The individual we spoke with thinks something may have happened on top of the cliff that caused Joey to fall to his death." Detective Meyer stared at me, waiting for any reaction. "Something between the two of you."

"Did this person tell you anything about that supposed altercation?" Mr. Fontane asked.

Detective Meyer clasped his hands. "We'd like to hear Maggie's side of this story."

I looked at Mr. Fontane, wondering if it was time for me

to speak. He stared down at the papers in front of him. "I've advised Maggie not to say anything today. I think it's best to have her therapist's approval before we proceed."

Detective Wallace cleared his throat. "We'd really love to settle this matter."

"So would we," Mr. Fontane replied. "But not at any risk to Maggie's well-being. She has been struggling to deal with the events that occurred on Memorial Day weekend, and Dr. Guest has advised her parents and me that we should not push her for any answers."

That part made me feel guilty. I hadn't told anyone about the memories that had flooded me on the Fourth of July. As backwards as it seemed, Adam was the only person I wanted to talk to about the cliff top. Since he'd been up there with me after everything happened, I felt like he would understand. But I couldn't get past my anger. All I could think was that he'd known everything and kept it from me, and I didn't know if I could ever face him again. So I'd held on to Joey's last moments for an entire week, keeping the secret my own, wondering how, and when, and if I would ever share it with anyone else.

The air conditioning kicked on with a *whir*, covering my arms in goosebumps.

"You were about to close the investigation?" my father asked. "Does that mean you have the results from the autopsy?"

Detective Meyer nodded his head. "We do."

"And if you were going to close the investigation, that means that you didn't find anything to indicate foul play." Mr. Fontane looked from one detective to the other.

"That is correct," Detective Wallace said with a curt nod.

"To be frank," Mr. Fontane said, sweeping his papers into a stack and leaning down for the leather briefcase that was propped against the leg of his chair, "I'm not exactly sure what we're doing here."

"I'm with you," my father said, his words tight. "You're keeping an investigation open because a girl who could be holding some kind of grudge against my daughter made some wild accusation?"

"We have not revealed the source of our informa—"

"We all know who it was." My father's voice rang through the room, shaking with anger. I was surprised by his insistence, by the way his hands had balled into fists, by how red his neck and cheeks had turned. But most surprising of all was how my mother just sat there, doing nothing to get him under control. Not that he lost it often, but when he came close, she was always the first person to reign him in. "If you look into Shannon's relationship with Joey, you'll find that she's not exactly known for her honesty."

"Regardless, *suspicion* is a strong word, Mr. Reynolds," Detective Meyer said, his belly rising with the intake of one deep breath.

"We'd simply like to know if there was any type of conflict between Maggie and Joey on the day of his death." Detective Wallace looked right at me.

"I've read the transcript from the first time you questioned my client," Mr. Fontane said. "She's already stated that Joey did not seem to be in conflict with anyone on the day of his death. Beyond that, she has complied with every one of your instructions." Mr. Fontane stood then, his briefcase thwapping against his leg.

"She most certainly has," my mother said, standing and placing a hand on my back.

"Then," Mr. Fontane said with a shrug, "we're done here."

"Understood," Detective Wallace said.

"Yes," said Detective Meyer. "And it should also be understood that this investigation will remain open until we have all the answers we need."

My father stood and pulled my chair back. I got to my shaky feet, wondering if my facial expression or body language or the fear radiating from me would tip anyone off. If it was obvious that I had remembered exactly what had happened up there on the cliff top and was keeping it a secret in spite of everyone wanting the truth.

Because if they could read me, I was screwed. Joey's death may have been a terrible accident, but it was one that I had caused. All because I'd trusted him too much and was too afraid of letting go.

"I made your favourite," my mother said from her perch on the side of my bed. "Pot roast, carrots, potatoes…"

I flipped over to face her, yanking my earphones from my ears. "I'm not hungry."

My father stepped in from the hall, his hands tucked into the front pockets of his jeans. "You have to eat, hon."

"Not now." I couldn't imagine eating. I was sure anything I swallowed would come right back up. "My stomach," I said, curling into a ball, "it's not right."

My mother sighed. "I can only guess why. That Shannon. What was she thinking?"

I heard the anger in my mother's voice. Solid, reckless rage. I loved her for it.

"We can't worry about it right now," my father said, leaning against the footboard of my bed.

"What are you going to do, sweetie?" my mother asked, her fingers swiping loose strands of hair from my face.

"Sleep," I said, my voice croaking the word out.

"You're sure you don't want anything to eat?" my mother asked. She smiled then. "I have peanut butter pie. What about a totally unconventional peanut butter pie dinner? I can come up and eat some with you. Right here in bed." She smoothed her hand over the patches of the quilt pulled up over my legs, looking them over, seeming to wish for the simplicity of the past, thinking of all those years, of the love, and pain, and acceptance those tiny little squares represented.

I sat forwards, hating the way her eyes lit up at the prospect of me accepting something as insignificant as a piece of pie. Had the rip tide of this whole thing pulled me that far off course?

"I'm going to be okay, Mom." I patted her hand, realizing how similar our long, slender fingers were, and even the shapes of our fingernails.

My mother sucked in a breath and tears filled her eyes. "I know you are, Maggie."

"You're one tough cookie," my father said, tipping back on the heels of his shoes.

My mother and I looked at him, then each other, and laughed.

"What?" he asked, throwing his hands in the air. "You are."

His confusion made us laugh even harder. The doubled-over, almost-pee-your-pants kind of laughter that sometimes surprises you in the strangest of moments.

It felt good, breaking open like that. And it lightened

the room by about a thousand kilos. I leaned back against the headboard, propping a pillow behind me, and asked my father to go get us all a slice of pie.

When he left the room, I pointed towards the end of my bed. "Tell me about that red one. The shiny patch of satin near my right foot." I wiggled my toes, bouncing the section of quilt up and down so she'd know where to look.

My mother's fingers found the square of fabric, traced its perfectly stitched border. "That one," she said, "is from the dress I wore to my senior prom."

"No way," I said, sliding further under the covers for her story. "You have to tell me all about it."

Her voice swirled around me then, a cocoon that gave me a much-needed reprieve from everything that had happened since Memorial Day weekend. We spent the rest of the evening together, hanging out in my room, my mother telling my father and me the stories behind each and every one of those worn swatches of fabric. As I listened, losing myself in each little tale, I realized that the quilt would not have been the same, not nearly as beautiful, without the sadness. The robin's egg blue patch from a baby blanket that had belonged to my uncle who died when he was two, the purple satin ribbon found after a tornado destroyed my grandparents' first home, the black silk from the dress my grandma wore to her father's funeral – those slices of life, they were just as important as the rest.

21 independence day

IT WAS FRIDAY THE THIRTEENTH and I knew a party was going on somewhere nearby. Tanna had invited me, but I'd said there was no way I was going to chance running into Shannon, who had never missed a party in her life. I'd watched a cheesy slasher movie on the couch before coming up to my room and falling into bed, my iPod in hand, ready to scroll through my music to find something that wouldn't remind me of Joey. Or Shannon. Or Adam, for that matter. After an hour, I yanked my earphones out, frustrated that the people I was trying to forget seemed to be attached to every song in my playlist.

It was a little after eleven when the text came through.

U know I luv u, right?

Yes, I replied. *I always feel the luv, T.*

Good. Bc I'm on my way over.

No, I texted back. *I'm going 2 bed.*

U can't, came the reply. *Adam's in trouble.*

I sat up, staring at the words, a feeling of dread spreading from my chest to the rest of my body until I felt numb all over.

I'll b there in 5, Tanna added. *B ready.*

Tanna's car pulled into my driveway and squealed to a stop. The windows were down, and the first thing I noticed was the lack of music pouring from the radio. Then I saw Shannon sitting in the passenger seat, her eyes locked on mine, her face void of expression.

"What the hell is she doing here?" I asked.

"Dude," Pete said from the back seat, "we don't have time for this. Just get in the car."

"No! I'm not going anywhere with her."

"What part of *'Adam's in trouble'* did you not understand?" Tanna asked, leaning through the open driver's side window. "Get in the freaking car, Maggie. We have to find him."

I crossed my arms over my chest and took a step back. "He's been missing in one way or another since Memorial Day weekend. What's so different about tonight?"

"His mom called." Shannon said. "She's worried because he had some appointment today that he missed. And then he never went home."

"He's not answering any of her texts or calls." Tanna ran her hands along the steering wheel nervously. "And even with everything we've seen, she said he hasn't totally ignored her until tonight."

"Blowing us off is one thing," I said, my level of anxiety exploding. "But it isn't like him to make his mom worry. Especially after Joey."

"So, you coming or not?" Pete asked, leaning between the front seats like he wanted to drag me into the car. "'Cuz we gotta *move*, Mags."

"Where have you checked?" I walked around the front of the car to the passenger-side door as Shannon swung it open.

"Nowhere yet," Tanna said. "We came for you first. We were thinking we could drive around to see if we can find his car."

"If he doesn't want to be found, he won't leave his car out in the open," I said.

Shannon stumbled out of the car, her shoes clicking on the driveway, and crossed her arms over her chest. The thick scent of liquor surrounded her, and I looked down to her feet, knowing that this was not the time to confront her about what she'd told the police. But, God, I was dying to. Instead, I pulled Shannon's seat forwards, lifting one foot so I could climb into the back, and my thoughts returned to Adam.

"He's hiding, so we have to think." I pictured him, then, the moonlight streaking his hair, his feet dangling over the rushing water. Heard his voice trailing through my mind: "*One* of my hideouts." "Wait! The creek. He's got to be at the creek." I shoved away from the car and ran around the side of my house, through my backyard, and towards the trail that led to the woods.

The wind picked up, rushing through the trees above, whispering in a frantic way that made me feel like we had to hurry, like Adam needed help and we were running out of time.

As we raced deeper into the woods, I heard someone stumble behind me. Then Shannon said, "Shit, Maggie, slow down already."

That only made me go faster. When we stepped from the line of trees to the edge of the creek, I fully expected to see Adam sitting there on the rock, right where I'd found him three weeks earlier, his green eyes flashing silver in the moonlight. But there was no moon – it had hidden behind a thick batch of storm clouds that raced overhead. And there was no Adam, either. The rock sat in a deep shadow, flat and cold, and so very alone.

"He's not here." The words exploded out of me, my breathing tight and quick as I turned in a circle, hoping he'd appear in the time it took me to spin back towards his rock. But it didn't work. "I thought for sure he'd be here."

The creek rushed by, curling in little waves, competing with the sound of the wind.

"We have to think," Shannon said. "We can't just run around like freaks all night."

"I'm not a freak," I said, turning to face her.

"I didn't say *you* were a freak, Maggie. Just that—"

"Whatever," I said, rolling my eyes. "What you think hardly matters to me any more, anyway."

"Well, the police seem to feel differently," Shannon said. "Thankfully, they—"

"Holy shit!" Pete shouted, jumping between us. "It's Friday the thirteenth."

"As if you didn't already know that?" Tanna asked.

"Yeah, but, it's Friday, *July thirteenth*." Pete's eyes were frantic, hardly focused, and I wasn't sure if he was really seeing any of us.

"Right," Shannon said. "And that matters because...?"

The wind tossed Pete's dreads up in the air. "It's Independence Day."

"Oh my God," Tanna said, her voice competing with the wind. "The cliff. There was something about a tradition with you guys, right?"

"July thirteenth is the day we took our first jump. And we swore we'd do it again, every year on July thirteenth. But it has to be a night jump to count."

"Oh, God," Shannon said. "That means we have to—"

"I can't go there." I backed towards the trail, shaking my head.

Tanna grabbed my hand and stopped me. "You have to, Mags. He's been so upset, pulling away from us, all because he's been keeping this secret from *you*. You need to hear him out, to listen to his reasons."

"Tanna, I—"

"Maggie, you're the only one who's gonna get through to him right now. It has to be you."

"Bro!" Pete shouted up the side of the cliff, his hands cupped around his mouth to be sure his words reached Adam. "What are you doing up there?"

We were standing in front of the Jumping Hole, the wind twisting around our bodies, all of us looking up. Adam was at the top, standing at the edge of the cliff, dark clouds rushing across the sky behind him.

"This isn't funny," Shannon yelled.

"I'm not trying to be funny," Adam shouted. He swayed a little, back and forth. "I'm trying to celebrate my freedom!"

"He's been drinking," I said. "What the hell are we supposed to do?"

"This isn't a *we* thing," Tanna said, turning and looking at me. "This has to be you."

"You're kidding, right?"

Tanna bit her lip. Shook her head.

"You have to go up there and get him," Tanna said. "He's not going to listen to any of us. He's hating himself right now because of what happened with you."

I thought of all the messages he'd left, all the texts I'd ignored since the Fourth of July. Adam had been trying to apologize and I'd shut him out. But then I looked to the ground, the wind tossing my hair wild, my eyes tripping over to the spot where Joey had been lying the last time I was here.

"This isn't my fault!" I screamed. "I didn't do *one thing* to cause this! Why the hell should I have to go up there?" Then the tears came, falling from my eyes faster than I could swipe them away. I did not want to be crying, but everything inside me had surged forwards and pushed its way out.

"Stop being so self-absorbed," Shannon said with a sneer. "Adam is up there and he needs you. Just like you needed him the day Joey died."

"Self-absorbed?" I shouted. "Did you really just call me—"

"Yes!" The wind carried the word and whipped it into the night. "You've been at the centre of this thing from the beginning, Maggie. With your boyfriend gone and your memory gone, everyone's been tripping over themselves to make sure you're okay. I've had to watch from the sidelines. No one knew how I really felt. And now that I have a chance to share how this has affected me, all I get is people talking behind my back about what a bitch I am. What I did might not have been right, but I loved him, too, Maggie."

"You expect me to care?" I asked. "After you ran to the police and tried to convince them I had something to do with Joey's death? Give me a fucking break, Shannon."

"Guys!" Pete yelled, his face twisted with irritation. "This is *not* the time."

"Where'd he go?" Tanna asked, her head tipped back, her words frantic. "Where's Adam?"

"All clear?" The voice trickled down to us, the meaning of the words slamming into me so hard they almost knocked me down.

"No!" we all shouted at once. The thunder of our voices crashing through the gorge brought Adam back to the edge of the cliff.

"It's as clear as ever," Adam shouted, waving a finger side to side. "It's not nice to lie, you guys. You should've learned that much by now."

"Stay there," I shouted. "I'm coming up."

"Maggie," Adam called. "I have to do this."

"Just give me five minutes," I shouted. "Please."

Adam swayed with a gust of wind. Then he sat down, dangling his legs over the side of the cliff. I was relieved and scared half to death. Adam was safe for now, but I had to get myself up to that cliff top and talk him down. All without allowing my memories to pull me into a total panic.

* * *

The creek was so swollen – the Jumping Rocks were almost underwater – and I had to hop carefully from one to the next as I made my way across the bridge they created.

When I got to the other side, the trail was dark.

Black-hole dark.

"You can do this." I whispered the words to myself over and over, the reassurance stringing out into the night, trailing up into the sky to be carried away by all those rushing clouds.

Branches cracked under my feet with almost every step. Leaves rushed and spiralled in the harsh wind, restless for a place to hide. As I hiked up the trail, I wondered if the wind was trying to keep me away. It seemed angry. Strong.

But tonight, I was stronger.

"You can do this."

The cadence of the repetition calmed me. Kept my mind from what I was about to do. If I thought about it, I might stop and turn around. And that was not an option.

Adam needed me.

I stumbled on the root of a tree. Fell to the ground, my hands catching me as a loud grunt escaped my lips. My fingers dug into the moist bed of the trail, the trail I had last travelled with Joey. No, wait. That had been Adam. I couldn't believe how mixed up everything still was, even with all my memories in place.

I smelled rain, a metallic scent that told me the clouds were about to break open. I needed to hurry.

I pushed myself from the ground, finding my footing. My hands shook as I dusted them off. My legs wobbled, threatening to buckle. I wanted to stop. But I couldn't. I *had* to do this.

My hands reached out for every tree that I passed.

A thin tree with smooth, silky bark.

A gnarled tree, bumpy like an old man.

An oak. Giant. Revered.

And all of them dancing, their limbs whirling in the air, their leaves hushing and shushing my mind.

The wind picked up, twirling my hair into the sky. I grabbed the mass of waves, twisting them into a bun, my fingers sinking into the silky strands as I took my last steps towards the cliff.

He was there. Sitting alone. Just looking down.

I walked to him, past the shrine of dead flowers that our classmates had brought here after Joey's death, trying not to think about why they were there, snapping in the wind, and put a hand on his shoulder. "Adam, what's this about?"

"I don't know any more, Maggie." He ducked his head. Shook it from side to side.

I wanted to sit next to him, knew it was the best thing to get him out of this place, but I couldn't. So I just stood there, my hair whipping into my eyes, wondering what the hell I was supposed to say.

"It's my fault," Adam said. "Everything with Joey."

I sighed. Squeezed his shoulder and let my hand fall away. "Nothing's your fault, Adam."

"It is, though. If I'd just told you, none of us would have been here. You and Joey wouldn't have been on top of this stupid cliff, and he wouldn't have fallen." Adam's words slurred together. He was in worse shape than I'd thought.

"Adam, there's stuff you don't know. Stuff that makes this my fault, too."

Adam looked back at me, his eyes tight. "What are you talking about?"

I shook my head. "I can't," I said, my words choking in my throat as I did everything I could to look into Adam's eyes and at nothing else. Not the treetops that had surrounded Joey and me right before the beads made me understand his betrayal. Not the feeling of my hand yanking out of his. Not the way his eyes had swelled with fear, and sadness, and regret as he lost his balance and pitched over the edge of the cliff.

"Maybe you can't tell me," Adam said. "But I should, shouldn't I? Just like you wanted me to the day of the funeral. When you tried to make that deal where we'd share everything. I need to tell you. All the shit I knew, and how I found out. You deserve to know, Mags."

I stepped back as he spoke. One step. Two. Three. Because I didn't want to know. All the details would slice me open again, and I couldn't face that. Especially not standing up there on that cliff top.

"No!" I said. "I'm not ready. Not for all of that."

Adam closed his eyes, burying his face in his hands. "I can't seem to get anything right any more."

"You can," I said. "I want to know. Just not right now. Right now, all I want is for you to stand up and walk down the trail with me. I want you safe, Adam."

"But I won't be safe, Maggie. I'm all messed up inside. Besides, tonight, I'm supposed to jump. It was an oath of our friendship." He smiled then, this thin smile that was so sad.

"Adam, you can honour Joey in a different way. Please. Don't jump off this cliff and leave me standing here all by myself. I can't face that again."

It was then that it seemed to register in Adam's brain. Where he was. Where he'd brought me. The recognition passed across his face like one of the bloated clouds that raced above us.

"Oh, Jesus, Maggie, I—"

"Adam, it's okay. Please, just—"

"So sorry. I can't believe I'm such an asshole." Adam twisted sideways, placing a hand on the dusty ground. He pulled his legs up and swung them around, skidding his feet along the little biting rocks that carpeted the earth.

And then he stood.

Way too fast with all the alcohol, and wind, and emotion.

He started to sway, his arms shooting from his sides, sweeping up and then down.

I didn't have time to think.

All I could do in the moment was react.

My feet rushed me forwards – one step, two, three – and my arms snapped forwards, my fingers gripping the front of his shirt. I yanked him into me before I took one single breath. Wrapped my arms around his waist as he fell against my body, his breath hot on my neck.

"Please don't hate me, Maggie." Adam's voice cut out on him, turning into a croaky cry. His shoulders shook, and he tipped his forehead onto mine, his eyes squeezed tight. As he slipped his face into the curve my neck, I sucked in deep, even breaths to keep myself under control.

Then the rain started, cool drops that made my skin tingle. I focused on each one, hoping they had the power to wash away everything, so we could just start over again.

I smoothed the loose strands of Adam's hair and he started to quiet down. His tears spilled down my skin, under the neck of my shirt, and into the places that only Joey had explored.

Adam pulled away slowly, looking right in my eyes. He cupped my face in his hands and shook his head. "I am so sorry, Maggie. For everything."

I nodded, feeling his fingers brush the skin of my jawline. He hesitated for a moment, his eyes focused on mine.

"I know you are." I sucked in a shaky breath, holding on to him tight. I wouldn't let him go until we were standing at the bottom of that trail, until we'd crossed over the Jumping Rocks and were safely on the other side. "And I could never hate you."

"You know we have to talk, right?" Adam raised his eyebrows. The rain was falling harder now, dripping down his face and onto the tangle of our arms and hands.

I nodded.

"I'm here. When you're ready, you just let me know."

I nodded again, because I wasn't sure if I could speak.

Adam ran a hand through his hair, pulling his fringe out of his eyes, and looked around, raindrops falling from his chin and nose. It's like he was looking for Joey, like he wanted to say one last goodbye. But we'd lost that chance. That moment had passed.

I wrapped an arm around Adam's waist and tugged him towards the trail head. He slung his arm over my shoulders, moving slowly, stumbling every few steps. His body was warm, solid, and so very alive. And I'd never been so thankful for anything in my entire life.

22 all the pieces

"IT'S OKAY, MAGGIE," DR. GUEST said in her most gentle tone. "You can tell me."

So I did. I let it all surge from deep within my chest, an angry storm breaking me open.

Dr. Guest sat still, taking it all in without moving.

When I was finished, I looked down, afraid of the disappointment I might see in her eyes.

"You're blaming yourself, aren't you?" Dr. Guest asked. "For what happened on Memorial Day weekend?"

"How can I not? He died because of me."

"Joey's death was a terrible accident, Maggie. It, however, was not your fault." Dr. Guest raised her eyebrows, waiting for her words to sink in.

"If I'd just kept running. If I'd jumped with him. If—"

"You can 'if' yourself to death – *if* you want – but I'd advise against it." Dr. Guest crossed one leg over the other and leaned back in her chair. "You have enough to sort through without simultaneously playing out every other possible outcome."

I nodded. Because I'd already thought of that. "What am I supposed to do now?"

"What do you think?"

"I hate when you do that," I said. "Turn a question back on me."

"Usually you have the right answers. I just encourage you to dig deep enough to reach them."

"I'm thinking I'll just ignore it. Pretend I still forget for the rest of my life. I haven't told anyone yet." I looked at her, narrowed my eyes. "Everything I say to you is confidential, right? So it's, like, against the law for you to tell?"

Dr. Guest smiled. "What do you suspect might happen if you try to ignore all of this? It's pretty big."

"Ignoring it might make it go away."

"What if it makes everything worse?"

I clasped my hands together, folding them in my lap. I thought of walking into school in the fall for my senior year with the grey cloud of Joey's death, all his lies, and Shannon's betrayal hanging over me. I knew it would suffocate me. Eventually.

"Maybe you should just tell everyone the truth." Dr. Guest threw her hands up in the air, like she'd just had some epiphany.

"The truth?" I asked. "As in, the *whole* truth?"

Dr. Guest shrugged. "It's just an idea. Sounds like there are already an awful lot of secrets."

"If I let everything out, if everyone knows the truth, people will hate me. It's *my* fault Joey died."

"Some people might be angry. But when they hear the entire story, I suspect most people will support you. And that support might just help you learn to stop blaming yourself, Maggie."

I shook my head. "You don't understand. Joey was this legend at our school. Bigger than all of us put together. Everyone knew him. And everyone loved him."

"Do you still wonder if anyone *really* knew him?"

I thought about that. Just a few months ago I thought I'd known Joey. All of him. But I'd been wrong. "Maybe Shannon did," I said, the words twisting around my heart and pulling tight.

Dr. Guest nodded her head, a serious look crossing over her face. "Then maybe she's the best place to start."

"Shannon?" I shook my head. "No way. I can't ever speak to her again."

"It might be worth a shot, Maggie. You still have your senior year to get through. She's been like a sister to you almost your entire life."

"No. I can't."

"Think about it," Dr. Guest said. "I'm not suggesting

that you try to rebuild your entire friendship. Just that you go to her and deal with the feelings that are making things so messy right now. Show her that you can face everything that's happened. Free yourself from this prison Joey and Shannon built around you."

I imagined myself walking into Shannon's bedroom. Sitting on her bed, where I'd slept so many nights. Where Joey may have slept…with her. I visualized opening my mouth to speak. But all I could hear was me telling her off.

"What about Adam?" Dr. Guest said. "Have you talked to him since the night you found him on the cliff top?"

I shook my head.

"That's another thing you'll have to figure out."

"This is one hot mess."

Dr. Guest chuckled. "It might feel like that, Maggie. But actually, you're doing very well – making monumental progress with your memories and ability to share. If you think about how you want it all to look in the end, if you take the right steps to get there, you might actually find yourself feeling happy again."

I snorted. "Doubtful."

"You have all the pieces in your hands," Dr. Guest said. "You just have to decide where to put them."

I thought about that, playing with the idea throughout the rest of our session. I knew I had all the pieces, I could feel the different textures sliding in my hands. The problem was, most of them were jagged edged, slicing into me when I tried to figure out how to order them, how to stitch them back together. So I envisioned throwing them all up in the air, running, and hiding from them for ever.

23 the very centre of our lives

I WASN'T GOING TO DO IT.

Not.

Ever.

But when I left Dr. Guest's office, new thoughts started pinging around in my head. If I spilled all my secrets, maybe Shannon would do the same. If I told her the one thing she needed to know, maybe she would tell me the thousand things I wished I could ignore. As much as I didn't want to hear about her and Joey, I knew ignoring them wasn't going to fix anything. Tanna had been right: the only way to the other side of this was straight through. And as much as I hated to admit it, I needed Shannon to help me get there.

It took a few days, thinking of how I would say all that I needed to. How I'd escape if she leaped towards me, assaulting me with the blame that I was trying to ease from my mind. Thinking of the insults I'd hurl if she attacked me with those words.

But even with two days of planning, I hadn't been able to prepare myself for her reaction when I shared the story of what had actually happened on top of the cliff.

Instead of rage-inspired threats, Shannon crumpled into a ball on the floor of her bedroom and stared at a patch of sunny carpet near her right foot.

"Shannon," I said. "Are you okay?"

I looked down at her, the way she'd started rocking slowly back and forth, her arms wrapped around her knees.

"It was the bracelet?" Shannon asked. "That's what did it?"

I nodded. "That's when everything clicked into place."

"It worked, then." Shannon looked up at me with tears dripping from eyes. "I *wanted* you to know."

I sat next to Shannon on the floor, leaning against the side of her bed, oddly numb in the moment of my big revelation.

"I left clues all over the place," she said. "My hairslide. His shirt. A pack of gum. My favourite pen. But you never figured it out. I had to think of something that I *knew* would work."

"Your random clues were kind of normal, though. We all have each other's stuff, Shan." I looked at the carpet, wanting to close my eyes and squeeze everything out. But I couldn't. Not any more. "Why didn't you just tell me?"

"Joey would have killed me. He wanted it to end

naturally between the two of you so it wouldn't seem so wrong when we ended up together. But then he kept dragging things out. Playing these games that made me think he was about to end it with you. Then we'd all hang out, and I'd hear some story about the great night the two of you'd had alone. I was so confused. And getting really angry."

"When did Adam find out?" I asked.

Shannon's eyes squinted tight. "I honestly don't know. I think he suspected for a while, but he wasn't sure. Joey kept stuff from me because he didn't want me to freak – and I *was* freaked about what we were doing to you – but I just had all these feelings and I didn't know what to do with…"

"Spare me, okay?" I said.

"Right." Shannon swiped her palm across her cheeks, wiping away her tears. "I know Adam was pissed off, Maggie, and he wanted Joey to tell you. Then Adam threatened to tell you himself, the night of Dutton's party."

"So that's what the fight was about?"

"Yeah." Shannon sighed. "I wanted you to know, too. But I didn't know how to tell you. I wasn't sure I could – so I just didn't."

"I don't understand the bracelet," I said. "If you knew Joey was going to tell me, why give him that bracelet to wear? It's like a slap in my face."

Shannon squeezed her eyes. Tight. "He broke up with me. The night of Dutton's party." Shannon sucked in a deep breath. "He said he'd been wrong. That he loved you, not me. He wanted it to be over between us before he told you."

"That's...crazy."

"I know." Shannon laughed, this choked sound that resembled a cry. "Joey was crazy. But I was, too. Crazy pissed off. He'd always been yours, and I thought it was time he was mine. So when he dropped me off that morning, I told him to wait. That if it was over, I wanted him to have something to remember me by. I ran inside and grabbed my necklace and tied it around his wrist before he left."

"Because you knew I'd figure everything out if I saw those beads."

Shannon nodded. "I'm sorry. I was just so...wrecked."

"And you wanted me to be wrecked, too?"

"Kind of. God, I know that's awful, but I couldn't believe, after all that time, he was choosing you. That I was so monumentally stupid to think he ever would have chosen me."

"It wasn't so stupid. You two had been together for a long time."

"Yeah. In hiding. Because I wasn't good enough to be seen with in public."

"I'm sure it wasn't about that," I said. "Sounds like, in his twisted mind, he just wanted to keep us all together."

"And look how it ended. A complete disaster."

I could not believe that we were sitting there just talking this whole thing over like it was nothing. But then I thought of all the emotion that had swelled up since Joey's death, the explosive night on the Fourth of July, how long we had been friends, and this moment somehow seemed to fit. It was the only way for us both to get what we needed.

"Mrs. Walther was furious when she found out." Shannon caved into herself as she said the words.

"You talked to Joey's mom?"

"Yeah. After the Fourth of July, when Rylan told her about me and Joey, she called and asked me to go over there. She'd heard about me going to the cops, and let's just say she was more than a little pissed off."

"I was, too," I said, thankful that Mrs. Walther wasn't angry at me, knowing that I needed to go see her soon. "Still am."

"I'm sorry," Shannon said. "I shouldn't have gone to the police. It was stupid, but I know everything now, so I can fix it."

"I don't know if it can be fixed," I said. But I didn't mean the stuff with the cops. I meant everything else – Joey's death, my memories of him, the lifelong friendship we all had shared. The important stuff had been ruined, and there was no way to get it back.

"Will we ever be friends again?" Shannon asked.

I shrugged. Thinking about it made me feel *all* that I had lost. Joey's death should have brought all of us closer together. Instead, it had ripped us apart.

"When I tied my necklace around Joey's wrist, making it into a bracelet for him, I didn't care about my friendship with you. I just wanted to shove the big secret out in the open. But now I hate myself for being so focused on the wrong thing. And I can see that this mess isn't just Joey's. It's mine, too. Problem is, I'm the only one left to clean it up."

"We can help each other, you know," I said.

"How?" Shannon asked.

"The cops. They still have lots of questions. I could maybe go to the station with you to tell them everything."

"The part where everything is *my* fault, you mean?" Shannon dipped her face into her knees. "If I hadn't given him that stupid bracelet, he'd be alive right now, Maggie."

"Shannon," I said, "I've been blaming myself in one way or another since the day he died. But the thing is, while we all played a part in what happened, it was an accident."

Shannon looked up at me, tears streaking her face. "Yeah," she said. "Maybe you're right."

"Does that mean you'll go talk to the detectives with me?"

I stood then, holding my hand out for Shannon to grab. She looked at me, her cheeks glistening with fresh tears, and grabbed on tight, letting me pull her up.

"Here," I said, shoving my hand into the pocket of my shorts and pulling Joey's bracelet out into the rays of sunlight streaming through Shannon's bedroom windows. The light winked off the smooth surface of the glass beads, splashing brilliant blue puddles into the space between us. "This is yours."

"Maggie, I—"

"Shannon. I don't want it."

Shannon didn't say another word as she tugged the leather strap from my fingers and turned, walking to her dresser, arm outstretched towards the velvet-lined box that had housed those turquoise beads for so many years. When she pulled the top off, I saw it buried snuggly within. The picture that had been taken the previous summer at Gertie's Dairy Farm. The one where all of us had gathered around Joey, arms raised in celebration of his defeating the Ten-Dipper Challenge, mouths spread in wide, carefree smiles. I realized as I stood there in the middle of Shannon's sunny bedroom that Joey had positioned himself right where he thought he belonged – in the very centre of all of our lives.

24 back to the beginning

"I LIKE THIS HIDING SPOT so much better than the other one,"
I said as I stepped from the trail, walking to the rock where
Adam was standing and looking down at the water. I kicked
my shoes off and sat back on the cool rock beneath us,
listening to the trickle of the creek as the sun slowly dipped
behind the thick of trees just off to our west.

Adam sat next to me, the movement stirring the air
enough that I smelled him – the soapy, sweaty, summery
scent making my vision swim. Adam tilted his head
towards me, his face glowing in the sugary pink tint of the
sky.

"I figured you'd never speak to me again," Adam said.
"After the cliff top last weekend."

"You're lucky," I said.

"I know I am."

We were silent for a while, the good kind of silent you
can only have with a close friend. I sat there next to him,
breathing in the scent of the summer, listening to the call

of the crickets, a lazy breeze blowing through my hair.

"You ready to tell me what happened at Shannon's house on the Fourth of July?" Adam asked, breaking the stillness that had settled around us.

I shrugged. "You were there."

"I'm not talking about the stuff I could see. You went into that strange daze again, just like the day of Joey's accident. Totally freaked me out. I'd appreciate it if you'd stop doing that." He poked me in the side with his elbow.

"Yeah. I'll try." I shoved my hand into the pocket of my shorts, strangely missing the feel of those three slippery beads.

"You remembered, didn't you?"

I nodded. And then I told Adam everything. He was silent as my words twined around us, soft and bruised, fading into the now velvety blue sky.

"There were so many clues, Adam. I can't believe I didn't see it before." I turned towards him as his arm wrapped around my side, pressed my face into his neck, feeling the steady throb of his pulse against my whispering lips. "I was so stupid."

"No, Mags. Our lives, our stuff, it's all mixed together. Seeing Shannon's things in his truck or his things in her room shouldn't have made you suspect a thing. With the six of us, that's just how it goes." He held me then. Let me cry. When I stopped, he sighed, but he didn't say one word.

"I just want to find an end," I said. "I want to reach the point where I know everything and can be okay with it all."

"You want me to tell you what I know?" Adam asked.

I didn't. Oh, God, I didn't. But I had to hear it. "Yes. I'm ready."

"You're sure?"

I tried not to be angry that he knew all the things I didn't. That he hadn't told me. I couldn't let the emotions get in the way. "I'm sure."

"Okay." Adam took a deep breath. "If I do this, I have to do it right," Adam said. "Which means we're going all the way back to the beginning."

Adam looked right at me, took in a deep breath, and then the words poured from him, trailing into what was left of the dim light. "Remember your first night with Joey?"

"The meteor shower?" I smiled. "Of course I remember. He drove me out into the field outside town, and that's where everything started." I pulled my knees to my chest and wrapped my arms around my legs, looking at a twisted pattern of rocks that was scattered across the trail. My movements felt disconnected from reality. Like this wasn't really happening, me sitting there, about to learn everything Adam already knew.

"He took that from *me*, Maggie. All of it. I'd told him that I liked you, that I wanted to ask you out. Told him my exact plan – the meteor shower, the crickets, the music. And he couldn't handle the thought."

"You… Wait, that was all you?" I thought of the stars shooting across the sky, how Joey and I had lazed under them for hours, kissing, and touching, and giggling. I'd felt so special, thinking that Joey had wanted to share that magic with me. With *just me*, and no one else. But now my favourite memory of Joey was tainted. Adam would for ever be in that field with us, standing off to the side, and I would never be able to push him away. "You're the one who told him about the meteor shower?"

"And the doughnuts. He never would have known what you liked and didn't like. He didn't pay enough attention. And he didn't have the patience to find a field with the least light pollution and best angle of the sky. I'm the one who spent weeks scoping out the best spot in town." Adam sighed. "I don't want to hurt you any more, but I have to tell you the whole truth. He challenged me. Said if I didn't ask you out by the Friday before the meteor shower, he'd do it for me. I had no idea he meant he'd steal the whole plan. And you."

My hands were shaking. My teeth chattering. My entire body started to shiver.

"When I missed his deadline, I didn't think anything of his stupid challenge. I figured I still had plenty of time before the meteor shower to work up my courage."

"But Joey asked me out, instead." I clasped my hands together to stop the shaking. "I remember it was exactly one week before the meteor shower, because I spent every moment of every day wondering what his surprise could be."

"That's about right."

"Why didn't you tell me?" I closed my eyes, not wanting to look into his.

"You were so excited, Maggie. I didn't want to ruin that. And I figured he'd screw it up in a few months, so I just let it go."

"But then we kept going, Joey and me."

"Right. You seemed happy with him. And I knew the way I felt about you didn't matter any more. You didn't feel the same. At least not about me."

Even with all the ways I'd learned to distrust Joey in the weeks that had passed since his death, even knowing that the last year of our relationship had been filled with secrets, I'd never considered that our very first moment had been a lie as well.

"Joey never gave me the chance to find out how I might feel about you," I said. "But I don't get what that stuff from way back in the beginning has to do with anything now."

"Even back then," Adam looked down at his hands, "I was trying to protect you from finding out who he really was."

I couldn't speak. The emotion riding the wave of his words scared me. Deep-down, can't-move kind of scared.

"It killed me, watching him with you, knowing that it should have been me. But there was nothing I could do."

"Until you found out about Joey and Shannon." The irritation that he'd known so much and never shared it with me rippled through my words. "You could have done something then."

"Yes. I could have."

"When did you figure it out?"

"Homecoming." Adam looked towards the creek. "I didn't know for sure, but that's when I started to suspect."

"The night his grandpa had the stroke?" I was confused, my brain trying to catch up with the information Adam had just given me. "Joey left town to go to the hospital that night, how could—"

"He wasn't at his grandparents', Mags."

Those words hit me hard, and I almost told him to stop. Because I knew from just that one sentence it had been worse than I had ever imagined.

"Where was he?"

"Home."

"The whole night?"

"I'm not sure. I saw the lights on when I drove past after the dance. Haley and I were on our way to the homecoming after party."

"I remember the party," I said. "Tanna tried to get me to go."

Everything in me flipped over everything else, twisted and writhed. One tangled mess. And then it all tripped over to Shannon. Where had she been? At the dance, with everyone else. She'd tried to get me to go, too. Called and called and called. Then, at about ten, Tanna stopped by before everyone in her group headed to the after party, asking if I wanted to join. She'd told me that Shannon was sick and had gone home.

"Shannon skipped that party," I said. "And she *never* misses a party. She was at Joey's, wasn't she?"

Adam nodded. "I saw her car parked against the house in the shadows where the driveway curves towards the backyard. I could hardly make it out, but I was sure it was hers."

"Is that when you called me?"

Adam nodded. "I'd been worried about you all night. When I heard that Joey had gone out of town – before I knew he *lied* about going out of town – I wanted to leave the dance to get you. But Tanna said I shouldn't. She said I couldn't afford to piss Haley off on our first date. Not that it mattered, since we never had a second date, but whatever."

"Then when you saw Shannon's car…"

"I didn't know what to think. I wondered if you were with them. If you'd at least heard from him."

"But I hadn't."

"That's when I knew something was going on."

"So what'd you do?" I asked. "Did you call him that night?"

"I did. After I dropped Haley off at the party. And again on my way to your house with the pizza. But he didn't answer."

"So you came to my house to cover for him?" I asked, anger blazing through my chest. "To keep me from finding out?"

Adam closed his eyes. "Don't compare me to him. I did it because I didn't want you to be hurt. And because I didn't know exactly what was going on."

"But you figured it out." I was quiet. Waiting. "Didn't you?"

"He didn't answer any of my calls the next morning, either. So I went to his house and when I confronted him, Joey admitted that she'd spent the night there. That he never went to the hospital." Adam sighed and ran a hand through his hair. "He told me it was one time. That they'd kissed, nothing else. He said she just showed up at his house, drunk and crying about some shit with her parents, and as he was trying to calm her down, it happened. He also said they'd talked, and that it would never happen again."

I balled my hands into fists, wishing for something to

hit. "Why didn't you tell me then?" My voice was shaky and taut with anger. "Some stupid guy code?"

Adam looked at me. "It wasn't like that, Maggie."

"So what happened next? I know there's more."

"I thought that was the end of it." Adam took a deep breath. "Until the day of your ACT."

"That day in Bradyville? Joey said he was grounded. That's why he couldn't—"

"He was with Shannon."

"When he was supposed to be picking me up? He left me stranded so he could have a morning play date with her?" My words echoed through the trees, angry and bursting with pain. I tried to stand up, but Adam stopped me with one hand on my knee.

"He told me she was upset about the kiss, that she felt guilty and wanted to tell you." Adam squeezed my knee. "I honestly thought it ended the night of homecoming. You have to believe me."

"Well, we know from those pictures that it was going on pretty steadily for most of the year," I said.

"The pictures," Adam said.

"You left them, didn't you? On my doorstep."

"Shannon was supposed to tell you after the funeral, but she didn't. And then you found those text messages. I had to do something. So I went to the Walthers' saying I needed some CD Joey had borrowed, and I searched his room for evidence. I didn't think I'd find anything quite so extensive, and I knew it would be hard for you to see the album Shannon made for him, but it was the only thing I could figure out."

"I don't understand why you didn't just tell me," I said.

"I didn't want to be a part of it, Mags."

"Adam, you already were."

"But to be the one to tell you? To be the one to take all of your memories and trash them? I didn't want you to remember that every time you looked at me."

I sighed. Gazed into the shadows that had overtaken the ground. "What happened the day of the ACT?"

"You can't hate me for this, Maggie. I did the best I could." Adam's voice shook with each word. "The day of your ACT, Joey was flipping his shit when he called and asked me to pick you up. His voice was all shaky, like he could hardly breathe."

"Of course he was freaking out. He didn't want her to tell me anything."

"Obviously, I told him I thought she was right. That's when the tension started between Joey and me."

I looked down then. At the way Adam's hand on my knee felt so normal that I almost didn't know it was there. Realized he'd scooted all the way up against me, his chest pressed against my side so hard I could feel his heart beating against my arm. Felt the way my hand itched to tuck his hair away from his face so I could see his eyes without their curtain.

"What'd he say?"

"He said nothing was going on, kept insisting it was just the one kiss the night of homecoming."

"You're kidding me."

"I believed him, Maggie." Adam looked right at me. "Until I saw them together the night of Dutton's party. Behind the garage. Kissing."

Adam's hand squeezed tighter. I wanted to say something, but I couldn't. The image of Joey and Shannon making out when I was right there, just around the corner, made me feel like throwing up.

"I confronted them," Adam said, "and Shannon ran away. That's when I told Joey he had to tell you. That if he didn't come clean, I was going to tell you myself."

"So that's what the phone call was about? The big argument the night of Dutton's party?"

"He'd texted me that he needed one more day. So I called him to say that he had until we left the Jumping Hole on Saturday, and not one minute more."

I buried my face in my hands. "He was pissed off?"

"So pissed off, Maggie. Like, I'm-going-to-rip-you-into-small-pieces pissed off. He didn't appreciate me telling him what to do. Said I had no right to butt in. That he had it under control."

"Oh, my God." The gorge. Adam was going to tell me after the gorge. And the accident, it kept everything buried deep. I went back to that cliff top. To Joey's smiling face. I heard his words ringing through my head.

You trust me?

"He didn't want anyone to tell me," I said. "He knew it would destroy everything."

"I told him then that he had to be the one to tell you. I knew you'd hate him, both of them, after everything. But if they came clean on their own, I thought that there might be a better chance of you forgiving them. I didn't want you to lose everything. I never thought all of this would happen. And when Joey died, I was torn. I thought it might be best if you never learned the truth. Then Shannon, she expected me to keep their secret, to say that Joey had been at my house the night of Dutton's party... But I couldn't. I thought if I told one truth, all the others would just follow, that Shannon would have to tell you."

"I don't even know what to say." My mind was like a thrashing whirlpool, churning each thought into the next before I could process anything.

"He never deserved you, Maggie. It was always supposed to be me."

I buried my face in my hands, stretching my legs out on the rock, swaying with the breeze. "Adam," I said, looking at him. "Nothing between us can ever be the—"

"Please don't say that." Adam's eyes were intense, glinting in the moonlight. Staring right into me. Those eyes. They were safe. As safe as Joey was dangerous. Everything about Adam was safe.

Adam tipped his head to the side. "I love you, Maggie. Always have. And I'm not going to apologize for doing what I thought was best for you." His voice was this raspy whisper that made my breath catch in my throat.

Adam grabbed both of my hands then. Squeezed tight. That's when everything fell away. It was just us. Sitting there together. The cliff top, the pain, the lies – everything – suddenly seemed behind us, somewhere where it didn't need to be found.

As Adam and I sat on that patch of cool rock, barely breathing, our hands tucked between our chests, I wanted to kiss him. Wanted him to kiss me.

It was this perfect moment of clarity. And I felt things. Things I'd never felt before. Things that didn't make sense. Until you flipped them over and they started to make the most sense of all.

But then I thought of Joey. Standing on Dutton's deck. Looking out at Adam and me dancing. The surprise and fear and anger splashed across his face making me feel as if he hadn't really been watching us in the yard that night, but that he'd somehow flashed forwards to this moment. Seen us sitting under the rushing leaves of the thick-barked trees, wanting to kiss each other and never wanting to stop.

That's when it hit me – the understanding that I wasn't much better than Joey.

I pushed him away then.

Adam.

Not Joey.

I felt like I had that part all mixed up.

But there was too much swirling around in my mind. I felt as if I might just explode.

"I'm sorry," I said in two breathless huffs as I scrambled to my feet, my fingers groping a tree trunk for balance, clawing at the rough patches of bark.

Adam shook his head. Ran a hand through his hair. "Maggie. You have nothing to be sorry about—"

"Adam –" I held a shaking hand in the air between us – "God, Adam, I don't even know what I'm doing any more."

"You'll figure it out." Adam looked up at me with a sad smile. "You always do."

I stumbled back, trying to get some distance between us. I was practically drowning in the waves of need and fear and hope crashing between us.

"Look. I just need some time. This is...*crazy*."

"Maggie. I understand." Adam's voice was steady. He hadn't moved from his spot on the ground. "I do. And I don't have any expectations, okay? No pressure. I just needed you to know how I feel."

I wanted to go home. To the only real safety the world had left to offer. I wanted to hide away in my bed, under the quilt my grandmother had made. I wanted to bury myself under the cover of all those years and erase everything that had happened.

But I couldn't.

I had to face this.

There really was no other option.

"THANKS, RYLAN," I SAID FROM the driver's seat of Joey's truck. I turned the key and the engine roared to life with a familiar sound that caused my chest to ache from missing him. It was strange, the things that brought the pain and loss rushing back to me. I was never ready to face the feelings. Not even now, a full two months after his death. "I owe you one."

"Thank you, Maggie. For telling me everything that happened the day he died." Rylan swiped his knuckles across his swollen eyes.

"I'm sorry," I said.

"At least it makes some sense now." Rylan pinched his lips together. "You'll come to the house? Tell my parents everything?"

I nodded. "Tomorrow," I said. "I promise I'll call and plan a time to visit."

"It'll be hard for them," Rylan said. "But good at the same time." He looked over his shoulder at the car parked one space away from Joey's truck, the one where three of his friends had been waiting patiently while I spilled everything I knew, then turned back to me. "You'll have it back here in the morning? Because if I don't have Joey's truck parked in the driveway by the time my parents wake up—"

"I'll have it here just after sunrise," I said. "It'll be in this exact same spot." I put the truck in reverse then, backed out of the parking space, and watched as Rylan hopped into the back seat of his best friend's car.

He didn't watch as I pulled around the side of Bozie's Doughnuts. Didn't see as I flicked on my turn signal and headed out onto Main Street, the bright lights of the restaurants I passed screaming into the dark night sky (Ha Ha Pizza, Ye Olde Trail Tavern, Carol's Kitchen). I was finally alone.

I sucked in deep breaths as I drove, Joey's scent so strong, even after all these weeks, that I practically tasted him. It was starting to get to me, what I was about to do, and tears burned my eyes. I'd spent so many weeks submerged in my anger, I wasn't familiar with the jagged edge of my pain. But tonight was about facing everything, no matter how difficult it might be.

I flipped on the radio and was shocked to hear the Dave Matthews Band. Dave's voice rippled from the speakers, filling the emptiness surrounding me. The stereo was set to CD mode, and I wondered if this song, *our* song, was one of the last Joey heard the day that he died. I felt like I was hearing the words for the first time, the line about disappearing and being gone, the other about the moon being the only one to follow.

I looked at the moon as I turned onto Blue Springs Road, moving further from the centre of town, the lights, the people, and wondered if Joey could still bathe in its light. I hoped so. He had always loved the night.

When I got to the field, I slowed the truck, flicked on the indicator, and almost drove past. It felt wrong somehow. Being there. All alone.

But it was the only way.

So I turned in, bumping along the uneven ground beneath the tyres as Joey's key chain clanged against the dashboard, and steered myself to the centre of the empty field.

"Okay, Joey," I said into the silent, too-still cab of the truck. "It's you and me. Let's do this."

I shoved the driver's side door open and reached behind me for all the things I would need. Yanked them free. Heaved them over the side of the truck's bed. And climbed in the back.

I made myself a little bed using Joey's inflatable camping mattress and the quilt I'd pulled off my bed, then I lay back, looking up at the sky.

"You here, Joey? Because I have some things to say to you."

The only response was a chorus of crickets. But that was okay. Easier, even, than if he'd still been alive and I had to face him – his eyes and his smile and the whisper of his touch – with all of this for real.

"You crushed me, Joey." I took a deep breath. Swiped at the tears that had begun to fall. "You crushed me into a million pieces. First by dying. Then with all of your lies. I feel like I don't even know who you were any more."

A batch of clouds floated across the deep blue-black sky, glowing from the backlight of the moon. I wanted a message, something I could be sure about. But I couldn't read anything in their shapes or outlines.

"I know everything now. All of your secrets."

I closed my eyes.

"I know you're not a bad person, Joey. You must have been very confused. But the thing is, none of this was fair to me. And I hate that a part of me hates you now. That you'll never be back to help me see you as something new. I just hope that one day I'll be able to forget this messed-up side of you that lied, and lied, and lied."

An owl called out to the night from the top branches of a nearby tree. I wondered if somehow it was Joey, trying to ease my pain.

"Hopefully one of these days, I'll see past all that. Get

back to the memories of before, when things were right and it really was just you and me. Back when I was stupid enough to think it would be for ever."

I sat up then. Reached into the bag of Bozie's Doughnuts and pulled out a devil's food.

"Shannon told me that you made a decision the night of Dutton's party. That you'd decided to drop the whole thing with her. That you'd chosen me."

I took a big bite out of the doughnut and concentrated on the burst of flavour in my mouth. Perfectly chocolate. And then I was ready.

"Joey, I gotta tell you one thing. I don't choose you. Not any more. And if you'd lived…if you'd been around long enough to play it all out, I'd have told you the same thing. I do *not* choose you."

I listened, waiting for a twirling ribbon of warm summer air to bring me a whisper. An apology. Some kind of understanding.

But still, there was nothing.

"It's over, Joey," I said. "I'm letting you go."

I lay back again, wiping the crumbs off my hands, remembering the taste of our first kiss. I played it back then. All the moments that made up our friendship and love and commitment. The way he had made me believe things were. And the way they were in reality.

I spent the entire night there in that field, lying in Joey's truck, my grandmother's quilt tucked around me. I dozed off a few times, but for the most part I simply let myself feel everything I'd been avoiding for weeks. Let it wash over me and take me where I needed to go.

I thought about Adam, too. Couldn't help it. He was there in the field, laced into all the memories in a whole new way.

I missed them.

Both of them.

Joey.

And Adam.

The thing was, while I missed Joey with a sadness so heavy its weight practically pressed me against the ground, Adam was the one I longed to see. It was Adam's voice I wanted to hear. His hands I was dying to touch.

But that part was crazy. Intense. And more than a little wrong.

So I pushed it away as I watched the moon cross from one side of the sky to the other and lost myself wondering if Joey was somewhere up there, spinning through the stars.

MEET ME @ THE CREEK? I typed into the keypad on my phone.

My stomach was all tied up. But I did it anyway. I hit Send.

I chewed on the nail of my right thumb, waiting.

I was worried I'd get nothing.

But then I did.

Ur ready?

I took a deep breath.

Yes.

It had been almost a week since Adam confessed everything. A lot had happened in that time, and I felt proud that I'd faced all of it on my own. I wished that it could go back to being simple between us, and that I could just spill it all out to him – my talk with Shannon, how she's still hanging on to Joey like he's coming back to her, our talk with the police, the relief I felt over their appreciation at our honesty, how the case was officially closed. But nothing would ever be simple between Adam and me, not ever again.

I stared at my phone, waiting for his response, panic flashing through me that I had waited too long.

But then my phone chimed, and his reply appeared.

B there in a few.

My entire body sighed with relief.

"I'll be back in a while," I said over my shoulder, hopping up from the couch in our living room, where my parents were watching a movie I'd chosen but couldn't get into.

"Where are you going?" my mother asked from her perch on the couch, a cup of iced tea in her hand.

"The creek," I said. "Just to...hang out."

"You look like you're up to something," she said, her eyes crinkling with a question. "Your cheeks are all red."

I waved a hand in the air as I walked past her, towards the sliding glass door that led to our back deck. "Nothing to worry about," I said. "I'm just sick of sitting around here."

"Good." My mother sat forwards, placing her glass on the coffee table.

"Very good." My father held a hand up in the air as I passed him, and I swatted it in a high five. "Stay out past your curfew or something. You deserve it."

"Noah!" my mother said, her voice high, but full of humour. "I don't know if that's the best idea."

"The girl needs to have some fun." My father looked up at me, his eyes sparkling with the fire of some explosion on the television, and winked. "But be safe."

"Yeah," I whispered as I slid open the door and stepped out into the darkness of the night, hoping I hadn't just made the biggest mistake of my life.

When my feet hit the dirt path at the edge of our yard, I started to doubt myself. There was nothing safe about what I was planning to do.

Above, leaves fluttered in the moonlight, and I wondered if their whispers were meant for me, if they were imprinted with a code that I needed to decipher. Some kind of important message that would help me get this right.

I focused, listening to their rippling cross over my head, hearing one word in the muggy wind.

Hurry.

Hurry.

Hurry.

I picked up the pace then, as that word echoed through my head. Hoped that I hadn't run out of time. I had to get it right. This last thing. I couldn't lose him, too. And there was only one way to protect what was left between us.

My arms pumped against my sides, helping me gain even more speed. The thick air rushed at me, pulling my hair over my shoulders, whipping it into the silver light of the moon. I wanted to be there, couldn't move fast enough. Each second felt like for ever.

But of course, when I turned that last bend and saw him sitting there, I almost stopped and ran back the other way.

Because there was no way to be sure which was the right choice to make.

But I had to trust myself.

There was no one else.

Adam turned as I kicked off my shoes. "Hey," he said.

"Hey." I folded my legs beneath me and took my place next to him on our rock.

"Didn't know if you'd ever call," he said with a half smile, "after everything I told you."

"Yeah," I said. "I needed to work some things out."

"Right," Adam said, turning his face to the rushing water of the creek.

"It was all pretty messy," I said.

Adam nodded.

"And I've been pretty pissed off."

"You have a lot to be pissed off about."

"I'm talking specifically about the parts that had to do with you."

Adam clutched his hands together in his lap. "Do you need me to apologize again?"

"No. I know you're sorry."

Adam didn't look at me. "I am."

"And I know that you were trying to protect me."

"I was."

"I'm ready to thank you for that part," I said. "For trying to keep me safe. And putting me first." I took a deep breath, noticing the air shift around me. I actually felt lighter.

He looked down then, nodded as though he understood something I hadn't even said, that shaggy blond hair obscuring my view of his eyes. Eyes I suddenly wanted to see more than anything.

"Maggie." Adam sighed. Bit at his lip. "I just want you to trust me again. I hope you can remember, even with everything, that you know me."

"I thought I knew Joey…" My voice trailed off as soon as his name hit the air between us. The single word soured things. Made Adam's face go hard.

"Don't compare me to him. Not ever." Adam held his hands out in the air like he was about to touch me. I wanted him to. So crazy bad. But he didn't. Instead, he used them to push himself to his feet and turn away from me, towards the water.

"I'm still trying to figure out what I'm supposed to believe. How much I can even trust myself."

"Let me help you, Maggie." Adam turned back towards me, into the moonlight. He hadn't shaved in a few days, and I wanted to rub my hand along the stubble on his cheek. To feel the warmth of his skin. But his words, they rushed me, flipping everything over one final time.

"I have wanted you as long as I can remember," he said. "And it's killed me, knowing what a screw-up he was, knowing that you deserved so much better than his lies.

But I've sat by and watched. And I've waited. Because I didn't want to be the one to take him away from you."

"Adam, I—"

"And now, when I finally have a chance, they've ruined it."

I looked into Adam's eyes. And I knew. Without a doubt. He was telling me the truth. The feelings between us, they were real. As suddenly as I realized that, it hit me that the most important parts of what I had with Joey were in my own mind. I'd built him up to be something he never really was. I'd kept the truth from myself, and that's why it all hurt so much when it came crashing down on me.

Adam chuckled. Twisted to face me. "Maggie. Just get it over with," he said. "It's nice and all, this little blow-off speech, but it's killing me. I know I screwed up. And that you'll never feel for me the way that I feel for you."

"Adam, I—"

Adam pressed a finger to my lips. "Just please tell me you'll still be my friend. I can't lose you all the way. Not now...not ever."

"Are you done yet?" I asked.

Adam nodded.

"Good." I stood up and stepped away from him. Pulled my hair from my face and looked right into his eyes. "Because it's my turn to talk."

Adam sighed.

"I've had all this crazy stuff swirling through my head lately. About Joey. And Shannon. All those memories and guilt that came rushing at me when I found that bracelet." I watched the way Adam's gaze had shifted down to my hands. Felt that he wanted to touch me. "But all the stuff with you, it's been there, too. Not just how you feel – have felt for so long – but how you make me feel."

Adam looked up at me then, his eyes flashing the brightest green.

I had to force myself to go on, to crash through the fear that was nearly suffocating me. "I've tried to shove it all down, but the parts with you, they bubble their way to the surface in the strangest ways. How, at the craziest moments, I just want to feel your hand on mine, or hear your voice whispering in my ear, or feel the tickle of your laughter against my cheek."

Adam smiled. Ducked his head.

Some of that fear melted away.

"I've been trying to sift through all the reasons we shouldn't try this, weighing them against all the reasons that we should."

"Yeah?" Adam asked, his voice hoarse.

I nodded. "There are about a zillion things going against us."

"True." Adam stood then. Held a hand out to me.

"And we shouldn't." I reached up and placed my hand in

his. So sad when I thought about everything that had led to this moment.

"Probably not." Adam squeezed my hand, pulled me up, and then let me go.

I stepped towards him, wishing I could cut a swatch of the cool, silky rock beneath my feet, wishing I could use it as the first patch of fabric in the quilt that would make up the rest of my life.

"But when I think about it really hard, when I push everything else away, I realize that I don't care." I grabbed both of his hands. "I don't care one single bit about any of it. I just care about you."

Adam raised his eyebrows, his eyes widening. "Wait. What are you—"

"I'm saying I'm ready. I am *so* ready. To try this thing with you. It's going to have to be slow, right? And I'm pretty sure that I'll have some total freak-out moments along the way. But I can't seem to get you out of my mind. And if you feel the same way, doesn't that mean we should just…"

"Give it a chance?"

"Something like that," I said, laughter curling over my words.

"You're sure? You're ready?"

I nodded. "I feel like I shouldn't be. Not so soon after my relationship with Joey. But there were so many lies. I needed to come to terms with that before I could move on."

"And you have? I don't want to rush you."

"You're not rushing me," I said. "I can't wait. Not one more minute."

Adam ran his thumb along my forehead, slowly pulling back my hair.

"Can I show you something, Maggie?" Adam's eyes lifted, his hands hovered in the air just under my chin.

I nodded. I hoped. But I didn't know.

We stepped closer then, our faces tilting together, closing out the rest of the world.

And this time, this moment, I got everything right.

So very right.

acknowledgements

The overall concept of this book was inspired by several people I've known who moved on before their time should have been up. In their honour, I want to acknowledge everyone who has lost a life too soon, and all of those who were left behind.

Writing a book is an incredible process that comes with many highs and lows. It's also something that I couldn't do on my own, and I'm grateful to have many people to thank for their support.

To Becky Walker, Rebecca Hill, Elisabetta Barbazza, and Sarah Cronin, the wonderful team at Usborne UK, for all of the time spent on the Anglicization of this novel. It has been a true delight working with you. / To Amy Eckenrode, who gave me excellent feedback on police procedure. Also to my team of medical advisors, Tim Beach, Jim Loki, Dr. Tim Schoonover, and Dr. Debra Sowald. Any mistakes in these areas of the book are mine and mine alone. / To Jason Behm for sharing his knowledge of all things motorcycle, and for finding me one that needed a key. And to his lovely wife, Lori for always being there and knowing the perfect thing to say. (It's time to celebrate, right?) / To Melanie Singleton, one of the only people I know who reads as much as I do, for always being there to brainstorm ideas, for your interest in my stories and characters (I know they keep you up for some late-late nights), and for always giving me incredible feedback. / To Jenny Cooper, for being one of my first readers and my number one musical advisor. Love all of our brainstormy dinners. Those SHS yearbookers rock, too! / To my very first reader, Janet Irvin, who ploughs through early chapters that should never see the light of day, for your skilful story problem-solving abilities, unwavering support, and for always giving me encouragement to keep going when I need it most. / To Katrina Kittle and Sharon Short, two very talented authors who have become like family over the course of writing this book. I am so lucky to have you to share and seek advisement when it comes to…well, *everything*. / To the remainder of my friends (who are like family) and my family (who are like friends) for always being there. / To all of the supporters who enjoyed *The Tension of Opposites* – your feedback keeps me going when I need motivation. Also to the Class of 2K10 and the Tenners, two groups of awesomely supportive authors – I am proud to be part of your lives. / To Jay Asher, my very first blurber, for a talk in the park, a salted caramel hot chocolate, and all of that lovely praise. / To Regina Griffin, Katie Halata, Mary Albi, and everyone else at Egmont USA for everything you do. Especially to Alison Weiss, whose phenomenal feedback, guidance and support helped me wrangle the earliest draft of this book into something I am proud of. / To my mom and dad for always nurturing my love of books. It's because of you that the first glimmer of this dream to become a published author came to life in my mind. / To my children, for your love and for always believing in me. Nothing beats having you in my life. / To Eric, my husband and best friend, you have this crazy way of getting better with each passing moment. Thanks for supporting this dream of mine. For so many reasons, I couldn't be happier. / To my kick-ass agent, Alyssa Eisner Henkin, for always being there, for always inspiring, and for always pushing me to do my best.

Thanks to all of you for believing in me, and for helping me believe in myself. Much love.

ANDY McNAB

I BROKE THE INTERNET

PHIL EARLE

ILLUSTRATED BY ROBIN BOYDEN

SCHOLASTIC

To all the teachers who have done an incredible job
teaching remotely over the past year, the parents
who have juggled normal commitments with the
pressures of homeschooling and to the children who,
I am sure, have all worked hard, been helpful around
the house and only said "I am hungry, what can
I have to eat?" a few times a day…

A.M.

To the real Miss D – Janet Doherty.
Everyone should have a teacher as brilliant as her.

P.E.

1

Fame is for weirdos.

No, hang on, Mum warned me about this —
about saying stuff without thinking it through first.
What I mean is: fame does weird things to people.

Yep, that's it.

What's also weird is that I even have to *think*
about fame. I never thought that anyone in my
class at school would ever be famous, but *all* of
us are.

Sort of.

Kind of.

1

We're not, like, Messi-famous — it's not like we did something proper skilful. We're not even YouTube famous, not like that baby who bit his big brother's finger, or that monkey who can whistle the American national anthem through his bum cheeks. But the video of what we did has been viewed *a lot* of times. 102,798 times, according to Giraffles. That's loads! It would take me *weeks* to count that high, if I could be bothered.

We didn't set out to do something brave, the bravery kind of happened by accident. We were meant to be on the coolest school trip ever — there was kayaking, rock-climbing and trekking, but there was also wiping my bum with nettles (by accident — I'm not a weirdo) and getting caught in booby traps set by my idiot big brother. And then there was the storm. A storm so wild that they ended up giving it a name: Nancy (not exactly the scariest name they could have thought of, but anyway…). A storm that saw us stranded on top of a mountain, fighting for our lives and having to zip line through the worst of it to get to safety.

I was the last one down, and, no, I wasn't brave and, yes, I was flipping terrified. Wouldn't you be?

What I didn't know was that someone filmed the whole thing. They captured me and some of the others flying down the zip line, hanging on for grim life, while the storm – straight from a Hollywood disaster movie – raged in the background.

I still don't know who filmed it, but they caught me, eyes bulging, legs flailing and mouth screaming rude words that I didn't even think I knew. Then they took that video, uploaded it to the Internet, and before we knew it, people found it. I don't know how or why, but they did. It ended up on Instagram and Twitter, then someone from the news saw it and the next thing we knew we had reporters knocking on our doors and TV cameras being thrust in our faces. One TV crew found out where we lived and climbed *seventeen* flights of stairs (the lift was broken, of

3

course) to bang on our door to interview us. And guess what? We weren't even home!

They found us all in the end though. We were in the paper and on the news. There were photos of Jonny and Lucky and Dyl on the zip line, looking brave. Even Giraffles looked brave (skinny, but brave). And then there was an image of me. And I looked … *terrified.* Like I was being chased by a mutant tarantula from Mars. Like I was literally pooing myself in fear. In fact, in the photo I swear my bum still looks swollen from wiping it with those flipping nettles.

Anyway, you get the message: I was a laughing stock. And that photo was *everywhere* – on the TV, on people's phones. It followed me around like a bad

4

smell — like a skunk that's never met a bar of soap in its life.

So, since it all blew up, I've kept my head down. I've not started wearing a disguise or nothing. I've not grown a beard or bought a false nose. But I'm the only one who is acting normally. Everyone else has gone well weird.

Fame hasn't just turned their heads. If anything, it's blown their heads clean off…

2

Eight a.m. on another boring school day and, as usual, Giraffles is waiting for me by the lift doors. I'm sweating from stomping down seventeen flights of stairs, only Giraffles is sweating MORE. But it's winter. And he doesn't even have a proper coat on.

"What's going on with you?" I ask.

"What do you mean?"

"Looks like you've been stood under a waterfall."

He shrugs, like he doesn't know what I'm on about, but I'm on to him.

Giraffles is ace – my best mate. And, all right, he looks slightly odd, what with his neck being as long as a giraffe's, but he's sound. Except, being in that video has changed him. Made him think waaay too much about how he looks.

"Am I really that skinny?" he asked, when he first saw it.

"Mate, the camera adds ten kilos…"

"But I still look…"

"Like a pencil on a diet?"

He'd flushed, and for a second I thought he was going to get angry. He didn't – Giraffles never gets angry – but since then he's been proper obsessed with his appearance.

He tried to join the gym, but they wouldn't let him cos he's too young.

He asked our Dyl if he could borrow his weights, but my brother is a scum bucket so he just laughed so hard that he broke wind fifteen times in a row.

That didn't stop Giraffles, though, and seeing

him sweating now, in the middle of flippin'
winter, I know he's still obsessed with it.

"You been running?" I ask.

"No."

"Sit-ups then?"

"No!"

"You've been doing star
jumps again, haven't you?"

"Leave off, Danny."

But I know there's
something going on. And then I
see it. He *does* look different – he's
all lumpy around his stomach.
And when I look harder, I see
his arms are lumpy too. And
his legs. I know I probably
shouldn't mention it – maybe
he's got a tropical disease or
something – but I can't help it.
He's my mate – I care about
him, don't I?

"What's that?" I ask, and I prod him in his belly. My finger pushes against something metal.

"Nothing," he replies, stepping backwards. But I'm faster than him, and I jab his stomach again. Then I jab his arm, and kick gently at his ankle as well. More metal!

"You turning into a robot or something?"

"Don't be an idiot."

"Then tell me what's going on, Giraffles."

He's having none of it, and turns to walk away, so I take my chance, lifting up the back of his school shirt to see he's wearing a kind of thick belt. Except, it's not really a belt, because he's actually strapped a load of tin cans to his waist with brown tape.

"Are they *baked beans*?" I ask. I don't know whether to laugh or call a doctor.

"Not all of them," he huffs. "Some of 'em are beans and sausages." As if that makes it all right.

"You planning on getting REALLY hungry?"

He slaps my hand away and pulls his shirt down.

10

"I'm trying to carry more weight around," he whispers. "It'll build up my muscles, won't it?"

I lift his trouser leg to find four tinned chocolate puddings. "It won't if you eat all these!" I giggle.

"It's all right for you, isn't it?" he hisses. "You didn't look like a streak of wee on that video!"

"No, I looked like I was being chased by a bear! Did you *see* my face? Plus Dylan's told everyone about me—" I pause to check no one is listening in before carrying on. "—he's told everyone about me wiping my bum with nettles."

A sudden giggle escapes his mouth. "Yeah well, I won't tell if you won't."

"Deal!" I agree. "Plus if I get peckish at playtime then I'll know where to come, won't I?"

He pushes me, but in a matey way, and we start the walk to school.

It's not long till the gang builds up around us and there's even more evidence of fame making people bonkers. Jonny is the first to appear.

Now. I like Jonny, he's a good lad – kind and everything – but it's fair to say that he's not the brightest bulb in the lamp. Probably because he spends half his life on his phone. You should've seen him on the school trip when he had no signal. It was like someone had died. And as for when his battery ran out? Well, I thought he'd *never* get over it.

"All right, Jonny?" I say, as he falls in beside us.

He grumbles something but we've no idea what it is because his head is buried in his Samsung.

"What you watching?" Giraffles asks, but Jonny doesn't reply. He just reaches into his pocket and pulls out a second phone, jabbing at that with his finger as well.

"Two phones? Why've you got two, mate?"

But it's like we don't even exist, because whatever he's looking for, he isn't finding it, so he reaches into his pocket again.

"He can't have…" I say to Giraffles.

"Nah," Giraffles replies. "No one has *three phones*."

12

But Jonny does! He pulls it straight out and starts bashing out a text while he's holding the other two. That's when we see that his third phone is plugged into a charger that looks almost as heavy as the cans Giraffles is carrying around. Me and Giraffles stare at each other, our eyes as big as beach balls. It'd be funny if it wasn't so bonkers.

"Jonny, mate, why have you got *three phones*? Isn't one enough?"

Of course, *this* is the question that breaks him out of his dream world, and he looks at me like I've just asked him why he prefers eating crisps more than cockroaches.

"Are you for real?" he asks. "Can't you remember what happened last time?"

"Last time?" I reply blankly.

"On the school trip!" he squeals, looking uneasy. "Don't make me say it!"

"What? You mean when your phone stopped working?"

Jonny stops dead in his tracks and throws his

head back, like he's a wolf about to howl at the moon.

"It must never happen again!" he shouts, and he starts to run off.

"Where are you going?" I shout after him.

"School! I'm down to three per cent on this one. It needs plugging in." He looks into his pocket. "And my charger is running low too. Laters!"

We watch him go without saying anything. I mean, what can you say to that anyway?

All I can do is thank my lucky stars that Giraffles, my best mate, is relatively sane.

Well, he would be if he didn't have half a supermarket strapped to his body...

3

I'd like to say that when we reach school,
everything becomes normal. Because nothing
weird happens at school, right?

WRONG!

In fact, from then it all gets weirder,
because when we troop into class, our teacher,
Miss D, steps up to the plate. Now, I think
Miss D is all kinds of brilliant, as well as
being properly kind (don't forget, she secretly
chipped in some money when I didn't have
enough to go on the school trip), but since

everything went wrong, well, she's been acting ... *differently*.

It started straight after the summer holidays, on a day when the weather wasn't just bad, it was like a monsoon outside.

"Right then, team," she cooed. "Out to the playground we go!"

We looked at the puddles, which were quickly becoming reservoirs. I couldn't be sure, but I *think* I saw the school cat cruising round on a windsurfer out there.

"Is she having a laugh?" Giraffles asked me.

But it turned out she was deadly serious.

"You all have coats ... and besides, you won't be cold or wet for long, not if I do my job."

So out we trooped, wondering why we couldn't just do PE in the school hall, where there were radiators. And walls. And a ceiling.

But that's not the way Miss D worked these days. I told you, didn't I? That trip changed her. When I told Mum, she wasn't surprised.

"All thirty of you could've perished on that mountaintop," she said. "Imagine being responsible for that, and knowing that you were at the mercy of the worst storm in a decade!"

She was right, I suppose, but that didn't help the fact that Miss D was definitely acting different and she was *definitely* obsessed with survival techniques.

"Fire," Miss D had said that day, as we stood in the playground getting pummeled by the rain, "is dangerous. But then again," she added, "so is hypothermia."

We nodded while Jonny googled "Hypothermia" and Miss D carried on.

"So, what three things do we need to create fire?"

Jonny shoved his hand up so quickly you'd have thought his armpit was ablaze.

"Oooooh oooooh ooooh, Miss!"

Now, Miss usually knew better than to ask Jonny for answers (because all he does is google them, and let's face it, even Wikipedia gets it

17

wrong sometimes), but as everyone else was too cold to take their hands out of their pockets, she told him to go ahead.

"Easy," he bragged. "All you need is a match, a firelighter and a fireguard."

Miss D tried to smile encouragingly, while the rest of us pulled our *Typical Jonny* faces.

"Yeeeeees," she cringed, "but what if you went into the wild *without* matches?"

"Well, I wouldn't do that, Miss."

"Why not?"

"Because you'd be cross. You've been telling us for ages that preparation is key. No way I'm going anywhere wild without matches!"

Miss D looked tired. "And why the fire guard?" she sighed.

Jonny beamed his proudest beam. "Because fire is dangerous. And the guard would keep it in check. In fact, forget the guard, I'd take a fire distinguisher instead."

By this point, none of us had a clue what a fire

distinguisher was, nor did we care. Though we would've been happy for Jonny to be taken away by a fire *engine*.

Or a police car for that matter – whichever was quickest so the lesson could be over and we could go hug a radiator. But Miss D wanted to keep us there till we'd learnt how to make fire.

It didn't go well.

The kindling was wet, the paper was wet, the sticks we were meant to be rubbing together were bloomin' *soaked*.

It still makes me shudder to think about it now.

So, you can probably understand why, when we walked into class today for a food lesson, I feared the worst.

Last term we'd have been making chocolate crispy cakes.

But not today. Oh no.

Today, Miss has different delicacies in mind. And on her desk, we can see jars of bugs and insects.

"Er … Miss? Where are the Rice Krispies?"

"Krispies? KRISPIES? There were no krispies
on the top of that mountain, were there?" she
cries. "If we'd been stuck for two more hours, we
would've been forced to live off the land."

"But, Miss," says Lucky, politely, because
Lucky Success is brilliant at everything,
including being polite. "We all had a packed
lunch in our rucksacks. You made them for us."

But Miss seems to develop that temporary
deafness that adults get sometimes. Mum does it,

usually when I tell her that Dyl has flushed my homework (or my head) down the bog.

"There are no supermarkets in the middle of the jungle…"

"But there might be coconuts," Lucky suggests.

"Or bananas," adds Giraffles.

"Or even guavas?" I suggest.

Poor old Jonny looks left out and suggests Coco Pops as well, which makes Miss turn instead towards the jars.

"Breakfast…" she smiles, "is served."

And any hope that there might be cereal, or even a piece of cold toast hidden inside the jars, is soon squashed.

"Mmmm," she says, seemingly serious, as she rips a lid off and pulls out a worm.

It's not an ordinary garden worm either – this one is so fat that it looks like it's been eating burgers and chips every day of its life.

"Protein is SO important when you're living on the edge," she says, like she's about to tuck into a chicken salad.

We stand there, mouths open, as she does the same with hers, sucking in the worm like a piece of spaghetti.

"Slides down a treat!" she says.

"Do you think we should call the head?" Giraffles whispers in my ear.

But we're all too stunned to move. Or even cry out.

"So, who would like to try?"

Jonny's stood next to me and tries to lift his arm, but I stop him. "Don't do it!" I hiss gently. Strangely enough, no one else volunteers.

So Miss carries on. She pulls out and eats crickets and grasshoppers, earwigs and maggots. She even has ants, but they're too smart for her, scuttling along her sleeve before she can hoover them up.

All we can do is watch her from behind our hands. I feel like I might never be hungry again.

And then … pudding arrives.

"This," she says, pulling out an insect that is most definitely dead, "is a stinkbug."

"You *are* kidding me," I say. I can't help it. A STINKBUG! *What* is she thinking?

"Oh, you're a squeamish lot," she chuckles. "Stinkbugs are considered a delicacy in Mexico. There's even a festival there that celebrates them. Just imagine, class: thousands of people, all munching away on these little beauties."

"I'd rather not imagine that, Miss." Lucky grimaces.

But Miss D is in her element. Tipping her head back, she chews the stinkbug *way* more times than she needs to before swallowing. She even licks her lips for maximum effect.

But then, before the cheese arrives (probably made from a llama's ear wax), something unfortunate happens. Miss D starts to turn a different colour.

Remember when that girl turned bright blue in Willy Wonka's factory? Well, it's like that, except Miss D turns green.

She doesn't say anything. She doesn't need to. We know what's going on when she grabs her tummy, bends double and runs as quickly as she can in the direction of the staff loos.

I sigh. I really, *really* like Miss D and her lessons (usually). But I'm hoping that one of the side effects of eating bugs and lice is memory loss.

Cos if she can forget about survival, well, she'll definitely live longer.

4

Why are parents always so obsessed with school?

Every day, without fail, when Mum gets in from work, she always asks me the same question:

"How was school?"

I mean, how do you answer that? Actually, I'll tell you how you answer it — in as few words as possible.

"Fine," I always say. But that's never enough for Mum.

"So, what did you do then?"

"Stuff," I say, which is true. We *did* do stuff.

"Like what?"

What does she want me to say? That we came up with a cure for cancer and a recipe for a sandwich that ended world famine? The truth is that we did sums and read and tried to speak French but just sounded like a load of plonkers.

Why is she even interested? It's not like I bombard her with questions about work, is it?

So I try to pretend I can't hear her, but I'm not good at that, cos she always tricks me by offering me a biscuit, which of course I say yes to, which means I then have to actually tell her about what we did at school.

Mums can be slippery.

So, I told her. Just the headlines.

"We did … stuff. You know, normal school stuff, like watching Miss D eat so many insects that she had to go and throw up."

Mum looks at me crossly.

"Daniel Mack, I am simply taking an interest in your life. You don't have to make up fibs! I get enough of those from your brother."

I suppose you can't blame her for not believing me, and she *is* right about my big brother, Dylan. He's a horror show, the devil made human and dumped in my life to make it a misery.

I can see him now, sprawled out on the sofa, TV blaring as he cuts his toenails with a blunt kitchen knife. Yep, you heard right.

"Dylan," Mum says seriously, "there are enough knives on this estate without you adding to the number. Put that away." And for once he does as she says, putting it down before taking his frustrations out on me.

"What's *your* problem?" he says, when he notices I'm looking his way.

"You are," I say under my breath, being as bold as I dare.

"You should be thanking me," he adds.

"How do you work that out?" I can't *believe* what I'm hearing – typical Dyl!

"Cos I made you even more famous today. Had

to tell someone else at college about how I saved you on the top of that mountain."

I feel the blood rush angrily to my cheeks, cos THAT IS NOT THE TRUTH! *I* saved *him*! *I* pushed him out of the way of a falling tree. *I* stopped him from getting squished. But Dyl has decided that *he* was the saviour that day and *that's* what he's said to anyone who will listen. I try to keep my cool and rise above it, but it's hard to do that all the time.

"You off to cadets?" I ask, more out of hope than anything. I've no chance of wrestling the remote control from him while he's sat there. He'd make me swallow it before letting me take control of the TV.

"Cadets is for kids," he scoffs, "like you."

This is a change of tune. For the past five years, Dylan has lived and breathed cadets. Most kids have hobbies like footie or free running or dance.

Not Dyl. He chooses to spend every free minute covering his face in camouflage paint, crawling through the woods and getting covered in mud. He also has a weird habit of ironing everything in his wardrobe. EVERY DAY. Anyway, he's army obsessed, has been ever since I can remember, so I can't work out why he's suddenly so anti it?

He holds up a piece of paper. I can't read it, but the paper is pristine flat, no folds or creases or grubby fingermarks, which makes me reckon he's ironed that as well.

"Today's the day! I got my date!"

I get excited for a minute. Maybe he's found a new family to live with. Hopefully one in Australia.

But, no.

"I've got my date. Your beloved big brother is joining the army! One month today, I start. Basic training – fourteen weeks of physical and mental torture."

"Sounds like what I've had for the past ten years."

"You what?"

"Nothing," I say. As much as I hate him, he's way stronger than me. His muscles have muscles.

"Anyway, that's the *good* news," he says, suddenly serious.

I get scared. "You mean there's bad news too?" They haven't lowered the joining age, have they? I don't have to go too, do I?

"Turns out basic training is two hundred miles away, kidda. I know this will be hard for you, but your big brother is moving out."

Turns out, I am a *great* actor. Not just great: the GREATEST.

Because, this is the best single moment of my life – the moment I can step out of his shadow and live a life without torment for the first time. But I can't show him that, can I? Not if I like my nose this shape and still positioned in the middle of my face. So I turn my tears of joy into wails of sadness.

"I don't know what to say, Dyl," I say, though inside I'm yelping *ZIPPEDY-DOO-DAH!* "It'll be a different place without you."

"I know it will," he says, smugly. 'That's why I'm going to give you every bit of my attention before I leave. Special brother time, eh?"

I shiver with fear. I know what this means: dead arms, kicks in the shins and kidney punches at every given moment.

I need something that gets me out of the flat. And I need it quick.

5

I like a challenge, I really do, and I rise to them …
usually, even if I have to fall on my face a few
times first. But twelve hours on from Dylan's
news, I know this is my toughest assignment
yet. How do I manage to not be mangled by him
between now and him leaving home?

It's not going to be easy, I know that. He made
a big show of affection in front of Mum last
night, going on about how much he was going
to miss me before pulling me into a hug that
morphed (as soon as she turned her back) into a

chokehold that was impossible to get out of.

It's clear I need a hideout. A safe house, somewhere his arms can't reach me, where he can't use my head as a punch ball, or shave off my eyebrows while I'm asleep.

I start with Giraffles, calling on *him* before school for once, which catches his mum off-guard.

"Hello, Danny love," she says, as she opens the door.

For some reason she's wearing slippers shaped like a giraffe's face. It messes with my brain. Why would she wear something that makes it look like she's trampling on her son's head?

I shake off the thought. I don't have time for this, I have to get straight to the point.

"Mrs Giraffles – I mean Raffles – I mean ma'am," I stutter.

"Spit it out, sunshine," she says cheerfully. It seems she has a radar just like my mum – I can see her bracing herself for a question that she really doesn't want to answer.

"I was wondering if I could come and stay?"

Her face softens instantly.

"'Course you can, Danny love. You're always welcome for a sleepover."

"Well … I wondered if it could be for a bit longer than a sleepover?"

Mrs Raffles frowns a bit. "We could do a whole weekend as long as you boys promise to get some sleep and don't eat everything in the fridge. Would that be better?"

I shuffle around. There's no easy way of saying this so I have to be blunt.

"I was thinking more like … four weeks?"

She doesn't say a thing, but her mouth does fall open and I see her doing the sums, working out how many nights that would be.

"Danny. Love. I know I say you're always welcome, but … well, that's a saying. You're a lovely lad, but I've a lot on my plate too."

I tell her I understand. That I don't want to get under her feet: then I think about being trampled by her slippers and figure that it's probably for the best. That might even be more painful than getting strangled by our Dylan.

Anyway, Giraffles tries to cheer me up on the way to school.

"It's only four weeks, mate. I mean, you've

survived nearly eleven years already. What damage can he do in only a month?"

I don't know where to start, but I give it a go.

"He'll write rude words on my forehead in permanent marker. He'll slip red-hot chilli powder into my porridge. He'll steal my homework and *actually* feed it to a dog. He'll dangle me off the balcony by just my shoelaces. He'll give me the worst wedgie in the history of undercrack—"

"—OK, OK, I get it!" he shouts, sweating at the thought of it. "Who else can you stay with, then? What about MandM?"

I frown. I mean, I like Marcus and Maureen. They're kind and smart and funny, but that whole twin thing can be properly freaky. I *swear* they can read each other's minds. And if I live with them long enough, maybe they'll start doing the same to me, and that would be weird, maybe even weirder than having to live with Dyl for another four weeks.

"What about Jonny, then?"

I stop and look at Giraffles with a stare that could melt an iceberg.

"Ignore me. Stupid idea. I know – crash with Lucky!"

As ideas go, it's a belter. Lucky's mum and dad earn a lot of money, so Lucky lives in a big house and has loads of stuff that I want but will never have unless we win the lottery. All of this is running round my head, as well as the fact that I could probably hide out in Lucky's house and his mum wouldn't even know, it's *that big*. But then I think of my mum, and how hard she works for so little money, and how she'd feel if I suddenly went to live with them. She might think I don't appreciate her, or love her, and then that makes me feel proper sad. Maybe the bruises I'll get from Dyl aren't so bad as long as Mum's happy?

By the time I've come to this conclusion, we're at school, so I have to park my daydreaming and survive whatever mad survival lesson Miss D has lined up for us today.

I start to sweat.

I was scared before, but now I'm flipping terrified.

6

I smile at Miss D as we trudge in and she smiles back, just like she always does.

But there's something different about her grin today. It's not as wide as normal. It's like she's nervous about something, and that makes me nervous too, which makes my imagination spin.

Why's she looking like that? Maybe her belly is still iffy from the jungle feast she forced down. Maybe she didn't manage to swallow the stinkworm properly and now she has a swarm of them breeding behind her teeth, which is why her smile looks so weird. Or maybe, maybe there's nothing wrong with her at all and I'm just totally terrified about how I survive Dyl's final month as chief tormentor.

Anyway, as Miss D begins a normal lesson about times tables and manages to speak without spitting out insects in the process, I realize it *is* me. I can't focus. So instead I look round the room and try and work out how I can organize to have tea at every one of my classmates' houses in the next month, and how I do it without my mum missing me or getting cross. Except, half of the people in my class are girls who look at me the way Dyl looks at me, so I don't reckon they'd want me round their house anyway.

It's all a bit much and my stomach starts to feel like maybe *I've* eaten a million stinkworms, so I think about going to the toilet and hiding in there for a while, but as I'm about to put up my hand, the classroom door flies open and in thunders our headteacher, Mrs Rex.

"Good morning, class!" she roars.

"*Good morning, Mrs Rix,*" we parrot in reply, making sure we get her name right.

You see, Rex isn't her name. It's *Rix*, but she's well terrifying and capable of shouting so flippin' loud that she makes the walls shake. Some days, when we're sat eating at lunchtime, the volume of her voice makes our water glasses ripple, like that mad killer dinosaur in *Jurassic Park*. No wonder, then, that everyone – *everyone* – even Mr Gash the caretaker, calls her Rex. Unless she's there in person, of course.

Want to know what's even weirder? Her initial for her first name is "T". I'm not making it up, it's true – it's on the school website and everything!

Anyway, here she is now, thundering in, looking around like she's searching for her next meal, and who does her gaze fall on? Me! It falls on me, which doesn't do much for my icky tummy, I can tell you! And she doesn't just look at me, she *stares* at me. And she *smiles,* which makes my brain race even harder, wondering what I've done to make her pay me attention.

"Miss Doherty!" she roars. "Didn't mean to interrupt, but something very exciting has just happened!"

A jolt of electricity ripples round the room, cos we love exciting things, especially as school has been scientifically proven to be 99% boring and 1% homework.

What could it be? we wonder, but we don't dare say that to each other, cos Mrs Rex EATS people who talk when she's talking. Or, if they're in Year 4, she just uses them as a toothpick – not enough meat on them to make 'em worth scoffing.

Then Mrs Rex does that thing that adults often do, where they talk to each other in hushed tones, so us, the kids, can't hear anything that's going on.

We sit there, all of us trying to lean forward and earwig without them noticing. But the problem is, they're almost in a two-person rugby scrum, whispering away, only breaking

44

off occasionally to look up. And when they do
that, the only person they look at is me! I start to
wonder if I've got a massive bogey hanging out
of my nose or something. And, you know what,
it's not just me noticing it, either. Others start to
as well. Lucky is staring at me, and so are MandM
(who are probably having a telepathic conversation
about it too), and then Giraffles leans over.

"What have you done, Danny?" he whispers,
like he's going to be in trouble too cos he's my
best mate.

"*Nothing!*" I hiss. "I mean, I may have
forgotten to flush the loo before assembly, but it's
not like that's the crime of the century!"

Giraffles wrinkles his nose and leans away. Fat
lot of help *he* is. Finally, after what seems like a
lifetime of whispers and stares, Miss D and Mrs
Rex stand up and face us.

"Class," says Miss D, and she coughs
nervously – presumably scared by whatever
punishment she's about to dish out. "We

have an announcement to make. A BIG
announcement. Danny Mack, would you mind
joining us at the front."

I don't move. I daren't, though I definitely do
need the loo again, only this time I *will* flush, I
will, honest! It takes every ounce of control I have
left to *not* scream this at the top of my voice.

"Daniel MACK!" Mrs Rex hollers when I
don't move. "Don't make us ask you again."

And that's it. I have no choice but to begin
the walk of shame, up to the front, straight into
the clutches (and the jaws) of the terrifying,
terrible T. Rex...

7

I don't know how Miss D does this every day,
standing up here. Everyone looks at you, all the
time, and right now all I can see is thirty pairs
of eyes all asking me the same, silent question:
What did you DO, Danny Mack?

Because I still haven't got a clue what's going on.

"Danny," Mrs Rex says as she leans into me,
her dino-breath hot and sour. "Would you say
you're a *hero*?"

I cringe. I mean, what do you say to that? Is it
a trap? One that she wants me to fall into so she

can pick the meat off my bones?

"Me, Miss? No, Miss."

"But think back. What was the last heroic thing you did?"

I try thinking, but I haven't got anything for her. Apart from surviving a chokehold from Dylan that would've floored a championship wrestler. Oh, and surviving when he tried to dangle me off the balcony of our seventeenth-floor flat.

I choose not to say these out loud, though. Not to protect Dylan. I'd dob him in in a heartbeat, but there's Mum to think about, isn't there? As well as my own dignity.

"Dunno, Miss. Can't think of nothing, Miss."

"You mean you can't think of *anything*."

"Yes, Miss, what you said, Miss."

"Well, let me help you. I'd say that allowing all of your friends to escape a terrible storm before you is pretty heroic. Wouldn't you?"

I feel my cheeks flush, so I look at the floor.

"I'd say saving your brother from a falling tree that's just been hit by lightning is pretty brave too, wouldn't you?"

I'm now looking at the floor so hard that my neck is hurting. If this is what being famous really does feel like, then you can keep it. I *hate* this feeling. Give me a life where no one looks at you *ever*, please and thank you.

"Well, Danny, *you* may be shy about being a

hero, but I'm afraid it's not something that's going to go away. In fact, word seems to be spreading…"

I don't look up, but my ears have pricked in that direction.

"You see, this morning, we received an email …"

OK, I'm listening.

"… about a prize …"

I'm DEFINITELY listening.

"… for *bravery* …"

I'm now listening only to the sound of T. Rex's voice so I don't miss a word of what she says.

"… that YOU, Danny Mac, have WON!"

I hear what she says, but I don't believe it. I don't win things. I never have. Actually, that's not true, I won the sack race at sports day in Year 3, but was then disqualified because it turned out my sack had holes for my feet to wriggle through and that apparently gave me an "unfair advantage" (even though I didn't even cheat!). You can imagine the shame, can't you? Dylan pushed me off the podium in front of the whole school.

"There must be a mistake, Miss," I stammer, trying to nip the idea in the bud before anyone – most of all me – gets carried away. I'm almost looking for Dyl, hiding in the shadows, just waiting to embarrass me yet again.

"Oh, no, Danny, there's *no* mistake. Would you like me to prove it?"

I shake my head, then nod, then shake it again. But that only draws a scowl out of Mrs Rex, who clearly expects me to be doing cartwheels of joy. So I say *yes please* before she decides to eat me alive and use my bones to make herself a new set of earrings.

"I'd be delighted," she says, before striding to the laptop that's hooked up to the whiteboard.

By now, the atmosphere in the classroom is electric. Everyone, barring me, is well excited, looking at each other and mouthing wild ideas, but doing it quietly so they don't bring on the wrath of Mrs Rex.

But me? Well, I almost don't feel anything.

I'm too scared to. And I know that sounds dead ungrateful, but if something good *is* going to happen then I almost don't want to know, cos if it's not mine, then I can't ever lose it, can I? It can't ever fall out of my grip and smash on the floor because I've been clumsy, or because there's actually been a mistake and it was never mine to start with.

Fortunately, Mrs Rex is on hand to do her best to keep me in the dark as she fiddles with the laptop.

What is it with teachers and technology? Do they have to take an exam where they prove that they can't even turn on a light, never mind a computer? Or is it even more sinister? Maybe teachers are part of a shadowy organization and when they sign up they have to have an operation where the techy bit of their brain is removed? I don't know why they'd agree to that, or even what use it would be, but I've never met a teacher yet who can operate a remote control without throwing it to the floor in a strop.

Today is no different, and Mrs Rex ends up

calling Lucky to the front. He brings the screen to life in a split second, making Mrs Rex blush.

"So class, as I was saying, this morning I received an email. A very *mysterious* email, a very, *very* mysterious email indeed…"

As a class, we roll our eyes, as she's done that other really annoying teacher thing, where they start talking to you like a baby. I almost expect her to start tickling me under the chin.

"The email didn't say very much; only that you, Danny, had come to their attention. You and your bravery. And that, as a result, they wanted to send you the following message. Lucky, be a poppet and click on the link, will you, and Miss D, drop the blinds."

They both do as they're told, quickly, before Mrs Rex flicks off the lights. I'm sweating. A lot. I don't even know why. All I can do is wait and watch, as two figures with deep orange tans and iceberg-white smiles appear on the screen, and begin to talk…

8

There's two of them, a man and a woman, filling
every inch of the screen, and it's like they've
been chiseled from the side of a mountain –
they're all tanned and slick and muscly, and as
they grin it actually looks like their chins have
six-packs, which I didn't even know was possible.

"Helloooo, Danny Mack!" They wave, grins
somehow becoming even wider and more
blinding. "How are you doing, my friend?"

I frown – I can't help it, cos as smiley as they
are, I don't know them so how can I be their

friend? Anyway, the woman doesn't pause. She doesn't even seem to take a breath (probably cos her lungs are properly muscly as well).

"You probably don't know who we are…"

Nope, I think.

"But believe me, we know *all* about you!"

OK, that's a bit weird.

"Me and my brother here—"

"—Hi!" booms the man, in a voice that's deeper than the Grand Canyon. "I'm Teddy!"

"And I'm Flick!" continues the woman. "We should've done that bit first, shouldn't we? It's just that we're so excited to meet you!"

"You see," Teddy says, "we've spent *a lot* of time lately scouring the internet for the bravest young people on our planet. And that's how we found you. And, boy, are you brave!"

"That storm that you had to survive," says Flick. "Not just survive, but *zip line through* … well, it was a beast, a BEAST, I tell you!"

"Plus, you had the guts to wait till all your

friends were safe before thinking of yourself. So we think – in fact, we *know* – that YOU are worth celebrating."

My cheeks are on fire now. And I can't help wondering if they saw an edited version of the video, one where I *don't* scream and cry and wail and threaten to make an awful mess in my trousers.

"So," says Flick, her smile somehow getting both whiter *and* wilder, "we have decided to honour you and one other lucky person as the joint winners of our new prize: the Silver Lining Award for Bravery in the Face of Adversity."

I grab on to Miss D's desk. I have to, cos if I don't, I'll be a mess on the floor, and, correct me if I'm wrong, but I don't think that's what brave people do. And anyway, did I just hear right? Did they just tell me that I've won an award?

I think I must've heard right, though, as there's a gasp from everyone around me, and someone shouts, "What does he win?"

"So, let's talk about your prize..." adds Teddy,

like he's in the room, which is a bit creepy but I don't care cos he's talking about MY prize, after all. "We want you and five friends, plus a couple of your teachers, to join us here at our resort, *Mountain High*, in Norway!"

"Yes, that's right," giggles Flick. "For the past year, Mountain High has been establishing itself as *the* place to rest and recharge your batteries. But in fact, it's been going SO well, Teddy and I want a new challenge, and have decided to open up a new side to the resort – EXTREME SPORTS!"

They both grin madly, so happy with themselves that I can't help thinking that if they were ice lollies, they'd be licking themselves to bits. I don't think about it for long though, as they continue talking … and grinning.

"You and the other lucky winner will have the chance to put your bravery to the test. Bobsleighing, ski jumping, big footing – every kind of thrill ride you can imagine is right here for you here at our five-star hotel. So what are you waiting for, Danny? You and your friends need to dust off your passports, dig out your ski jackets and put on your earmuffs, as this is a prize that you are NEVER GOING TO FORGET!"

And with that, the video ends and the excitement begins. For, when I tear my eyes away from the screen, there are thirty faces looking at me, thirty-two if you include Miss D and Mrs Rex, and all of them are wearing the same expression that begs…

PLEASE TAKE ME WITH YOU!

I should be celebrating. I should be dancing on the ceiling, and I *am* excited, of course I am! But also, I'm thinking, how do I choose who gets to join me…?

What on earth do I do now?

9

First thing Mum does when I tell her about Norway is dive for her phone.

Not to tweet about it — she's no twitter-er or tweeter-er, or whatever they're called — no, I know what she's checking: her bank balance.

Mum works her bum off. Always has. As many jobs as she can fit into the day: cleaning mostly, but she'll paint people's houses if they ask her, or do the filing, or do their nails (not with the same paint). She can do *anything*, my mum, she's ace, which is why I don't want her to worry.

"It's OK!" I yell, snatching the phone off her and throwing it on to the settee. "It's all paid for. The flights, food, activities – everything! Not just for me, for five mates too."

She looks like she's remembered how to breathe again, which is good, but she still has worries.

"But you'll need warm clothes! And gloves … and a hat!"

"Er … last time I checked, we don't live in Australia. I have a ski jacket."

It's an old coat of Dyl's (a bargain Mum snapped up in the local charity shop), but I'm used to that. And anyway, I washed it twenty-three times before wearing it for the first time, just to get rid of all traces of him.

"Anything else I need, I'll borrow, Mum, I promise. Or I'll raise the money myself, like last time."

"Er, no you won't. Last time you nearly cut off five ears shaving kids' heads, and I'm a cleaner, not a bloomin' surgeon."

I hate it when she brings that up. I didn't mean to do it — I was nervous, my hands were shaking.

"And besides," she says, "I *want* to be able to buy you the stuff you need, but after new uniform and Dyl's army kit … well, there's not a lot left over this month."

I give her a hug and remind myself to buy her a flipping massive mansion when I become a world-famous and mega-rich explorer. One with a pool and a helicopter landing pad and a tennis court … oh, and a cell for Dyl to be tortured — I mean, *live* — in.

Unfortunately, just at that moment, Dyl decides to crawl out from under his rock.

"Hey, Dylan." Mum smiles. "Say well done to your brother. He's just won a massive trip to Norway!"

"I heard," he says, face straight, not a trace of a smile.

And then he does it. He says the worst words imaginable. Words I should've expected if I'd been smart enough to think ahead.

"So, when are we going?"

And that's it. My life is over. Just when I think that there has been a chink in the clouds and I'm going to escape from him before he leaves home for good, here comes Hurricane Dylan, intent on maximum destruction and ultimate unhappiness. I could weep, fall to the floor, bite the settee in anguish, but I know I have to come up with a decent argument to put an end to this before it starts.

"You…? Dylan…? Come…?"

"You certainly didn't win the prize for speech-making, did you?" he sneers. "And anyway, what's brave about squealing your way down a zip line? If they wanted to choose a real hero they should've come looking in my direction."

He lifts his arm and flexes his bicep, nearly hitting me in the face with it. What *is* it with him? Isn't it bad enough that his fists are lethal weapons, without his muscles themselves being the equivalent of a boxing glove?

Just as I think things can't get any worse, they do. For some weird reason, Mum decides to take Dyl's side.

"You know, if you're allowed to choose who goes with you, maybe Dylan *should* be on your list. After all, he *was* up there at the end with you, and besides—"

Here they come, I think, *the worst four words in the world, the ones I never want to hear…*

"—he *is* your brother."

"I knew you'd understand, Mum," Dylan brags, "because, dear little brother of mine, Mum knows what *really* went on up on the top of that mountain. Only a mother could possibly know the truth." And he gives her a look, which is meant to show what an angel he is, but at that moment I swear I can see the horns popping out of the top of his head. Not to mention his eyeballs glowing red.

It makes it difficult to come up with a decent argument, I can tell you that, but just as despair sets in, Mum shows her true colours.

"Mind you, Dyl, I have to say, it's a bit of a risk, isn't it? An extreme sports holiday so close to your basic training."

She lets the sentence hang there for a minute and I see the cogs in Dyl's brain start whirring. Slowly. They could definitely use some oil, that's for sure.

"I mean," Mum continues, "I know the idea of Norway and mountains and bobsleighing is appealing … but then again, how long have you wanted to join the army?

I watch as Dyl tries to remember, but he doesn't have enough fingers to do the job.

"Ages," is all he can manage.

"That's what I thought," says Mum, nodding, "so really it's up to you, son. You can go wild in Norway, put your body on the line and possibly come home in a plaster cast, miss your sign-up date, maybe rule yourself out of a career in the SAS, or…" Mum lets the alternative hang in the air.

I see what she's doing, and boy do I like it.

"Yeah," says Dyl, nodding way too hard for it to look realistic, "I was thinking the same thing. Why go to the playground with the little kids when there's a whole world of adventure out there with the big boys and girls? Sorry, little brother, but it looks like you'll have to survive this one without me."

And he punches me in the arm so hard that it

feels like a bomb's gone off, before going back to his grubby little lair.

I could cry. I really could. Yes, because my arm hurts. But mostly because of relief, and love for my mum.

"Thanks, Mum," I say.

"For what?"

"For getting me out of that ... for keeping him away from my trip."

"That's all right, Danny love. I can see what it means to you. Plus, I know that one day, the two of you will get on and be friends."

I look at her long and hard. How can someone so smart get something so horribly and terribly wrong?

"Yeah, Mum, sure," I smile, and go back to what I was worrying about ten minutes ago: how am I meant to choose who goes on the trip without everyone hating me?

10

Three days on, when I get to my desk in class, there's a present waiting for me. Plus, another two on my chair. There's also a balloon tied to my desk which says, *You've got a friend in me*, and when I open the drawer, an invite to laser quest is hiding inside from a lad who barely ever speaks to me.

I sigh, then feel ungrateful, then feel a typhoon of pressure building in my brain that makes me want to scream, *AAAAAAAAARRRGHHHHH, THANKYOUBUTSTOPITNOW. IDON'TKNOWWHOTOCHOOSE!*

It started the day after the news broke. A big box of chocolates from James Hickton and a really nice note saying how he'd love me to come for tea one night.

By the end of lunch that day I had another box of choccies, a bag of liquorice as big as my head and a pizza made entirely out of sweets nestling in my bag.

I mean, it's all very flattering, but:

A. I know what people are *really* after, and

B. Being popular is going to make my teeth so rotten they'll fall out of my head.

I mean, I know who I'd like to choose, but how do I do that without upsetting everyone else? I've no idea, and it's getting to me, all of it. I'm so

YOU'VE GOT A FRIEND IN ME!

nervous that I haven't managed to eat my packed lunch in three days, never mind a pizza made entirely out of sugar! I realize I'm not hiding it very well when Miss D pulls me aside at the end of the day.

"You must be excited about the trip, Danny?"

"I am," I say, pasting on my best *I'm really grateful and lucky* smile.

"It's created quite a buzz in class, hasn't it? Everyone wondering who's going to be joining you?"

I nod, not knowing what to say.

"So … have you thought about it? Who to take? It's quite a responsibility."

And that's it. That's all she has to say to make my chest feel weird and a mahoosive lump to appear in my throat.

I try to swallow it down but it feels like a watermelon and I look for words but none appear, though a stray tear or two *does* escape, so I brush them away pronto. I mean, what would

73

Dylan say if he saw this? I'd never live it down.

Then Miss D does what Miss D does best: she smiles. Not in a cruel way – she's not laughing that I'm sad, she's proper kind (when she's not eating weird bugs).

"You know, Danny, I was thinking, perhaps I could help you with the big decisions. Because, and you can stop me if I'm wrong, I know there are definitely people you'd love to join you …"

I nod and manage a smile.

"… but how do you choose those people without upsetting everyone else? Wow. To be honest, Danny, I don't think I could carry that responsibility on my own. I think I'd need someone's help, someone to be the fall guy, to take the heat off me when it all gets announced."

I nod so hard I pull fifteen muscles in my neck.

"Hm, so I wonder, who might that person be, Danny? Who might be the fall guy?"

"Well…" I murmur, "Maybe, well, could you… I mean, *would* you… I mean, would—?"

"I'd be delighted," she says, interrupting. "Tomorrow morning, after register, I would be delighted to do that for you. After all, you took plenty of hits on our last school trip, didn't you? Enough for all of us."

And with that, she walks off to break up a baked bean war at the other side of the canteen. I've no idea how she's going to pull this off, but for now I can breathe slightly easier and feel my stomach awake for the first time in days.

Now, where did I put that pizza?

11

Next morning, Miss D becomes a living, breathing saint. "Class!" she says. "Quiet now. I have news."

Silence falls, freakishly fast.

"Now, I'm sure you have all been wondering who will be joining Danny in Norway."

There are whoops and yelps and hollers and I'm pretty sure someone breaks wind as well, but Miss D ignores all of it, though she does wrinkle her nose when the waft hits her.

"So I'm delighted to announce who the lucky

individuals are … though there *has* been a slight change of plan."

Silence descends again, though it's a different type as the people who bought me the prezzies are suddenly frowning and shuffling in their seats.

"Mrs Rix and I have spoken to the very kind organizers, who agree with us that being on such a trip is a HUGE honour and responsibility, and as a result they have agreed that it will be *us*, Mrs Rex – I mean, *Rix* – and I, who will be choosing the winners, and not Danny."

I don't know how to react. Should I look cross, like this is the most outrageous thing to happen since they served us parsnips in the canteen and tried to pass them off as chips? If I do that, it'd be cruel to Miss D, wouldn't it? When she's doing me a massive favour. Anyway, turns out I don't need to do a thing, as everyone else looks cross on my behalf, booing and shouting, "Not fair!" and stuff like that.

"ER!" barks Miss D – and it's not often she

looks cross. "Outbursts like that are NOT going to convince me that ANYONE deserves to go!"

Silence again. I want to drop a pin and hear it perforate everyone's eardrums. Miss D can be well powerful when she wants to be.

"So. In no particular order…" (she makes it sound like *The X Factor* or something) "the children joining Danny in Norway, are…"

(Cue a pause that goes on so long that I reckon I could celebrate three birthdays.)

"For his bravery in saving our tour leader on the last school trip: Thomas Raffles!"

Giraffles is out of his chair and trying to floss, which is nothing short of disastrous. I mean, who flosses any more? Plus, his arms are so long that he's in danger of tying them into knots that even a chief scout couldn't untangle.

I'm well chuffed though, obviously. Cos he's my best mate, yeah, but it's true what she said. He saved old Geri from sliding off that cliff and he wasn't even wearing a cape!

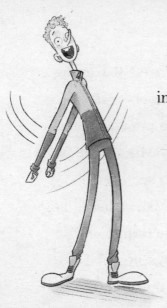

"Next, for academic excellence in *every* subject: Lucky Success!" Bless Lucky, he doesn't celebrate like a loon, just smiles his best smile, knowing that his super brain is going to help him get to a lot of places other than Norway.

"For excellence in co-operation and collaboration: Marcus and Maureen!" The twins embark on a handshake so elaborate that only their telepathic minds could manage it.

There are plenty of disappointed faces already, but mine's not one of them. Miss D is doing me proud here. She knows full well that these are the guys I would've invited, and she's taken every bit of heat off me! But then I realize there's

still one place to be claimed. And all my mates have already been chosen. So I'm a bit stumped about the name she's going to throw into the mix.

"And finally, the last place to be filled falls to a young man who never, ever gives up ... and never, ever fails to make us laugh. And that, in itself, is a trait that we should celebrate..."

My heart stops. My stomach lurches. She isn't? She hasn't? She couldn't be ... could she?

"So congratulations, Jonny Walker. You'd best get your suitcase packed as you're on your way to Norway!"

I want to groan, but that would be way selfish given the bullets Miss D's taken for me. Instead I look to Jonny, who hasn't got a

clue why people are staring at him, or why there are evil eyes looking in his direction. He was too busy, as usual, sneaking a look at his phone under his desk.

"Norway?" he asks, stunned. "Is that a place?" before googling it on one of his phones, his eyes widening in concern. "'Will I get a signal there?"

Thirty people fight the urge to bash their heads repeatedly against their desks, but Miss D does what she always does and looks on the bright side.

"Well, you lucky few. Mrs Rix and I will look forward to the adventure that lies ahead!"

And at that moment, nothing can dull my enthusiasm. Not even our terrifying headteacher joining us.

In fact, it could be fun. I mean, imagine a T-Rex on skis!

12

OK, so airports are pretty exciting!

Or, at least, they are once you manage to finally say goodbye to your evil older brother.

He's been like a limpet for days, offering advice and the occasional threat (of course), trying to come with me and Mum down the charity shop to find cheap jumpers and gloves. Dylan's helpfulness is harder to trust. He even tried to help me pack. Not that I want him anywhere *near* my bag: knowing him, he'd probably booby-trap it.

In fact, I don't properly relax till we get

past passport control and Miss D assures me that Dylan can't hurt me now. As I turn the final corner though, I see him laughing in my direction. And not just chuckling either. Proper, full on, bending-double-like-you're-about-to-weep guffawing.

I think about how he managed to get himself invited on our last school trip at the very last minute, posing as a responsible adult, and the tricks and torture he inflicted on me. And even now, as we reach the security checks, I still reckon he's going to find a way. He'll end up being the air steward, or even worse the pilot. He'll make us loop-de-loop till I throw up my breakfast. He'll lock me in the tiny loo and refuse to let me out till I've cleaned the bowl with my tongue. Before I know it, I'm sweating like I'm in the Sahara, not on the way to the Norwegian mountains.

"Chill out, mate!" says Lucky, before kindly buying me a bag of crisps from the vending machine, which I never normally can cos they're well expensive.

He's right about Dyl, I guess, but I realize it's not just that plonker that I'm nervous about.

"How many times you flown before, Lucky?" I ask.

He looks stumped. "Dunno, mate. Quite a few I suppose." He doesn't say it to be cocky, cos that's not his way. Not like our Dyl, who could eat takeaway chicken for tea and pass it off as a five-star feast.

"It's just … well … I haven't flown before, have I? And to be honest I haven't got the foggiest—"

"—how the plane even stays in the air?"

"Exactly!" I yell, so grateful that someone understands. "How does it *do* that?"

"Beats me," he replies. "But my dad always told me you're statistically more likely to be involved in a car crash than have a problem on a plane."

"We're more likely to have another nightmare trip than lose a wing then!"

"Danny," Lucky smiles. "*Nothing* could be

worse than last time. Our plane could have one wing and no engine, and it'd still be safer than the last school outing!"

That makes me relax a bit, not even fretting when we have to empty our pockets at the security point. It never takes me long to fish all the loose change out of my pockets, but I didn't expect to have to take my shoes and belt off too. I have to keep hold of the waist of my jeans and waddle through the body scanner. They used to belong to Dyl, like most of my clothes, and they don't fit me very well – like most of my clothes.

Once we're dressed, we sit and wait for the others.

It takes three guards to explain to MandM that they can't go through the scanner at the same time despite them being twins, and Giraffles gets an extra-long stare from them as well. Maybe they think his long limbs are fake or something? Maybe they think he's got hidden stolen cash rolled up inside 'em. Who knows, but they definitely scan him twice to make sure, much to our amusement.

It's Jonny next, and of course we expect him to do something daft.

"Phone in your pocket, son?" he's asked.

He nods reluctantly and palms it into the tray, but when he walks through the scanner the alarm goes mental.

"You haven't got another, have you?" the scowling guard says.

"A few," he replies.

"A few? How many is a few?"

That's what causes the biggest delay – Jonny rifling around until he pulls out three more smartphones and a handset so old that it looks like it was made by a caveman. It's that big it doesn't even fit in his pocket. The wally has got it tucked into his flipping sock.

The guard shakes his head and waves him through. Not that Jonny cares. He doesn't take his eyes off the basket his beloved phones are nestled in. I swear, before he pockets the last one he actually gives it a little kiss.

"Won't be long now," Lucky says, as we watch Mrs Rex prowl through the gates. The alarms buzz angrily, but the guards look so petrified of her that they give her the briefest of body searches before waving her through.

Which just leaves Miss D. And she's hardly going to be any bother, is she? What with her being so bloomin' kind and jolly.

But as she walks through the gate – off goes the alarm! So she takes off her belt and tries again.

SQUEAAAAL! goes the siren.

Blushing, she pulls a compass from her pocket.

"Anything else?" she's asked. She reluctantly pulls out a first aid kit.

And a GPS device,

and an emergency sewing kit,

and an avalanche whistle,

and some tweezers,

and an eye patch,

and some rubber gloves,

and a torch,

and a miniature fishing kit,

and a lighter,

and some kindling.

"Madam?" the guard asks. "Are you going on holiday or hoping to survive a nuclear attack?"

"Don't be silly," she replies like it's the daftest question ever. "We're going on a school trip."

"So you don't really *need* these items, do you?"

She looks at him like he's gone mad.

"Are you kidding me? You should see what's in my suitcase!"

"If you don't mind, madam, I'll give it a miss.

Though when the zombie apocalypse finally arrives, I'll be sure to knock on your front door," and he waves her through, after confiscating nearly everything that was hidden in her pockets.

By the time she reaches us, they're calling us over the tannoy to board our plane, but it's hard to run quickly when you're laughing so hard.

13

I imagine the view out the plane window is going to be amazing.

I don't get to find out, as from the second it takes off and throws me back into my seat, I shut my eyes tightly. I don't care if crashes are rare; this plane must weigh more than a herd of rhinos, and there's no reason it should stay in the air other than witchcraft. And as I didn't see Dumbledore putting his wand through security, I don't even have faith that a spell is keeping us off the ground.

There's one point, about an hour in, that I open my eyes a touch, but can't see out the window anyway as Jonny is filming on all his phones at the same time. Not that he'll be able to watch any of them back once we crash into the flipping sea.

Instead I grip the armrests so hard that they start to mould round my fingers. I ignore offers of food and drinks and little boiled sweets to stop my ears popping as we start to land. And I try to do it while retaining my cool to my friends. Do I manage it? How the heck do I know – I've got my chuffin' eyes closed, haven't I? But I can't hear them laughing, so maybe they just think I'm asleep. Or dead from fright.

As soon as the wheels roughly touch the tarmac (I scream, before turning it into a sneeze like a flippin' genius) and the plane comes to a stop, I'm on my feet and ready for the doors to open. Two minutes later, after hugging the air steward way too hard, I'm running down this little corridor, only stopping when a big man with a very bushy beard sitting behind a desk asks me for my passport.

By the time the others catch me up I've calmed down a bit. You can't actually see my heart thumping through my shirt any more, though you *can* still see the waterfall of sweat forcing its way through my jumper, which is now so sodden it's as if I've been carrying Dylan on my back.

"All right, Danny?" Giraffles asks, patting me on the back and then regretting it.

"Perfect! Ideal. A–1! What could possibly be wrong?!" I say, way too enthusiastically and in a voice that sounds like a pig that's just inhaled a shedload of helium.

"Dunno. You just seem a bit … jumpy?"

"Me? Jumpy? HAHAHAHAHAHAHA, whatever makes you think that?" I say, before jumping into his arms as Miss D taps me on the shoulder.

"Goodness, Danny, are you OK?" she asks.

"I'M FINE!" I yell, making sure everyone in the airport and indeed the whole country of Norway can hear. "I'm *fine* and I am definitely NOT freaked out by being stuck in a plane that clearly had no business staying in the air for so long!"

Miss D looks at me sympathetically. "Well, that's great, Danny. Now listen, I want you all to go to the loo before we leave the airport."

"But I don't need to go, Miss," I say. And it's true. I've sweated so much there's not a drop of liquid left inside my body.

"Not to … you know … have a wee. Have you looked outside?"

I haven't. Mainly because I've been panicking so much about the fact that I survived the plane journey. So when I look outside it's a relief, cos I'm no longer worried about the plane – now I'm worried about freezing to death! It's snowing, and not like in a Christmas card where the flakes fall occasionally and are all proper beautiful flakes. Oh no. These flakes are coming down in their squillions, whipping around in the howling wind like a snowstorm and a typhoon have joined forces.

"I think everyone could do with looking in their cases and putting on some extra layers, don't you?"

I nod, hard, and run off to the bog, pulling my case behind me.

Lucky is already in there, pulling on the coolest-looking ski jacket and thermal trousers. They're all shiny, so much so that they almost seem to be changing colour as he turns in front of the mirror to check himself out.

Giraffles isn't far behind him, pulling on a polo neck that I swear his mum has knitted especially for him: the neck is so long that it could probably keep my tower block warm from October through to April.

I don't want to open my suitcase in front of the others though. The clothes in there are OK. They're aren't holey or anything; Mum sewed up anything that looked a bit tired, but none of it's new. They're either borrowed, or handed down, or found in the charity shop. And even then Mum has a habit of arguing the prices down with the old ladies that work in there. It's embarrassing! They look at me like I'm a right sad case. Anyway, I can't compete with Lucky, or Giraffles, or probably even Jonny. Though, knowing him, he'll have a massive thick woolly jumper with a mobile phone knitted on to the front of it.

So I pull my case into the toilet cubicle, which is a squeeze, and lift it on to the loo seat, before opening the zip.

And then?

Then, I do ... nothing.

Except stare into the case.

And it's lucky there's no liquid left in my body, cos if there was, I'd probably cry you a river, or more likely an ocean.

Cos Dylan has gone and done it again, hasn't he?

He's not even in the same country, but he's

still with me, stitching me up, laughing in my ear.

I hate him. He is the devil in human form. And I want him to hear me, hear how angry I am, so I let rip with a single word that is so loud it shatters every bit of glass in the building. "DYYYYYLLLLLLLAAAAAAAAAAAAAAAN!"

14

I'm not dressed for the weather but I'm not cold either.

No chance. My embarrassment, as I sit on the coach that's crawling through the blizzard, is keeping me tropically warm.

I wouldn't mind, but it's not even very easy to sit down: the rubber ring around my waist, unicorn shaped for maximum humiliation, makes it properly difficult to even slump against the seat.

Yes, you heard right.

A rubber inflatable ring shaped like a unicorn.

But you know what? It ties right in with the bright pink armbands, plus the goggles and snorkel that sit on my head instead of a woolly hat. Not to mention the lime-green mankini that is stretched over the top of the few warm clothes that I was already wearing.

Everything else that me and Mum bought is missing from the case, though Dyl did include a couple of bricks that made the case *feel* as though it was full.

I mean, what is it with him? What evil lurks inside his head that makes him so hell-bent on making my entire life a misery? I asked myself this while hiding in the loo. Even when Miss D and Mrs Rex were outside telling me to come out *immediately.*

In the end, Mrs Rex went proper prehistoric on me, just stopping short of threatening to rip me limb from limb like she would a helpless raptor.

"Daniel Mack!" she roared. "I don't care what is in that case of yours. You will put on *everything* in there *this instant*, and you will *not* take it off until we reach our destination. Do you hear me?"

So I did. I did what I was told, which explains why I'm sat here like the biggest wally to ever walk the planet. I had to walk through the airport too, while people pointed and stared and laughed and whipped out their phones. I'm probably on the Internet already. Probably got a squillion views and every single one of 'em is another arrow to my wounded heart. Honestly, this makes wiping your bum with nettles seem like a tiddly, honest mistake.

The others were kind. Well, they were once they'd picked themselves off the floor and stopped laughing. Even Giraffles, my best mate in the whole world, couldn't suppress a giggle, which is rich given that his polo neck was longer than the plane we flew over on.

Jonny didn't make it any easier either. As we walked through the airport, he papped me every step of the way, with every phone he had, which was impressive as I was practically sprinting to get my sorry backside out of there.

And so here I am, face burning red like I've been on a tropical beach all day, but Mrs Rex is sticking to her word and making me wear my costume all the way there as punishment for not coming out of the cubicle the second she told me to.

It's all right for her, she's wearing a proper ski jacket (although it's patterned with scales, which makes her look even more dinosaur-deadly than normal).

All I can do is sit here and hope. Hope she'll change her mind soon. Hope that my embarrassment will burn a hole in all my inflatable gear and they'll deflate before we reach where we're heading.

But they don't. The journey takes hours, and I watch every mile of it. These huge beautiful lakes called "fjords" appear, and the water is calm – so calm it looks like a mirror that me and my unicorn can float on. But beyond the water, that's where we're heading. Up into the hills. In fact, they're not hills. That's like calling a marathon *quite a long way*.

These are mountains! And they make the ones we saw on our last school trip look like molehills.

I'm not going to need a snorkel at the top of that mountain – I'm going to need an oxygen mask!

But then I think about our last school trip AGAIN, and I get the fear AGAIN. Cos it was only when we got there that everything started to go wrong. We had to pitch our own tents with no instructions. If we wanted a glass of milk we had to pull it straight out of the cow. We had to poo in a bucket!

I mean, what's going to happen *here*? Am I going to have to build my own igloo whilst wearing swimming gear?

It's going to be a nightmare. It's going to be hideous, it's going to be the worst few days of my entire life.

But then we arrive.

And my jaw ... just ... drops.

15

I wish Dyl hadn't pinched the sunglasses out of my case, cos right now I definitely need them, and not just because of the snow.

OK, so there's loads of it – metres and metres of the stuff, all powdery and bright, begging to be played in (if you weren't wearing a mankini). You could make a *billion* snowmen – an army of them – and you still wouldn't use even half of it. But it's not just the snow that's gleaming. It's the *whole place*: the buildings, the resort, *everything*.

It looks brand spanking new.

There's no tents, no cows waiting to be milked, and, if first impressions are anything to go by, you can bet that you won't have to go to the loo in a bucket. If anything, it'll be a white-gold throne with toilet paper so soft it'd make an angel sing. And cry. Simultaneously.

I can see an indoor swimming pool with water slides sticking out the side of the building, a pack of obedient huskies stood by a sled that looks as sleek as any Porsche, and another gleaming building that I'm guessing is our luxury lodge. I'm guessing this cos in red neon, on the side of it, is a sign that beams "Luxury Lodge". Sherlock's got nothing on me, I tell you.

"Whoa," we all sigh, even Lucky, who is well used to the luxury life.

But if we think the future looks bright, it's nothing compared to the grins that move into view.

"Friends! Welcome to our hotel! Our pride and joy!" two voices sing in unison from the doorway, and I have to guess that it's our hosts, Teddy and Flick. I can't be sure because I have to hide my eyes behind both my eyelids and hands to stop my retinas from burning, but as I said, my detective skills are seriously good these days. A lot better than my fashion sense. I mean, what must they be thinking as they look at me?

The only thing that makes me feel better is how gingerly they approach our bus, slipping on the ice half a dozen times each, hanging on to each other for dear life.

"Ha," chuckles Giraffles. "You'd think they'd have got the hang of slippery bits by now, living up here?"

It is a bit weird, I suppose, but I can't think anything of it for long, as two hands start pumping my own with an elaborate handshake. I can see through squinted eyes they're doing the same to everyone, except Jonny, who is doing a strange kind of dance.

"What are you doing, Jonny?" I ask.

He holds his phones aloft like they were the

World Cup. "Whaddya think? Celebrating! Full signal, every phone. In fact…" He grins, staring at them in turn. "Wi-Fi! Must be fibre optic! Superfast, baby!"

He sinks to his knees and kisses each of his handsets in turn.

"I'm sorry," I say, as my eyes start to work again and I find Teddy and Flick towering over me like another couple of mountains. "You'll have to forgive my friend. He's…" I search for the right word. I don't want to offend Jonny, even though he's oblivious to the fact that we're talking about him.

"Different?" they suggest together.

"I'd say *bonkers* covers it more accurately," I whisper, cos I do like Jonny, underneath all of his … weirdness.

"Bonkers is GREAT!" they say, again together, which is good as I remember about the rubber unicorn, and slither awkwardly out of it. "You're going to have to be a little bit crazy to try out everything we have lined up for you here," says Teddy.

"Yes, we're going to take you all the way to the edge ... and then ... we're all going to jump off!" adds Flick, and she looks like she really, really means it.

Now, I'm no chicken (well, not completely). OK, OK, so I may have got wigged out by the whole aeroplane thing, but let's not forget whose bravery got us here in the first place.

I always thought, though, that the edge is probably far enough to go. Why not take your nerves all the way to the edge, then shuffle back from the huge gaping precipice and have a nice cup of hot chocolate to celebrate? Isn't that enough?

Anyway, I don't say this out loud, course I don't, I do it in my head, as everyone else is grinning and beaming and whooping in excitement. Especially Miss D, which really, REALLY scares me.

Everyone is so happy that Flick pulls her

phone out of her pocket and starts snapping
endlessly with the camera. "Don't mind me,"
she beams, "I do this all the time. For our social
media. Instagram, Snapchat, Twitter – we're
huge on them all. HUGE!"

Doesn't mean a lot to me, to be honest. The only
phone I have is a burner. No games, no Wi-Fi, you
have to talk really nicely to it to persuade it to even
send a text, so snap-wotsit is a bit out of my reach
and over my head.

Anyway, the photos go on and on – for a bit
too long to be honest, especially as my mankini
isn't thermal. Just as my extremities are starting
to frost over, we hear a cough from over Teddy
and Flick's shoulder. And, as they turn round, we
see six more kids, all our age, though all of them
are dressed way more sensibly then me. There
isn't an inflatable unicorn or inappropriate swim
costume in sight.

"Aaah, forgive me," smiles Teddy. "Danny
and friends, let me introduce you to our other

guests, the wonderful students of St Virtuous International Prep School."

At first glance, they look brave (and warm – not that I'm jealous). They're all wearing matching ski jackets, with a crest of two hearts on them that looks so real that for a second I think I can see them beating in tandem. Unlike Teddy and Flick, they also seem completely at home on the ice and snow – not a single slip or slide between them.

The two teachers are no less impressive. Both are six feet tall and look more like professional weightlifters than anything else. They aren't so good at smiling though, despite how widely Miss D beams at them, which makes me cross – no one disses our teacher without it being noted.

Anyway, in that second, I know, *KNOW*, that whatever these guys did to be here, it was WAY more impressive than the sight of me bricking it as I came down that zip line. They probably fought off a pride of ravenous lions with only the use of a paperclip, or survived a flood by fashioning a life raft out of the Year 1 students or something.

Turns out, as Flick starts to speak again, that I'm (nearly) right…

16

"Danny, let me introduce you to Blaize. Blaize Cosmo, this is the wonderful Danny Mack."

Blimey, I think, *what a name!*

At least I *think* it's a name. It's so exotic and out of this world that it sounds more like a space rocket that's off to probe the outer reaches of the solar system. That, or a Las Vegas magician who can make Big Ben disappear up his sleeve.

Anyway, this lad steps forward confidently, a fire in his eyes that matches his name. He's not bigger than me, just broader (and warmer)

and when he shakes my
hand it's like I'm being
gripped by a polar bear.
He has a grasp of steel
and he's not afraid to
use it. I try to squeeze
back, in a friendly way, but
every time I do, he does it
harder, in a mean way, until I
actually think that my poor
frostbitten pinkies are about
to snap off and fall to the ground.

As I don't want to spend the rest of my life
searching the snow for my weedy blue fingers, I
do the decent thing, and gently pull my hand away.

Well, I do when he lets go of me.

"You two are the *bravest* young men we have
ever come across. Danny, to put your friends first
during one of the most savage storms on record
was incredible. And Blaize, what can we say? To
run back into a classroom when it's on fire? Well,

some would say it was reckless and stupid, but it was also INCREDIBLY brave."

I. Am. Gobsmacked. And, man, do I feel like a fraud now. Me, brave? Next to what he did? Er … hello?

"You …" I stammer, "you ran back into a burning classroom … to save your friends?"

He looks at me, eyes still burning, and I swear I can almost picture him dashing bravely into the room.

"Nah," he says, like it's nothing, like all he did was cut his toenails on a wet Tuesday afternoon. "They were all out and safe. I went back in for Fluffball."

There's a moment when I think I've misheard him, then I realize he really did say "fluffball", so I do what anyone would do, and I laugh a bit, cos, well it was an unexpected word.

"Fluffball? What is that, a nickname for your teacher or something?"

His eyes narrow and the flames snuff

themselves out, only to be replaced by the iciest of glares.

"*Fluffball*," he spits, "is our class mascot. Our guinea pig. He has been with us since reception and HE IS TOTALLY WORTH SAVING FROM A BURNING BUILDING!"

Well, I don't really know what to say to that. I'm not sure I'd help Dyl if he had a splinter in his thumb, so the whole, well, you know, risking-getting-burnt-alive-to-save-a-guinea-pig thing seems extreme. (Maybe cos we've never had a pet? The insurance was too expensive, never mind the food.)

So I do the decent thing and congratulate him. I don't shake his hand though, not after last time. I playfully thump him on the bicep instead, then have to hide the pain that shoots through my fist and into every single cell in my body. He's built like our Dylan, which makes me like him even less.

"Meet the others," says Flick, taking attention away from the fact that my fist is now shattered into a squazillion pieces.

We're introduced to Milo, who
is just as big as Blaize (I wave
instead of shaking – wouldn't
you?), plus Andreas, August
and Amelia, who I instantly see
are triplets. Not cos they look
similar, they kind of do, but
not identically so. I know cos
they're not even looking at us.
They're reading. The same
book. And I don't mean, three kids, three books.
Oh no, they're reading the same copy, and they
must be reading at exactly the same speed, since
August, who's in the middle and holding the
book, turns the page without asking the other
two if they're ready.

"Hello," I say, but they say nothing. Instead
they just suddenly all laugh and point at the
same line on the page. At exactly the same time.

And I thought MandM were freaky! Marcus

and Maureen don't look impressed though. They
don't say anything, not to us anyway, though
they're probably having a telepathic conversation
about how triplets are weird and twins are
WAAAAY better.

The two teachers have odd names too.
Something long and regal sounding. I'm pretty
sure one of their surnames was triple-barrelled,
never mind double. Anyway, I don't give it much
space in my brain, as there's still one person to
meet. A girl, stood at the back. Like the triplets,

she *doesn't* look impressed to meet us. She's got her head stuck in something too, but it's not a book. It's a phone.

"And this is Jasmine. Jasmine Denim. Say hello, Jasmine," says Flick excitedly.

I wait for a response, but … nothing. Not a flicker, apart from the flicker that comes from her phone as she scrolls down the screen.

"She only answers to Jasmina Denima," Blaize explains with a tut.

"Why?" Giraffles ask. "What is it, her superhero name or something?"

"Hardly," replies Flick. "It's her Insta handle. She *lives* on Instagram. The only way you'll ever learn anything about her is by following her online."

Me and Giraffles share a shrug. It doesn't do it for me, that social media stuff, but as I turn around I see Jonny has eyes like soup bowls. He's staring, staring, staring and not blinking. It's like someone has removed his eyelids or something.

"It ..." he gasps, "it's ... *beautiful.*"

"Mate," I whisper. "You can't call her an *it*!"

"But it's ... it's a Goldvish Eclipse. 64GB of onboard storage and a Snapdragon quad-core processor."

"She's called Jasmine. Or *Jasmina* if you want her to talk to you."

"I never thought they actually existed. I've only seen them online."

"What, girls? Jonny, you go to school with loads of 'em!"

He looks at me like *I'm* the wally, not him, and staggers forward towards both Jasmina and the thing he *really* fancies ... her phone. But he hides his own phones first. Next to hers, his look like antiques.

Oh man, I think. I never realized love looked like this. Then I feel a bit sick and make myself think about something else. Like how much my hand still hurts.

"The most important thing," says Flick, interrupting my pain, "is that you settle in, and have the most *amazing* experience. We want you to have the *time of your lives* these next few days. And we don't want it to feel like school, for the students *or* the teachers." I see the St Virtuous teachers share a smile as they're told they can relax if they want to, or hit the gym, though I see from Miss D's face that she wants to put her new love of adventuring to the test. Plus, I know Mrs Rex will be watching us like a hawk (a prehistoric one).

"So, make yourselves at home," calls Flick, "because the biggest adventure of your lives, is almost … about … to begin!"

17

"This place is unreal!" laughs Giraffles, as we sit on chairs that are actually *in* the swimming pool. "Another drink?"

I nod, cos that's how we roll these days: we sit on chairs in a swimming pool and lean against the bar, which is *also* inside the pool. I want to text Mum about it, but she'd never believe me.

We order two more mocktails called "Icebergs" and lick our lips as they glide down our throats.

"S'alright here, innit?" I sigh.

"I'd rather be home on the estate, obviously,"
Giraffles grins, "but I'm doing this for you,
mate, just remember that."

I finish my drink and smile. "Aw, cheers, pal.
Shall we have another one?"

"As long as we can clobber a water slide
while they make it?" he asks.

"Be rude not to," I reply. And off we slide.
There's no need to queue; we have the whole

pool to ourselves.

The first few hours are all as good as this. The "Luxury Lodge" does exactly what it says on the tin. We don't have to carry our own cases (never mind put up our own tents!) and we're even offered rooms of our own! Not that me and Giraffles take them up on it. I mean, what's the point of living in luxury if there's no one to giggle with about it?

"Look!" we yell, as we walk into our room. "The towels!"

Me and Mum have watched loads of travel programmes where they fold the towel into the shape of a boat or something lame, but on my bed there's a white towel which has been sculpted into a flipping ski-jumper, while Giraffles' is a snowboarder.

There's a little box of chocolates on each pillow, and bottle after bottle of fizzy pop in a little fridge, while the showerhead is as big as our entire bathroom at home.

"Teddy and Flick must be minted!" I say.

"Yeah ... and well generous!"

We fill our gobs with chocolates and bottles of fizz. I even think about having a shower, before realizing I don't need one. I had one two weeks ago, after all.

The thing that really gets me, though, is that there's a suitcase waiting on my bed with my name on it. And when I open it, there's clothes in there that'll fit me. And they've still got the tag on. Not a charity shop tag neither, ones from the shop. There's a ski jacket and matching trousers: there's jumpers and jeans and gloves and socks, and just about everything I could possibly need for *summer*, let alone winter. I'm so shocked (and ever so tin-ily guilty feeling – Mum could NEVER afford to get me all this) that I have to take a deep breath before even daring to believe it's mine, never mind consider trying it on. It'd take Mum years to earn enough for all this!

Finally, once I've got over myself, me,

Giraffles, Jonny, MandM and Lucky go exploring, just around the grounds. There's so much stuff to do that you could live here for a month and not manage to do it all. There's an inside footie pitch and tennis courts. There's a sauna, Jacuzzi and beauty salon, a nightclub, a cinema *and* a music room where the walls are lined with guitars that have been signed by proper famous singers. It's out of this world, all of it!

We pass the gym, see all the mega-posh kit in there, as well as two people working out furiously.

"That's Teddy and Flick!" I say, pointing. "What are they doing in the gym? I thought they were outdoor types? Into extreme alpine sports?"

Giraffles shrugs and smiles. "Looking at the tans on them, it's like they exercise on the surface of the sun." And we laugh, though if I was into skiing and that, there'd be no way I'd be wasting my time inside, no matter how cold it was.

We decide, finally, on a game of ten pin bowling, but change our minds when we see that the St Virtuous lot are already in there.

It's not like they're unfriendly or nothing: the triplets all wave and shout welcome (in triple stereo, obviously) and Milo manages a wave with his big fat ridiculously strong sausage fingers.

But we can see that they're all really good at bowling, and, well, none of us barring Lucky has even tried it before. So we smile politely and say we're going to keep exploring.

As we walk, something niggles at me. Even having a niggle when I'm in such an amazing place makes me feel guilty but, as it doesn't just disappear, I say it out loud.

"Giraffles?"

"MMMM?" he says with a full mouth – he'd brought his choccies with him.

"Where's everyone else?"

"In the bowling alley. We just left 'em there."

"No, you nugget, not *them*."

"You're not telling me you want to hang out with Mrs Rex, are you?"

"Er … *no*! She's probably having her claws sharpened at the salon or something."

"Who are you on about, then?" he asks.

"Everyone else! The other guests! It's a hotel, isn't it? I haven't seen anyone else since we arrived."

"So?"

"Well, it's a hotel halfway up a mountain, perfect for skiing. And it's the middle of winter? It should be *bursting* with people. So … you know…" and I pause, cos I don't want to sound like a plank. "Where *is* everyone?"

Giraffles looks at me like my mum does when I say something that is apparently *daft*.

"Mate, what are you on? Are you telling me, seriously, that's it's not busy enough for you? What do you want? A room that's not as good cos someone else is already in it?"

"Course not."

"Or queues to stand in? To get in the way of all the laughs we're having?"

"Er … do I look daft?"

"No," he grins, "you just talk like you are." And he shoves another chocolate in my mouth to stop me banging on any more.

I don't say no to the chocolate (would you?) but I can't help wondering *why* the resort is so empty. I mean, I've only been here a few hours, and I *never* want to leave. Surely every other guest who's been here felt the same.

It's teatime in an hour, and I can only imagine the delights that are going to be on offer.

And after that, we aren't ever going to want to go home!

18

Dinner was amazing, by the way, though they
scared us a bit at first, bringing us a menu that
just said:

HERRING, cooked any way you wish:
Dried
Smoked
Grilled
Fried
Pickled

"What's herring?" Giraffles asks.

"Think it's a big long-legged bird," I say quietly, but not quietly enough to stop Blaize hearing, and snorting through his nose like a bull.

"That's a *heron*, you numpty. Herring are foraging fish, mostly belonging to the family *Clupeidae*. They often move around in large schools around fishing banks and near the coast."

There's not a right lot I can say to that kind of show-off knowledge, but thankfully Jonny does the hard work for me.

"I didn't know fish went to school," he says, which leaves Blaize's eyes as wide as his mouth, and me feeling not quite as thick as I did a second ago.

Anyway, the waiters put a bit of it on our plate, so we can choose, and all I can think, while trying not to vom, is *stinkworm*! I look to Miss D, who does this awkward smile when they put it in front of her, even daring to put a tiny bit in her mouth. I can see she's trying to be brave, like she's trying to set a good example.

None of us lot try it, but the St Virtuous mob are all over it, practically licking their lips, which makes me turn a bit green, but not with envy.

"Don't look so worried, Danny!" beams Teddy. "We're only playing with you," and turns the menu over, which has just about everything you could ever dream of on it … except herring.

So, with our heart rates falling again, we have the meal of our lives, before being packed off to bed. Well, we are after having our photographs taken by Flick a billion more times, though who wants to see me with a gob-full of triple cheeseburger with bacon, I do not know. Even Mum might pass on framing that one.

That night, I sleep well. Though I do dream a lot, about skiing and sledging and husky racing. Whichever it is, I'm always at the back, watching Blaize and his mates race off into the distance. Still, it could be worse, I suppose – I could be dreaming about Dyl, or he could actually be here with me.

When I go down to breakfast I have a spring in my step, but with a still-full tummy. That is, until I see what's on offer.

Oh MY *LIFE*!

You should see it.

There's, well, *everything* you could possibly want to eat. It's like they've bought *all* the food in *every* supermarket in Norway and laid it all out for us to choose from.

So we do. We get stuck in. Though I can't help wondering what will happen to the fresh stuff that won't get eaten. They won't throw it away, will they? Makes me wonder if I should stash some of it in my pockets. I could take plenty back to Mum, fill up the cupboards a bit. I put a small packet of cereal in the pocket of my spanking new hoodie, then feel a bit daft so put it back and fill my plate with every chocolate pastry ever invented. And an apple. Which I don't end up eating, as once I've cleared my plate I'm on a massive sugar high.

"Right then, troops!" shouts a friendly and excited Flick, while Teddy takes photos of her and us (what is it with these two and photos?). "If your bellies are full, then it's time we filled up your sense of adventure too. So, bring your warmest clothes and every bit of bravery packed in your case, and meet us in the lobby in thirty minutes. It's time to get in the game!"

There's whooping from the other lot; the triplets are high-fiving and Blaize seems to be doing star jumps as a post-breakfast warm-up. In fact, only Jasmina looks calm in any way, though she's glued to her phone, frowning. Unlike Jonny. Who's looking in her direction with absolute adoration. Though probably for her phone, rather than her.

Half an hour later, there we are, huddled in reception, and even though we're inside, it's still flippin' cold. Not that anything can freeze the excitement coming out of Teddy and Flick.

"*Are you ready for this?*" they chant.

As always, the shout from the St Virtuous lot is loud and confident, whereas us lot are mostly nervous and in the dark about what's going to happen.

Teddy looks around the lobby expectantly. "Blaize, are your teachers sitting this activity out?"

Blaize nods. "Said they were going to swim and sauna and gym it instead," he says, without a care, and a brief look of disappointment passes between Teddy and Flick.

"Oh. That's a shame," says Flick through a tight smile. "I imagine they are excellent snowboarders?"

Blaize nods again. "Skied for their country. Olympics, I think." He says it casually, like it's as impressive as brushing your teeth.

"Oh, *shame.*"

There's another weird look between them.

"...But never mind. You still have us to guide

you!" Teddy beams. And he tries to lead us outside, before Miss D pipes up.

"Er, excuse me, Teddy," she says, "but before we go outside, well, I think we need to take extra precautions. Against the cold."

Teddy looks confused, checks he's got his gloves on. "Really?"

"Well, yes. I've been researching life hacks for surviving in extreme cold. And I think we might be missing something. Something vital."

I can see Blaize and co smirking, but Miss D either doesn't notice or doesn't care.

"Firstly, you all need to take your boots off, and your socks too."

Weird, I think, but we do it, unlike Teddy, Flick or the Virtuous lot. They just look at her like she's a loser, especially when she pulls a load of supermarket plastic bags from her rucksack.

"Amazing!" yells Jonny. "Barefoot food shopping! My favourite!" which earns him a carnivorous stare from Mrs Rex.

"*Hardly,*" answers Miss D. "These pieces of high-tech kit are going to save your life today. Or at the very least, your feet. You know about this, don't you, Teddy and Flick?"

They nod their heads keenly, though their eyes don't look half as sure.

"It could get as cold as minus twenty degrees Celsius today," Miss D goes on. "Maybe even colder if the wind's blowing. And if you're wearing thick, warm socks, your feet are likely to sweat."

"So?" says Blaize, cos it's becoming clear he knows everything about everything. The fact that he's aiming it at *our* teacher makes me like him even less, but Miss D isn't put off.

"Well, your feet are in constant contact with the freezing ice and snow, so as soon as your feet sweat into your socks, that sweat will turn into ice. In fact, within minutes your socks will be like icebergs, with your feet trapped inside them. Thirty minutes like that and you'll risk hypothermia. Much longer and you'll be at risk of frostbite. But these bags trap the sweat next to your tootsies and keep your socks dry! So, if you're fond of your feet, then I'd wrap these bags round them. Pronto!"

As warnings go, it's hard to ignore and even though we feel daft, we do it. Miss D offers some bags to Teddy and Flick.

"Already got ours on," says Flick.

"Never go out without them," adds Teddy, though all their gear looks so expensive and barely worn that I can't imagine them *ever* strapping a carrier bag to their feet. Blaize and co certainly won't, waving the bags away with a sneer.

"Ready now, everyone?" asks Flick, impatient to get outside.

"Almost," says Miss D. "Does anyone need the toilet before we go?"

There are groans of embarrassment all round.

"I'm not a baby," moans Blaize.

"Clearly not," replies Miss D, "but if you try to go to the loo out there, your wee would be an icicle hanging off you before it hits the floor."

I look to Teddy to see if it's true, but for a second he looks as shocked as me, before adopting what looks like his best *Yes that is also true* face.

Just when we think Miss D can't shock us any more than she already has, she lets loose with another golden nugget.

"And don't even think about pooing out there. Frostbitten bums are not easy to treat."

At this point, Jonny decides to add his own unique wisdom.

"You should talk to Danny about that," he beams. "He likes to wipe his butt with nettles."

This obviously draws loads of grimaces and weird looks in my direction. Even Jasmina lifts her head from her phone long enough to shake it in my direction. Mrs Rex hoiks Jonny away to give him a piece of her mind, which he clearly could use as his brain is obviously, completely empty.

"I'm going to the loo," I say quickly, hoping everyone will have forgotten what was said by the time I've been.

The sooner we get outside into the bitter cold, the better. I'd rather die of frostbite than humiliation.

19

We're outside now. And Miss D was right: it is
F-F-F-FREEZING out here.

Despite wearing two pairs of gloves, I can feel
the cold nipping at my fingers, and even though
my breath is being captured by the balaclava *and*
a scarf pulled round my face, it's cold the second
it leaves my mouth.

I'm not saying it isn't fun though. It is. All
right, so it's cold and windy, but even stood
halfway up the mountain, it feels like we're
standing on the top of the world. The sun's out,

and all I can see is mountains and snow and birds I've never seen before, soaring and swooping and circling. Beats the estate by a mile.

Next thing I know, despite already being on top of the world, we're taken even *higher* in a cable car. It swings in the wind, but that makes it even more exciting, like we're in the middle of a James Bond movie chasing the bad guy to the top of the mountain, before racing him down again on snowboards.

Only problem is I can't snowboard, and boy, am I in for a shock when I try to.

The boards are waiting for us at the top of the mountain, all gleaming and sleek and sprayed with the sort of graffiti we have on the tower blocks at home (well, minus the rude words).

"They look like they've never been used!" gasps Giraffles.

"Bet they cost a fortune too," I add.

"So, how many of you have done this before?" Flick asks.

One hand goes up on our side – Lucky's. All six of the St Virtuous kids have theirs in the air.

Teddy and Flick frown for a second.

"OK…" says Teddy, sounding slightly disappointed but trying to cover it up. "Well, I'm sure you'll all be fine. And besides, falling down is the fun bit."

He tells us to clip ourselves into the boards, while the pair of them walk over to a couple of gleaming skidoos.

"Er…" says Mrs Rex. "Are you not boarding yourselves?"

Flick looks at her like it's the craziest thing she's ever heard.

"*Us?*" says Flick, but Teddy nudges her in the ribs before interrupting.

"We'd *love* to," he beams, "but both of us are carrying injuries, you know, from being so EXTREME!" He makes a sign with his fingers that I think is meant to look cool, but all it does is make him look like a complete doofus.

"Funny," I whisper to Giraffles, "I didn't see them limping in the gym yesterday. They were properly going for it."

But Giraffles just shrugs, probably cos he can't work out for the life of him how to fix the board to his boots.

"Doesn't mean we can't coach you from onboard these, though," Teddy smiles, pointing at the skidoos. And I *really* hope he's right, because I haven't a clue how to do this!

The next hour is ... what's the word? Oh yeah...

CARNAGE!

Oh, and here's another one:

NIGHTMARE!

And a third:

OUCH!

I mean, how do people *stand up* on these things – some kind of black magic?

Blaize and that lot are off instantly, and so is Lucky. He looks back a bit guiltily as he weaves and sways his way effortlessly down the hill – the nursery slope, I heard them call it.

University slope, more like! The rest of us are way, waaay out of our depths.

Flick and Teddy are ecstatic that the Virtuous lot are all so good – so ecstatic that they seem to forget we even exist – following them down the slope, filming endlessly, shouting excitedly as they pull off tricks and cool jumps.

"Higher!" they shout to Blaize, but from where I'm sprawled, he's already nearly touching the sun.

Mrs Rex agrees. "I hardly think you should be encouraging them to go higher!" she yells at Teddy, but Teddy can't hear her. He's too busy shouting "HIGHER!" at Blaize again.

Which leaves us to fall and tumble and skid our way down the mountain, pretty much ignored. Miss D tries to coach us, bless her, but given she's never done it before and is spending just as much time on her bum as us, well, it hardly makes her an expert.

We try anyway, we really do, and at first, the

falling over is kind of fun. But after a hundred and sixty-three times, it starts to get a bit irritating. And cold. And I've found there's a gap between my ski jacket and trousers where some snow has got in, and it actually feels like a small patch of skin is on fire. I mean, how does that work? Snow is made of water and water puts out fire, so why does my back feel like it's chuffing burning?

And it's not just me who is struggling; I feel for Giraffles. I mean, kids with arms and legs (and a neck) as long as his shouldn't even be allowed to *look* at a snowboard, never mind try and ride one.

What he needs, what we ALL need, is some expert tuition and a dollop of kindness, but when Teddy and Flick FINALLY remember about us, they don't seem very good at that either.

"The children really could use some help and guidance," Mrs Rex snarls, rubbing at one of her many bruises.

So Flick and Teddy try but, to be honest, they

are *lousy* teachers. The only thing they seem to say is, "Stand up, STAND UP!"

And when we get worse instead of better, I see a change in them. Like we're disappointing them, or letting them down. I can see it in their eyes, which go narrow, like they're irritated, while their eyebrows start going higher and higher till they disappear into the hoods of their jackets.

"Sorry," I say – after trying to get up yet again – and I mean it. "We're holding everyone up, aren't we? It's just, well, most of us don't even have a sledge at home."

"Oh, it's fine," says Flick, softly, but again, her eyes are hard, and as she and Teddy zoom off, I think I hear her say, "Remind me, Teddy, how is this going to help us? It's a disaster, this whole idea!"

I wonder what she's on about, and turn to Giraffles, but he's too busy rubbing the sleeve tattoo of bruises that he's probably collected all over his body to have heard.

"There's something weird about this," I say.

"Definitely," he replies. "Remind me again how this is fun?"

And we keep trying, but after another fifteen minutes of tumbling, falling, skidding, screaming and blushing as the others try to hide the fact that they're laughing at us, I snap.

"That's IT!" I yell, wedging the board into the snow. "I'm done! Finished. Kaput. You can count me OUT. I don't even care if I'm putting my BIG FOOT in it or being rude, I AM. NOT. DOING. THIS. ANY. MORE!"

It's a tantrum on an epic scale and it's not like me at all, but I don't like being humiliated. And as I stand there, sulking, my face burning red enough to melt the polar icecaps, I expect a telling-off from one of the adults. But it doesn't come. Instead, Teddy skids up on his skidoo next to me and slaps me on the back.

"Bigfoot, you say, Danny? Well, just wait there. Don't move. Any of you."

So we don't. Actually, we couldn't even if we tried. We're aching all over.

20

"Bigfeet!" shouts Teddy.

"Not really," replies Jonny. Then, pointing at Giraffles, "But he's got a long neck."

"*No*," frowns Flick, "*these* are Bigfeet." And she points at the pile of things that her brother has dumped in the snow.

We look, and they're right: they look just like big feet. Different sizes, and made out of the same stuff as skis, but they're shaped like feet with toes and a heel, and the same kind of clip the snowboards had, where your foot slides in.

"What are we meant to do with these?" Jonny says.

"Wear them on your head like a hat," snigger MandM together, while cuffing Jonny on the bonce for being the world's biggest doofus.

"They're like skis," says Flick, all cheerful again, "but because they're only a bit bigger than your actual foot, it'll be way easier to stay upright."

"Easy enough for you two to try it as well?" I say under my breath. I don't feel like being laughed at again.

But within minutes, due to Teddy's sheer persistence (which borders on desperate), I'm stood at the top of the slope wearing a pair of dumb Bigfeet, preparing to throw myself down the hill.

Teddy tries to help. "Tell you what, Danny, start by doing a tandem run with Giraffles here. It'll help both of your confidence."

"Wouldn't it be better for his confidence if he tried it with someone experienced like you?" Miss D asks, which prompts Teddy to limp and grimace like he's just remembered that he's in pain.

"I'd love to, believe me, but this injury isn't going to heal itself. Especially when you're born to be extreme like me!"

He positions himself between me and Giraffles, and grabs hold of our arms.

"Here," he says, as he crosses our arms at the wrist like we're about to dance Gangnam-style, before telling us to hold hands.

"Away you go, then," he says.

"What?" we reply.

"…Spin."

"What do you mean *spin*?"

"Well … *spin*. Down the mountain."

"Are you kidding me?!" I shriek. I mean, what sort of coaching is that?

"It'll be fine. Honest."

I want to tell him *no*. That it sounds like lunacy to even try, but as I'm about to say it, Blaize and his cronies arrive at the top of the ski lift.

"Perhaps Danny Mack isn't as brave as he makes out," he sneers.

And that leaves me no choice, does it? I feel inferior enough to Mr Run-back-into-a-blazing-building Cosmo as it is. Plus, suddenly I feel like I have to prove it to myself too.

So, squeezing Giraffles's fingers, I ask. "Shall we show 'em what we're made of?"

"Let's do it," he replies, and before we can change our minds, we allow the Bigfeet to start to slide down the slope.

And then?

Well … I yell. Actually, it's more of a scream, and for the first few seconds it smells like a fear fart, but then something brilliant happens. My scream turns into a *ohmygodthisisthegreatestfeelingintheworldandIloveit andneverwanttodoanythingelseeveragain* type of scream.

Because you know what? We *don't* fall over. *I* don't fall over. Instead, my feet glide effortlessly

across the snow. The Bigfeet are only just bigger
than my own, so its WAY easier and when I
wobble Giraffles kind of keeps me stable. It feels
like we're travelling at a million miles an hour,
and my goggles are steaming up, but it doesn't
even matter cos it's just brilliant. We're zigging
and zagging, forwards and backwards, and then
we're spinning, spinning so fast it's like we're
trapped in a food blender, and it's dizzying and
epic and brilliant and the only downside is that
eventually, we run out of slope and when we stop
I pull off the Bigfeet and try to run back up the
hill to do it all over again.

"Why don't you try the lift instead?" shouts Flick from her skidoo, her eyes all smiley again. "Only, next time, do it quicker! You know, for the camera!"

And you know what, for once I don't mind the idea of being filmed, because all I want to do is slide down the hill again and again and again. For the rest of my flipping life if they'll let me. Seriously, it is THAT good.

It's just as good the second time, and the third (with Miss D for a change), though I manage to avoid a spin with Mrs Rex, cos as a T-Rex (in disguise), her arms are too short to hold on to without being uncomfortably close to her and her dino-breath.

I don't know how long we're doing it for, but I know I'm not cold any more, and even when I see Blaize and his mate Milo smirking at us like we're a bunch of circus freaks, it doesn't matter, cos I know how bloomin' good this feels right now. All I do is smile at him, and give him a thumbs up, which prompts him to slide over to us on his board, coming to a stop with a skid while coating us from head to foot with powdery snow.

"Fast learners, you," he says, though his face isn't kind, even if his words seem like they are.

"Maybe," I reply, all cool, like I'm not even bothered what he thinks.

"Makes me think, we should, you know, have a race, prove who's the king of the mountain."

Well, the answer to that is simple, isn't it? It's a *Nah, you're all right, ta*, like it doesn't matter, like we're too cool to race, like taking part is all that counts, but as per normal, we have Jonny on hand to balls things up.

"You're on," he says toughly while eyeballing Blaize, which actually just makes him look a bit cross-eyed and even dafter than normal.

'This is brilliant!" gasps Flick, overhearing the tail end of the conversation. "Extra dessert tonight for those who pull off the most EXTREME tricks for the camera! In fact ..." she says, looking ecstatic with herself, "what about a *team relay?*"

Teddy looks equally pleased, pulling out a load of brand new GoPro cameras from his bag. "I love it! Each team can go down in pairs, setting off a flare when you reach the bottom to signal to the next couple to begin. And if you all wear the cameras we'll get some EPIC footage!"

There's whooping and hollering and so much excitement that I get caught up in it too, forgetting entirely that there's no way in the world that us lot, after a few hours of practice, could beat a team who could almost compete at the Olympics.

But it's too late to back out now. Cameras are being attached to helmets, flares are being planted at the bottom of the slope, and before you know it, Flick is shouting,

"On your marks!

Get set!

...GO!"

21

And we're off!

Or at least MandM are, screaming and spinning their way down the slope, pitted against Andreas and August from St. V's, who cut through the snow effortlessly. MandM aren't going to win any medals for technique, basically cos they don't have one, but they pick up some serious, epic speed and by the time they crash into the flare at the bottom, setting it off with a dramatic KABOOM! they're only a few seconds behind the opposition.

The flare sets Lucky and Jonny into action against Amelia and Jasmina on the other team. It feels like all of a sudden we're in with a chance of taking the lead, cos Lucky's done this before, and Jonny's brain is so brilliantly different to anyone else on the planet that he doesn't realize he could break every bone in his body by going as fast as he currently is.

By the time they reach halfway I could swear that we're neck and neck, and then somehow, we edge into the lead!

"Why is the other team going so slow?" I say, peering down the slope. Then I work it out. Amelia and Jasmina seem to be arguing. It looks like, even now as she flies down the slope, Jasmina STILL has her phone out, and I swear down she's looking at her screen!

"Don't look at her, Jonny, don't look!!" I whisper to myself, fearing that if he does, he'll get the look of love again and manage to fall over. And if that happens? Well, we're

stuffed, aren't we? Cos there's no way that me
and Giraffles can outrun Blaize and Milo, who
both look like they were born with a snowboard
attached to their feet.

Anyway, as it turns out, Jonny manages to
focus for longer than a goldfish for once, and,
unbelievably, they set off the flare a good five
seconds ahead of the opposition.

Incredible!

As me and Giraffles push off into the abyss,
I realize that the only people who can mess up a
glorious victory now is us. But there's no way
I'm going to let that happen. I haven't known
Blaize for more than two minutes, but I know
he'll make my life as unbearable as our Dyl would
if St. V's beat us. So I grit my teeth, flex my
knees and shout at the top of my voice,

"Spin, Giraffles, SPIN!"

And we spin. Slowly at first, but with every
metre we pick up momentum, so much so that
everything starts to blur as my squeals get

louder and louder and louder. I hope the camera on my helmet doesn't have a microphone on it: in fact, I can't imagine the footage will be any use, it'll just be a whirlwind of movement, we're going that flippin' fast.

But just as I think we've got it in the bag and imagine the bragging rights on offer, I feel an icy presence, and it's not cos the weather's changing. It's Blaize and Milo, hammering up behind us, casting a shadow that looms larger and larger and larger. I feel the temperature drop by five degrees and grip Giraffles's hands so tight, to make us spin faster, that I see him grimace in pain.

"They're gaining on us!" I yell, and we double down, ignoring the nausea that lurches in our tummies as we go even bloomin' faster. We're going so quick now that I imagine the snow melting beneath our Bigfeet. Any quicker and they'll have to call the fire brigade, if that exists up here.

But as fast as we go, Blaize and Milo seem to be going faster, and they know it. As they close in behind us, I can hear them laughing, mocking, knowing that it's only a matter of time before they zip past us and set off the final flare.

Finally, they pull alongside us, deliberately spraying us with powdery snow to try to make us veer off sideways or lose our balance as they overtake.

"Arrrgggghhhhhhh!" we yell, using all our strength to not lose our footing, knowing if we do that the race will be lost.

"They did that on purpose!" Giraffles yells in anger. "Let's give 'em some back!"

He grips me hard, harder even than Blaize's first handshake, and with a bend of his knees, he starts us spinning again, and we continue our career down the mountainside towards our opponents.

It pays off. The ten-metre gap between us halves to five, then halves again, and I see Blaize look over his shoulder – see the grin slide off his face and slither down the hill, as he realizes that, against all the odds, we might just manage to beat them.

But in that second, we learn something about Blaize – and Milo too, I suppose. We learn that they aren't used to losing. We learn that they don't like the idea of it, and most importantly, we learn that they aren't prepared to let it happen. For, as the gap between us closes even further, they do the unspeakable and cut us up, zipping across our path, knowing full well that it will mean the end of us. We're going too fast and are too out of control to adjust our bodies and stay on course, and instead, all we can do is flail and squeal and accept the fact that we're no longer going to pull off a dramatic victory. The only thing we're going to embrace is the snow and ice underneath us.

It doesn't hurt much at first. The snow is deep and not packed too tightly. But after skidding for another twenty metres, we're finally stopped by a large rock. Giraffles hits it first, then I hit Giraffles, at such a speed that he cries out.

For a second or two, we forget about the race,

we're more worried about whether we're still attached to our limbs, but then we hear a bang and see a flash of orange, as Blaize sets off the winning flare.

The St Virtuous lot celebrate wildly, singing songs and dancing despite the fact that they're still attached to their Bigfeet, and suddenly I'm angry, which doesn't happen often.

"Mate," I say to Giraffles, "can you stand?"

He shakes his head, and even through his trousers I can see that is knee is starting to swell up.

"I need you to, mate, even if it's only for a second."

"Why?" he asks.

"Cos we need to show this lot what we're made of." And I hoist him to his feet and on to my back. "Hold tight," I say, nervous that his damaged leg is so long that it'll end up dragging in the snow.

Then I do what we HAVE to do. I show them that we might not be used to being on snow, but that we still have skills, and I manage to ski, with Giraffles on my back all the way down to the finishing post, much to Miss D's delight, who gets to put into practice all the first aid she's been learning about for months.

All right, so we didn't win. We might have actually been beaten all ends up, but when Giraffles sets off our flare and the sky turns blue with a single epic firework, it feels good. Better than good — it feels flipping brilliant, and I look right at Blaize Cosmo, cos I want him to see just how amazing it feels.

22

There's a weird atmosphere on the way back to the hotel.

All the way down in the cable car, the St Virtuous lot look proper pleased with themselves, like they've won the World Cup, not just a race against a group of kids who've mostly never even skied before.

Blaize is gloating BIG STYLE. All blinding-white grins as he leads the singing, sparing me the occasional look, mouthing *loser* at me, but subtly, so Mrs Rex or Miss D don't see. I still don't like it though. Feels like the gloves are off and he's properly gunning for me.

They're too busy sorting out Giraffles to notice anyway, placing an ice pack on his bruised knee. Teddy and Flick are just as distracted. From the second we got back in the cable car it was like we didn't exist; all they were interested in was looking at the footage they got on the GoPros. Within minutes they'd downloaded it on to an iPad, and were crouched over it, pointing and smiling and punching the air.

It isn't easy to hear what they're saying over Blaize and co's wailing, but I do overhear bits and pieces.

"Think of the exposure!" Teddy says, more than once, but I've no idea what they mean by that. Anyway, Flick looks well happy too, and although I can't hear everything, she definitely says "bookings" more than once before staring at her phone without blinking for what seems like minutes. For a while, she looks more like Jasmina than Jasmina.

In the end I switch off from it all. Adults are weird and I don't bother wasting any more energy trying to work out what they're going on about.

I try to forget about Blaize and co too. Who cares if they beat us? All I know is that while we were spinning down that mountain it felt like the best rush ever. We didn't need to *win* to feel that, and we don't need any camera footage to remember how it felt neither.

So instead, I let my forehead rest against the glass, and watch as the trees whizz by.

I can't say the rest of the evening is boring. I mean, we're staying in the poshest place on the planet, with more stuff to do than I ever thought possible. And since there's *still* no one else staying here, we *still* don't have to queue for a thing!

When we get back, we hit the water slides and the hot tub and Jacuzzi, before ordering the

world's biggest hot chocolate on room service
and watching a movie on a screen that's bigger
than any cinema I've ever been to. Talk about
living your best life!

To top it off, we have dinner to look forward
to, all million courses of it, nearly every one of
them involving chips or burgers or chocolate –
just the sort of food needed to take my mind off
my aching body.

It's brilliant as well, cos we get to watch the St
Virtuous lot wolf a load of herring down again.
Honestly, you should see 'em. Can't get enough
of it, they can't. It tickles us, with Jonny taking
endless snaps of 'em on his phone, adding icons
and beards and hats till they look even more
ridiculous.

"For a winning team," smiles Lucky, "they
don't half look like a bunch of losers."

"Never mind them, check out Teddy and
Flick!" says Marcus and Maureen together.

And it's true, they look like someone who

thinks they've ordered a chocolate sundae only to be served Dog Turd Surprise. They're huddled on the other side of the restaurant, scowling at their iPad, scrolling endlessly through the screen and arguing.

"What's their problem?" Giraffles asks.

"Dunno," says Jonny.

"Beats me." I shrug.

"Isn't it obvious?" says a voice behind us.

It's Jasmina, which takes us by surprise, as she hasn't said a word since we met.

"Er ... no?" we reply, as one.

"Honestly," she huffs, "if you spent less time in the real world, and more time on your phone, you'd realize what was going on around here."

And she struts off, like that was the smartest thing she'd ever said, tray of food in one hand, and her phone in the other.

"Wow," mouths Jonny. "What a beauty."

"The phone or her?" I ask.

"Both," he says, before staring at his own

phone so hard, as if it contained the secret to everlasting life.

We sit and chat and wonder what the morning will bring. Bobsleighing? Ice hockey? Paragliding? Whatever it is, after the day we've had, we know it won't be dull...

23

Twelve hours later, with plastic bags strapped to our feet and every inch of us covered in clothing, we're trudging through the snow back to the cable car.

The pace is brisk, like Teddy and Flick can't get up there fast enough, though they do still manage to slip around way too much.

Poor old Giraffles is limping, struggling to keep up, so I slow down to keep him company.

"You OK?" I ask, offering my shoulder as a crutch.

"Can hardly feel it. Miss D wrapped that

many bandages round my knee it's thicker than my waist."

I look back at our teacher, who's finding it harder to walk than old Giraffles. But not cos she's injured, more cos her rucksack is as big as she is, and heavier too by the looks of it.

"What has she got in that bag?" I ask him.

"Just the basics, apparently."

"Like what?"

"Life raft?"

"To use on snow?"

"Collapsible hospital, then."

"Nah," I reply. "I reckon she just volunteered to carry Mrs Rex's packed lunch. You know how hungry dinosaurs get."

"That explains the zebra she was shoving in her bag at breakfast…"

"Bet she didn't dare pack any of them disgusting herrings…"

"None left, was there, old Blaize over there ate 'em all."

The mention of Blaize makes me shiver a bit, and when I glance in his direction he's already looking at me and scowling, doing a Dylan impression that's so good it makes me shiver again.

"Cold?" he sneers.

'Toasty," I answer, cos I don't want him to know the truth, do I?

"Ready to eat some snow?"

"Yeah, I reckon. Tastier than herring."

He calls me a pleb, but I don't know what that means, so I thank him sarcastically and make a mental note to stay out of his way. After the trick he pulled yesterday, I reckon he's planning something else and I know it'll be at my expense.

For the next half hour I try not to give him any oxygen and just get excited by the view instead. It's amazing up here. There's been a fresh dump of snow overnight and the cable car climbs higher – way higher than we were yesterday. It literally looks like no one's ever walked, skied or snowboarded these slopes before

– and, to be honest, I'm well excited. They won't make us ski again, they've said it's something different, and whatever it is I'm going to show Blaize and his muppets that anything they can do, we can do way better.

Though, Miss D isn't quite as confident.

"Do you not think we've gone high enough already?" she asks our guides.

"Nowhere near!" grins Teddy.

"But it will be safe up here, won't it?" says Miss D. "I mean, we don't want any more injuries, do we?"

"Yesterday was just a warm-up," adds Flick, waving her concern away instantly. "After all, we promised you guys EXCITEMENT. UNLIMITED EXCITEMENT. That's what we do. And that's what you're going to get!"

They're smiling still, like they always do, but there's a moment – a flash of a look between them where their eyes aren't smiling.

They look, I dunno, not *scared* exactly, but worried.

"Did you see that?" I ask Giraffles.

"See what?" he replies. "All I see is snow!"

I shrug and watch Miss D instead, chuckling to myself as she checks her first aid kit about seventy-three times before we reach the end of our journey.

"Right then!" Teddy booms through his scarf as we stand in the wind and sunshine. "Who here knows about zorbing?"

Straight away, Jonny's hand is in the air, and I wince in advance.

"He's the Greek ice-cream-van man on our estate. Best ninety-nines in the world!"

The look on his face is sheer pride, and he's looking right at Jasmina. For a minute I think he's going to ask her on a date to share an ice cream. Until Lucky puts him straight.

"Mate, that's Zorba. And you do know that's only his nickname, don't you? His real name's Nigel."

Jonny shrugs like he doesn't care, and just carries on staring at Jasmina (or her phone, it's hard to tell), much to the amusement of Blaize and co.

"Good guess!" says Teddy, looking slightly frustrated, cos as always he's filming us and we've just messed up his vid. "But THIS is zorbing!"

From nowhere, Flick appears, rolling before her what looks like an ENORMOUS hamster ball.

"If you thought Bigfeet were extreme, wait till you get in here! Zero skill needed, just bags of bravery!" she says. "Now, who wants to go first?"

"Er…" interrupts Mrs Rex, "shouldn't you demonstrate how it's done first? You *are* the instructors after all."

But Teddy disagrees, throwing his arm around her in a well smarmy way. "Oh, there's no need for *that*. It's as easy as falling off a log."

"Hhhhm … or a mountain," Mrs Rex says, which makes him laugh falsely.

"You are one funny woman," he adds, "as funny as your students are fearless. Now, which of you wants to lead? Show us what you're made of."

My hand goes up before I or my brain know

it, and Giraffles leans over to me. "Mate, do you know what you're doing?"

"Not a clue," I whisper back, "but I reckon it's time we show Blaize's army what we can do."

And I stride forward, to the whooping and hollering of my mates.

24

Adrenalin is the greatest thing in the world.

Fact.

Period.

There is *nothing* like it.

I know this cos, right now, at this second, my body is absolutely pulsing with the stuff.

An hour ago I was a bit nervous about making a fool of myself; about proving myself in front of Blaize and the others but, right now, rolling around inside a ten-foot inflated rodent ball, I feel like I could do anything. And everything. At the same time.

All right, so at first it feels weird. Will I be able to breathe in here once they zip the ball up? Will it hurt when I fall over? What if I bang into a rock, or shoot off the edge of the mountain? After all, we must be about five miles off the ground up here. I swear the moon is proper, proper close right now.

But all that changes when the ball starts to roll — and, all right, it feels a bit weird at first, and yep my tummy feels like it's being thrown around inside a washing machine. But at the same time, it feels FLIPPIN' AMAZING. It makes my heart thump and race to speeds I didn't know existed, it makes my scream so high-pitched that only dogs can hear me, and my legs feel like they're not actually attached to me, but there's not one thing that I'd change about it, and the second I reach the bottom of the slope, the only thing I can do is squeal "AGAIN! AGAIN!" like I used to do aged three when Mum threw me up in the air.

It is AWESOME.

So I do it again.

And again.

Twenty, thirty or forty – I don't know how many times I do it. I give up counting and just enjoy it!

It's not just me, either. It's Giraffles, and Lucky and the twins. Jonny even keeps his phone in his pocket at least the first few times; even Teddy and Flick are beaming again, skidooing alongside us as they film our every scream.

"Danny," they yell, when our teachers are out of earshot, "do you think you could do the next run a bit faster? There's a really big jump down to the left that we think you'd love. We want to get it on film. Show the world how brave you are."

"Have you done the jump before?" I shout back.

"Hundreds of times!" they reply emptily. And I don't believe them.

"And it's safe?"

"Would we put you in danger?" Flick replies,

like she's the biggest saint on the planet.

I think back to the rubbish snowboard coaching they gave us yesterday, how Giraffles got hurt – and any of us could've hurt ourselves, really – and how they didn't seem to give a monkey's: were way more interested in filming the Virtuous mob being all alpine-extreme.

"Maybe I'll do it in a bit," I answer, which doesn't seem to please Teddy.

"Make sure you do. After all, we don't want anyone thinking you're a chicken now, do we?"

There's an edge to the way he says "chicken". Like he's taunting me, trying to make me do the jump out of fear of being branded a coward. And I don't like it. So I roll away, back to Giraffles and Lucky, where we can have fun our own way, like normal.

Course, at some point the fun has to stop, and Teddy sees to that ten minutes later with one simple sentence.

"Right, everyone. Let's turn this into a bit of a

competition, shall we? Turn the extreme dial up to MAXIMUM!"

My shoulders sag at the thought of yet another challenge, plus I feel Blaize's eyes burn into me, a big old weaselly grin on his chops too. This is his chance to torture me again, though how he'll do it from inside a huge ball I've no idea.

"Now then," continues Teddy. "If you look down to the bottom of the slope, you'll see Flick, and near her, a set of ten pins. But not normal ten pins – this is no normal game of bowling. These pins, as you'll see, are as big as any of us. Bigger, even! And all you have to do is roll down the hill and knock over as many of them as possible!"

My heart eases a bit. *OK. Good*, I think, *no chance of Blaize ruining that, is there?*

"Only thing is," adds Teddy, "to REALLY max out the adrenalin, it's going to be a duel too! Winner takes all! Time to go hard, or go home!"

I want to roll my zorb clean over Teddy's head.

"Yes, this will be a one-on-one race. One person in a zorb, one on foot, with a thirty-metre head start for the runner. Whoever knocks the pins over first, wins!"

There's a cheer, but not from me. Not from any of my mates, though of course all the Virtuous ones are whooping and hollering like they've just won Olympic gold.

Blaize pauses to say something in Teddy's ear, pointing at me.

"Of course!" Teddy says, already strapping a camera to Blaize's head. "I think you racing against Danny would be an amazing idea! Our two heroes, head to head!"

Now, there have been a lot of amazing ideas in the history of the world. The person who woke up one day and decided to invent the wheel was a proper smart cookie. So was the genius that invented the Internet – and don't get me started on the mastermind who dedicated themself to invent the all-you-can-eat-buffet.

But this? You can NOT call this an amazing idea. You can call it an absolutely stinking turd of an idea, and nothing else.

I don't say that of course, cos I'm meant to be this all-action hero, aren't I? The brave one. The legend.

So it feels like the only option open to me is the one I take: I puff out my chest and go, "Yeah, I'm up for a race."

It'll be OK, just as long as I'm the one in the zorb and not the one being chased on foot. If that happens, I'm stuffed. Buried alive.

"Here you go, Danny," smiles Teddy, handing me a helmet with a GoPro already attached.

I gulp, and turn around to see Blaize already inside his bubble, grinning like a bonkers Cheshire cat.

I know then that I'm the mouse.

He's Tom. I'm Jerry.

And he's not going to stop until he's caught

me and crushed me into a slush puppy (OK, slush mouse).

And right then, in that moment, every drop of my adrenalin is gone and I definitely want to go home.

25

This is the worst moment of my life.

Worse than being stuck up a mountain during the most terrifying storm in a decade.

Worse than wearing a mankini and rubber ring in an arctic climate.

Because both of those times I didn't know what was going to happen next – didn't know I was about to be in agony, one way or another.

But today? Right here, right now?

I know that in a minute or so I'm going to be liquidized. Squished to a pulp by a snow-zorber with a vendetta.

And I know it's going to hurt. So, forgive me if I'm feeling a bit sorry for myself.

I turn my head, the helmet feeling like it weighs an absolute ton, and clock Blaize in his ball, fifty metres up the mountain. But, even from that distance, I can see him sneering and laughing, knowing full well that I am *toast*, at his mercy – however you want to put it, I'm in serious trouble.

"No good looking at him, Danny boy," smiles Teddy, filming yet AGAIN. "Keep your eyes on the prize," and he points at the ten pins that seem so far away that they look the size of pins you stick in clothes.

"You can't run your fastest if you're constantly looking over your shoulder. Now, any last words for the camera?"

And that's when I actually ask the question that's been in my head since we arrived, partly to delay the start of the challenge, but also cos, to be honest, it's bugging me!

"What IS it with you and cameras? Why are you always filming us? Is there something going on here that we don't know about? Cos, to be honest ... it's weirding me out!"

Instantly, I know I've hit on something, as he can't keep eye contact with me. His eyes dart around, focusing on anything apart from me.

Flick says otherwise, course she does.

"We're just documenting your bravery. That, and the fun you're having here, that's all."

But there's more to it than that – Teddy's reaction showed me that. I still don't know what it is, but I know now that my hunch is right.

But I don't get the chance to say anything else, because from the top of the hill a horn blares. Blaize is on his way and I have a choice: stay to interrogate Teddy and get pulverized by a huge hamster ball, or run. Run like the flipping wind.

Strangely enough, I choose the second option.

I'm moving, but not as quick as Blaize. I don't

need to turn around to test that theory, I just know. I'm not a numpty.

To be honest, running isn't easy. My legs are short to start with and the fact that I'm wearing four layers of thermals, a pair of tracky-bums and also some snow pants means that my brain has to work super-hard to get the message through to them.

The snow doesn't help either: it's not exactly a running track, is it? Though it's obviously had the snow-plough crushing the powdery stuff down, making it semi-hard. Anyway, there's no point in wailing. There'll be plenty of time for that if Blaize catches me.

So I sprint, the sound of my heavy breathing building a rhythm in my head, spurring me on. I try to imagine I'm Usain Bolt, tearing down the track, whereas in reality I'm just a terrified school kid doing his best not to face-plant, whilst shrieking his head off.

Anyway, I'm moving. In fact, I seem to be

moving pretty well. The ten pins are getting closer, and I'm starting to realize just how HUGE they are.

I can do this, I think to myself. I can defeat the odds and show that muppet Blaize what I'm made of.

But just as I start to write the victory speech in my head, I slip. Ice. Somehow, despite being in subzero temperatures, I'd forgotten it exists. It kindly decides to remind me by throwing me into the air, and I land on my bum.

It hurts, but I haven't time to rub it better. Instead I'm back on my feet and haring on. In front of me, I can see MandM, cheering me on, and I speed up, much to their delight. But as I pass them, I see Lucky further on, and he doesn't look so confident. He's doing an *Oh my word we're going to have to get a bike pump to inflate Danny back to life* face, which means Blaize is catching up. So I run even faster. Cue another reminder from the ice that it's there, flooring me.

"OW!" I yell, before limping on again, if only for a second, as here comes another bump, then another, then another then another. I am like the worst jack-in-the-box ever invented, and I'm spending so much time on the ice that I realize that there's only one way I am going to reach the pins before Blaize.

Channeling all the footballers I've ever seen celebrating a goal, I sprint and throw myself on to my belly, headfirst, allowing the ice to embrace me.

The results are A-MAZING.

Within seconds, I'm whistling down the slope. Seconds more and I'm screaming down it. Bobsleighers have got nothing on me!

I hear a whoop of delight as I zoom past Jonny, then a strangled, terrified yell from what I can only presume is Giraffles (everything is a blur now!), but I can't worry about Blaize any more. I know he must be right behind me, but there's nothing I can do about it. All I can do is lie still and trust gravity to get me there first.

The pins are closer now, and I push my right arm in front of me, like Superman flying, but as I do so, Blaize's zorb makes contact with my toes, then my ankle, then my calf. He's literally going to run over me! I stretch myself even flatter in the hope of picking up more speed, but as I do so he reaches my waist, so close I can hear his laughter jabbing at my ears.

"ARRRRGGGGGHHHHHHH!" I scream, pushing my other arm in front too, going full-on superhero, faster than the speed of light and sound combined.

Can I do it? Can I do it? Can I do it?

I have no idea!

All I can do is close my eyes and scream my head off until I feel the most incredible impact. I feel myself being thrown in the air before crashing (fortunately!), into a pile of powdery snow. I don't know which way is up or down, what my name is or where I am, and I certainly don't know if I won.

Well, I don't until there's an almighty roar, and I'm plucked from the snow and hoisted skywards. The light is blinding, I've got snow everywhere, including down my pants, but I don't care any more, cos I can hear Mrs Rex, of all people, chanting,

"WE ARE THE CHAMPIONS!"

It's then that I realize I'm sat on her dinosaur shoulders, and she and Giraffles and Jonny and everyone are doing the dance of victory.

We did it! *I* did it!

And, boy oh boy, does Blaize look unhappy…

26

Man, winning feels good. And I'd be lying if I said it didn't feel good to show Blaize that I'm made of tough stuff, too.

First thing I do, once we stop celebrating that is, is to try and shake his hand.

"Good race," I say, "thought I was toast there at the end."

But he doesn't say anything; in fact, he doesn't even *look* at me. It's like I don't exist, like I never even opened my mouth. All he does is shoulder past me back to the ski lift, making enough contact to knock me off balance.

"He took that well," laughs Lucky, still patting me on the back. But it makes me feel uncomfortable, and ... well, sad, I suppose. I don't know what his problem is. If he had managed to turn me into an icy puddle, would that have put a smile on his chops? Was I supposed to just lie down in the snow and let him bounce on my head? I dunno, I just don't get people sometimes, and it makes me even sadder, putting me on a downer that lasts all the way back to the top of the slope.

"Come on, mate," sighs Giraffles. "Don't let that idiot get to you. I'm going to need you cheering for me if I'm going to win my race."

He's right. It's daft letting Blaize upset me, so I pull myself straight and yell and cheer and laugh (a lot) as Giraffles narrowly loses his race. It's brilliant though, to see him try and fold his ridiculously long limbs inside the zorb. Giraffes were never meant to exercise in a hamster's ball, that is for sure, but he gives it a proper good, heroic stab.

And the races go on. We win some and lose some, we celebrate and sulk, but not like Blaize does. Honest, it's like this is the world cup or something. I can see him itching to have another go at me, like he won't be able to sleep again unless he gets his revenge.

In the end, he gets his chance to put things straight, only this time, it's me in the ball, chasing *him* down. And you know what, I feel pretty good about it. Like *I'm* Tom, and *he's* Jerry. Plus being inside the zorb is pretty cool. It's proper padded, though there's not a lot of room in there, despite me being way smaller than Giraffles.

I can do this, I say to myself. I can catch him; make it two-nil.

But as I get ready for battle, something unexpected happens. Blaize appears in front of me, faced pressed up against the rubber.

"Good luck," he barks, which is weird given the fact that he's been giving me death stares for the past thirty minutes.

"Er … thanks?" I say.

"No, I really mean it. May the best man win."

And then, if that's not weird enough, he sticks his hand through the gap and offers his hand.

I frown. Has the ice frozen his brain? It's completely out of character. But then I see Mrs Rex, nodding at me, encouraging me to do the decent thing and shake it, so I do.

The first thing I think is *OW!* cos I've forgotten how strong he is, but that's not all, cos as he crushes his palm against mine, I feel something crack, and it's not my knuckles.

At first I'm confused; what was that? What just happened? But as he pulls his hand away and zips up the zorb with a flourish, I see "nice guy Blaize" disappear, and "evil, possessed Blaize" loom over me.

"Eugh," he grins demonically. "What IS that SMELL?"

I feel something on my hand and look down to see a tiny crushed bottle smeared on to my palm.

Instinctively, I go to smell it and almost throw up in repulsion.

"What … is … *that?*' I gasp, though I know what it is really: a stink bomb.

And not just any stink bomb – this is the devil's stink bomb, the stink bomb of *nightmares.* I swear, it is *so* powerful and eggy and rancid that I can almost see green smoke snaking off my palm. Within seconds, the smell has filled every square centimetre of the space around me.

I gag, then choke, then gag again, trying to breathe through only my mouth, but the smell is worse than anything I have *ever* smelt in my life – and I've shared a room with Dylan and his killer socks.

I need to get out, to escape, to shove my head in the snow until my nostrils either clear or freeze, but as I fumble with the zip it's clear that the smell is affecting my ability to do anything except want to vom.

The zip won't budge and my brain won't work and even if it did, everyone's walked off ready to cheer me on.

Then, as if this wasn't bad enough, I hear another chuckle from beside me. It's Milo.

"Jeez, you stink!" he says with great delight. "No one's going to want you anywhere near them."

"Help me. Please…" I mouth, but he ignores me.

"Tell you what," he leers, "why don't you wait over there? Just till the smell passes." And while no one is watching, he kicks my zorb off to the left, where the slope is steeper and icier … and much, much deadlier.

It looks like the equivalent of a black run, the sort that would have Olympic champions secretly parping themselves. But as I start to roll, I don't parp. I'm well beyond that. It's taking every bit of willpower not to cover myself in my own puke as the ball dashes and bounces and skids and careers off in every direction possible, speeding up with every second.

I see a huge cliff rushing towards me and I actually scream, throwing my body weight to the right, thanking the snow gods as the zorb changes direction.

I'm moving at such a pace that I don't know where the snow ends and the sky starts. It's kind of like doing the hokey cokey, but on mega fast forward – I've never been shaken about so much in all my flippin' life!

And when I try to yell, the smell chokes me. As I spin round I see Flick racing on a skidoo to catch up with me.

"Stop me, PLEASE!" I squeal, but as the ball spins and she comes into focus again it's clear she's going to do no such thing. In fact, she's pointing into the distance.

"Big jump, that way!" she shouts, eyes wide with excitement. "It'll look amazing on film. *Trust me!*" And I see her phone in her right hand,

trained on me. I'm about to either die or vom up
my entire stomach, and she's actually *filming me*!

WHAT IS IT WITH YOU AND FILMING?!
I want to yell, but I can't cos I'm trying to
work out how to make it all stop. My brain is
blancmange and the smell is so bad and my
nostrils are burning and the speed is so fast and
then I see a big rock racing towards me closer
and closer and closer and then…

And then?

Well, then I don't remember anything, cos
everything …

turns …

black.

27

When I come around, I'm in the cable car, with concerned-looking faces staring right at me. Suddenly, everything starts to spin and lurch. Then I smell the stink bomb, and think I'm going to chunder, before my stressed brain decides to make me pass out.

When I come around again, I feel like I'm laid on a massive fluffy comfortable cloud, and for a second I panic that I'm dead. Then I realize it's actually my luxury bed in my luxury room in my luxury hotel. After a few seconds, my head starts to throb like a family of woodpeckers are pecking my brain into a statue of Blaize Cosmo, just to top off my lousy day.

"All right, Danny?" whispers Giraffles, though it feels like he's trying to compete with the woodpeckers.

"Water," I gasp, cos that's what people say in the movies when they wake up from a coma. And also cos I'm proper thirsty.

He sits me up carefully and does the honours.

"Head aching?" he asks.

"Just a bit."

"Gave us a shock, you did. Thought you were going to roll right off the side of the world. Doctor says you'll be OK, though. They checked you out like a million times already, while you were resting."

"That's good."

"Strange thing you did though, mate, what with Blaize running in the opposite direction."

I look at him like *he's* the one who's had a

blow to the head.

"Well, I didn't *mean* to, did I? Milo shoved me in that direction. On purpose!"

"He what?!"

"Yeah — Blaize crushed a stink bomb inside the ball, then Milo gave me a shove!"

It takes a lot to get old Giraffles rattled, but the second I get my words out I see his eyes flare in anger. Just as he's about to reply we're interrupted by Miss D, who's carrying the world's largest first aid kit and the galaxy's most concerned face.

"Oh, Danny, thank goodness you're back with us. I only stepped out to see how long it might be until the doctor arrives. How are you feeling?" She rattles in her bag and finds a tiny torch, shining it into my eyes without warning.

"Er ... fine? Blind?" I offer, which sees her blush in embarrassment, hide the torch and my face with a cooling wet cloth.

"Whatever happened, Danny?" she says. "You

had us all worried sick, rolling off like that!"

I'm about to tell her EXACTLY what happened, but for some reason, old Giraffles dives in first, with a fury I've never seen before.

"He's no idea, Miss! Not a clue, not a sausage. But I'll tell you what. Me and the others are going to make sure it never EVER happens again, that's for sure." And without warning, he sprints from the room, leaving Miss D wide-eyed and mystified.

"I think he's the one who needs his head read, Miss, not me," I say, trying to play it down.

But I make a deal with myself to be up as soon as possible, cos I want to know what Giraffles will do next...

For once on this trip, things go my way. The doctor comes back and, after like a million tests, declares I wasn't concussed. Apparently I just fainted, which is fine by me, as it means I can dash (kind of) down to the hotel restaurant.

It's a strange experience watching Giraffles eat as quickly as he did tonight.

He ditches the spoon, lifts the bowl to his mouth and drinks his soup in one long slurp. Then he puts his chips inside his burger bun to cut down time, and as for his ice cream? Well, I can't imagine the brain freeze he has after shoveling it in at such a rate.

"Mate," I say, "we go home tomorrow night. Don't you want to enjoy the grub? It'll be a while till we get fed like this again."

"You finished?" he asks, ignoring me. I'm not really hungry anyway. My head's still throbbing. I look around the dining room. There's only us and the Virtuous lot in there: no other guests, obviously, and Blaize and co have only just started, licking their lips as they tuck into their herring (again!). They look well pleased with themselves: Blaize and Milo sniggering in my direction between every mouthful.

"Don't worry, they won't be laughing for

long," smiles Giraffles, and I spot Lucky by the door. He's clutching a carrier bag, and wearing a grin that matches Giraffles's. They are both properly up to something, and whatever it is, I flipping love it already.

28

I know something is *definitely* going on when
Giraffles and Lucky both pull balaclavas out of
their back pockets.

"We're not going outside, are we? It's chuffin'
freezing out there," I say.

"Shhhh!" hisses Giraffles.

"This mission is all about stealth," says Lucky.
"No one can know it's us under here – and there's
cameras everywhere."

"Hmm…" I say. "Fair enough, but it's not like
there's any other guests, is there? Plus, there's no

one else whose neck is longer than a ladder, so, to be honest, whatever we're about to do, I reckon people will know it's us…"

They look at each other shocked, like they haven't thought of that.

"Plus, I don't have a balaclava on me, and whatever you're about to do, you're not doing it without me."

They shove their balaclavas back in their pockets, and pull me quickly down the corridor.

"Then we have to do this *quick*," whispers Giraffles. "Lucky, how many did you get?"

"*Loads.*"

"They're not fresh, are they?"

"No chance. I saw the chef throwing them in the bin with a peg on his nose."

"Perfect."

I've no idea what they're talking about, but I am now officially DESPERATE to know.

"What is it, what is it, what is it?" I yell, before remembering the stealth bit.

"Shhh! You'll see."

We run down corridor after corridor; so many that it dawns on us just how HUGE this resort is. Weird how much space there is when there's hardly any of us staying here.

"Did you get the key?" Lucky asks Giraffles.

"Course. Reception was deserted."

We go down four more corridors, but finally we stop outside a room and Giraffles touches the key card to the sensor, which swiftly sends the door sliding open.

As soon as we're inside, I know it's Blaize and Milo's room. Somehow it smells of them: unpleasant. Like they've sprayed fifteen cans of deodorant each, but the unpleasant smell is still there. Also, there's clothes everywhere. Enough to clothe a family for a two-week holiday, never mind two boys for just three nights.

Most surprisingly, there's a teddy bear on each of the pillows, which makes Giraffles snort and point.

I'm not so comfortable.

"What are we doing here?" I say, panicking that we're going to be caught.

"Herrings," grins Giraffles, "are like revenge: best served cold."

"Nah," says Lucky, "soon as we get these bad boys warm, they are gonna STINK!"

And he pulls from the bag a big old gloopy handful of herrings. But they don't look like the ones that get served at every meal. These look old and stale at the edges. Even from across the room, I can smell them.

"They're perfect," sniggers Giraffles. "They think they're the only ones who know how to handle a stink bomb? They can think again! Now, where are we going to put 'em?"

"Suitcases?" says Lucky, after surveying the room further.

"...Nah."

"In the wardrobe, then?"

Giraffles still isn't convinced.

"We've only got one night left. They need to reach maximum stink in the next twelve hours."

And that's when I see it. "There," I point.

They look at a metal grill that sits in the wall between the single beds.

"Is that the central heating vent?" Giraffles asks.

"Looks like it."

"And tonight's going to be cold, isn't it?" he asks.

"F-f-f-reezing," I answer.

"Then it's perfect," he giggles with a twinkle in his eyes, before dropping to his knees and pulling a screwdriver from his pocket.

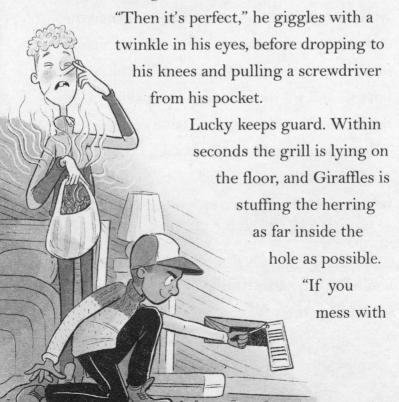

Lucky keeps guard. Within seconds the grill is lying on the floor, and Giraffles is stuffing the herring as far inside the hole as possible.

"If you mess with

my mate, you mess with me," he mutters with a grimace. The fish smell is awful already!

Once the grill is back in place, Giraffles takes a couple of deep breaths.

"See the thermostat over there?" he asks me.

I nod.

"Crank it up to eleven. We can't have Blaize and his teddy getting cold tonight, can we?"

Now, I'm not evil, I'm really not, but I'd be lying if I said I didn't smile when I turned the dial as high as it could go. After all, the smell of that stink bomb was still buried deep in my nostrils. All we were doing was repaying the favour. Settling the score. Getting revenge. Whatever you call it, it felt good.

We closed the bedroom door behind us without being rumbled, and gave each other a high five.

"Skills," I say to them both. "Thanks."

We turn and almost walk straight into Blaize and Milo, who are striding back to their rooms after filling their faces.

"Nice food, was it?" smiles Lucky.

"Why are you looking so pleased with yourselves?" sneers Blaize.

"No reason," I reply. "We're herring — I mean *having* a lovely time, that's all. Sleep well!"

And we stroll on, laughing to ourselves, leaving them clueless.

For once, I don't mind going to bed. I want our last day to be memorable, and I can't *wait* to see the colour of Blaize's face in the morning.

Can. Not. Wait.

29

His face is green.

Greener than green.

It is GREEN, with a capital everything.

So is Milo's, and the triplets', whose room, we now realize, is next to theirs.

I do actually feel a bit guilty that they've copped a nose-full as well, but not for long.

"I didn't see the triplets giving Blaize a hard time about what he did to you, so why worry?" says Giraffles.

And perhaps he's right, so I focus on laughing quietly at Blaize as he sits queasily in the breakfast room, head in hands, like he's stuck in the smelliest nightmare ever.

Me, Giraffles and Lucky do our best to make it worse for him, walking slowly past with the smelliest food imaginable. Kippers, poached eggs, you name it, but it's not until we amble past with three platefuls of curried herring (that we OBVIOUSLY aren't going to eat) that it's too much for him. He rushes from the room with a hand over his mouth.

"And that, my friends, is mission complete!" smiles Giraffles, as we high five subtly, so as not to give ourselves away.

Blaize is not the only person with a green tinge to him, though. Teddy and Flick look decidedly peaky as well: like they've lost a million quid down the back of the sofa and can only find one sock, a button and a Monopoly pound note hidden there instead.

It's really starting to get under my skin now. This place, the lack of other guests, the weird way they've acted towards us – all of it. I'm *convinced* they're hiding something, and the more I let it rush around my head, the more I feel that I *have* to know what they're up to. So while they chunter to each other in hushed tones, I stand by the waffle machine and pretend to make one whilst expertly listening in.

"What do you *mean* there've still been no bookings?" Flick is saying.

"Exactly that."

"Not even one? Even after yesterday? I mean, how extreme does the footage have to be to attract people?"

"This is a disaster, the whole th—"

At that exact moment, Jonny walks by with the biggest plate of pancakes known to man. But instead of focusing on not dropping them, he's also staring at his phone, which leads to him tripping and accidentally tipping them over Teddy's head.

I want to go ballistic at him. Firstly, because

he's flipping embarrassing, and secondly cos obviously I was on the verge of overhearing something *really* important.

But all I can do though is walk back to my seat and try to figure out what is going on. I mean, it's our last day and I want to enjoy it, but at the same time, I'm getting a weird feeling in my stomach, and it's got nothing to do with rotten herrings.

Teddy and Flick are up to something, and it feels like I have to keep an eye on them, when I already have to watch out for Blaize.

Honestly, since when did school trips get so flippin' complicated?

By the time we pile into the cable car, there are at least *some* happier faces amongst us.

Not Blaize – most of the time we can't even see his ugly mug, as it's buried inside a paper bag that he's chundering into. Teddy and Flick look cheerier, even if I know they're faking it.

I turn it all over in my head again and again, what they're up to, what they're even getting out of this whole trip apart from feeding us up then scaring the lives out of us, but then I wonder if it's just me being paranoid.

"Last day!" chirps Teddy. "And we want to make it one you'll never forget. The sort of adrenalin-packed day that'll make you dash home and force your parents to book you in again!"

I laugh quietly to myself. Not much chance of that, I think. Not on Mum's wages, though I have absolutely no idea how much a trip like this would cost.

"Have you worked it out yet?" says a voice in my ear, and I turn to see Jasmine, staring into her phone, of course. She must be talking to someone else, so I turn back around.

"I *said*, have you worked it out yet?" she says again, and she gives me the shortest of glances.

"Worked *what* out?" Does she mean how much it costs? And if she does mean that, then how does she know I was even thinking about it? Can her phone read my mind or something?

"All of it. What we're doing here, what's in it for those two muppets." She points at Teddy and Flick. "Because we both know it's got nothing to do with celebrating you and Blaize being heroes."

I pretend not to know what she's on about, cos actually, I LIKE being a hero. Makes a good change from being just little Danny who lives on the eighteenth floor.

"*Come on*, Danny – you're smart. Surely you've put two and two together?"

"I never was any good at maths," I say, which makes her actually look at something other than her phone for once, though her stare makes me feel even more uncomfortable.

"Haven't you wondered why the resort is so empty?" she asks.

"Since the first day we arrived." I nod, my ears pricking up.

"I mean," she says, "it's amazing, isn't it? Five

stars, no expense spared, luxury *everything*, but there's only us staying here. Isn't that…"

"…Weird?" I finish for her. "Yeah, it *totally* is. It doesn't make sense. It should be rammed full."

"And what about Flick? And Teddy?"

"Where do you want me to start?" I whisper.

She leans in closer. "Do you not think it's odd that they're apparently alpine sport mad but they've not skied or snowboarded or zorbed even *once*?"

"Well, I don't believe they're injured, that's for sure."

She shoots me a conspiratiorial look. "If they want us to believe that line then they need to practise their limping."

I sigh. "I'm just confused why *we're* here. Because I don't believe anything they say any more."

"And you're right not to," Jasmine says. "*Look.*" And she sticks her phone under my nose.

"What's this?" I say, squinting.

"The prices to stay here – on the hotel's website."

I look closer, and there are numbers and pound signs and more zeros than I've *ever* come across in any maths test. *Loads* of 'em.

"Whoa," I gasp, my mouth shaped like one of the zeros. "*That's* what it costs to stay here?"

She nods and I feel sick, suddenly paranoid that they're going to give us a HUGE bill when we leave later.

"Are they insane?" I stammer. "Who has that sort of money?"

"Judging by the emptiness of the place? No one. That's why we're here."

"B-b-but I haven't got any money to pay!"

"No, but we're *kids*, aren't we? Cute, adorable and, in yours and Blaize's case, BRAVE."

I blush. "So, what's that got to do with it?"

"They're going to milk us for every bit of publicity they can."

And with that, she wipes at her screen and brings up a video on it, ready to show me.

"Come on, Danny, it's *obvious*," she sighs as I try desperately to make all the pieces fit together. "They're about to go bust," she says. "Bankrupt. Because they've made staying here too expensive. So they've panicked and bought as much swanky alpine sport stuff as they can, to make the resort fit for adrenalin junkies. Only problem is, they don't know the difference between a husky and a snowboard."

"All the Bigfeet and zorbs and kit, none of it had been used before…" I say.

"Course it hadn't, because no one has booked to stay. So they turned to us. We're the last resort for their resort!"

And even though it's all starting to make sense, I still feel confused.

"But I don't see what help we are," I say, so Jasmine leans in even closer, like she's about to tell me the secret of how to turn bogeys into gold.

"Because kids are *watchable*. They can make stuff like zorbing look easy and fun and EXTREME! In fact, there's only one thing better than cute kids, and that's *brave* kids. Because, if they can get us doing brave stuff on camera, even if actually it's totally reckless and dangerous, then they can use it to drum up business – to save their own backsides."

"You mean they'd put us at risk just to line their own pockets?"

Jasmine shrugs. "Money makes people do

reckless things. Look at this." And she shows me her phone.

The video is of us, on the first day. Blaize boarding, me falling, Blaize soaring, me tumbling, over and over again. But something has been done to the video. Someone's messed with it somehow, because the slope looks WAY steeper than it was. And they've added sound, loads of it, the sound of me wailing and squealing as I fall again and again.

"That is not my voice!" I protest. Jasmine frowns at me. "It's not. I mean, I did scream … a bit … maybe once … but that's *definitely* not me."

"Doesn't matter anyway." She shrugs. "No one's seen it."

"What do you mean?"

"You really aren't the sharpest, are you? They've *used* us. Invited us here as guinea pigs to try and drum up business, show people how generous they are. But no one's interested. This video only got ten shares. It's pointless."

Why would they use us like that? *Why?*

I ask Jasmine exactly that, which draws another sigh and another video, then another and another, all of them featuring me and Blaize, going head to head: on snowboards, on Bigfeet, in the zorbs. And each video has been messed with, edited, so it looks extreme and dramatic and properly, properly dangerous.

"The videos *are* clever," she says. "Well edited, good music – but they can't change the fact that no one cares. At least, not at the prices they charge. Still, it makes you wonder, doesn't it?"

I look at her. "Wonder what?"

"What lengths they will go to, to capture some REALLY extreme footage. Today is their last chance, after all. Our last day. If I was you, Danny, I'd be a bit careful."

I gulp, and shiver. And not because it's freezing cold.

30

I never thought I'd say this, but right now I wish
school trips still meant a day at the sewage plant.

How rubbish is that?! But I can't help it. I feel
like I need three pairs of eyes: one for Blaize, one
for Teddy and one for Flick.

It'll be OK, I tell myself. *You can do this. You've
survived one extreme school trip, so what's the worst
that could happen?*

But then images of broken legs and air
ambulances and crutches flash into my head, and
before I know it I'd rather be in one of Dylan's

headlocks than on top of this beautiful mountain.

"Come on, Danny," scowls Mrs Rex, "it's our last day. Breathe in this air, will you?"

I want to tell her what I know, but she's hardly approachable, is she? I chew it over, before deciding that I *have* to try.

"Miss, I think we should go back down. I think this is a bad idea. I don't think it's safe."

She gives me that special look that adults save for kids who they think clearly don't know what they're talking about.

"Is that right?"

"It is. Teddy and Flick, they're up to something. Honest."

"They are indeed — Miss D and I have already spoken to them about the plans for today, and they've assured us it will be good, exciting, safe fun!"

And that's it as far as she's concerned. Case closed. She's always going on about us making up stuff and telling tales, so there's no way she's going to buy anything I say.

So I turn to Miss D instead, try to get her ear, but she looks so weighed down by the MASSIVE first aid kit on her back that if I fear she'll sink into the snow.

So I decide to do nothing. Instead, I suck it up, paint on a smile to cover my nerves and do whatever I'm told, which on any other day would be pretty flipping awesome. But not today.

We spend the morning sledging. The sledges are brand new and top of the line (of course), the snow is deep and fresh and proper fast to slide on, and all of it gets your heart racing and feeling good about the world.

But every time Teddy whips out his phone to film us, I shudder, and every time Blaize flicks me an evil glare, I shiver, and it's happening so much that by the time it gets to lunchtime I feel like I'm freezing to death.

Of course, they roll out the biggest, fanciest packed lunch imaginable, with hot chocolate that is so hot you could poach an egg in it (though that would taste pretty rank), and while the others talk about all the amazing things that we've done, I'm just worrying about getting off the mountain without being pulverized by Blaize or being made to do something life-threatening by Teddy and Flick, all in the name of publicity.

"So ..." says Flick, interrupting my thoughts, "before we say goodbye to you, there *is* one last little surprise left."

And, from nowhere, a thudding noise starts to echo, slowly getting louder and louder and louder, till it feels like a gigantic mutant vulture could be flapping its wings into our earholes.

"What is *that*?" Lucky asks, but there's no time to answer, as from behind the mountain thunders a golden helicopter, coming to land on a helipad thirty metres away.

"Your carriage to heaven awaits!" beams Teddy. "It's going to take us all to the highest spot in this whole mountain range, where it will drop us to ski, board or sledge, all the way back to the hotel."

There are whoops and cheers and gasps, but all I want to do is break wind. Imagine the revenge Blaize could wreak, for starters? And what on earth might be waiting up there thanks to Teddy and Flick's incompetence?

Avalanches?

Snowstorms?

Yetis?

I don't mind admitting it: I'm scared. But fortunately Miss D is *even more* terrified.

"Is it ... would it ... is it ... safe? I mean, it's h-h-*high* up there?"

Thank the lord, I think. *Finally, someone responsible on my side!*

But Teddy sleazes over to her and drapes an arm round her shoulder. "Dear lady, the safety of your children is *everything* to us, and I know about the *awful* experience you all had before. We have checked and quadruple checked. The weather is set fair, the chopper has a full tank of gas, and *every one* of us will be wearing top-of-the-range avalanche detectors."

And the problem is, Teddy is completely believable, and after showing Miss D and Mrs Rex all his weather charts and apps, I see Miss D bow down to his "expertise" and we're all herded on to the helicopter and whisked so high into the sky that I expect us to collide with a satellite.

It *should* be amazing, but all it actually is, is terrifying and terrifying all at the same time (did I mention how terrifying it is?). The mountain just keeps going and going and going, and the snow just gets deeper and deeper and deeper, until finally the chopper starts to hover only metres above the top of a peak.

"OK!" shouts Flick. "This is where we get off!"

But this doesn't make sense – there's nowhere to land. It's *literally* the peak of a mountain.

"Where are we going to land?" someone asks.

Flick looks around, like whoever asked has no

brain. "We *can't* land, *obviously*. We can only jump."

For a second I think she said we are going to jump out of a still-flying helicopter, but that's obviously just a joke, obviously … until she repeats it.

Of course, the Virtuous lot are *all over* the idea, as if they do this sort of thing every day of the week and twice at weekends, and one by one they pile out, whooping in delight when the fluffy snow below pulls them into a welcoming hug.

Us lot aren't quite as up for it. Well, Lucky is and he dives in happily, but Giraffles and the twins look terrified. Mrs Rex only does it cos headteachers are meant to be tough, but Miss D won't go unless Teddy goes with her, so he picks her up and carries her before jumping. *So much for his injury*, I want to scream, not that it would be heard above the din of the chopper.

Which just leaves me.

"Anything you want to say to the camera?" Flick asks, her phone thrust in my face. But the

only words in my head are rude and I'd only get told off using them.

So I say nothing. Well, nothing intelligent, though I do let out a scream as I finally pluck up the courage to jump.

31

The snow is soft and welcoming, but *cold*.

Yeah, all right, I know it's meant to be, but this is *really cold*: the sort of cold that freezes any piece of skin left showing so it feels like a burn. This only adds to my sense of fear. I know it's daft and that I should just enjoy myself, but I can't help it, it feels like something I really won't like is about to happen, and I've no idea what to do about it.

"So, there are two aims to our final activity," beams Flick, as her brother films her (obviously).

"Firstly, get down the mountain in one piece. There's sledges, snowboards and Bigfeet. Take your pick! Secondly, don't be afraid to go large! The more extreme, the better! And I *wouldn't* advise walking. The sun will go down in less than three hours. We'll have a break at the rest point together. But don't stop too often. You do NOT want to be outside after dark."

"Cos that's when the yetis come out," pipes up Jonny, like he's an expert or something.

"More because you'd freeze to death," answers Teddy.

"Yeah, and yetis do like their food cold too," Jonny adds, though where he got that from I have no idea.

Teddy's not listening to him any more though, he's waving his arms at a second chopper that's whoomped into view, delivering a skidoo each for him and Flick.

Jasmine and me exchange a knowing look as we think about their mystery "injuries" all over again.

There's a scrum for the equipment. The Virtuous lot dive in for snowboards, which suits me fine – they're welcome to them. But I can't decide whether to sledge or BigFoot it down.

"Do both," says Giraffles, shoving a couple of pairs of Bigfeet in my rucksack. "There's plenty to go around. And you can carry a set for me too."

Despite the sense of fear gnawing at my belly, I try to make the next hour feel like fun.

I keep well away from Blaize and Milo, picking really easy runs on the sledge that I know they'll laugh at cos they're too simple. And it works – they dive off to look for bumps and jumps, pursued by Teddy and Flick, and I breathe easy again.

Or I would if it wasn't so cold. I don't know if it's because we're so high up today, or if it's cos the air is thinner as a result, but I can't hide the fact that I'm freezing my bits off.

The sledging, fun as it is, doesn't really help either, because I'm not exactly moving about, am I? I'm just sitting there, steering, face-planting into the snow every now and again, which just adds to the fact that I'm becoming a human icicle.

An hour in and it's getting worse. My fingers are struggling to grip inside my gloves, and I'm falling off the sledge more and more. Also, the snow is deeper. No one's walked on it or trodden it down, so the sledge sometimes sinks into it instead of gliding over the top. It's becoming hard work, and that's crazy cos sledging is meant to be easy, isn't it?

It comes as a relief, then, when Teddy and Flick pull us together and give us some good news.

"Our rest point is up ahead," Teddy says, squinting at a map in his hand. He's staring at it hard, like he's looking at it for the first time. "Only a quick one. The temperature is only going to drop, and I can see that some of you are cold."

"Not me," sneers Blaize in my direction, as Teddy goes on, reading what's written on the map, word for word.

"Look down and to your left, about a kilometer

on. You'll see a patch of brown."

I strain through my goggles and see it.

"That's an opening to a cave. The *perfect* place to refuel. Approach it from the right though, not above. The snow there has been warmed by the sun and will be soft. Doesn't need us ploughing over it and making it slide."

I don't believe Teddy or Flick have *ever* been here before in their lives, but still I don't need telling twice. I know they haven't said the actual word, but sliding snow is an avalanche, and that alone makes a massive alarm go off in my head.

So, taking a deep breath and bashing my hands together to get them working, I push off my sledge, feeling a whoosh of cold, then another, as Blaize and Milo zoom past, spraying me with snow.

"Better get used to that!" Blaize shouts, but just when I think he's going to wait and spray me again, he puts the pedal down and speeds off, his laughter not getting any quieter, despite the increasing distance between us.

32

The cave's approaching, but I'm taking it slow.

Maybe it's the cold, I don't know, but I'm *tired*. And the problem is, trying to slow down the sledge takes way more effort than letting it speed up. Plus, my hands are biting with cold, and my back is freezing too. Must be sweat turning into ice pops. Maybe I can feed one to Blaize without him realizing what he's eating…

But before I can laugh at my own lame joke, I'm the one eating snow as the sledge capsizes and makes me face-plant yet again.

I want to shout in frustration, but I think my tongue is icing over too, and it doesn't make me feel any better to see a large crowd gathering in the mouth of the cave. Maybe I'm hallucinating, but it looks like they're drinking something from a flask. Hot chocolate again probably, but I'm SO COLD I can't even imagine how warming that would taste right now.

I grit my teeth and decide to let the sledge glide quickly down to the cave, but as the runners speed away, I realize all is *not* as it should be. Maybe it was the last crash, I don't know, but the sledge doesn't seem to want to be steered any more. I pull one way, then the other, but it doesn't matter – and soon enough, instead of running down below the cave, I'm veering up above it, exactly where they told us NOT to go.

I say a word that I shouldn't know, never mind say, but that doesn't help, nor does trying to jam my feet into the snow, as it's so deep and powdery it does little to slow me down.

Before I know it, the cave is disappearing beneath me, and it dawns on me that I don't know what lies in the path ahead. It could be the edge of the mountain or a yeti's lair! So, with panic buzzing inside me, I choose to bail out, belly-flopping into the snow with so little style that I hope to god no one was filming it.

Any thought of humiliation is replaced instantly by a sheer, awful, terrible cold feeling. I'm not kidding, it feels like I'm naked, like I'm in an ice bath, like I will never EVER be warm again.

I feel scared, try to shout down to the cave to get someone to help me, but no words come out. I try again and again, and finally, there is a noise, but it doesn't sound like me, it sounds like Blaize, which is weird. It happens three more times before I realize I have company, and as my neck turns against the cold, I see him, twenty metres above me, or at least, I see his head. The rest of him is hidden behind the biggest snowball I have ever seen. You should see it: it's practically the size of a ten-bedroomed igloo.

"Think you're so clever, don't you?" he hisses. "And brave. Well, let's just test that theory, shall we? Let's see how you cope with *this*."

And with a monumental effort, he pushes off the snowball so it starts rolling in my direction, and with every turn it gets closer, and it also gets bigger as more and more snow sticks to it.

I try to run, well, I think about it, but the ice has seized my brain. I try to scream but my throat's still on strike. The only thing I can do is panic, and even that, I have do silently. And slowly.

It's rumbling closer and closer and getting bigger and bigger, and although I'm already covered in snow, I don't want to be wearing any more of it, so at the last moment, using energy I didn't know I had, I dive to my right, feeling the wind rush past me.

I should celebrate, I should dance and whoop and holler, but I don't do any of those things, as that big old snowball doesn't realize that it was only meant to be hunting me. Now it's rolling on, still growing, still spinning ever faster and still, I realize, heading right above where the others are hiding, warming up with their hot chocolate.

"IT'S COMING!" I yell. "TAKE COVER!"

But as I shout it, it sounds like the rambling of a lunatic and, besides, they probably can't hear me anyway. But that doesn't stop me, I shout it again and again, until I see the most terrible thing. The snowball has loosened all the snow between me and the cave.

They warned us, didn't they, whoever actually put the map together? They warned us to stay off, that the snow would be soft and could give way, and now all I can do is lie there, mouth open, eyes disbelieving as the snowball, and then what looks like half the mountain, falls firstly over the edge, and then over the mouth of the cave as well.

Before I know it, there's a voice in my ear. A soft voice, a scared voice and a voice belonging to Blaize.

"I didn't mean to," he whimpers. "I didn't mean to."

But there's nothing I can say to that, is there? All I can do is stumble, as quickly as I can, to the mouth of the cave. Or at least, where the mouth of the cave once was, because now, the mouth is sealed entirely shut.

33

The snow covering the cave's mouth is thick, but moveable, despite how cold my hands are. It feels more like I've got five brittle twiglets inside my gloves than fingers.

The only problem is, every time I clear away a wedge of snow, more of it slides down from above us. It feels like one step forward, seventeen back.

I get frustrated, and scared to be honest, and I turn to Blaize, who, for the first time since I've known him looks nothing like his name. There is no fire in him at all, he's all shivers and snot icicles.

"Are you going to help me or what?" I ask. "We've got to clear this snow, and quick." But he doesn't move. Well, his mouth does, but no words come out. He's like the worst ventriloquist ever. Or maybe just his dummy. Either way, he's no chuffin' use.

So I dig again, but get nowhere. I look up, but can't see the sun any more, it's dipped behind one of the peaks, and immediately I shiver and pull my phone from my pocket. I need to text one of them. Giraffles or Lucky. Jonny, even. He'll be glued to it in there, obviously. And I still have battery.

Phew!

But no signal. I curse it and look at the time. No wonder the sun's dipping; it'll be dark soon, and if it's cold now, it's nothing to how it'll be in two hours.

I go back to digging, but shout over my shoulder at Blaize.

"Have you got any signal?"

He mumbles something, and I hear him

rustling in his pockets, so I keep on pawing at the snow. "Have you?" I say, turning.

He's stood there, squinting at his phone through his goggles, then he shakes his head, and I realize he's only gone and taken his gloves off.

"Oi!" I shout, trying to sound cheerful. "Put your gloves back on, you muppet. Don't you remember what Teddy and Flick told us? Especially now it's getting late. You're going to need those hands to dig the others out."

I walk to him, then push him gently in the direction of the cave. I need to him to help me and I need him to do it now.

"We can do this!" I say to him, all cheerful though my insides are jelly. "With two of us we'll have 'em out in no time. Twenty minutes from now we'll be sipping hot chocolate, mate."

The thought of it powers me on, and we scoop and pull and, well, I do most of it, but just as I think we're starting to get somewhere, there's a rumble and a groan from above before a whole huge stack of fresh snow tumbles down on top of us, and of course, on top of the cave's mouth.

I pull myself clear and look around for any kind of hope and see the rear end of a skidoo sticking out of the snow. I stumble to it on hands and knees.

"Come on!" I shout to Blaize. "Dig this out and we can get down the hill for help in no time." I paw at the snow, my hands transformed into super shovels, but no matter how quickly I pull the stuff away, more slides down and I'm left back where I started.

I don't weep. I can't, cos I'm so freezing and have been bent over so long that my coat has ridden up and there's snow hitting what feels like every part of my back. I feel it harden and stick to my skin, which shakes me into action. So I pull myself up, do a bizarre war dance to shake as much snow off of me as I can, before pulling Blaize out of the drift too. He looks broken.

"Blaize," I say, gently. "Mate! We've *got* to

come up with a plan. The digging, it's not working, is it?"

I deliberately ask him a question, just like teachers always do, to try and make him do some of the work here. Try to make him think! But he doesn't offer me a single word, never mind an idea!

So finally, I crack. I've tried to be nice. Nice since the second I met him, and what have I got in return? Pranks and stink bombs and a ginormous pain in the bum. So much pain that at that exact moment I consider checking if his face is a mask and that our Dyl is hiding underneath.

"Blaize!" I say, sternly, but not so sternly that he doesn't suddenly decide to punch my face off. "Come on! We've got a problem here. Everyone else is stuck in there. The cable car is about a mile uphill, and before we know it, it's going to be dark. Now I don't believe the yeti's going to come out and pull off our arms like they're chicken legs, but I do believe we could freeze to death. And, strangely enough I *don't* fancy that today … or any day in fact. So I need your help, mate, don't I?"

And I look at him, but there's just a big icicle of fear where his face should be.

"Come on!" I beg him. "You're meant to be a hero! You ran into a burning building to rescue a Guinea pig, didn't you? So where's that Blaize now? Cos wherever he is, I need him, mate, and I need him quick."

He doesn't say anything for a few seconds. Then, finally, he does. Not that it makes much sense.

"Never happened."

I have no idea what that means. But I know he needs to tell me quickly, so we can get down off this flippin' mountain.

34

"What never happened? The fire? The guinea pig? The stupid name for the guinea pig? What!?"

"The hero bit," he says quietly, and he looks at me with the eyes of a dog who's just guiltily eaten the turkey leg you've been looking forward to all Christmas day.

"I didn't run back in to save it," he says.

"Does that really matter?" I ask, but he doesn't listen, he just carries on talking while I stamp my feet to try and keep them from freezing.

"I *was* the last one out of the classroom," he says, "but not because I went back in. I was last one out because I was too scared to move in the first place. No one else was. Everyone else knew exactly what to do and where to go, and so did I, I suppose. Only difference is, I was too much of a coward to do it."

"Why don't we talk about this as we keep moving?" I suggest. "Seriously, Blaize, the clock's ticking and that sun is not sticking around."

But now he's started, he doesn't want to stop.

"I *did* move in the end though. The flames were getting bigger and the path to the door was getting smaller, and, in the end, I just shut my eyes and ran forward, which is when I … well, when I…"

"What? When you *what?*"

"When I stood on Fluffball."

I try not to smile, then remember I'm covered by a scarf, so it doesn't matter.

"I didn't pick him up because I wanted to *save* him. I picked him up because I thought I'd squashed him flat. Then, when I got outside and everyone saw me carrying him, they presumed I'd rescued him. I was so embarrassed and ashamed that I just went on with it. It was easier than telling them the truth."

"OK," I say, "so you didn't rush back in, but he wouldn't have got out in one piece if you hadn't carried him!"

Blaize's eyes brighten behind his goggles for just a second.

"Then this trip came up," he says, "and suddenly I'm the hero all over again, and you were here and what you did WAS brave and so I felt rubbish again and, well … I've not been particularly nice to you, have I?"

I feel myself blush, which feels great cos my cheeks are warm for a second or two, and I realize that this is the closest to an apology from Blaize that I'm going to get. It feels good too, though it does jolt me back to the fact that we're stranded on the side of the highest mountain in Norway, without our guides, friends, and, soon, without any light whatsoever.

"But it's just a word, you know?" I say. "Brave, or hero, or any of that. Do I *look* like a hero? Half the time this week, or on my last school trip, I was bricking it but trying to not let anyone else see!"

He lets out a snort of laughter, but it's kinder than normal. "You didn't exactly hide it well!"

"Tell me about it," I say, and I look at him,

all serious all of a sudden. "The bravest thing we can do now is get our backsides down this mountain and fetch help. They'll be warm in there for now. They'll probably be warmer than us, plus they've got food and hot chocolate." I'm not sure I actually believe what I'm saying, but I need Blaize to be in a positive mood.

Blaize pulls a single chocolate bar out of his backpack. "And we've only got this."

"Exactly. And I'm getting hungry. Not hungry enough to eat a herring, but hungry!"

I pull off my backpack and take out my pair of Bigfeet. "My sledge is busted, and I can't go as fast as you on a board."

"Doesn't matter," he says, snapping his boots on to his snowboard. "I'll find us the easiest route, but I won't go fast, I promise."

And with that, he pushes off and I follow him, hoping beyond hope that Blaize Cosmo is all out of practical jokes and, more importantly, all out of revenge!

35

I'm sure the sunset views are lovely, like
something off a postcard probably, but all I
can focus on is the back of Blaize Cosmo as he
weaves his way down the hill. I can't say I've felt
at all envious of him over the past few days, but
watching him right now, I do. We'd be moving a
heck of a lot quicker if I had even a quarter of
his skills. I'm doing my best, though: following
his lead, avoiding the bumps, or "moguls" as
he calls them. I don't think he's showing off, as
every time I fall over he stops to wait for me.

He's even side-stepped back up the mountain once or twice to get me back on my feet.

What we both know, but aren't talking about, is the fact that the light is fading. *Fast.* And with every minute that passes and every bit of darkness that slides over us, the temperature drops, which makes me stop more often than I want to: to shake loose snow from out of my boots or down my neck. I'm worried — bloomin' terrified — that if I don't get the snow out then it's going to sit there and stick to my skin like an icy slug.

So, what with the stopping and starting and falling and rising, our progress is slow. *Too slow.* And we know it.

It doesn't help that the fading light is drawing out the nightlife. I mean, I'm no David Attenborough, but the sound of howling somewhere behind me can only mean one thing.

"That a wolf?" I shout over to Blaize.

"No," he replies. "There's definitely more than

one of them, so it's a pack more likely."

They're hardly comforting words, but motivational at least, as they make me move quicker than I ever have before. Of course I'm scared, and of course I keep looking over my shoulder and OF COURSE I see a dozen pairs of red eyes in the gloom that may or may not exist.

"There's not enough meat on me," I yell over my shoulder. "Go eat someone else!"

But then we see something that I hope isn't a mirage. Can you get mirages with snow? Or is that deserts? I don't know, but what I *do* know is that we both think we see, way down in the distance, a cluster of twinkling lights.

"Where there's lights, there's life!" sings Blaize, like it's the wisest thing he's ever said, and it gives us extra energy, my Bigfeet sliding over the snow more effortlessly than before.

As long as we follow the lights, we'll be OK! I tell myself, but just as hope starts to grow, we find ourselves sliding towards an obstacle way bigger

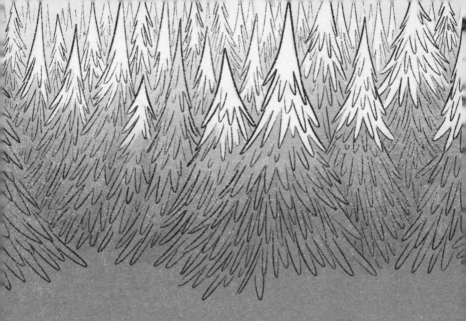

than both of us: a forest with trees taller than anything we've ever seen.

"Who thought it was a good idea to plant them up here!" gasps Blaize, sounding more like Jonny than Jonny himself.

"I don't think it works like that, mate," I say. "You got your phone still?"

"Yeah."

'Then fire up the torch. It's going to be proper dark. Plus, maybe the light will scare off any wildlife."

I don't tell him that my phone's too old to

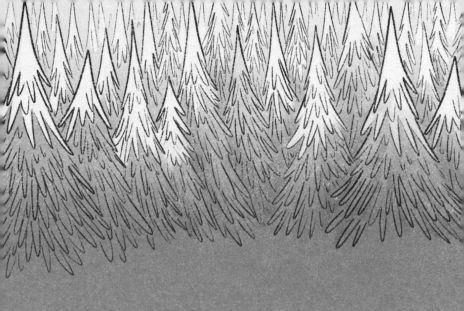

even have a torch, not when he's finally looking at me like a normal human being.

Anyway, Blaize does as I've asked, and slowly, nervously, we edge our way through the trees, trying to avoid the tree roots beneath us and the snow tumbling from the branches above.

"Slow down a bit," I shout, cos the torch is lighting the distance instead of the stuff I'm skiing over now, but even as I say it, I tumble, my helmet taking the brunt of a whack from a tree trunk that I hadn't seen looming in front of me.

"You all right?" Blaize shouts, and I want to

throw a proper fit and scream and sulk, but I can't, can I? Not when I lectured him on being brave, plus sulking isn't going to get us to safety, is it?

So I do the only thing I can think of, which is to pull myself back to my feet, shout "I'm fine!" and plough on until I catch Blaize up.

On we go, tree by tree, metre by metre until suddenly, I see it — light! Well, kind of. Maybe it's not light *exactly*, but it's less murky for sure, and our spirits lift.

"That's the end of the trees!" Blaize shouts, and we both speed up, our hearts thudding and spirits soaring.

But just as we get to the last tree, Blaize hits it, literally, and does a quadruple front somersault with tuck, pike and swallow dive, before landing painfully on his right knee.

He says a word that even Dylan wouldn't say, and I think one myself, cos now the twinkling lights are closer than ever, but so is the darkness.

If I can get Blaize on to his feet, then I reckon we can make it before we freeze to bits, but without him… Well, I can't *leave* him here, can I? What if I have an accident too, and there's two of us left stranded in different places to the mercy of the wolves? And what about everyone else stuck in the snow cave?

"Can you stand?" I ask him, and he can. But he can't put any weight on his left leg.

"How am I going to board now?" he gasps. And I've no idea. Could I carry him? He's too heavy. Could I strap his knee up? Well, for starters I haven't got bandages, and we were told to never, EVER expose our skin to the cold, so that's a no-no from word go-go!

Then I have a thought. That's all it is – a thought. It's certainly not an idea, it's got way too many holes in it to be one of those. But as it's all we have, and cos I can barely feel my hands or feet any more, I decide to run with it.

"What are you doing?" Blaize asks, as I rip the

rucksack off my back. And when I pull a single Big Foot from inside it, he looks at me like I'm bonkers.

"You're not expecting me to put that on, are you?" he says. "I can barely stand up!"

"Course I am," I reply, like it's a completely normal thing to say. "Cos you're a hero. And heroes don't lie down on mountains till they freeze to death – they ski on one leg. Until they reach the bottom, at least."

It's not exactly a good speech, and I'm so cold now that I don't even know if it makes sense. But it's enough for Blaize, who straps the big foot in place and stands beside me.

"So how do we do this?" he asks, and I face him, with my arms stretched out towards him.

"You grab me, I grab you, and we'll try and keep each other on our feet."

Blaize's face tells me he was expecting more of a plan than this, but he grabs my hands anyway. "Good luck," he says, "and thanks, you know, for—"

"—I haven't done anything," I cut in. "Not yet anyway." And before it gets any colder, I let my feet slide down the hill, and slowly, carefully, we start to spin.

At first it's carnage. We fall, slip, skid, do everything *except* stay on our feet, and every time we fall, I hear Blaize yelp in pain.

But it doesn't put us off. I can see it hurts him more every time, but Blaize grits his teeth, puts his weight on his good leg and his faith in me as I carve a route down.

I can feel his arms trembling as every bit of strength and energy leaves his one good leg, but I can't let him fall again, cos if he does, I doubt he'll get back up. We can't even use the torch because we're clinging on to each other with both arms, so now it's blacker than black. Even the snow seems to have changed colour.

But then, just as I feel the tears rise in my throat, I see a light, closer than the others, and this one is moving. Moving up the hill fifty metres to our left. I've no idea what it is or where it's going, it doesn't matter. All that matters is that we get to it, so, pulling Blaize with me, I start to change direction, and we spin and lurch towards it.

I try to shout but no noise comes out, try to speed up but there's not enough left in us. But we don't give up. We spin on and on *and on*, until we can hear an engine and see that it's a beast of a machine: a cross between a tank and a snowplough. They'll never hear us, not above the noise, so all we can do is skid in front of it, hope the driver sees us in the darkness, and hope its brakes are in good nick.

So we do it – we veer straight into its path, shouting ourselves hoarse, eyes widening as its bulk rumbles close and closer and closer. And just as I think we're done for, that we've come all this way only to be squished by a snowplough, I see my own wide eyes mirrored in the driver's, and she slams on the brakes and the beast veers and skids and burps, and comes to a halt not even a metre from where we stand.

She yells something in a language I don't understand, but imagine it means:

"What on EARTH are you doing out here? Do you want to freeze to death?"

"Do you speak English?'" I reply, my voice a painful whisper. "It's just … we just … we need your help."

And this time I know, I just know, that help is definitely on the way.

36

Hot chocolate makes *everything* better.

In fact, that's not true. Hot chocolate, headache tablets, a six-course dinner, a blinding hot shower and the comfiest bed in the world makes everything better.

The only thing that would make things perfect is news of everyone else, but the food and the bed…? Well, it knocks me out no matter how hard I try to resist, and I sleep so deeply that when I first wake up, I feel guilty. How could I sleep when the others aren't back safely?

But I've woken up for a reason, because there above me is the goofiest set of faces I've ever seen in my life. And boy, am I happy to see them.

Giraffles, Lucky, the twins, Jonny, Miss D – even Mrs Rex – they're all there beaming, wrapped up in foil like they're about to be covered in oil and roasted in the oven.

"You're safe!" I yell, my voice still scratchy.

"We were always safe," laughs Giraffles. "You know, Miss D had EVERYTHING we needed in that bag of hers."

"Though, strangely, no one really wanted to play Monopoly," laughs Lucky, which makes Miss D blush as she says, "Failing to plan to planning to fail!"

"We're just pleased," interrupts Mrs Rex, "that YOU are safe, Danny. What you did was *incredibly* brave. Without you, who knows how long it would've taken them to find us."

"It was Blaize really," I say. I mean, he *was* injured, after all.

"Well, whoever it was, it means we can go home. Flick has found us a flight back tonight, so get your bags packed pronto."

I bet *she has*, I think. I bet they can't wait to see the back of us now we failed to fill up their hotel.

But when we get downstairs, things aren't what we expected. There are people *everywhere*. People with cameras, people with notepads, people who are DESPERATE to speak to us about our "Alpine Ordeal", whatever *that* means.

And there, mingling, talking, showing all the journalists just how amazing their hotel is, are Teddy and Flick. And before I know it, they're pushing me in front of the cameras, whispering reminders for me to say how "top of the range" and "extreme" the hotel is.

And I'm so bewildered that I don't know what to say except what happened, and yes I do manage to say how amazing the place is, because, well, it's true, isn't it?

Then, as quickly as it began, it ends, and all of

us, including the Virtuous lot, are all piled on to a really posh bus.

Teddy and Flick wave us off. Well, they do until one of their phones starts ringing and they dash off to start taking bookings.

But the weird thing is, on the bus, Blaize and Giraffles are sitting together, laughing and joking like they're mates.

"What's going on?" I ask them, ever so slightly worried that I might have lost my oldest friend.

"Oh, nothing," laughs Giraffles. "It's just, well, me and Blaize, we decided that we should say thank you to Teddy and Flick, you know, for tricking us into going there in the first place … and for not being, well, honest."

And with that, Blaize pulls out a screwdriver from his pocket and shows me the screwdriver attachment.

"The herring hidden in reception won't start smelling for a few days," he grins, "not until their first guests start to arrive. But when they *do* go off … well, they're in for a shock. Believe me, I know."

He goes to shake my hand.

And of course, I accept.

ANDY McNAB

GET ME OUT OF HERE!

PHIL EARLE

ILLUSTRATED BY ROBIN BOYDEN

HAVE YOU READ DANNY'S
FIRST GREAT ADVENTURE YET?

"Easy," I tell myself. "Simple. Piece of cake."

Then ... I don't move.

Minutes pass. So many that I start to feel sick from nerves.

"Don't be a plank," I say out loud. "You've seen plenty of others do it."

I have as well, kids older and younger, plus I've jumped waaay further myself. Only thing is, those jumps were at ground level, and this isn't.

All right, I'm stood on a brick wall that's only three times my height, but right now it feels like

I'm wobbling on the top of an electricity pylon that someone's plonked at the highest bit of Everest.

So here I am, heart sweating, forehead pounding: it might be the other way around, but I don't know any more. All I know is these two things:

A. I'm not getting down until I jump the gap to the wall opposite.

And…

B. I no longer WANT to jump the gap to the wall opposite.

I should've brought a hat, coat, sleeping bag and pillow up here with me, because by the time I finally do jump it's going to be dark … and cold.

I look down at my trainers, high-tops with built-in swoooosh, made to be springy. The sort of trainers you slam-dunk in.

The only trouble is, my feet aren't the first ones to wear them. At least one other pair lived in them before Mum found them in the charity shop, and now they feel more like concrete wellies than Nike Airs.

The glue holding the soles to the leather probably weighs a few kilos alone, and as much as I love them (second-hand or not) I reckon it'll be these trainers that will see me fall to my death (or at least graze my knee), not the fact that I'm a clumsily short-legged chicken.

My brain does this for ages, whirring and clunking until I'm pulled back to reality by a gentle tap on the shoulder that nearly shocks me off the wall and into the void.

"You jumping or not?" a voice asks.

A voice that belongs to a boy two years below me at school. "Cos if you want, we could go first." He points to another four lads behind him, one of them even younger than he is.

I feel my cheeks flush, like I've been blowing up balloons non-stop since the day I was born. I want to ask them why they aren't in bed yet, or in front of the telly in their 'jamas. I don't say anything, though. Just wave them through, like I'm doing them a favour by letting them get their jump in before their mums call them in.

One by one they jump. All of them make it. One even does it with a spin and I instantly hate him, but also want to be him. Even though he's only eight.

And I have to do it now, don't I? Especially as they're all stood there watching, with big beaming grins on their faces.

I close my eyes and breathe in, then feel a bit dizzy. *Come on, Danny,* I tell myself. Then the boys tell me the same.

I open my eyes – it'd be daft to jump with them closed – then count to three in my head, launching off my right foot before I change my mind.

Air rushes past me, and I'm skyward for what seems like ages. I'm going to smash it – probably fly right over the boys themselves. I even get ready to salute as I pass them.

But then something weird happens.

The air turns to treacle and my legs turn to lead. I start falling instead of soaring, and I grapple with the air as if I'm trying to find an invisible ladder that quite clearly isn't there.

The wall's close, but not close enough and, most importantly, my feet are miles from it. No way are they going to land on top. My fingertips do though, biting into the bricks, giving me just enough of a grip to hang on. The rest of me slams into the wall, but I don't feel it. There's not enough room in my brain to know whether I've hurt myself or not.

I can't let go – I'd look like the biggest loser ever. One of the kids even tells me so. Another one offers me a hand but I ignore it, pulling myself up with every bit of strength I have.

It feels like it takes me ages. Like someone could build a wall quicker than I could climb this one, but, eventually, with a grunt so loud it belongs in a zoo, I pull myself on to the top, every